zero sum game

S. L. HUANG

zero

sum

game

TOR

A TOM DOHERTY ASSOCIATES BOOK • NEW YORK

ZERO SUM GAME

Copyright © 2018 by S. L. Huang

A Tor Book
Published by Tom Doherty Associates
175 Fifth Avenue
New York, NY 10010

www.tor-forge.com

Tor® is a registered trademark of Macmillan Publishing Group, LLC.

Library of Congress Cataloging-in-Publication Data

Names: Huang, S. L., author.
Title: Zero sum game / S. L. Huang.
Description: First edition. | New York : Tor, 2018. | "A Tom Doherty
    Associates Book."
Identifiers: LCCN 2018023931| ISBN 9781250180254 (hardcover) |
    ISBN 9781250180261 (ebook)
Subjects: | GSAFD: Science fiction.
Classification: LCC PS3608.U22485 Z34 2018 | DDC 813/.6--dc23
LC record available at https://lccn.loc.gov/2018023931

Our books may be purchased in bulk for promotional, educational, or business use. Please contact your local bookseller or the Macmillan Corporate and Premium Sales Department at 1-800-221-7945, extension 5442, or by email at MacmillanSpecialMarkets@macmillan.com.

Originally published, in substantially different form, as ebook in 2014.

First Tor Edition: October 2018

Printed in the United States of America

0 9 8 7 6 5 4 3 2 1

TO MEL.

WITHOUT YOU, I'D BE LIKE WATER WITHOUT CESIUM—

USEFUL FOR TEA, BUT SADLY UNEXPLOSIVE.

zero sum game

one

I TRUSTED one person in the entire world.

He was currently punching me in the face.

Overlapping numbers scuttled across Rio's fist as it rocketed toward me, their values scrambling madly, the calculations doing themselves before my eyes. He wasn't pulling his punch at all, the bastard. I saw exactly how it would hit and that the force would fracture my jaw.

Well. If I allowed it to.

Angles and forces. Vector sums. Easy. I pressed myself back against the chair I was tied to, bracing my wrists against the ropes, and tilted my head a hair less than the distance I needed to turn the punch into a love tap. Instead of letting Rio break my jaw, I let him split my lip open.

The impact snapped my head back, and blood poured into my mouth, choking me. I coughed and spat on the cement floor. *Goddammit.*

"Sixteen men," said a contemptuous voice in accented English from a few paces in front of me, "against one ugly little girl. How? Who are you?"

"Nineteen," I corrected, the word hitching as I choked on my own blood. I was already regretting going for the split lip. "Check your perimeter again. I killed nineteen of your men." And it would have been a lot more if Rio hadn't appeared out of nowhere and clothes-lined me while I was distracted by the Colombians. Fucking son of a bitch. He was the one who'd gotten me this job; why hadn't he told me he was undercover with the drug cartel?

The Colombian interrogating me inhaled sharply and jerked his head at one of his subordinates, who turned and loped out of the room. The remaining three drug runners stayed where they were, fingering Micro-Uzis with what they plainly thought were intimidating expressions.

Dumbasses. I worked my wrists against the rough cord behind my back—Rio had been the one to tie me up, and he had left me just enough play to squeeze out, if I had half a second. Numbers and vectors shot in all directions—from me to the Colombian in front of me, to his three lackwit subordinates, to Rio—a sixth sense of math-ematical interplay that existed somewhere between sight and feeling, masking the world with constant calculations and threatening to drown me in a sensory overload of data.

And telling me how to kill.

Forces. Movements. Response times. I could take down this idiot drug runner right now, the way he was blocking his boys' line of fire—except that concentrating on the Colombians would give Rio the in-stant he needed to take *me* down. I was perfectly aware that he wasn't about to break cover on my behalf.

"If you don't tell me what I want to know, you will regret it. You see my dog?" The Colombian jerked his head at Rio. "If I let him loose on you, you will be crying for us to kill your own mother. And he will like making you scream. He—how do you say? It gives him a jolly." He leaned forward with a sneer, bracing himself on the arms of the chair so his breath was hot against my face.

Well, now he'd officially pissed me off. I flicked my eyes up to Rio. He remained impassive, towering above me in his customary tan duster like some hardass Asian cowboy. Unbothered. The insults wouldn't register with him.

But I didn't care. People pissing on Rio made me want to put them in the ground, even though none of it mattered to him. Even though all of it was true.

I relaxed my head back and then snapped it forward, driving my forehead directly into the Colombian's nose with a terrific crunch.

He made a sound like an electrocuted donkey, squealing and snorting as he flailed backward, and then he groped around his back to come up with a boxy little machine pistol. I had time to think, *Oh, shit,* as he brought the gun up—but before firing, he gestured furiously at Rio to get out of the way, and in that instant the mathematics realigned and clicked into place and the probabilities blossomed into a split-second window.

Before Rio had taken his third step away, before the Colombian could pull his finger back on the trigger, I had squeezed my hands free of the ropes, and I dove to the side just as the gun went off with a roar of automatic fire. I spun in a crouch and shot a foot out against the metal chair, the kick perfectly timed to lever energy from my turn—angular momentum, linear momentum, bang. Sorry, Rio. The Colombian struggled to bring his stuttering gun around to track me, but I rocketed up to crash against him, trapping his arms and carrying us both to the floor in an arc calculated exactly to bring his line of fire across the far wall.

The man's head cracked against the floor, his weapon falling from nerveless fingers and clattering against the cement. Without looking toward the side of the room, I already knew the other three men had slumped to the ground, cut down by their boss's gun before they could get a shot off. Rio was out cold by the door, his forehead bleeding freely, the chair fallen next to him. Served him right for punching me in the face so many times.

The door burst open. Men shouted in Spanish, bringing Uzis and AKs around to bear.

Momentum, velocities, objects in motion. I saw the deadly trails of their bullets' spray before they pulled the triggers, spinning lines of movement and force that filled my senses, turning the room into a kaleidoscope of whirling vector diagrams.

The guns started barking, and I ran at the wall and jumped.

I hit the window at the exact angle I needed to avoid being sliced open, but the glass still jarred when it shattered, the noise right by my ear and somehow more deafening than the gunfire. My shoulder smacked into the hard-packed ground outside and I rolled to my feet, running before I was all the way upright.

This compound had its own mini-army. The smartest move would be to make tracks out of here sooner rather than later, but I'd broken in here on a job, dammit, and I wouldn't get paid if I didn't finish it.

The setting sun sent tall shadows slicing between the buildings. I skidded up to a metal utility shed and slammed the sliding door back. My current headache of a job, also known as Courtney Polk, scrabbled back as much as she could while handcuffed to a pipe before she recognized me and glowered. I'd locked her in here temporarily when the Colombians had started closing in.

I picked up the key to the cuffs from where I'd dropped it in the dust by the door and freed her. "Time to skedaddle."

"Get away from me," she hissed, flinching back. I caught one of her arms and twisted, and Polk winced.

"I am having a very bad day," I said. "If you don't stay quiet, I will knock you unconscious and carry you out of here. Do you understand?"

She glared at me.

I twisted a fraction of an inch more, about three degrees shy of popping her shoulder out of the socket.

"All right already!" She tried to spit the words, but her voice climbed at the end, pitched with pain.

I let her go. "Come on."

Polk was all gangly arms and legs and looked far too thin to have much endurance, but she was in better shape than she appeared, and we made it to the perimeter in less than three minutes. I pushed her down to crouch behind the corner of a building, my eyes roving for the best way out, troop movements becoming vectors, numbers stretching and exploding against the fence. Calculations spun through my brain in infinite combinations. We were going to make it.

And then a shape rose up, skulking between two buildings, zig-zagging to stalk us—a black man, tall and lean and handsome, in a leather jacket. His badge wasn't visible, but it didn't need to be; the way he moved told me everything I needed to know. He stood out like a cop in a compound full of drug runners.

I started to grab Polk, but it was too late. The cop whipped around and looked up, meeting my eyes from fifty feet away, and knew he was made.

He was *fast*. We'd scarcely locked eyes and his hand was inside his jacket in a blur.

My boot flicked out and hit a rock.

From the cop's perspective, it must have looked like the worst kind of evil luck. He'd barely gotten his hand inside his coat when my foot-flicked missile rocketed out of nowhere and smacked him in the forehead. His head snapped back, and he listed to the side and collapsed.

God bless Newton's laws of motion.

Polk recoiled. "What the hell was that!"

"*That* was a cop," I snapped. Five minutes with this kid and my irritation was already at its limit.

"What? Then why did you—he could have helped us!"

I resisted the urge to smack her. "You're a *drug smuggler*."

"Not on purpose!"

"Yeah, because that makes a difference. I don't think the authorities are going to care that the Colombians weren't too happy with you anymore. You don't know enough to gamble on flipping on your crew, so you're going to a very faraway island after this. Now shut up." The perimeter was within sprinting distance now, and rocks would work for the compound's guards as well. I scooped up a few, my hands instantly reading their masses. Projectile motion: my height, their heights, the acceleration of gravity, and a quick correction for air resistance—and then pick the right initial velocity so that the deceleration of such a mass against a human skull would provide the correct force to drop a grown man.

One, two, three. The guards tumbled into well-armed heaps on the ground.

Polk made a choking sound and stumbled back from me a couple of steps. I rolled my eyes, grabbed her by one thin wrist, and hauled.

Less than a minute later, we were driving safely away from the compound in a stolen Jeep, the rich purple of the California desert night falling around us and the lights and shouts from an increasingly agitated drug cartel dwindling in the distance. I took a few zigs and zags through the desert scrub to put off anyone trying to follow us, but I was pretty sure the Colombians were still chasing their own tails. Sure enough, soon we were speeding alone through the desert and the darkness. I kept the running lights off just in case, leaving the moonlight and mathematical extrapolation to outline the rocks and brush as we bumped along. I wasn't worried about crashing. Cars are only forces in motion.

In the open Jeep, the cuts on my face stung as the wind whipped by, and annoyance rolled through me as the adrenaline receded. This job—I'd thought it would be a cakewalk. Polk's sister had been the one to hire me, and she had told me Rio had cold-contacted her and strongly suggested that if she didn't pay me to get her sister out, she'd never see her again. I hadn't talked to Rio myself in months—not until he'd used me as his personal punching bag today—but I could connect the dots: Rio had been working undercover, seen Polk, decided she deserved to be rescued, and thrown me the gig. Of course, I was grateful for the work, but I wished I had known Rio was undercover with the cartel in the first place. I cursed the bad luck that had made us run into him—the Colombians never would have caught me on their own.

In the passenger seat, Polk braced herself unhappily against the jounces of our off-road journey. "I'm not moving to a desert island," she said suddenly, interrupting the quiet of the night.

I sighed. "I didn't say desert. And it doesn't even have to be an island. We can probably stash you in rural Argentina or something."

She crossed her spindly arms, hugging herself against the night's chill. "Whatever. I'm not going. I'm not going to let the cartel win."

I resisted the urge to crash the Jeep on purpose. Not that I had much to crash it into out here, but I could have managed. The correct angle against one of those little scrub bushes . . .

"You do realize they're not the only ones who want a piece of you, right? In case our lovely drug-running friends neglected to tell you before they dumped you in a basement, the authorities are scouring California for you. Narcotics trafficking and murder, I hear. What, were all the cool kids doing it?"

She winced away, hunching into herself. "I swear I didn't know they were using the shipments to smuggle drugs. I only called my boss when I got stopped because that's what they told us to do. It's not my fault."

Yeah, yeah. Her sister had tearfully shown me a copy of the police report—driver stopped for running a light, drugs found, more gang members who'd shown up and shot the cops, taking back the truck and driver both. The report had heavily implicated Courtney in every way.

When she'd hired me, Dawna Polk had insisted her sister wouldn't have hurt a fly. Personally, I hadn't particularly cared if the girl was guilty or not. A job was a job.

"Look, I only want to get paid," I said. "If your sister says you can throw your life away and go to prison, that's A-okay with me."

"I was just a driver," Courtney insisted. "I never looked to see what was in the back. They can't say I'm responsible."

"If you think that, you're an idiot."

"I'd rather the police have me than you anyway!" she shot back. "At least with the cops I know I have rights! And they're not some sort of freaky weird feng shui killers!"

She flinched back into herself, biting her lip. Probably wondering if she'd said too much. If I was going to go "feng shui" on her, too.

Crap.

I took a deep breath. "My name is Cas Russell. I do retrieval. It means I get things back for people. That's my job." I swallowed. "Your sister really did hire me to get you out, okay? I'm not going to hurt you."

"You locked me up again."

"Only so you'd stay put until I could come back for you," I tried to assure her.

Courtney's arms were still crossed, and she'd started worrying her lip with her teeth. "And what about all that other stuff you did?" she asked finally. "With the cartel guards, and the stones, and that cop . . ."

I scanned the constellations and steered the Jeep eastward, aiming to intersect the highway. The stars burned into my eyes, their altitudes, azimuths, and apparent magnitudes appearing in my mind as if stenciled in the sky behind each bright, burning pinprick. A satellite puttered into view, and its timing told me its height above Earth and its orbital velocity.

"I'm really good at math," I said. *Too good.* "That's all."

Polk snorted as if I were putting her on, but then her face knitted in a frown, and I felt her staring at me in the darkness. Oh, hell. I like it better when my clients hire me to retrieve inanimate objects. People are so annoying.

By morning, my madly circuitous route had brought us only halfway back to LA. Switching cars twice and drastically changing direction three times might not have been strictly necessary, but it made my paranoid self feel better.

The desert night had turned cold; fortunately, we were now in a junky old station wagon instead of the open Jeep, though the car's heater managed only a thin stream of lukewarm air. Polk had her bony knees hunched up in front of her and had buried her face against them. She hadn't spoken in hours.

I was grateful. This job had had enough monkey wrenches already without needing to explain myself to an ungrateful child every other minute.

Polk sat up as we drove into the rising sun. "You said you do retrieval."

"Yeah," I said.

"You get things back for people."

"That's what 'retrieval' means."

"I want to hire you." Her youthful face was set in stubborn lines.

Great. She was lucky I wasn't choosy about my clientele. And that I needed another job after this one. "What for?"

"I want my life back."

"Uh, your sister's already paying me for that," I reminded her. "But hey, you can pay me twice if you want. I won't complain."

"No. I mean I don't want to go flying off to Argentina. I want my *life* back."

"Wait, you're asking me to steal you back a clean record?" This girl didn't know what reality was. "Kid, that's not—"

"I've got money," she interrupted. Her eyes dropped to her knees. "I got paid really well, for someone who drove a delivery truck."

I snorted. "What *are* the going rates for being a drug mule these days?"

"I don't care what you think of me," said Polk, though red was creeping up her neck and across her cheeks. She ducked her head, letting her frizzy ponytail fall across her face. "People make mistakes, you know."

Yeah. Cry me a river. I ignored the voice in my head telling me I should take the fucking job anyway. "Saving the unfortunate isn't really my bag. Sorry, kid."

"Will you at least think about it? And stop calling me 'kid.' I'm twenty-three."

She looked about eighteen, wide-eyed and gullible and wet behind the ears. But then, I guess I can't judge; people still assumed I was a teenager sometimes, and in reality I was barely older than Courtney. Of course, age can be measured in more ways than years. Sometimes I had to pull a .45 in people's faces to remind them of that.

I remembered with a pang that my best 1911 had been lost back at the compound when I was captured. Dammit. Dawna was going to get that in her expense list.

"So? Are you thinking about it?"

"I was thinking about my favorite gun."

"You don't have to be so mean all the time," Courtney mumbled into her knees. "I know I need help, okay? That's why I asked."

Oh, fuck. Courtney Polk was a headache and a half, and clearing the names of idiot kids who got mixed up with drug cartels wasn't in my job description. I'd been very much looking forward to dumping her on her sister's doorstep and driving away.

Though that small voice in the back of my head kept whispering: *Drive away where?*

I didn't have any gigs lined up after I finished this contract. I don't do too well when I'm not working.

Yeah, right. Between jobs you're a fucking mess.

I slammed the voice away again and concentrated on the money. I like money. "Just how much cash do you have?"

"You'll do it?" Her face lit up, and her whole body straightened toward me. "Thank you! Really, thank you!"

I grumbled something not nearly as enthusiastic and revved the station wagon down the empty dawn freeway. Figuring out how to steal back someone's reputation was not my idea of fun.

The voice in the back of my head laughed mockingly. *Like you have the luxury of being choosy.*

two

I PULLED the station wagon into a grungy roadside motel near Palmdale, the type with a cracked plastic sign of misaligned letters misspelling the word "VACANCY." I'd detoured again, and we'd circled around enough to be coming in from north of LA, through the dusty shithole towns of meth gang territory. Courtney's friends, on the other hand, had been smuggling coke, which I supposed made them the classy drug dealers.

I didn't need to rest, but I suspected Courtney did, and I wanted to think. I had no idea how the hell I was going to approach her case. The obvious plan was to find enough evidence on her old employers to give the DEA some sort of smashing takedown, let Courtney take the credit for it, and broker a deal to expunge her record. That would involve dealing with the police, though, and that sounded about as appealing as driving two-inch bamboo splinters under my fingernails.

I ushered Courtney ahead of me into the motel's threadbare office; her jaws cracked with a yawn as she stumbled in. The clerk was stuttering into the phone. I crossed my arms, leaned against the wall, and waited.

The clerk stayed on his call for another ten minutes, and kept giving us increasingly nervous glances, as if he expected me to bawl him out for not helping us straightaway. I supposed that made sense, considering my messed-up fatigue-style clothes and my messed-up face, which had to be turning into a spectacular rainbow of color by this point. Or maybe he saw brown skin and thought I was a terrorist—I've been told I look kind of Middle Eastern. Goddamn racial profiling.

I tried to smile at him, but it ended up more like a scowl.

The clerk finally got off the phone and stammered his way into assigning us a room on the first floor. He dropped the key twice trying to give it to me, and then dropped the cash I gave him when he tried to pick the bills up off the counter. If he'd known I'd pulled the money from a succession of stolen cars that night, he probably would've been even more nervous.

I pulled Courtney back into the sunlight after me, where we found the right door and let ourselves into a stock cheap-and-dirty motel room, the type with furnishings made of stapled-together cardboard. Apparently relieved by my promise to help her, Courtney zonked out almost before her frizzy head smacked against the pillows on one of the dingy beds. I tossed the cigarette-burned bedspread over her and went to push open the door to the small washroom.

Only to be met with the muzzle of a .45. "Howdy," said the black cop from the compound from where he sat on the toilet tank, feet on the lid. "I think we need to have a talk."

Well, shit.

No matter how much math I know, and no matter how fast my body is trained to respond automatically to it, I can't move faster than a bullet. Of course, if the cop had been within reach, I could have disarmed him before he could fire—but the bathroom was just large enough for the math to err on his side, considering he already had his gun drawn and pointed at my center of mass.

"Don't mind me," I said, inching forward and trying for flippancy. "I'm just going to use the—"

His hand moved slightly, and I froze.

"Good," he said. "You stand still now, sweetheart. You move and I'll put a bullet through your kidney."

I knew two things about him now. First, he was smart, because not only had he tracked us here and then gotten into our bathroom before we had reached the room, but he also wasn't underestimating me. Second, he didn't give a rat's ass about proper police procedure, which meant he was either a very dangerous cop or a very dirty one— or both.

I let my hands hover upward, showing I wasn't going for a weapon. "I'm not moving."

"Pithica," he said. "Talk."

"You have me confused with someone else," I said. Mathematics erupted around me, layering over itself, possibilities rising and crumbling away as the solutions all came up a hair short of the time the handsome cop needed to pull the trigger.

"Talk," said the cop. "Or I shoot you and break your pet out there."

Courtney. Shit. Stall. "Okay," I said. "What do you want to know?"

In the bathroom mirror, I saw the rising sun peek above the sill and through the almost drawn curtains.

Specular reflection. Angles of incidence. Perfect. As long as the cop wasn't going to fire blind, I had him. Hands still raised in the air in apparent surrender, I twitched my left wrist.

At the speed of light, the glint of sunlight came in through the window, hit the bathroom mirror, and reflected in a tight beam from the polished face of my wristwatch right into the cop's eyes.

He moved fast, blinking and ducking his head away, but I moved faster. I dodged to the side as I dove in, my right hand swinging out to take the gun off-line. My fingers wrapped around his wrist and I yanked, the numbers whirling and settling to give me the perfect fulcrum as I leveraged off my grasp on his gun hand to leap upward and give him a spinning knee to the side of the head.

The cop collapsed, out cold, his face smacking inelegantly into the grimy bathroom floor.

I checked the gun. Fully loaded with a round in the chamber, as

I'd expected. I gave it points for being a nice hefty .45 with an extended magazine, and points off for being a Glock. Typical cop. I hate Glocks.

I searched him quickly and found three spare mags fully loaded with ammo and a little snub-nosed Smith & Wesson tucked in his boot. No wallet or phone—and, more important, no badge or ID of any kind. I was right; he was dirty.

I dragged him out into the room, yanked the sheet off one of the beds, and began tearing long strips from it. In the other bed, Courtney stirred and squinted at me sleepily. When she saw me tying a tall, unconscious man to the radiator, she came fully awake and shot bolt upright. "What's going on?"

"He followed us here," I explained. The guy must have regained consciousness fast enough to track our escape back at the compound, and must have been the one on the phone with the motel clerk when we checked in, making sure someone let him into our room before we got the key. This time I'd make sure he couldn't track us. By the time he woke up and got himself loose, we'd be long gone.

"Who is he? Is he with the Colombians?"

I frowned at her from where I was securing my knots. "He's the cop from back at the compound. Remember? As to whether he's with the cartel, I don't know. I think he's dirty."

"How do you know he's a cop in the first place?"

"Police training makes you move a certain way." It came to me in numbers, of course, the subtle angles and lines of stride and posture. But I didn't feel like explaining that.

"Oh." Courtney's hands had tightened into fists on the threadbare bedspread, her knuckles white.

I finished my work and moved toward the door. "Come on, kid. We've got to hit the road."

Courtney scrambled up and stayed behind me while I checked outside. The sun gleamed off the cars, the dusty parking lot completely still. If our police friend was dirty, it was unlikely he'd have a partner nearby, fortunately. I glanced around to see if I could spot his car, figuring it might have some nice toys in it—as well as maybe his badge and ID, which could give us some leverage—but no vehicle stood out as promising. Instead, I led Polk over to a black GMC truck so caked with dust and grime it looked gray. In my business, getting into a car and hot-wiring it are such necessary skills I could literally do them with my eyes closed, and I had the engine coughing to life in fourteen seconds. We left the motel behind in a cloud of dust.

I flattened the accelerator, and the desert sped by around us, the morning sun flashing off dust and sand and rock. I drew a quick map of this part of the county in my head, calculating the best way to travel so that even if the cop woke up quickly and used the most efficient search algorithm he could—or had supernatural luck—the probabilities would drop toward zero that he'd be able to find us again.

Courtney's subdued voice interrupted my calculations. "Was he after me?"

"Yeah," I said. I brooded for a moment. "What do you know about something called Pithica?"

She shook her frizzy head. "I've never heard of it."

"Are you sure? You never heard a whisper from your former employers? Think hard."

Courtney winced away from my harshness. "No. I swear. Why?"

I didn't answer.

What the hell was going on? Why was a peace officer on the take after Courtney Polk? She'd been a drug mule, for crying out loud, one the cartel had ended up locking in a basement. She hadn't exactly been high on the food chain. And what the hell was Pithica?

I didn't go straight into LA; instead, I continued zigzagging through the brown desert of the northern outskirts and switched cars twice in three hours. I didn't know if our dirty cop could put out an APB on us—he might even have enough resources to have his buddies set up roadblocks. Best to err on the side of being impossible to find no matter what.

Once the morning hit a decent hour, I stopped at a cheap electronics store and picked up a disposable cell. I stood under the awning of the shop, watching Courtney where she sat in the car waiting, and dialed Rio.

"Pithica," I said as soon as he answered.

There was a long pause. Then Rio said, "Don't get involved."

"I'm already involved," I said, my stomach sinking.

Another pause. "I can't talk now." Of course. He was still under-cover. I'd assumed he was just taking down the whole gang for kicks, but now . . .

"When and where?" I said impatiently.

"God be with you," said Rio, and hung up.

I should've known, I thought. Undercover wasn't Rio's style. His MO was to go in, hurt the people who needed hurting, and get out. If taking down the gang had been his only objective, a nice explosion would have lit up the California desert weeks ago and left nothing but a crater and the bodies of several eviscerated drug dealers. *That* was Rio's style. And why had he referred Dawna to me to get Court-ney out in the first place? Why not do it himself? He was more than capable; in fact, I was sure he could have done it without even blow-ing his cover.

Unless things were way more complicated than I had realized, and this wasn't a simple drug ring.

"Who were you calling?" asked Courtney, getting out of the car and squinting at me in the glare of the Southern California sun.

"A friend," I said. Well, sort of. "Someone I trust." That part was true.

"Someone who can help us?"

"Maybe." Rio was clearly working his own angle, and didn't want help—even from me. Which hurt a little, if I wanted to be honest with myself. I'm good at what I do. Rio didn't mean to hurt me, of course; he didn't care about my feelings one way or another. He didn't care about anyone's feelings. I wondered what it said about me that he was the closest thing I did have to a friend.

Suck it up, Cas.

Rio wasn't the only resource I had. I contemplated for a moment, then dialed another number.

"Mack's Garage," said a gravelly voice on the other end.

"Anton, it's Cas Russell. I need some information."

He grunted. "Usual rates."

"Yeah. I need everything you can get on the word 'Pithica.'"

"Spelling?"

"I'm not sure. There might be some ties to Colombian drug run-ners. And the authorities might be investigating already."

He grunted again. "Two hours."

"Got it." I hung up. Anton was one of several information brokers in the city, and I'd hired him not infrequently over the past couple of years, whenever I wanted to know more than a standard internet search would give me. If "Pithica" had a paper trail, I was betting he could find it.

"Come on," I said to Courtney, shepherding her back to the car. "We're going to hit rush hour as it is."

three

"Do you have cash, or is your money all in the bank?" I asked Courtney as we inched forward through the eternal parking lot of the 405 freeway, the heat beating down through the windshield and slowly cooking us. The temperature had catapulted up by a full thirty-four degrees Fahrenheit with the rising sun as we finally headed into the city: Los Angeles at its finest. Our current junkpot car didn't have air-conditioning, and the still air and stalled traffic meant even rolling down the windows didn't help one whit.

Courtney fiddled with the end of her ponytail self-consciously. "They paid me in cash. I didn't—taxes, you know, I thought it would be better if . . ."

"Oh, yeah," I said, trying not to laugh at her. "No sign at all they weren't on the level. I can see why you thought it was a legitimate delivery service." I dealt only in cash myself, of course, but I wasn't exactly a yardstick for legality. "Where is it, under your mattress?"

She grimaced, red creeping across her cheekbones again. "A floorboard."

"All right. We'll swing by. Let's hope the cops didn't find it." I had a fair amount of my own liquid capital stashed in various places throughout the city, but I preferred to use hers. She was supposed to be the paying client, after all.

"You think they searched my place?" Courtney asked, going tense and sitting up in the passenger seat.

"You're a murder suspect," I said. "You think?"

Her whole face had gone flushed now. "I—I just don't—I have some things—"

"Relax, kid. Nobody's going to care about your porn collection."

She choked and broke out in a coughing fit.

"Unless it's children," I amended. "Then you'd be in big trouble. Bigger, I mean. It's not kiddie porn, is it?"

"What—? I don't—*no*, of course not!" she stammered. Her skin burned tomato red now, from her neck to the roots of her sweat-dampened hair. "Why would you—I don't even—"

I laughed for real as traffic started creeping forward again. She was too easy.

Courtney's place was only a few miles from Anton's, and I decided to drop by the information broker's first. Anton's garage was a constant of the universe. A ramshackle mechanic's outfit, the place had never changed in all the times I'd been there. The words "Mack's Garage" barely showed through a decades-thick layer of motor oil and grime on a bent-up metal sign, and the junkers in the bays were the same derelict vehicles I'd seen the last time. No customers were in sight. Anton did know cars, as it happened, but he wasn't an auto mechanic.

I knocked on the door to the office and Anton opened it himself, a faded gray work coverall over his considerable bulk. Anton was a big, big man in every way—six feet five and beefy all over, he had a thick neck, thicker face, and steel-gray hair shaven to a strict quarter inch, which for some reason made him seem even bigger. Considering I was already short, I tended to feel like a toy person next to him. But as much as I was sure he could open a can of whoop-ass on someone if he wanted to, I always thought he was kind of a teddy bear. A surly, taciturn teddy bear who never smiled, but a teddy bear nonetheless.

He grunted when he saw us. "Russell. Come in."

Courtney and I followed Anton through the outer office and into his workshop. Computers and parts of computers sprawled across every inch of the place, some intact but many more in pieces, and bits of circuitry and machinery I couldn't name hummed away all over the room in various states of repair, with teetering mountains of papers and files stacked on every marginally flat surface. A huge office chair sized for Anton's bulk stood like a throne in the middle of the chaos, and perched in its depths was a twelve-year-old girl.

"Cas!" Anton's daughter cried, leaping up to run over and throw her arms around my middle. Even for twelve, she was tiny, and with her dark complexion, I always figured her mother must have been a four-foot-ten Asian or Latina woman whom Anton could have picked up with his little finger.

"Hey, Penny. How's it going?" I said, ruffling her dark hair.

"Good!" she chirped. "We've got an intelligence file for you!"

"Thanks. Hey, I've got a present for you." I pulled the cop's little Smith & Wesson out of my pocket. "Look, it's just your size."

"Ooo! Cas! Thank you!" Eyes shining, she took the gun, keeping it pointed down. "Daddy, look what Cas gave me! What caliber is it?"

"Thirty-eight Special, for a special little girl," I said. "Take good care of it; it'll last you a long time." What can I say, I have a soft spot for kids.

"You're giving her a *gun*?" squawked Courtney from behind me. "One you stole from a *cop*?"

"She knows how to use it," grunted Anton.

Courtney quailed. "That's not what I—"

"You think I don't take care of my daughter right?" said Anton quietly, looming a bit. "That what you saying, girl?"

Courtney stared up and up at him. Then she said, "No, sir," very meekly.

"Didn't think so," rumbled the big man. "Russell, I got that info for you. Not much to go on, mind."

"I appreciate anything you can get us," I said.

He pulled a file folder from among the machines. "Some fishy things here. Could be more we ain't hit yet. You don't mind, me and Penny'll keep digging on this."

"Sure," I said, surprised. It was the first time he'd said something like that in all the times I'd hired him. "If you think there's more to find, go for it. Usual rate." I opened the file and gave it a cursory glance—the contents were puzzlingly varied; I'd have to sit down with it later.

"I bet we get more," said Penny optimistically, hopping back up on her dad's chair and rolling it over to a computer keyboard. "Hey, Cas! I cracked an IRS database yesterday. All by myself!"

"She's got the talent," murmured Anton in his quiet, gravelly way, but anyone could see he was glowing with pride.

"Nice job," I told Penny. "Too bad you don't pay taxes."

"Well, Daddy does, but he told me not to change anything. I want to try some White House systems next."

I turned to Anton in surprise. "You pay taxes?"

"I use this country's services," he said. "I pay the taxes them people we elected says I owe. Only fair."

Wow. "Your call, I guess."

He gave one of his trademark grunts. "Want to teach my girl right."

Courtney made a squeaking sound. I decided I'd better get her out of sight before Anton felt the urge to reach out his thumb and crush her like a bug. Besides, Anton's reference to more weirdness was amplifying the alarm bells that had been going off in the back of my head ever since the cop had cornered us at the motel.

The feeling got about a hundred times worse when we got to Courtney's house.

"That's—that's my . . ." She trailed off, her hand shaking as she pointed. Two white men in dark suits were standing on her doorstep talking, the front door cracked open behind them. As we watched, one of them pushed open the door and went inside. The other stubbed out a cigarette and followed a minute later.

"What are they doing in my house?" whispered Courtney weakly.

We were still a block away. I pulled the car over and turned off the engine. Courtney's place was a little guesthouse-type cottage, and most of the blinds were shut, but one of the side windows was the kind of slatted glass that didn't close all the way. Through it, we could see more suits—and they were in the midst of tossing her living room. Thoroughly.

"Who are they?" asked Courtney. "Are they police?"

"No." Some of them moved like they might have military backgrounds, but I wasn't sure; we didn't have a good view and I didn't have the numerical profiles of every type of tactical training memorized anyway. Definitely not cops, though.

"Do you think—are they with the Colombians?"

"Possibly." The men were the wrong ethnicity to be on the Colombian side of the cartel, but maybe they were American connections. Why would the cartel be searching Courtney's place, though? If they were after the girl herself, they would be lying in wait, not turning the rooms inside out. "Did you steal anything from them? Money, drugs, information? Anything?"

"No!" Courtney sounded horrified. "I have money there like I told you, but it's what they paid me. I'm not a thief!"

"Just a drug smuggler." As someone who did dabble in what one might call "stealing," when paid well to do it, I resented her indignation a bit. "Let's keep our moral lines straight and clear, now."

"I didn't know," repeated Courtney hopelessly.

I reached for the car door handle. Maybe these men were only burglars after her little stash of savings, but I wasn't going to bet on it. "I'm going to get closer. Stay here and keep out of sight."

"What if they come this way?" Courtney had gone pale, her freckles standing out across her cheekbones.

"Hide," I said, and got out of the car.

I still hadn't had a chance to clean up my face, and despite this not being the best part of town—unkempt, weedy lawns buttressed trash-filled gutters, and most of the houses sported cracked siding and sun-peeled paint—I got a few looks from people on the street as I strolled toward Courtney's cottage. I ran a hand through my short hair, but it was a tangled, curly mass and I was pretty sure I only made it worse. Undercover work has never been my forte.

I meandered down the sidewalk, keeping a sidelong view of Courtney's house. The dark-suited men became points in motion, my brain extrapolating from the little I could see and hear, assigning probabilities and translating to expected values. As I drew up to the house, the highs and lows of conversation became barely audible, but I ran some quick numbers—to decipher the words, I'd have to be so close I'd be the most obvious eavesdropper in the world. The plot of half-hearted grass between the street and the houses didn't have any handy cover I could use to sneak closer, either.

I ran my eyes over the surrounding scenery, a three-dimensional model growing in my head. A stone wall curved out from just behind Polk's house and ended in a tumble at a vacant lot, and it very nearly fit the curvature of a conic.

Sound waves are funny things. They can chase each other over concave surfaces, create reinforcing concentrations of acoustics at the focus of an architectural ellipse or parabola. Some rooms are famous for the ability to whisper a word on one side and have it be heard with perfect clarity on the other.

I only needed a few more sounding boards.

I wandered back down the street and kicked at a trash can as I went by so it turned slightly. Ran my hand along the neighbor's fence, pulling the gate closed with a click. Flipped up a metal bowl set out for stray cats with my foot so it leaned against a fire hydrant. Tossed a rock casually at a bird feeder so it swung and changed orientation. I ambled down the street twice more, knocking the detritus of the street around, making small changes. Then I ran my eyes back across the house, feeding in the decibel level of normal human conversation.

Close. All I needed was an umbrella. It wasn't raining, but plenty of cars were parked on the street, and I found what I needed after a quick survey of back windows. I jimmied my way in, retrieved the umbrella from the back seat, and left the car door cracked at an angle for good measure. Then I headed over to a tree at the edge of the next lot, one that stood exactly at the focus of my manufactured acoustic puzzle, put up the umbrella, and listened.

The voices in Courtney's house sprang up as if they were right next to me.

"—utter rubbish, that's what it is," a man was saying in a British accent. "FIFA's got no right to blame Sir Alex. They got a scandal, it's their own damn fault."

"You two and your pansy-ass soccer players," put in an American voice. "You're in fucking America, you know. Watch some real football."

"Oh, you mean that boring little program where they prance around in all the pads and take a break every five minutes?"

"Aw, fuck off. At least we score more than once a game."

"Gentlemen. Focus." This man's voice was smooth, deep, and oozing charisma, and it cut off whatever the American's retort would have been like he'd hit a switch.

"I don't think it's here, boss," said a fourth guy in a nasally voice with an accent I couldn't place. "I think she stashed it somewhere else. Or she—"

"'Stashed it'?" cut in the talkative Brit. "Where? She doesn't have a safe deposit box, they made it so she's got no friends—"

"So she buried it in the front yard, or spackled it into a wall," said the American. "Who knows what she was thinking?"

"The only place left to look here is if we come back with a sledge-hammer and a shovel," agreed the nasally man.

Their words fell off while they waited for the leader to make a decision. I found myself holding my breath.

"Hey, momma, it look like rain to you?"

I was jerked out of listening to see an arrogant teenage kid wearing far too many chains laughing in my face. "You expecting rain? Ha! Whatcha do to your face, or were you born that way?"

My first instinct was to knock him on the head and get him out of my way. But he was only a kid—a shrimpy Hispanic teen, probably part of a gang considering the area and the colored bandanna knotted around his bicep, and aching to prove himself. Even if he was doing so by picking on a small woman who resembled a disturbed homeless person at the moment.

"Are you trying to pick a fight with me?" I asked evenly, lounging back against the tree and letting the grip of the cop's Glock peek out of my belt. The kid's eyes got wide, and he stumbled back a step.

I glanced back at Courtney's house. The men in dark suits were filing out the front door, either leaving for good or planning to return with a sledgehammer. Either way, I had missed it. I sighed and turned back to the gang member. "Hey, kid. Watch this." I leaned down, pried up an old tennis ball from where it was embedded in the dust, and threw it hard off to the side.

A series of soft pings sounded—across the street, behind us. The kid looked around, confused. Then the tennis ball came rocketing from the other direction and bopped him lightly on the head.

"Whoa!" He stared at me. "Fuck, momma! How'd you do that?"

"Learn enough math, you might find out," I said, keeping tabs on the suits out of the corner of my eye. Conveniently, this conversation provided a neat cover if they happened to look this way. I no longer appeared to be lurking. "Stay in school, okay?"

"Yeah, okay. Okay." He nodded rapidly, eyes wide. Then he turned and hurried off, looking back over his shoulder at me.

Like I said, I have a soft spot for kids.

The Dark Suits had headed off at the same time, appropriately in a dark van. I glanced around the street and walked casually over to Courtney's front door. The jamb was already splintered next to the bolt; I nudged the door open.

The living room looked like a herd of rambunctious chimpanzees had been invited to destroy it. Cushions had been torn off the furniture and rent open, their polyester filling collecting in puffy snowballs on the floor. Every chair and table had been upended. Cabinets and closets stood ajar and empty; clothing was tangled with DVD cases and broken dishes in haphazard piles amid the chaos. True to the Dark Suits' lack of sledgehammer, however, the walls and floor were still intact.

I hesitated on the threshold, wondering what the chances were that the Dark Suits or anyone else might have left surveillance devices behind, but if so, they had probably recorded my skulking already. I picked my way through the destruction to the corner Courtney had told me about, a growing sense of urgency making me hurry. What the fuck was Courtney Polk mixed up in?

I didn't have any tools, but breaking boards is all about the right force at the right angle. With one well-placed stomp from my boot, the floorboard splintered, and I pried back the pieces and fished out a paper bag filled with neat piles of loose bills.

My gaze skittered around the room as I wondered where else Courtney might have hidden something . . . something small enough to spackle into a wall. But the only option I could see was breaking every floorboard and then tearing down all the drywall, and that would take far too long. If Courtney still insisted on claiming ignorance, maybe I could stash her somewhere and then get back with tools before the Dark Suits did.

And maybe I could get some of my questions answered another way before then. Tucking the paper bag under one arm, I headed out, pulling out the cell phone as I did so and dialing Anton.

"Mack's Garage," chirped a girl's voice.

"Penny, it's Cas. Can you put your dad on?"

"Sure!" She shouted cheerfully for her father, and in moments Anton grunted in my ear.

"Anton, it's Cas Russell again. I need you to look up something else for me."

Grunt.

"That client who was with me today. Courtney Polk. Check her out for me."

"Anything else?"

"No, just—"

A deafening explosion tore through the line. I heard a girl's scream, and Anton shouting, and then any human sound was swallowed by the chaos of more explosions, multiple ones at once—and the call went dead.

four

SHIT SHIT shit shit shit!

I tore back along the street, my boots pounding against the asphalt, the math blurring and every other thought evaporating as I dove toward the car. I yanked open the door and ignored Courtney's panicked questions as I wrenched the transmission into gear and spun us out into traffic with a squeal of tires; a cacophony of horns deafened us as other drivers swerved and slammed on their brakes, but I only heard Penny's scream, echoing endlessly, high and terrified—we had to move—*faster faster faster faster faster—*

LA traffic is forever fucked, but it helps to know the calculus of moving objects—and to drive like a maniac. I slewed between lanes, skidding in front of other cars by a hairbreadth, cutting it as close as the numbers told me I possibly could, and when I started hitting traffic lights, I laid on the horn and popped the wheels up over the curb to sheer down the sidewalk, horrified pedestrians hurling themselves out of my way and traumatized citizens howling expletives in my wake. Courtney made small sounds in the passenger seat, bracing herself against the dashboard and trying to hang on.

This part of town didn't have a huge police presence, but if I'd seen blue lights behind me I wouldn't have cared. Or stopped. Within minutes, I was careening around the last corner toward Anton's garage.

A tidal wave of heat and light and smoke crashed over the car, overloading every sense, blasting, overwhelming. We were still a block away, but I jammed my foot down on the brake, sending Courtney tumbling against the dash.

Anton's building was a roaring inferno, the flames towering into the sky, black smoke pouring from the blaze and rolling thick and acrid over the street. I scrabbled at the door handle and stumbled out—the heat slammed into me even at this distance, an oppressive wall of blistering air. My skin burned as it flash-dried, and every breath scalded, as if I were swallowing gulps of boiling water.

The building was melting before my eyes, collapsing in on itself, the walls and roof folding with slow grace in massive flares of sparks. My brain cataloged materials, heat, speed of propagation . . . this horror had used chemical help; it must have. I did a quick back-of-the-envelope timing in my mind, holding my breath and closing stinging eyes against the smoke that clogged the air.

I ran the numbers three different ways, and succeeded only in torturing myself. Even with the most generous estimates, nobody had made it out.

Fucking math.

I stumbled back to the car. The metal of the door was already warm. I slid into the driver's seat, wrenched the steering wheel around into a U-turn, and accelerated back the way we had come. We'd ditch this car a block or two from here in case any traffic cameras had glimpsed my vehicular stunts, then put some distance behind us before the authorities arrived.

"Did they . . . are they . . ." Courtney asked timidly.

"Dead." My eyes and throat scratched from the smoke.

A small sob escaped her. "Are you sure?"

"I'm sure." I couldn't help wondering if it was her fault.

Or mine.

My mind buzzed. I'd contacted Anton a little over five hours ago—the traffic going into the city had held us up for a good chunk of time, but then I'd headed straight here. Five hours. Ample time to set this up, if someone had caught on to Anton's search. If that someone happened to be motivated enough.

I tried to tell myself Anton's work had encompassed a multitude of other projects, any of which might have generated enemies. Whoever had targeted him had overcompensated like fuck to take all of his data and information with him, but even so, a case from months or years ago might have provoked this. Some old client with a grudge. This didn't have to be because of what I'd brought him.

Did I really believe that?

The platitudes curdled in my head.

Jesus Christ. This was supposed to be an easy job. Rescue the kid, get her out of the country, be home in time for dinner.

Nobody should have died on this one, least of all two people sitting at a computer looking things up for me.

My grip tightened on the steering wheel until my fingers hurt.

I studied Courtney out of the corner of my eye. She was hugging her knees to herself, her shoulders shaking, her ponytail falling across her and hiding her face.

She was involved in this somehow.

"What aren't you telling me?" The words came out too harsh. I didn't care. "Those men at your place were looking for something. What was it?"

She raised a blotchy, tear-streaked face to look at me. "I don't— I don't know. I swear I don't."

Right.

My client might be lying to me. My client, who was already on the run not only from the authorities, but from a drug cartel who wanted her dead, government men in dark suits, a dirty cop, and some unknown player willing to commit arson and murder to cover its tracks.

And, on top of everything, I'd lost my information broker. I tried not to think about Penny, the twelve-year-old kick-ass hacker who'd been taught to pay her taxes on time.

Courtney cried softly in the passenger seat the whole way to the bolt-hole I drove us to. If she was playing a part, laying it on thick in the hope I'd buy the tearful façade, she deserved some sort of acting award.

Maybe she really was just a naïve kid who had gotten in too deep, too scared or too stupid to tell me what was going on.

Still, the crying pissed me off. What right did she have to sob her eyes out for people she'd barely met and seemed to judge from moment one? "For Christ's sake," I growled as I swung the car into a grimy alleyway. "You didn't even know them."

"How can you be so cold?" she murmured tremulously.

I slammed the car's transmission into park. "Are you feeling guilty? Is that it?"

Tears swam in her red-rimmed eyes. "Guilty? Why would I—" Her face contorted in horror. *Could someone really fake that?* "This was about us? Oh, God—that was only this morning!"

Maybe I could turn her guilt to my advantage, I thought. Come at her from the side, maneuver her into revealing whatever she was hiding—

The thought was exhausting. I wasn't any good with people, and I definitely wasn't good at subtlety. I could threaten her, but . . .

Courtney rubbed the ends of her sleeves across her face, sniffling.

She was just a *kid*. Or near enough. Even I wasn't willing to go there, at least not yet.

I picked up the file from Anton and the paper bag of money with stiff hands, and we got out of the car. The alleyway ended at a rusted back door; I led the way up a narrow, dark stairwell that climbed into a dilapidated second-floor loft. The furnishings were basic: mattress in the corner, some boxes with food and water in them, not much else.

I dug through one of the drawers in the kitchenette area where I remembered having thrown medical supplies and unearthed a bottle of expired sleeping pills, which I tossed at Courtney. "Here. Take those and get some rest."

"I don't like drugs," she said unhappily.

I didn't comment on the irony of that.

She swallowed the pills dry and stumbled over to the pallet in the corner. "Where are we?" she slurred, the drugs already kicking in.

"A safe place," I said. "I have a few around the city. Keep them stocked, in case I need to lie low."

She cocked her head at me for a long moment, smearing her sleeve across her face again, her eyes glazed. "You're scary."

Her frankness took me aback. "You hired me to get you out of all this, remember?"

"Yeah, I guess," she mumbled. "I wish . . ." She was already starting to slump into a doze, her exhaustion combining with the pills.

"What do you wish?" Maybe, with her half-conscious state, I could get her to tell me something she otherwise wouldn't have.

"I wish I didn't need someone like you," she said, and her eyes slid closed.

Yeah. Sure. I was the bad guy here.

I left my client a docile, snoozing form on the blankets, grateful for the respite. My stupid body was starting to feel the last thirty hours, but I rummaged through the drawers again and found a box of caffeine pills. I ached for a shower and a quick nap, but first I needed to see if I could put together what Anton had found—what he might have died for.

The file was thin. I pulled the lone stool in the flat up to the kitchenette counter and opened it, turning over the first few sheets of disconnected information and wondering how I would make sense of them, only to be hit in the face by a blandly unassuming document: a funding memo from the Senate Select Committee on Intelligence. I sat and stared at it, feeling as if someone had kicked my legs out from under me.

Pithica was a project. Possibly a highly classified government project. I closed my eyes, trying to get a grip. *It could be anything,* I told myself. *The United States has any number of operations the population doesn't know about; it could be anything.* Anything . . .

I saw lab coats and red tile in my mind's eye. Whispers of weapons and a better future. I slammed down on the vision before my imagination ran away with me.

It could be anything.

There was a reason why I stayed off the government's radar. Why I didn't like the police, why I willfully ignored the law, why I didn't have a Social Security card, why—unlike Anton—I refused to pay taxes, aside from the obvious. The government scared me. Too many secrets. Too many bits of darkness I'd seen hints of over the years.

People with that much power . . . too big. Too dangerous.

Too real.

What was I getting into?

I forced myself to keep looking through the other documents. The Senate memo referenced the word "Pithica" only incidentally, as if the mention had slipped in by accident, and included no details on the mission of the project or who might be running it. I rifled through the rest of the pages: a report of an investigation into California dockworkers' conditions, marked with a sticky note that said it had come up in cross-referencing; a transcript from a radio transmission with half the text blacked out, giving no clear reference points; another memo with the phrase "Halberd and Pithica"—Halberd must be another project, but I found no other mentions of the word. . . .

A few other documents turned up similarly frustrating bits and pieces. The file proved Pithica existed—or had existed; the most recent document dated from more than five years ago—but nothing more. Underneath the last page was a note in Anton's blocky handwriting: "Should be more. Dead ends. Scrubbed? Will keep digging."

The papers made no reference to Colombian drug cartels or anything else connected to Courtney Polk, and no hint of why the LAPD—or any other local police force, for that matter—would be looking into this.

I sat back. What did I know? The dirty cop chasing after us had expected me to have information on Pithica. He had followed us from the compound, which meant the cartel was involved somehow, and he had also said that if I didn't talk, then he'd expected Courtney to be able to answer his questions.

Why? As far as the cartel's chain of command went, Courtney Polk had been rock bottom. What did the cop think she knew? If this was about drugs, why had the cop come after her rather than anyone higher up?

And who were the people who'd been at Courtney's house? The suits and the way they operated had screamed government type, which fit with what Anton's intelligence had revealed, but at least two of them had been European. What had they wanted from Courtney?

Every piece of this mess pointed back at my skinny twenty-three-year-old and her hard-luck story. Either Courtney Polk had lied to me from the first moment I met her, or a whole slew of people, from the dirty cop to the Dark Suits, were mistaken about her importance.

And I knew someone who might be able to tell me which it was. Someone who could give me an idea whether I should be protecting my new charge or pulling a gun in her face and demanding answers. Someone who, if Courtney was more than the naïve kid she seemed, might have had ulterior motives about sending me on this mad chase in the first place.

I picked up the phone.

"I said don't get involved," said Rio flatly by way of greeting.

"Answer me one question." I glanced over to the corner, where my would-be client was curled up into a ball and wheezing lightly in her sleep. "Did you have some other reason for sending me after Courtney Polk?"

Heavy silence deadened the line. Then Rio said, "Who?"

five

I HOPED the line we were on was insecure as hell, and that Rio knew it and was answering accordingly. Otherwise . . . otherwise, someone had been playing me like a fucking marionette. "We need to talk," I said. "Now."

"Camarito," Rio said. "Main and El Zafiro. Midnight."

Camarito was a small town near the compound I'd pulled Polk from the night before. "I'll be there," I said, and hung up. My skin felt itchy and too tight all of a sudden, as if a thousand hidden eyes were watching me.

Rio had been willing to make a meeting, which meant our phone call wasn't compromised—at least, not to his knowledge. Which meant he hadn't contacted Dawna.

Who *had*? Dawna Polk was a middle manager at an accounting firm. She wasn't exactly well connected to the criminal underworld. It was very like Rio to decide her sister needed out—he judged people, decided what they deserved, and made it happen, and I had no trouble believing he would have disinterestedly come to the rescue of a scared kid suffering from one bad decision too many.

If Rio hadn't called Dawna, however, then someone else had a motive for rescuing Courtney—and this mystery conspirator had kept me from being suspicious of the job by using Rio's name. Which meant said unknown person not only knew way too much about Rio and me and our strange not-friendship, but was one hundred percent aware of Rio's cover.

Rio was compromised. I felt sick. Our conversation would have tipped him off, and he could take care of himself, but still . . .

I picked up the phone again and called Dawna's work number.

Her secretary answered, and hemmed and hawed about her boss being in a meeting, but apparently Dawna cared a lot more about her sister than whatever she was doing at work, because mere seconds later her voice came fast and breathless over the line. "Did you find her? Is she okay? Oh my God—did they hurt her?"

"She's fine!" I raised my voice to cut in over her frantic queries. "*Fine!* She's sleeping right now."

"Oh—Ms. Russell, I don't know how to thank you. I just—she's my little sister; I can't—*thank* you—"

"Yeah, okay, okay." I had trouble squeezing a word in. "Dawna, we need to meet. Your sister—she might have gotten in deeper than she realized."

"I don't under—what happened? Is she still in danger?"

"We'll talk in person," I said. I didn't want to give away too much—the way this case was going, someone was probably listening in on Dawna. Or following her. "Remember the coffee shop where we met before? Meet me there in an hour."

"I—of course—of course I will. Will Courtney come? Can I see her?"

"Not yet." No way I would let Courtney out into the world before I had a better handle on the situation. "It's better if she stays here for now. She's safe here. I'll see you in an hour."

"Oh—yes, of course," Dawna said, her words tumbling into each other. "I'll be there—and *thank* you—"

I hung up on her.

Courtney was still out cold. I did a quick differential equation, my eyes measuring her body mass, and figured she'd be gone for a while—three hours at the very least, probably a lot longer. Enough time for me to make it to Dawna and back.

Still . . .

A couple of naked pipes ran along the base of the wall next to the mattress. I pulled the handcuffs back out of my pocket and locked one side around a pipe and the other side loosely around one of the girl's scrawny wrists. Then I stuffed some cash and other supplies in my pockets and pulled a .40-caliber SIG Sauer from behind the false back of one of the kitchen cabinets, replacing it with Anton's file and the rest of the paper bag of money from Polk's place.

I borrowed a motorcycle from a nearby parking garage, one with a layer of dust that told me the owner had last ridden it forty-two days ago, plus or minus a few hours. Probably a rich guy who took it out for a spin every few months; he'd never miss it. The helmet clipped to it was two sizes too big, and I made a face as I put it on—I don't crash. But I also couldn't afford to get the highway patrol on my tail. Stupid California and its stupid fascist helmet laws.

Motorcycles are a joy to ride in LA traffic. I wove between the cars, zipping past long lanes of stopped vehicles and leaning into a tight curve to fly up the ramp onto the freeway, frustrated motorists idling in line behind me. Widths and speeds and movement danced in front of my eyes as I rocketed the huge sport bike through spaces that didn't look wide enough for a cat to slip through, dipping and looping around other drivers and gunning between them down the asphalt, an untouchable point in motion.

On the bike I made it across town in thirty-four minutes, which would have been impossible in a car. I also managed to find parking on the street in Santa Monica, which likewise would have been an exercise in futility for a larger vehicle—I squeezed in against the curb behind a little Honda, not worrying myself about the niceties of a legal parking space. My friend I'd borrowed the bike from would be the one to see the fallout from any tickets.

I was early, but my client already sat at a table waiting for me, some-how looking both relieved and tense at the same time as she fiddled with the strap of her purse and ignored the cold paper cup of coffee in front of her. Dawna Polk looked nothing like Courtney, and with her height and fine bones and Mediterranean coloring, she could have been beautiful . . . except that she wasn't. She was . . . worn, and faded, and looked like someone who stared glassily at tedious minutiae all day in a featureless cubicle where she let her personality leach slowly away.

Yes, said a taunting voice in my head, *drinking your way through life is so much better, isn't it?* Hypocrisy, thy name is Cas.

Dawna leapt up when she saw me, almost knocking her purse off the table. "Ms. Russell!"

"Dawna," I greeted her. "Walk with me."

She jerked her head in a rapid nod and scooped up her belongings to trot after me, tottering slightly as she tried to hurry in stupidly high heels. "Where are we going?"

"Somewhere else. I need to make sure you weren't followed."

Dawna's eyes got wide, and she came with me without any more questions.

I led her down a few bustling, crisscrossing streets, surveying the trendy crowds of midday shoppers in all directions and staying alert for watchers and tails. A few blocks over, I took a sharp right into another coffee shop with a mostly empty sit-down section. A hipster on a laptop in the far corner was the only other customer; given that this was Los Angeles, he was probably working on the next Great American Screenplay.

"Sit down," I said to Dawna, dropping onto one of the chairs at a small wooden table as far as possible from the other patron. The rich smell of brewing coffee mingled with warm baked goods made my stomach start a riotous clamor about not having been fed; I pulled out an energy bar I had pocketed back at the loft and tore it open. A lanky young employee made a hesitant movement toward me as if he were about to say something, but I glared at the kid, and he meekly turned back to wiping tables.

I pulled out a little electronic gadget I'd also grabbed when I'd dropped off Courtney and pushed a button on it as I chewed. A light flashed green, which meant it wasn't picking up any electronic interference likely to be a bug. I let my eyes flick around the shop, measuring distances and figuring sound propagation in air; the lone employee had gone back behind the counter and the laptop-engrossed hipster wasn't close enough to eavesdrop over the folksy wallpaper music. Excellent.

Dawna watched me anxiously, not asking questions. She wasn't the curious sort. "How is Courtney?" she said at last.

"I left her right after I talked to you," I said. "So, sleeping. She's fine, like I said."

Her fingers clasped at each other in worried little twitches of movement. I realized she was literally wringing her hands. I'd thought that was a figure of speech. "When can I see her?" she asked.

"When I figure out what's going on here," I said evenly.

"What do you mean?" Her eyes were wide and frightened.

"Dawna." I lowered my voice, even though we had already been speaking quietly. "Tell me everything about how you knew to contact me."

Her forehead wrinkled in confusion, but she obeyed anyway. "A—a man called me." She swallowed, as out of her depth as the first time she'd told me the story. Dawna Polk was not a woman built for uncertain times. "He knew my name. He told me Courtney—" She lowered her gaze to her nervous hands, blinking rapidly. "He said if I wanted my sister to live, I would—I needed to get her out. He was very convincing." She shivered. "He gave me your phone number, said to call you and tell you—to tell you Rio had sent me."

"What did his voice sound like?" So far she hadn't said anything she hadn't told me in our first conversation, when she'd initially contacted me.

She gave a tense little half shrug. "A man's voice? What—what are you asking?"

"Any accent? Distinctive pitch? Anything?" Jesus, I needed *something*. If Dawna couldn't give me a clue, I was at a dead end.

"No. It was very flat."

Which did sound like Rio, but it also could have been someone else. Someone meaning anyone. "Can you remember him telling you anything more specific? Anything might be helpful."

"He said—he said they would kill Courtney if I didn't—" She started to tear up. *Honestly, woman, get a hold of yourself.* "He said you were very good, that you were the only one who could save my sister. He said to pay whatever you asked."

Well, that had been nice of Not-Rio.

"I knew she'd been taken," whispered Dawna. "The police, they interviewed me about what happened. The news stories about the cartels, what they do to people—the police wouldn't help; they already thought she—" Her voice broke. "I was scared to go to you, but if I hadn't and Courtney had—I couldn't bear that."

Yes, yes, I was such an intimidating person. Dawna had given me exactly zero new information. "Aside from the drug stuff, was Courtney mixed up in anything else?"

"Of course not!" Fire flooded Dawna's eyes. "My sister is a good person! How could you even think—?"

"Okay, okay, I get it." This interview had been useless. The woman didn't know a damned thing.

"Ms. Russell." Dawna reached out, taking me by surprise, and grasped my hands in her own slim, birdlike ones. "Please. What's going on? I thought Courtney was safe."

"She is. Now. But . . ." I sighed. "It turns out my friend Rio wasn't the one who called you. There may be more going on here than we thought."

"What are you going to do?"

In spite of myself, I felt sorry for her. "I'm meeting with Rio tonight," I said, trying for a soothing tone. "I'll see if he knows anything. And then we'll figure out why everyone is after your sister."

Dawna's eyes widened further. "Everyone? After her?"

"Well, we know why the cartel is and why the cops would be, but I think someone else . . ." I frowned. "Dawna, have you ever heard of something called Pithica?"

She shook her head. "No. What is it?"

"I don't know yet. But some people think Courtney's involved in it."

"Who? The cartel?"

"The cops. Or at least, a cop we . . . ran into. I don't know about the cartel."

"And this Pithica thing, it's . . . bad?" hazarded Dawna anxiously.

"Considering people seem pretty willing to kill her over it, yeah." She started tearing up again.

Oh *geez*. "Look, Dawna, I'm going to get her out of this."

She tried to nod, but she was trembling with the effort of not breaking down. She brought her fine-boned hands up to cover her face, breathing raggedly.

I'm not great with people, but I tried. I reached out and put a hand on her thin shoulder. The motion felt very contrived. "Hey, don't worry. We're going to find out what this Pithica thing is, and why people think Courtney is involved in it, and then we're going to shut them down."

She managed to nod, face still in her hands.

"Here, I'll buy you a coffee."

I finally got Dawna calmed down; she drank her latte with small, dignified sips, dabbing at her ruined makeup with a napkin. "I'm sorry, Ms. Russell," she whispered, her voice shaking only slightly. "It's so overwhelming."

"I understand." I didn't, but whatever.

"I, ah, I have to get back to work," said Dawna softly.

I wondered where she worked that she couldn't take time off right now. Well, maybe she needed the distraction. It wasn't like I was unfamiliar with that myself.

"To meet with, uh, Mr. Rio—are you going back to the—to where you found my sister?" Dawna asked in a quiet, fearful voice as she cleaned herself up.

"Yes," I said. "To a little town nearby."

"Be careful, Ms. Russell. Please."

"I will," I assured her.

It wasn't until I had left Dawna tottering back toward work and was back on my borrowed sport bike that I realized I'd forgotten to ask her about payment.

Huh. That was unlike me—I never forget about money. This case must be getting to me more than I thought.

six

WHEN I got back to the loft, Courtney was still asleep, her skin pale and tight with ashy smudges under her eyes. I hesitated, then left her cuffed to the pipe, locked the door and zip-tied it shut on the outside, and set off for Camarito.

I took a straighter—well, slightly straighter—route this time, but full night had fallen by the time I hit the desert, and when I slung off the exit toward Camarito, it was well after eleven. This far from civilization, pitch blackness swallowed the road. The bike's headlight beam hit a wall of cavernous darkness only a few meters in front of me, a maw of nothingness threatening to swallow me whole; I revved the engine and sped into it even faster. I'd left the helmet behind at the apartment, and the wind sliced harshly against me, taking everything but thought.

The sound sparked against my senses first, a low rumble just at the edge of my hearing. The neurons in my brain fired with *Warning! Danger!* and I slewed off the road before I even identified the noise as other motorcycles—a *lot* of other motorcycles—

A *crack* split the darkness, and my brain spasmed with a disbelieving *Holy fuck, mines in the road!* even as the charge caught the edge of the bike and the frame contorted and leapt like a living thing. I twisted with it, the forces and variables splintering and erupting in every direction until I snapped into alignment and counterbalanced to slam the heavy motorcycle into a controlled skid.

Metal screamed as the bike took off the top layer of the rocky desert, the headlamp blinking to darkness and fairings snapping off in an explosive cacophony. I balanced the mathematics and rode the dying motorcycle to a crashing halt amid the rocks, levering off right before inertia flung me free, and I hit the stony ground on one shoulder to roll up into a crouch, the cop's Glock in one hand and the SIG I'd grabbed in LA in the other.

I snapped my eyes around the darkness, straining to adjust to the pitch black of the night without my bike's headlamp. Someone had *mined the fucking road* in an effort to assassinate me—what the *fuck*— and it sounded like they were bearing down to finish the job—

The motorcycle engines I had heard on approach built to an overwhelming thunder. Making a few safe assumptions with regard to engine size, I knew I had about four seconds before they closed. My mind flipped through options and found precious few—these people knew my location; they had been waiting for me; they were undoubtedly armed. I couldn't outrun them on foot. I had to fight, which meant finding some cover and attempting to pick them off with the handguns. Considering my marksmanship, the plan wasn't as stupid as it might sound . . . the one flaw being that cover is severely lacking in the desert, and pitch darkness isn't the best place to go looking for it.

With no better choice, I dove behind my downed bike as a dozen heavyweight motorcycles roared off the road in my direction. The blackness was still total; they must've clipped the wiring on their headlamps and been riding with night vision gear, which boded even worse for me. But I'd been listening, and I popped off my first shot before I even hit the hard-packed ground behind my improvised cover. A shout and a shriek of metal rewarded me. I listened and fired again, and again, the brilliant muzzle flash in front of my eyes blinding in the darkness.

Bursts of light lit up the night in front of me as my attackers fired back—and then a white flash burned my retinas and a deafening concussion shoved me down so hard I cracked my chin on a twisted fairing of the motorcycle.

Holy Christ on a cracker, they have grenades? Shit!

I focused past the ringing in my ears as I got the handguns up again, but the Glock was an inert lump—it must have gotten slammed against something when the grenade hit and jammed, *dammit, typical Glock!* I swept the SIG across the wave of attackers, firing over and over; I could take down one enemy per shot, but there were *too damn many of them*—

And suddenly there were fewer.

White light flashed across the scene with a roar, blinding me. I had a vague impression of massive, hulking silhouettes on monstrous Harleys as chaos tore through the gang; shouts and grunts became panicked screams as shadows I hadn't aimed at twisted and fell. Not wasting time in surprise—*thank you, Rio*—I took out one more, then half saw a snarling shape lob another grenade toward me and fired without thinking about it. The bullet found its mark on the little bulb and the grenade bounced off course to detonate halfway between me and my enemies. The tooth-jarring concussion slammed into all of us; I ducked back behind the cover of the bike just in time and sensed more than heard the explosive fragmentation as it chewed up the metal.

I peeked out again and snapped off another shot, but the fight was almost over. One last would-be escapee revved a bike to life, seesawing wildly; I fired a hair before another gun also rang out, and bike and man jerked and went down together. The motorcycle's engine sputtered for a final few seconds and then died, leaving the desert a still and silent graveyard, the glaring headlights of a truck throwing the edges of leather-clad corpses into shadow and relief.

My ears rang in the sudden stillness.

I rose cautiously from my crouch behind the downed bike and stepped out gun first, my boots crunching on sandy gravel and the shards of my shredded motorcycle. I had expected to see Rio striding toward me, tan duster swirling around him; instead, the silhouette of my assist was shorter and darker—and was transferring his gun from the defeated biker gang to me. My own SIG snapped over in the same instant, and I found myself facing the cop who had held me up earlier that same day, who was apparently *really fucking good at tailing me,* and who was quickly becoming the bane of my existence.

We stood for a moment pointing guns at each other.

"Someone wanted you super-dee-duper dead," the cop said finally, almost idly. His eyes flickered down to the muscle-bound corpses, then back up to me. "You piss off some one-percenters?"

One-percenters? I searched my memory. That was cop-speak for the outlaw motorcycle gangs, wasn't it? The answer to his question was no, I wasn't at odds with anyone in the outlaw biker crowd—in fact, I'd had a few as clients before, and they'd all been perfect gentlemen. I did have enemies who might have hired these guys, but . . . well. If this attack wasn't related to Courtney Polk somehow, I would eat my gun.

I kept the SIG pointed at the cop and didn't say anything.

"This wasn't exactly random lawlessness," the cop mused. "This was a hit. A real overboard hit. Either these fellas had a big ol' beef with you, sweetheart, or someone out there—"

I was about to mete out fair punishment for calling me "sweetheart"—in the form of a high-velocity .40-caliber bullet—when someone behind the cop coughed wetly.

I moved before the sound had registered. With two possible threats and only one weapon, a quick slip to the side put the cop and the cough in the same trajectory so they formed one neat line in front of my gun.

The cop himself hesitated for half an instant. Then, apparently making a split-second judgment call that I wouldn't shoot him in the back compared to the definite threat if one of the biker gang was still alive, he too spun toward the noise, weapon first.

"First rule," I growled, annoyed. "Make sure they're dead when you kill them."

"He's not getting up," said the cop, though instead of sounding defensive, he only sounded grave.

I sidled cautiously up beside him. He was right. For starters, an eight-hundred-pound Harley pinned the guy solidly to the ground.

Still, considering he was a spectacular specimen of an outlaw motorcycle gang, as enormous as a mountain troll and with tattooed biceps as big around as my waist—literally, which was kind of scary—he might have been able to rescue himself except for the professional double-tap in the center of his chest leaking a black stream of wetness through the leather.

Typical police technique, I thought derisively, but still, the marksmanship impressed me. If the guy hadn't been the size of a yeti, he'd be dead already. As it was, he was well on his way, nerveless fingers scratching weakly at the metal trapping him. I knew the math, but it was still somehow fascinating that two comparatively tiny holes could take down such a giant.

I did a quick visual survey of the carnage to make sure no one else had survived—I knew all mine were dead; I never mess around with that center-of-mass crap—then stepped over to stand above my erstwhile attacker and put the barrel of my SIG in his face. "Who hired you?"

He glared at me, glassy-eyed and hateful. "Cunt," he whispered, blood bubbling in the corner of his mouth.

I quashed the urge to quip that he'd noticed my gender; I could already hear something of a death rattle in that one word. "Who hired you?" I repeated.

"No one," he spat. "We wanted to."

Well, that was new. People who wanted to kill me for fun.

"Who told you she'd be here?" the cop asked next to me.

"Go . . . fuck . . ." the gang member managed to hiss, and then he choked on his own blood and went still, the hate in his eyes unfocusing, blood still oozing from his mouth and chest.

Death is never pretty.

"Real pleasant dude," commented the cop.

We no longer had our weapons pointed at each other, and reinitiating that situation seemed like a bad idea. Still, I kept the SIG out and pointed in a direction that wasn't quite down as I turned to face the man who had both threatened my life and, I reluctantly admitted, probably saved it in the same day. "Who are you?"

"Name's Arthur Tresting."

"And you're a cop."

"Not anymore," he said, and something I couldn't read flickered through his eyes. "I'm a PI. Lady, I think we might be on the same side here."

I resisted the urge to haul off and sock him one for calling me "lady." "You didn't think so this morning."

He glanced at the carnage surrounding us. "That was before Pithica tried to kill you."

Pithica again. I thought of Anton. Two people I liked were dead, and this Arthur Tresting knew something about why.

And he was going to tell me.

"What's the Polk girl to you?" said Tresting.

I hesitated. As a general rule, I didn't give out information—any information, to anyone, and particularly not to a person I had every reason to mistrust. Still, I wanted to keep him talking, and the value of a few low-intelligence tidbits . . .

"Purely fiscal," I answered. "Someone hired me to protect her."

"Who?"

"Quid pro quo," I shot back. "What's your interest?"

"Guess you could say money started it for me, too. A woman hired me to find out who killed her husband and the father of her eleven-year-old boy."

"What does that have to do with Polk?"

Tresting studied me. "Well, she did it, you see."

What the hell? The desert silence blanketed us. "One of the cops on the drug bust," I guessed. But the police had already blamed Courtney for those murders. Why would the widow feel the need to hire a PI?

"No," Tresting said, overly casually. The word fell between us—soft, final, incriminating. "A busy young woman, our Courtney Polk."

I'd already known she wasn't on the level, but I'd been assuming some combination of fear and naïveté. That maybe she hadn't realized what she'd gotten into, or had been too scared to face it. "She doesn't seem the type," I offered, stalling.

"Nah, she doesn't, does she?" said Tresting. "Was an odd sort of crime. Odd in the same way these lovely motorcycle gents discovered an irredeemable hatred for you. Makes you think it wasn't their idea."

"Maybe they thought it was a fun night out," I said, stubbornly not thinking of the mines in the road or the freaking *grenades,* or the fact that all the biker guys I'd known had a code against baseless killing. Okay, something fishy might be up with the bikers, and it very well might have to do with Courtney Polk, but a mastermind theory that cast her as a hired assassin alongside them? It didn't wash.

"Might agree with you, if there wasn't a pattern," said Tresting.

"A pattern of what?"

"Murders. And other things."

"I don't have time for riddles," I said, my gun hand twitching.

"Well. Hypothetically, let's say Miss Polk and your new friends here aren't the only ones acting out of character. Let's say it's more. A lot more." He cleared his throat. "And let's say it's senators and grandparents and the folks next door."

I squinted. "Are you even listening to yourself? What, so every killer who doesn't fit the profile is part of some shadowy conspiracy? Newsflash, Einstein: Sometimes people are violent. A lot of times for no other reason than they want to hurt people."

"A lot of times." He gave a noncommittal half shrug. "Maybe not all the time."

This was far too fantastic for me. "And Pithica?"

"Far as I can tell, it's them pulling the strings. Can't pin it any closer than the word, though." He seemed to make a sudden decision and holstered his gun. "So. What do you say? Can I give you a lift into town? Maybe share some intel?"

My first impression was that the PI was one hundred percent cracked. But whatever else he was, Tresting was a lead, and I needed all the information I could get.

"Fine." I slid the SIG back into my coat. I could still kill him in a fraction of a second if I needed to, as long as he didn't have a gun on me.

Tresting jabbed his thumb at the source of the white headlights. "My truck. And I'll pretend I didn't see the extended mag."

"It's legal two hundred miles east of here. 'Sides, you should talk."

"Yeah, speaking of, where is it?"

I waved vaguely toward the desert scrub. "Back there somewhere."

He rolled his eyes and jogged over to where my bike had gone down, flashing around the white beam of a penlight. A few minutes later he returned, banged-up Glock in hand.

"Afraid your bike's a lost cause," he told me.

"Wasn't mine."

He shot me a look. "Didn't hear that, either."

"I thought you weren't a cop anymore."

"Old habits, blah-dee-blah." Examining his jammed handgun, he dropped the mag out and racked the slide a few times, clearing the chamber, then stuck it in the back of his belt without reloading. I watched with some approval—I wouldn't have trusted a weapon that had nose-dived into the desert dust either, not if I had another choice. He patted his Beretta. "Lucky for you, I had another backup."

"Yeah, nine-mil?" I scoffed. "Did a little girl give that to you as a party favor?"

"Best gun is the one you have with you," he quoted at me mildly. "And someone stole my forty-five. Can I get the snubby back too, by the way?"

"Can't," I answered breezily. "I gave it to a little girl as a party favor." Something in me twinged, and the quip felt hollow as I remembered what had happened to both Penny and her new present. "Let's go."

We did one last once-over of the bikers to look for anything out of the ordinary, but aside from some frighteningly high-tech night vision gear and more armaments I wouldn't have expected this kind of gang to have—not that I was an expert or anything, but still, plastic explosives?—we found nothing. No clue indicating what might have brought them here, except that they really, really wanted me dead. Fun.

I snagged a saddlebag off one of the Harleys and loaded up some of the nicer toys. A girl can never have too many grenades, after all. Tresting gave me a severe look but didn't say anything, fortunately for him.

seven

TRESTING'S TRUCK was a beat-up old clunker that looked like it had come out of its share of brawls not only still kicking, but bragging about how tough it was. I stowed my bag of toys on the floor of the passenger seat and climbed in.

"Seat belt," said Tresting as he coaxed the ignition to a shuddering rumble.

I didn't explain that I could buckle up plenty fast enough if I calculated it would help with anything. Tresting had seen too much of my skills already. I fastened my seat belt, muttering, "Yes, Mom," under my breath.

Tresting revved the engine, the tires spinning against the sandy ground before they found enough purchase to rocket the truck forward with an almighty lurch. We bounced back onto the dusty highway, the headlights sluicing through the empty darkness.

"So," I said. "GPS tracker?"

Tresting's eyebrows jumped in surprise, and his teeth flashed in a sheepish grin. He put one hand in a jacket pocket and held up the tiny device between two fingers. "Smart gal."

"On the bike," I guessed, sure I was figuring this right. "You retrieved it when you got the Glock. And you knew to trace the bike because . . . you had another tracker on Courtney."

He looked surprised again. "Quick study, too."

"Which is how you found us at the motel. And you must have been watching where Polk is in LA. When I came back on the bike before leaving, you slapped another GPS on that. Smart."

"Thanks."

"Unless your clumsy surveillance gets my client killed, in which case I will not be amused. In fact, I'll be so unamused I'll put a bullet in you."

"Ouch. And we were just getting to know each other."

"I'm serious. If someone else figured out you're tracking her, all they have to do is follow the same signal."

He was silent for a moment. "She's your client," he said finally. "I only want to see where she leads."

I scowled. "Compassionate man." Pot, kettle, it was true, but he wouldn't know me well enough to point it out.

Tresting's knuckles tightened against the steering wheel. "Rather she not end up dead. But she murdered *my* client's husband, and I'm gonna find who put her up to it."

In fairness, he had a far guiltier conscience about putting Courtney in danger than I would have, had our positions been reversed. "One thing I don't understand. If you got close enough to plant the tracker, why not interrogate her then? Why wave a gun at me so unsuccessfully at the motel?"

He didn't rise to the bait, only let a frustrated breath hiss out through his teeth. "Didn't get close enough. Got the opportunity to slip one into her food when the drug runners had her."

And he'd figured a GPS would cover all bases in case he had to follow Courtney back to . . . well, to her masters, if Tresting was to be believed.

"Your turn," Tresting said. "Who are you?"

I'd forgotten I hadn't introduced myself. "Tell me more about Pithica."

"Hey, I told you about the GPS."

"You didn't tell me; I guessed. And considering you were using it to track *me,* I think it was about time I knew."

"Whatever," he muttered. "In for a penny, I guess. Pithica's some government project or other."

"I know that. What else?"

He cut his eyes at me suspiciously.

"I did some digging after you mentioned it while pointing a gun barrel at my face," I explained impatiently. "What else?"

"It's buried deep. I got a tech guy. He can only find bits and pieces. But it's far-reaching. My client's husband, he was a journalist. Started digging into some things. Political decisions, that sort of stuff, ones that didn't make sense. Nutso crime spikes. Chances are they could've left him alive; I don't think he ever saw the connection."

"What connection?"

"Pithica. Just the word. Buried deep. Didn't find it linked up to all the things he'd been looking at, but it was enough to be, uh, a 'statistically significant correlation.' Or so says my tech guy."

His tech guy must be good. Anton had been able to find almost nothing. "And you think Pithica killed him. The journalist."

"Sounds crazy, but yeah. Some of what we found, it was a pattern— it's too similar, the MO of his murder. Can't prove it, not yet, but his death's got Pithica all over it."

"So Courtney Polk is, what, some sort of secret government agent?"

"Always the ones you least suspect, right? She's the only one who could have done it. We managed to figure out she saw my guy day-of."

"Wait. So you don't have any hard evidence?" I narrowed my eyes at him. "If you can prove Polk committed cold-blooded murder, why aren't the cops investigating her for it?" I'd seen her police record. Nothing about being a person of interest in a prior crime.

Tresting kept his eyes on the empty highway. "There was a suicide note."

I almost laughed. Or screamed. One of the two. "Great. Just great.

You've got quite the case there. You ever hear of something called Occam's razor?"

"He didn't kill himself," Tresting ground out. "His wife—"

"Is probably in denial," I interrupted. "It sounds to me like you've invented a conspiracy—"

"He didn't kill himself," Tresting repeated, louder. "And Polk's the only one who could have. Besides, why was she there otherwise? The kid was a trailer park migrant who ended up smuggling coke. Why was she there?"

"Maybe your guy was interviewing her for some other story," I pointed out sarcastically. "Since he was, you know, a *journalist*."

"Yeah, you'd spend the few hours before you dose yourself to death trying to meet a deadline. That makes sense."

"Murder's still a stretch. Like, a bungee-level stretch. I'm not buying it."

"'Cause I'm giving you the short version. Lot of other details didn't add up. The whole scene was fishy. Best part is, I don't think this is the first time Polk's done it."

This was too unbelievable. "Wait, so now you think she's a *serial killer*?" Jesus. I knew some serial killers. Courtney wasn't one of them.

"Maybe," said Tresting doggedly. "Or maybe she's someone's patsy. I'm telling you, I spent months building up this case. Didn't start out trying to make it nutso, I promise you."

"You just happened to see the bright light in the sky and realized your client had been abducted by aliens."

"You don't have to believe me, sweetheart," he said. "But that's the lowdown of what I got."

"Mysterious crimes you say form a pattern."

"Yeah."

"Does this phantom Pithica group have a motive? Or do they just go around convincing biker gangs and driftless twenty-three-year-olds to kill random people?"

"Right now they're protecting themselves, obviously," Tresting said. "And I got no idea what they're trying to do. All I know is there's too much evidence, spread over the last dozen years or so. This is real."

"Yeah. Right."

"Like I said. You don't gotta believe me." He ground the truck's gears as we jounced around a curve. The pickup bitch-slapped him with a hard jolt in response. "Your turn."

I debated. Tresting's summary was far too outlandish to be useful, but he did have one thing I didn't: data, and a lot of it, though right now he was using it to wallpaper his fantasy with completely fallacious "patterns." *Humans, we like to see patterns. We see them all the time, even when they don't exist.* I wasn't sure whether I was repeating what someone had told me once, or if it was an observation.

I couldn't work from Tresting's fanciful conclusions; I needed the raw data. I tried to come up with an angle from which a minimal dialogue with a loony PI might endanger either my case or my client, and decided a few cautious words were safe enough. Besides, the underground had a gossip chain with the efficacy of the internet. He could probably ask around about a brown-skinned, curly-haired, angry-looking chick who could kick his ass, and he would find out who I was soon enough.

I sighed internally. I don't like giving up information. Ever. "My name is Cas Russell."

"Hey," said Tresting. "Heard of you. You do retrieval stuff."

Oh. I had a reputation?

"And good at it," he acknowledged. "Word is you get things done."

Well, that was nice to know.

"Nobody mentioned putting up with the sass, though. That new?"

I stared at him incredulously. "Sass? You want to see sass? I'm still armed, you know!" I sputtered to a stop. Tresting was laughing.

"Didn't expect you to be so young, either."

"I'm older than I look," I bit out. I hate being patronized.

"So how'd you get shanghaied into bodyguarding, then? Not your usual shtick, is it?"

"I was hired to get Polk back from the cartel," I explained stiffly.

"I admit it was a guess, but I figured 'alive and unharmed' was implied in the contract."

"See? Sass." When I shot him a look that could have splintered his skull, he took one hand off the steering wheel and raised it in mock surrender. "Sorry, girl, sorry! I mock because I, uh, because I have respect. For your badass retrieval skills. Happy?"

"Only because from here I could kill you in less than half a second."

Okay, maybe it wasn't the smartest boast to make. But it was worth it to see that glib look in his eyes stutter into discomfort, and for the truck to fall into blessed silence. When Tresting spoke again, his tone was back to businesslike. "So, who hired you?"

I wasn't in the mood to cooperate. "Client privilege."

Anger clouded his features. "Hey, I told you—"

"A whole big sack of nonsense," I cut in. "Here's the deal. You show me all your precious data. If I agree there's something there, then we can work together, and *then* you get to know everything I know. Not before."

"What happened to quid pro quo?" demanded Tresting.

"I'm young and sassy," I shot back. "This is all just a game to me."

"Come on, I didn't mean—"

"Hey look, we're here." The dirty handful of buildings that constituted Camarito slumped jumbled around us in the darkness. "This is where I was going. You can drop me anywhere."

Tresting stepped on the brake a trifle harder than he had to, and we jerked to a halt. "You owe me," he said tightly. I'd forgotten how dangerous his tone could get. It was edging back toward that now.

"I told you," I said. I wondered if I had let myself get needled into being ornery, and whether that was wise, but it was too late to second-guess myself now. "I want to see your data. Prove to me that what you told me wasn't the ravings of some crackpot, and I'll share what I know."

I unbuckled the ridiculous seat belt, collected my saddlebag full of toys, and swung down from the truck. Tresting got out as well, apparently deciding for annoying. He came around the hood to face me.

"You can find me here." He flicked a business card at me, probably intending for it to flutter to the pavement, but I caught it out of the air without thinking about it—projectile motion with a nice muddle of air resistance mixed in; please, challenge me. "I think you still need what I got on this. And you owe me. I saved your ass today."

I offered him a one-shoulder shrug. "Maybe."

"We don't have to end up enemies. Don't think either of us wants that." He brushed back his leather jacket to lay a hand not-quite-on his holster.

He wasn't going to draw. The movement was all wrong. It was the posturing of the street, an unsubtle reminder that he was smart enough and good enough to be a threat to me if he wanted to be. Besides, if he had been intending to pull his weapon, I would have had him dead or incapacitated before his gun cleared. He was far too close to get away with trying. I lounged, leaning my weight back, content to let him posture.

Someone else wasn't.

A step crunched on the gravel behind Tresting, and Rio's voice said, "Hand away from the gun, nice and slow."

The PI didn't need to see Rio's sawed-off pointed at the back of his head from five feet away. He knew danger when he heard it. Especially when it was behind him. Very slowly, making no other movement, he lifted his hand away from his gun.

"All right?" Rio asked me, not taking his eyes from Tresting.

"Sweet of you," I said, "but I had it covered."

Rio nodded. He didn't lower the shotgun, though.

Tresting was looking at me, his eyes unreadable, and I relented slightly. "Besides, he wasn't drawing on me. It's okay."

Rio hesitated a moment longer, and then the sawed-off disappeared whisper quickly into his duster. He stepped carefully around Tresting, still keeping half an eye on him. "You're late," he said to me.

"Ran into some complications."

Rio twitched his head at Tresting. "He one of them?"

"Sort of."

"I think the motorcycle gang hit squad I helped *run off you* has me beat," Tresting said. I could tell he was trying for lightness, but his tone was strained, and a muscle in his cheek twitched as his eyes flicked back and forth between me and Rio. Rio—you don't have to know what Rio's capable of to realize how dangerous he is. People underestimate me sometimes. Rio, on the other hand—the only reason people ever underestimate Rio is a lack of imagination.

"This is Arthur Tresting, PI," I said. "He was following me."

"And he's still alive?" asked Rio mildly.

Tresting swallowed.

"Didn't seem worth it," I admitted. "Plus, I think he has information."

"What kind of information?"

I opened my mouth.

"Hey," cut in Tresting. "I shared my intel with *you*, Russell. You." His eyes flickered to me and then to Rio and back again. "You don't gotta believe me, but I'm telling you, if you spread it around it'll get us both killed."

"I trust this man," I answered, adding a trifle flippantly, "but you should know, it's not the best way to keep something secret, telling a girl you only just met all about it."

He glanced at Rio again. "Maybe not."

"Besides, you're the one who wanted to work together. You work with me, you work with my—the people I trust."

Tresting hesitated.

"You're the one who keeps telling me we might all be on the same side here."

Still he hesitated, and it occurred to me—Tresting might be an excellent PI, but when it came to this case . . . I remembered him saying he'd been on it for months, and I realized that despite all his bravado, he was desperate. Desperate enough to go out on a limb and try to ally himself with someone he had only the most tenuous of reasons to believe might not sell him out to the highest bidder. He probably didn't trust me to offer him a drink of water in a rainstorm, but he was taking a risk to break whatever deadlock he had found himself in.

Which put me at a definite advantage here. Excellent.

Tresting wet his lips and stepped forward, holding out a hand toward Rio. "Arthur Tresting. Sorry we got off on the wrong foot, brother. From what Ms. Russell says, I think we might have some similar goals." His voice was tense, but civil.

Rio stared at the hand, and then looked askance at me. I couldn't tell whether he was calling me an idiot or calling Tresting one. He looked back at the PI, not taking his hand. "Rio," he said. "I work alone, though Cas keeps what company she likes."

At least, that's what he started to say. As soon as he said his name, Tresting's face twisted, and before Rio was halfway through his next sentence the other man had gone for his gun.

I was faster, but Rio was closer. Tresting might be a ridiculously quick draw, but his gun hadn't even cleared when he cried out, and the gun was suddenly in Rio's right hand while the left whipped forward into Tresting's face. I heard a sickening crunch as Tresting staggered back, but I was already diving in; I came up alongside Rio and twisted with his movement as he brought the Beretta up—the vectors of force and motion lined up and clicked into place and then the nine-mil was in my hand instead of his. I raised it and pointed it at Tresting myself.

Not that I truly thought Rio would have fired—at least, not without getting all the information we could first. But just because I didn't think he would have pulled the trigger yet . . . well, you know, I would have felt bad if he had.

Rio had let me take the weapon as soon as he realized I was going for it—which, truth be told, wasn't until after I already had it off him, but the whole thing happened so fast it made little difference. He relaxed and stood looking at me calmly, which was pretty much what I had expected him to do. Rio and I had never gone head-to-head, and I couldn't imagine a scenario in which we would. I wasn't sure what would happen if we did. I was better than he was, but Rio was . . . more willing.

"Okay," I said, pointing Tresting's own gun at him as he hunched against the side of his truck. He had his hands to his face, blood streaming freely through his fingers. I hoped Rio had pulled the blow enough that he hadn't, well, killed him with it. I knew he could hit hard enough to do it. "Talk, Tresting. What was that all about?"

He tried to focus streaming eyes on Rio. "I know who you are," he croaked thickly, through the blood. "Heard of you, too."

"Have you now," said Rio.

"I know *what* you are," spat Tresting. "Would've done the world a favor to blow your goddamn head off."

"I would prefer it," said Rio, "if you did not take the Lord's name in vain. Particularly when speaking of blowing off heads. It seems a poor choice for your soul."

Tresting stared at him. It wasn't, generally speaking, the kind of thing people expected Rio to say, unless they knew him.

"And *I* would prefer it," I said, with all the menace of someone holding a gun in another person's face, "if you not insult people I like."

"Chivalrous, but unnecessary," Rio said to me as an aside.

"Oh, I don't know. I think it's just necessary enough." I raised my eyebrows at Tresting over the gun. "You meet a guy, you pull a gun on him—or, well, try—and then you insult him . . . Mr. Tresting, that's just rude."

"Russell," Tresting managed, and his voice was thready and desperate. "Russell. You don't know what he is. Get away from him. Please."

"I know him," I said, "and I trust him. If you want me on your side, deal with it."

He stared at me, long and hard, blood still streaming from his face. Then he straightened up with an obvious effort, mopping a handful of the blood off in a fruitless effort at cleanup. The man had steel in him, I'd give him that.

"I will never," he said, "be on the same side as someone like that."

He spat on the ground, the expectorant a bloody mess but the message clear, and, still using his truck for support, got around to the driver's side, levered himself in, and roared away.

"It occurs to me," said Rio, "that being acquainted with me is not the best decision for your social network."

"Screw my social network," I said.

eight

CAMARITO WAS barely more than a truck stop, a ramshackle collection of buildings pretending to be a town. The gas station lighting up Main Street tried very hard to be a travel center and almost made it before giving up. A couple of truckers hunched over coffee at the mostly deserted tables outside; Rio and I took one far away from everyone else. I sat back and watched the night while Rio went inside to pick up some coffees.

The childish part of my brain wanted to write Arthur Tresting off entirely. Nobody who threatened and belittled my friends—or my not-friends, whatever—deserved my help, or even my acquaintanceship. But a small, insistent voice pointed out that Tresting's distrust of Rio was not outrageously unreasonable, and was maybe even an indication that Tresting might be a good guy, or something. I was never quite clear on where the gray ended and the black and white began, but it wasn't a stretch to put both Rio and me among the condemned, whereas Tresting . . . I wasn't sure. I didn't like him, but much as I wanted to, I couldn't dismiss him or the information he might have just because of what he'd said about Rio.

After all, he wasn't wrong.

Rio . . . Rio came into this world not quite right. He doesn't feel emotion the way other people do. Doesn't empathize. He honestly does not care about other people.

The one thing that drives him is inflicting pain. He craves it. He *needs* it. Some people are born for certain careers in this world; Rio's talents mold him to excel at the worst of them all, the man with his tray of silver instruments whose mere presence in a room will cause people to scream and confess, the man who will smile through the spray of blood and revel in how much he loves his work.

I have no illusions about Rio.

In some strange joke of the universe's, however, he was raised with religion. Lacking his own internal moral compass, he substituted Christianity's, and became an instrument of God.

It's twisted, of course. I freely admit it. Any Christian you stop on the street would pale with horror at the way Rio follows the Bible, because it doesn't stop him from hurting people. Only as a Christian, he seeks out the people he judges deserve God's vengeance, and he doesn't bother with the little sins, the unfaithful husbands or petty thieves. Rio searches for people like himself. Or worse.

And then he introduces them to God.

Rio doesn't have friends. It's not part of his makeup. Some people hire him, usually people who aren't very nice and can live with themselves after hiring someone like Rio. He's choosy about the jobs he takes, and in between times, he freelances. For him, the payoff is never about the money anyway.

Rio and I had known each other a long time. As far as I could tell, he put up with me because I didn't actively annoy him, and as for me, well . . . I understood him. Hell, he was a lot easier to understand than most of humanity. He practically had axioms. And because I understood him, I could trust him.

He was the only person I did trust.

And though I might not delude myself about the type of person Rio was, that trust had bred loyalty. Even if it didn't bother the man himself, other people talking smack about Rio made my trigger finger real itchy, and I didn't care who knew it. You didn't knock my not-friends in front of me and expect to walk away unscathed.

Rio came back outside and set two paper cups on the table, taking one of the metal chairs for himself that allowed him to see almost every angle. Usually I would have taken that seat, but I always felt Rio outranked me in the paranoia hierarchy, so I ceded him the vantage point.

"What was Tresting's information?" he asked as he sat.

I passed on everything the PI had told me, from the methods he'd used to track Polk and me to his nebulous theories about Pithica, not reserving judgment on the latter's credibility. Rio listened silently.

"So, what's the deal, then?" I demanded. "You've heard of whatever this Pithica thing is."

"I told you not to get involved," said Rio.

"Exactly," I agreed. "Which means you know something."

He sipped his drink. "On the whole, I know very little. Far less than I would like. What I do know suggests Arthur Tresting is more correct than not."

"What?"

"I, too, have followed some unusual patterns. What interests me more," he continued, "is who made such a concerted effort to draw you into this. That, I think, is a question worth answering."

I was still trying to take in the fact that he didn't think Tresting was a raving lunatic. "I take it you didn't call Dawna Polk ever," I said slowly.

"No. In fact, I have no idea who that is."

"Courtney Polk," I explained. "The girl I mentioned before, the one I got out. Kid who says she 'accidentally' became a drug mule for the Colombians. She got caught, the Colombians threw her in a basement, and then her sister Dawna contacted me and said that you called her and told her to hire me."

"Yet I never made such a call. Interesting."

"Did you see Courtney in there?"

"I remember thinking her rather stupid." His voice was matter-of-fact. "It did not occur to me that she would be worth risking my other goals for."

"Well, whatever your goals are, it sounds like you've been compromised."

"So it would appear." He took another sip of his drink. He was taking it very in stride—but then, I'd never seen Rio flustered about anything.

"Somebody in there is on to you," I continued, feeling it out aloud, "and somehow knew about your relationship with me, and called Dawna impersonating you. I don't know why, but I intend to find out."

Rio tilted his head slightly, as if considering. "That is one theory."

"It's the only possible theory," I contradicted. Rio just kept looking at me. "What? You have something better? Nothing else fits all the facts."

"Odd," he said. "You're usually better at this."

"Better at what?"

"You say the only possibility is that someone else contacted Dawna Polk using my name."

"Well, yeah." I searched for the flaw in that logic, puzzled. "That *is* the only possibility."

"Unless she lied to you."

"Who?"

Rio regarded me as though I were speaking a foreign language. *"Dawna."*

I laughed. "She wasn't lying to me. Jesus, if you'd seen her—she was practically in hysterics about this whole thing."

"Did you do a background check on her?"

I frowned. I background check all my clients if I have the time. But . . . "I didn't need to. Seriously. You're being ridiculous. Let's concentrate on the real possibilities."

"Cas. You're acting strange."

"What do you mean, strange? Because I'm not jumping to suspect the least likely person in this whole tangle?"

"No. Because you're disregarding it as an option."

"So?"

"So, that is very unlike you."

I found myself becoming annoyed. Which was unheard of—I couldn't remember ever having gotten annoyed at Rio. Why was he insisting on being so infuriating over this Dawna thing? "Oh, so you have my deductive process axiomatized and memorized, do you?" I said.

"You will not acknowledge her deception as possible?"

"No!"

He sat back in his chair. "Odd."

I didn't like the judgment I heard in that word. "What's that supposed to mean?"

"Ordinarily, you acknowledge every possibility. It is part of what makes you good at what you do," Rio said evenly, and if I hadn't been feeling so hostile toward him at the moment, I might have been flattered by that. "Logic, yes? It's how you're wired."

"How I'm *wired*?"

"I do not mean it as an insult."

"Well, maybe I'm taking it as one!" I snapped. "I'm allowed to have a gut instinct about people, you know!"

"Cas, you detest reliance on gut instinct."

"And maybe you don't know everything about how I work!" My voice was rising, a biting fury building in me by the second. "It's such a bad thing *not* to suspect an innocent woman? Oh, right, I forgot—*you* wouldn't know anything about valuing other human beings—"

"This isn't like you, either," Rio observed calmly. "Something's affecting you."

"Something's *affecting* me?" I cried incredulously. "Well, yes, genius, *things affect me*! You think you're such an expert on emotion all of a sudden? *You*? Did you ever think that maybe I'm reacting like a *normal human person*?"

"Cas—" Rio tried to cut in, but I wasn't having any of it.

"The poor woman has done nothing but care about her little sister, and she's being dragged into this whole violent mess with drug dealers and cops, and now we find out someone very dangerous called her and lied to her, and you want to dump it all on her? Maybe while we're doing that, the people we *should* have been investigating will take their sweet time to come kill her and Courtney!"

"Cas, sit down—"

"No, fuck you, Rio!" I spat. I wasn't sure when I had stood, but I was looming over him, so angry I felt like my skin was splitting open, my insides seizing. "I don't owe you a goddamn thing! What, does it ruin your sick little masturbatory fantasies that I might care what happens to someone else? Too bad! Because unlike some fucked-up people, I have emotions, and morals, and a sense of right and wrong that doesn't come from some demented version of the Bible!" Red was fuzzing around the corners of my vision. I wanted to hit him, to hit him so hard that he wouldn't get back up. The math pricked my senses all over, whispering of all the ways I could strike. Maim. Kill. "And you? You *dare* preach to me about how I should or shouldn't act, well, *fuck you*, because I'm not a *fucking psychopath*!"

My final words rang in the air between us, echoing in the space between trust and history.

"Oh, God . . ." I whispered.

"Do you believe me now?" Rio asked dryly.

"Oh, God, Rio . . ." I couldn't move.

"I'm not angry," said Rio. "Sit down."

Of course he wasn't angry. Somehow, I wished that he *would* be, that he would get up and slug me, fight back, because I . . . I had stabbed him as ruthlessly and effectively as I knew how, and it didn't matter that he was pulling the knife out and dismissing it as a flesh wound, because I had crossed the line, *that* line—

"Sit down," said Rio again, his voice calm and even and without injury.

I couldn't sit down, but I was leaning on the table to keep from falling. "Rio, I can't . . . I'm so sorry . . ."

"You are not usually so blunt," said Rio, "but we both know what I am."

"But that wasn't even true, I—" I was having trouble speaking. Everything was wrong, twisted and crumpled. "I owe you my life, I owe you everything . . ."

"And on that we shall agree to disagree, since I will insist on giving the credit to the Lord." He gave me a small smile. "Be careful, Cas. It would perhaps not be a good thing if you were to give me an ego."

I laughed before I could stop myself; it came out half a hiccup. It wasn't *funny;* Rio without boundaries was about the most unfunny thing I could possibly imagine—not to mention nightmarish and heartbreaking and absolutely fucking *terrifying*—but it was either laugh or turn and walk away and never speak to Rio again because *I* couldn't deal with what I'd said, and as appealing as that sounded, it also sounded really fucking dumb.

So I sat down, my face in my hands, and said, "Rio, I think something's affecting me."

"An astute observation," he replied with a straight face. "Considering the context, I suggest we look into Miss Dawna Polk."

I still felt a strong ridiculousness at the idea, to the point of defensiveness, but now I shoved it aside angrily. Something had interfered with my logic here, had made me lash out irrationally against the one person in my life I could depend on, say things to that one person I would have laid out anyone else for so much as thinking. The *one person.*

I was going to figure out what was going on here if it was the last thing I did. Whoever had done this to me—Dawna Polk or Pithica or some shadowy government organization of people in dark suits—I was going to take the bastards down so hard it would register on the Richter scale. I realized I was literally growling, deep in my throat, a low, animal sound.

"I have a conjecture about what might be happening," said Rio. "Tell me, Cas. Did you tell Dawna Polk you were meeting me here?"

"Yes, I—" My head suddenly started ringing as if I'd been clocked, and I felt as if I were seeing double. *I told her.* . . . But that wasn't like me either. I hardly ever told anybody *anything.* Why would I have told Dawna I was meeting Rio? And where?

Well, she was crying and wanted to know you were doing something for Courtney, and you're clumsy with people so you were probably just talking in order to say something. . . .

I didn't know what shocked me more: that my brain was trying to rationalize this, or that this type of rationalization might have worked a few minutes ago. A deep and furious self-loathing thrummed through me.

I had told Dawna everything because she had asked. And then I'd been attacked.

"Jesus Christ," I mumbled into my hands. "What the hell?"

"I believe Dawna Polk might answer some questions for us," said Rio.

"I know how to find her." The shock and horror were coalescing into rage in the pit of my stomach. Dawna had done something to me. A drug? I hadn't drunk anything with her, only eaten an energy bar that I'd brought with me, but there were other ways. *Dawna Polk, you are going to give me answers. And after that . . .*

Well. I wasn't a forgiving person.

"I think, perhaps, it would be better if I took that part of the job," said Rio smoothly. "It appears I cannot go back to my role here, and there is the chance you are . . . still affected."

I made an angry noise. "I'll be on my guard."

"Even so. Let me take Dawna. Your time may be spent more profitably by talking to your new detective friend."

I almost laughed. "Tresting? I think you might not have a good grasp of the word 'friend.'"

Rio smiled slightly, and I felt myself flushing at the unintentional truth. "Doubtless," he said. "But Tresting will have other contacts. And it is quite clear he will not talk to me. You can find out more of what he knows. I'll track Miss Polk."

I swirled the dregs of my coffee in the paper cup reluctantly. What he was saying made too much sense not to agree. "I guess this means we're working together on this one, huh."

"It appears you have become involved despite me."

"Yeah, I'm irritating like that. I suppose there's no getting around the fact that Tresting might be useful."

"It seems not."

I groaned and stood. "Best get it over with, then. I'll call him in the morning. You want me to set up a meet with Dawna for you?"

"Perhaps, but not yet. For now, whatever contact information you have will suffice."

I gave him everything I had on her. Embarrassingly, it was precious little, much less than I would usually be comfortable with. Rio didn't comment, for which I was grateful.

"Off to try to talk to people, I guess," I said. "Wish me luck."

Rio touched his forehead in a brief salute. "Go with God, Cas."

"Yeah. You too."

"Oh, and Cas." I turned back. "Do not concern yourself with defending my honor. It serves no purpose."

"La, la, la," I sang. "I can't hear you." I threw him a grin, hoping it looked remotely genuine, and strode off.

I managed to find a flashy sports car to steal for the trip back to LA. I wanted to go fast, to feel the wind in my hair and watch the desert whip by too fast to see.

Dawna Polk had attacked me. Whatever she had done had wormed its way into my brain somehow, twisted my thoughts, manipulated me . . . beneath my fury lurked a sick sense of violation, an oily stain on my soul.

Dawna Polk was going down for this.

When I got back to the neighborhood my safe house was in, I yanked the e-brake and spun, sending the trendy speedster into a sideways skid against the curb between two SUVs with less than twenty centimeters of clearance. Yup, I'm that good at math: I can parallel park in Los Angeles.

Despite my anger, exhaustion overtook me as I climbed the stairs to the flat. I was going on two days without sleep. I needed some rest, some real rest, and I couldn't call Tresting till the morning anyway. Well, I could, but I didn't figure annoying him in the wee hours of the morning to be the brightest move at this point. I cut the zip tie I'd secured the knob with and nudged the door open quietly so as not to wake Courtney if she was still sacked out.

The loft was dark and quiet.

Shit.

My subconscious knew something was wrong before I registered the computations that told me the silence was too absolute. I hit the lights, dreading what they'd show me. The loft's single room was empty, its small bathroom open and vacant as well. The other side of the handcuffs lay open and impotent on the mattress.

Courtney Polk was gone.

nine

No TIME to coddle people with sleep. I'd ditched my old phone on the way home, having burned the number with Dawna, but I had a new one in one of the kitchen drawers. I pulled out Tresting's business card and dialed.

He answered on the second ring. "Yeah."

I swallowed something I was pretty sure was my pride. "Tresting, it's Cas Russell. Polk is gone."

There was a pause over the line. Then: "Shit," he said eloquently.

I hadn't been sure Tresting himself hadn't abducted Polk or ordered someone else to while we were in Camarito, but he sounded so surprised and defeated that I relegated the possibility to slightly-less-likely. "My thoughts exactly. You still got a GPS on her?"

"Yeah. Give me a sec." His words sounded muffled, and with a slight pang of guilt I remembered he had just had his face bashed in. His night wasn't going terribly well either.

A minute later, Tresting's voice came back on. "I got it. South of LA, and moving."

"I'm going after her. Where are you?"

"Receiver won't help you."

My suspicions swung back the other way. "You do realize you want her found, too, right? So help me, if you don't give me the—"

"Whoa, hey, not what I meant. Meant you can't catch her. Moving too fast to be in a car."

"Train?" I asked, my stomach sinking.

"Faster. Guess again."

Shit.

"Won't be able to do anything until they land. But hey . . ." He hesitated. "Listen, if you still want to share intel, come meet me. Might be we can still get ahead some."

If he had Courtney himself, I thought it unlikely he would want a face-to-face. On the other hand . . . "You're awfully calm about this," I said.

He sighed, and when he spoke again he sounded frayed. "Not surprised. This case has been fubared six ways from Sunday ever since I took it. Think I'd die of shock if something went right."

I squeezed my eyes closed. I needed sleep, even a good hour of it, but time wasn't on my side. I decided it didn't matter whether Tresting had taken Polk or not—either way, I needed to take the meet. "All right. Where?"

He named an intersection in a part of town I was vaguely familiar with. "And, Russell? Please. Come alone."

What he meant was *Don't bring Rio*. I snorted. "Your delicate sensibilities are safe. He's working another angle." I paused. "I won't be unarmed, though."

He took a quiet breath that sounded like relief. "Not a problem. Good. Thank you."

"Whatever. I'm surprised you still want to work together, after that show you made."

"Not sure I do," he admitted frankly. "But I made a few calls. Like I said, I'd heard of you. Your rep's solid."

Well, that was nice to know. I wondered which of my former clients he'd talked to. I wished I had a way to check *him* out, but I'd lost my information guy, and I hadn't made a whole lot of friends in the past couple years I could check a reference with and trust the answer I got.

For all I knew, I could be walking into a trap. It didn't feel like one, but I had no way to know.

.·.˙·.·.˙·.˙·.

TRESTING WAS waiting when I arrived, a lean silhouette in the darkness. He'd cleaned up his face, and the damage didn't look as bad as it probably was thanks to the darkness of the night and the dark shade of his skin, but I could still tell he'd been hit by a truck the shape of Rio's palm.

"This way," he said.

"I want to see the receiver first."

"Thought you might," he said, taking it out of his pocket and handing it to me.

I studied the display. Nothing said this couldn't be faked, but it supported what Tresting had already told me. The red dot indicating Courtney crept forward somewhere over New Mexico. I measured its speed with my eyes and glanced at the scale. Slower than most commercial jets went—private plane, I figured.

Apparently presuming I was satisfied, Tresting started to walk, letting me keep studying the display as I fell in step beside him. I extended the plane's trajectory in my mind, thinking through probable destinations, but there were too many variables. I sighed and handed the receiver back to him, a small gesture of cooperation. "Where are we going?"

"My office. Meet with my tech guy."

I was pleasantly surprised. I'd been feeling Anton's loss keenly every time this case took another left turn. From what he'd said, Tresting's guy was good. "Can he be trusted?"

"With my life."

I still wasn't sure the PI himself could be trusted, but I liked the sound of that.

Tresting led me up a hill of close-packed buildings leaning against each other in the darkness, storefronts crammed in against ancient apartments with barred windows and rusted security grilles. We turned down an alley at the top of the hill that led between a tall brick building and a revamped warehouse with cement blocks for walls; bars were bolted across the windows here too, even the second-story ones. Tresting led the way up a narrow metal staircase climbing the side of the warehouse and stopped at a second-floor door reinforced with sheet metal. The stenciling on it read ARTHUR TRESTING, PRIVATE INVESTIGATIONS in clean, professional lettering, and he unlocked it and pushed it open.

Part of me had still been suspicious of a trap, but instead we were in a tastefully furnished office with a broad wooden desk backed by several comfortingly decorative tall houseplants. Plants. It was absurdly normal. The only thing in the place that hinted the office didn't belong to a tax lawyer was a tall gun safe abutting the file cabinets against one wall.

"Come in," said Tresting, going behind his desk and pulling one of the client chairs around with him so he could gesture me to sit. He powered on a sleek desktop computer with dual monitors that booted into some Unix-based variant of an operating system. I squinted at him in surprise.

"My tech guy set it up," he explained.

"Speaking of, when is he getting here?"

"Right now," said Tresting, opening a video chat link.

A clear image of a room snapped into focus on one monitor, and my immediate impression was the lair of someone who was one-third hacker, one-third supervillain, and one-third magpie. Bundles of wiring and edges of hardware I didn't recognize filled the whole view, and multiple monitors showing abstract screen savers backlit the darkened space, racked one over the other to create a wall of screens. The dim light silhouetted a man who sat presiding over his nest of computers, and as the chat link came alive, he turned to face us, levering one side of what I realized was a wheelchair around to bring himself closer to the camera. He was surprisingly young, probably Tresting's junior by two decades, and was one of the skinniest men I'd ever seen, with a skinny lean face, a skinny little goatee, and skinny long fingers, which he steepled under his chin as his eyes flicked over us. A manic grin lit up his narrow face.

"Well, well, well, Arthur," he said. "What do you bring to stimulate my genius today?"

Tresting gestured to me. "Checker, meet Cas Russell."

I nodded to him. "You have the data on the Pithica stuff?"

Checker narrowed his eyes at me behind wire-framed glasses. "I do."

"I want to see it all."

He affected surprise. "What, all of it? And you haven't even bought me a drink first?"

"I'll pay your rates," I assured him, thrown by his flippancy. Most business deals were a quick and easy exchange of money and services. I wasn't used to a bantering preamble.

"I charge double for new clients," Checker said cheerfully. "Discounts for beautiful women and anyone who can quote the original *Doctor Who*. I can see you aren't going for the former, but if you offer me a jelly baby I'll take off ten percent."

"Hey," said Tresting. "Behave. Didn't anybody ever teach you not to insult a woman's looks?"

"I'm not insulting her looks, only her deportment," said Checker. "So I like good scenery. At least I'm willing to offer financial incentives for it." He winked at me. "Want to come back in something slinky and ask again?"

"Are you fucking kidding me?" I sputtered. "You know we're on the clock here, right?" We didn't have time for clowning around, but more than that, it was . . . off-putting. Besides, it was objective fact that my looks fell on the lacking side of any aesthetic scale. Symmetry and proportions—who cared?

Checker pulled a face that made him look about five years old. "I don't know if I like her, Arthur."

"Cut her some slack," said Tresting. "We've all had a rough night." He cleared his throat, then said carefully, "She might have some more pieces of the puzzle, too."

Checker perked up immediately. "Well, why didn't you say so?" He rubbed his long, thin hands together and reached out to start clattering on one of his many keyboards, his fingers so fast the clack of the keys was almost indistinguishable. "What've you got for us, Cas Russell?"

I blinked. I'd had Tresting's relationship with this guy all wrong. Checker wasn't merely his information broker. This wasn't just a business deal. The two of them were *friends*. And Checker was as invested in this case as Tresting himself was.

Which meant, duh, of course they were much more interested in what I could bring to the table in terms of the case than they were my money. That was new.

I supposed this was the time to toss in. If I wanted their resources, I would have to be a part of that—that team effort. It felt . . . completely and horribly wrong to me. After all, I reminded myself, Arthur Tresting had introduced himself to me by threatening to kill me and torture my client, and had tried to point a gun at me no fewer than three times. I wasn't sure I wanted to tell this man or his friend anything at all.

Except my client was winging her way away from me on a jet plane, and a motorcycle gang had just tried to wipe the desert with me in a high-tech hit, and *Rio* was weirded out by this whole case—and, overshadowing everything else, I had told my plans to a woman I barely knew and then attacked the only person I trusted in the worst way I knew how.

I needed information. I was desperate for it.

I felt a distinct sympathy for Tresting's instant decision to trust *me* earlier.

Perhaps thinking along the same lines, the PI took pity on me. "Start with the basics," he suggested. "Who hired you to protect Polk?"

Dawna had waived her client privilege when she had drugged-or-whatevered me anyway. I unstuck my tongue and said, "Her sister. Dawna Polk."

Tresting frowned at Checker. Checker was frowning at me. "She doesn't have a sister," the skinny computer guy declared authoritatively.

"What? Yes, she does," I said.

Checker was already shaking his head and turning to his keyboards. "I did deep background on this girl. Thoroughly, for Arthur here. She hasn't got a sister."

I gripped the edge of the desk, fighting off a massive, almost desperate sense of foreboding. "What about a half sibling or something? One she didn't grow up with?"

"Nope. Not unless the person was entirely off the grid, which is so unlikely as to border on the impossible," Checker answered. "Otherwise there would be paternity tests, or adoption papers, or birth certificates, or—or *something*. You can never disappear completely, unless maybe your parents were hippies who went off the grid before you were born and raised you with wolves in the wild." He wrinkled his nose. "Courtney's parents, on the other hand . . . if I remember rightly, they were a boring little high school romance turned into a boring little small-town marriage, and then they died in a combine accident. Right, Arthur?" He was typing rapidly, his attention on a screen I couldn't see as he continued talking. "Yeah, a combine accident. Hey, can you believe we still have those? I thought combines were from the Laura Ingalls days or something. You know, back when they still had farms."

I shook my head, trying to get back on track. "But Dawna says Courtney's her sister, and Courtney says Dawna's *her* sister—why on earth would they both be lying about that?"

Tresting shrugged and looked at Checker.

Checker raised his eyebrows. "You're not asking me, are you? Because, yes, I am all-powerful, but some questions—"

"Maybe they could be, I don't know, really close childhood friends," I broke in. "So they started calling each other 'sister,' or something."

"Except you said they're both using the name Polk," Tresting pointed out. "Unlikely coincidence for unrelated friends, unless they're running a game."

He was right. Shit. *You already know they aren't on the level, idiot. Why are you still looking for honest explanations?*

My head started to hurt, an aching, buzzing pain behind my eyes. I pushed it away. "What else did you find on Courtney?"

"Born and raised in rural Nebraska, moved out to Los Angeles a few years ago," recited Checker. "On paper, totally boring until the arrest warrant for murder. She grew up with an aunt and uncle in Nebraska after her parents died. They didn't have any kids who could have been a 'sister' either," he added, preempting the question I'd been opening my mouth to ask. "And aside from them, all her living relatives are of the distant variety."

"Does she have a psych record?" I asked.

"What part of 'totally boring' didn't you understand?" said Checker.

"We ought to look into Dawna," said Tresting. "Whoever she is."

The buzzing pain got worse, the strange insistence of *wrong, no, Dawna's all right!* still tugging at my consciousness.

I beat it back savagely with a mental crowbar. What the hell was going on with me? "Yeah," I forced myself to say. "I agree."

Checker levered one of the wheels of his chair and spun to a different keyboard, then looked back expectantly at the webcam. "Okay, Cas Russell. Give me what you've got on her."

I took a breath, ignored the headache, and recited all the contact information I had, again with a flush of embarrassment at how little it was. I barely had more than her work and cell numbers. A slight pause followed my rundown, as if the two men were waiting for more, and part of me wanted to explain and defend myself—she had *done something* to me!—but my humiliation at being bested was stronger than the mortification of not having done a good background check, and I bit back the information.

Checker's fingers danced over his keyboards. "Cell's a prepaid disposable," he announced. "And the work number . . . is also a prepaid disposable."

I avoided looking at them, my face heating.

"Let's try something else," said Checker, and I tried not to feel like he was working to spare my feelings. He hit a few more keys, and Tresting's second monitor lit up to show an array of photographs, mostly poor head shots. I realized they were driver's license photos, women named Polk with the first name Dawna or Donna. I didn't even know which way she spelled it. "Do you see her?" Checker asked. "If she backed up the alias with paperwork, I might be able to track it."

Eighty-seven photos had matched his search, and I took a good minute to scroll through them all, even though I didn't need that long. After all, bone structures are only measurements, and measurements are only math. None of the eigenvectors of the feature sets were even close to Dawna's, but I compared the isometric invariants anyway, delaying the conclusion I already knew was true.

Dawna's face wasn't there. I shook my head.

"Color me shocked," murmured Tresting.

My embarrassment was hardening into a cold fury. The anger gave me a focus, made it easier to think. "What about a picture?" I said. "Would that help?"

Checker brightened. "Sure! I've got the best facial recognition software out there. I know because I wrote it."

"Pull up a map of Santa Monica." One was up on Tresting's other screen in front of me before I had finished the words. I reached over to the mouse and traced the cursor along the streets. "I met Dawna here at about four P.M. yesterday. We walked this way." I carefully followed the walking route we had taken. "Then we sat and talked here for . . ." I thought. I'm capable of measuring time down to the split second if I want to, but I hadn't been paying attention. "About half an hour."

Checker had begun grinning more and more broadly. "Oh, Cas Russell, good thought. Good thought!" His fingers did their mad dance again, and the map on Tresting's other monitor disappeared to be replaced with a flickering slide show of grainy black-and-white shots. A color photo came up in the corner of my own face, a frowning mug against the background of Tresting's neat office—clearly a screen grab from our video chat—and digital lines traced and measured my forehead, cheekbones, nose, chin. The black-and-white security camera footage flashed by next to it faster and faster and then finally disappeared, leaving three still frames arrayed across the top of the screen.

"Downright disturbing, how much they see," said Tresting.

"What are you talking about, Arthur? Security cameras keep us nice and *safe*," said Checker sarcastically. "But it's okay. As long as I can use their power for evil." We took a good long look at the three frames that showed clear shots of both Dawna and me.

"That's her," I confirmed.

"'She,'" said Checker.

I blinked. "What?"

"Predicate nominative. It should be 'That's she,' though I admit some allowance can be made for colloquialism because it does sound frakking weird to say that."

Tresting flicked a finger at the computer screen. "Go back to being a computer nerd."

"I'm a pan-geek," Checker said loftily. "Besides, it's your fault for giving me the Kingsley research to do."

I stared at them, utterly confused. "That's Dawna," I repeated.

"Yes, yes, I know, supergenius on it," Checker muttered, waving dismissively at me over the webcam. Dawna's face replaced mine on Tresting's screen, the digital markers now measuring her fine Mediterranean cheekbones. "I'll start with the California DMV."

The photos flashed by too quickly to see. A minute or so of suspense later, Checker sighed. "No matches, kids. We'll go national. This might take a minute."

"Somehow I'm doubting she's a licensed driver at all," Tresting said.

I slouched in my chair. "So we're back to square one."

"Not so fast, Cas Russell," Checker crowed. "You gave me a photo! Do you have any idea what I can do with a photo? If she doesn't show up in a DMV photo, or a passport photo, or on a private security ID or a student ID or in a high school yearbook photo—well, it doesn't matter, because as we speak I am tracking her from your meet." He gave me another manic grin. "See? You can never disappear from me!"

And then, God help me, he threw back his head and gave a textbook evil laugh.

"You're a maniac," Tresting said with affection.

"Really?" Checker was still grinning. "What gave it away?"

To be honest, I was getting slightly uncomfortable with the knowledge the little hacker had *my* photograph and voiceprint now, but there wasn't much I could do about it. I tried to stay focused on the case. "Okay. What can we do in the meantime?"

Tresting stretched, yawning. "Wait and get some sleep? Unless you know of anything else we can pursue."

I thought of Dawna's humiliating ability to get into my head. I thought of the men in dark suits at Courtney Polk's house. I thought of Anton's workshop erupting into flames, the heat searing my skin.

I thought about how much I still didn't know about Arthur Tresting and his information guy.

"Nothing else comes to mind," I said.

The headache continued to pound away behind my eyes.

ten

"WAIT," I said as Tresting moved to sever the connection. "I still want to see your data, remember? Whatever led you two to believe in the whole Pithica conspiracy in the first place."

Checker laughed. When I only stared at him stonily, he said, "Wait, really?"

"Yes, really. Is that funny?"

He waved his hands limply. "It's just, you know, there's a lot of it."

"So?"

He glanced at Tresting. "Okay."

"And I want to see your algorithms, too."

He crossed his arms. "Those are my intellectual property."

"Then show me on Tresting's machine now," I said. "I don't have a photographic memory."

"They're not very understandable, you know," he shot back. "I refuse to document my code."

"I'm very smart."

Checker's jaw jutted out, and I thought he was going to argue further, but instead he broke eye contact and stabbed at his computer keys. "Fine. Knock yourself out."

The other monitor filled with dense programming code. I scrolled, letting my brain relax into it, my headache finally dissipating as the mathematics rose in ghostly shadows, the edges of the algorithms sharpening and focusing into the barest outlines of a skeleton. The code wasn't a language I recognized—possibly it was one Checker had invented himself—but the structure was familiar; it filtered through my senses and solidified, the commands looping and interlocking through layer after layer of abstraction, the elegant constructions jigsawing deep into the program.

Checker was watching me closely. I ignored him and kept scrolling.

"Well, I'm going to get some sleep," said Tresting to no one in particular. "You kids have fun." He meandered over to a couch against one wall of the office and stretched out, sagging to unconsciousness right away.

Checker was still watching me through his screen. I pretended to be too absorbed to notice. After a few minutes he turned his attention back to his own machines and began working on something on a monitor out of frame, but he left the video link open and kept glancing over at the camera. I refused to give him the satisfaction of asking any questions.

Checker didn't say anything else, but other windows eventually popped up on my screen with notes on the murder they were pinning on Courtney, followed by file after file of data tables. The numbers sorted themselves in my head and fell into place, matching up with variables in the algorithms until the statistical analysis unfolded before me. Yet another document appeared a short time later, this one tracking instances of the "Pithica" reference.

Tresting and Checker had started with the journalist's research. Reginald Kingsley had been considered top-notch in the journalism community, Pulitzer Prize and all. He'd had his fingers in a lot of different stories, and at some point he'd started keeping a log of mysteries that didn't quite add up, events that didn't jibe or were short a solid explanation. He had been in Los Angeles researching an article when he reportedly decided life just wasn't worth it anymore.

Kingsley's suicide had made a big splash in journalistic circles, the newsworthiness exaggerated by the insistence of his wife, Dr. Leena Kingsley, that it was one hundred percent definitely faked. Other than her sworn declaration her husband wouldn't have taken his own life, she cited two grammatical mistakes in his supposed suicide note as her proof. The "mistakes" weren't anything I would have recognized as wrong, and I understood why segments of the press had started to mock Dr. Kingsley's adamant assertion that her husband never would have split an infinitive in a hundred billion years and this should be proof of a nefarious cover-up.

It turned out the suicide (or murder) had happened almost six months ago now and had led to a lot more tragedy than a wife losing her husband. Dr. Kingsley, who had been a professor of Asian studies at Georgetown University and had just been tapped as a Foreign Service Officer by the White House when the tragedy struck, developed a reputation as slightly mad and her previously illustrious career fractured and tanked. She became obsessed with solving the mystery of her husband's death, moving herself and her son out to Los Angeles permanently after losing her State Department commission and resigning her professorship. Once the LAPD threw her out as a distraught crackpot enough times, she hired multiple private investigators, but from the file, I gathered Tresting was the only one who had stuck it out and given her story any credence.

Tresting had gone back through every story Kingsley-the-husband had been working on, systematically analyzing lists of possible enemies and one by one eliminating them all as suspects in his murder. And then, with Checker as his computing partner, he dove into evaluating Kingsley's journal of inconsistencies.

I skimmed the entries. A senator making an about-face decision on a key issue. The FBI discarding a star witness and screwing themselves out of a titanic RICO takedown. An entire notorious human-trafficking ring simultaneously deciding to turn themselves over to the police. Tresting's notes showed a massive amount of legwork—phone calls and meetings and tracking people down—but he had reached no conclusion other than that he had stumbled into the Twilight Zone.

The strange cases went back years, and in a statistically significant percentage, Checker's digging had found one common thread: the word "Pithica." Scraps of memos, snatches of conversations, a whisper of a whisper with six degrees of separation from the actual event . . . but a connection.

Checker had tried researching the word. Like Anton, he had discovered a few blink-and-you-miss-it references to a shadowy government project in scattered classified documents. Unlike Anton, however, he'd also found a few brushes with CIA paperwork, including a comparison to a covert ops project code-named Black Gamma, which a notation in Checker's colorful hyperbole explained was "well-known for collapsing spectacularly in the faces of its creators." Pithica had been a failure, too, then? That didn't seem to match up with the rest of the data, Pithica's ghostly reach appearing to affect events from the local to the national to the global.

I sat back and rubbed my eyes. Tresting's wild conspiracy theories were becoming a lot harder to dismiss.

Checker swore softly, interrupting my thoughts. "Arthur. Wake up," he said.

I turned to call to Tresting, but the PI had woken at the sound of his name. He came back over to stand behind me. "What is it?"

Checker reached out and smacked the side of a screen I couldn't see. "The GPS tracker. We lost the signal."

Tresting cursed as well and dug into his pocket, pulling out the receiver to check for himself. He cursed again. "What happened?"

"Dunno," said Checker. "Could be a malfunction. Could be inter-ference. Could be they went down in the Gulf of Mexico." His atten-tion was still on one of his other monitors, his fingers clicking so rapidly on a mouse that he resembled a telegraph operator. "Me, I'd bet on the cynical side. Even if our girl passed the tracker and it landed in a toi-let, it still should've kept the signal on the plane for us."

Tresting sank into his office chair. "After all that, she disappears."

I wondered if my client was dead. I tried not to think about it.

"They didn't file a flight plan, but the great circle trajectory would have led over Colombia," Checker said. "It's only a possibility, but . . . just saying."

"Colombia," Tresting mumbled. "Right. Of course."

I tapped the screenful of data still in front of me. "I haven't finished going through this. Did you find the connection between Pithica and the drug cartels?"

Checker leaned back, for the first time looking tired. "Who knows? Sometimes they seem to want to shut the cartels down. Sometimes they keep them from getting shut down. I'm starting to think they're just Chaotic Neutral."

"Doesn't help us much now, anyway," Tresting said softly. "A country's an awful big place to find a few ghosts, even if we knew for sure it was Colombia." He raised his head to me. "Your gal killed Mr. Kingsley. Got no doubt on that. But me, I wanted whoever put her up to it." He closed his eyes, his body slumping.

"Hey, chin up, Detective," said Checker. "Before you fly into a fit of despair, I might have another lead for you here in the City of Angels. While you have been snoozing, I have been managing, with an impressive degree of success, to track Dawna Polk."

Tresting and I both sat upright simultaneously. "What?" Tresting cried.

"Yes, yes, you may worship me." Checker affected a statuesque pose, one hand canted in the air. "The line for autographs starts on the right—"

"Checker!" said Tresting.

"You won't even let me bask? You horrible man," Checker scolded amiably. "I tracked her to an unregistered car, and tracked that car to a parking garage in an office park. Hitting your phone now, Arthur."

I waved my disposable at the screen. "What about me?"

Checker gave me a penetrating stare as if sizing me up. I gazed evenly back. "Fine," he said, stabbing a button. My phone buzzed in my hand with a new text message.

I didn't show how unsettled I was that he had the phone's number already. After all, I'd called Tresting on this cell; it was the simplest explanation. Checker was not omniscient. He wasn't.

"I don't know what office, but I will soon," Checker said. "I still have a lot of security footage to fast-forward through, and all the leases and backgrounds of the businesses in the building. Give me a few hours and I'll narrow it down for you."

"*Atta* boy!" Life flowed back into Tresting. He jumped up with entirely too much enthusiasm and gripped Checker's screen with both hands. "You are brilliant. Brilliant!"

"I know," said Checker with a smile.

Tresting whipped around to address me. "How d'you want to play this, then?"

Part of me was surprised he wasn't trying to keep me out of things. Not that he would have succeeded, but still. "I say we bust in, bash some heads, and find out what's going on here."

Tresting's eyebrows lifted. "You really aren't a detective, are you."

"Nope," I said. "That's not my job. People tell me where something is, and I get it back for them, no detecting necessary." It was almost true; every so often I had to do research for a case, but rarely much. Clients hired me for the extraction part.

"I suppose brute force does have a certain elegance to it at times," put in Checker. I couldn't tell if he was being sarcastic.

"Why, what would you do?" I demanded of Tresting.

"Usually? Stake it out first. Bug the place. Gather intel without getting seen, have Checker here hack into their systems. Go in undercover if I have to."

"Like the delicate approach you used with me," I said pointedly.

"Totally different. Lone woman spiriting away my target? Far as I knew, I had the upper hand on that one."

"Far as you knew," I said.

Tresting shrugged ruefully.

"Dawna could still be in there," I argued. "And so far, they've been ahead of us. Trying to kill me, taking Courtney, the GPS signal going out—we can't play this thing safe and slow." I thought of Anton's death and the Dark Suits at Courtney's house, and started to wonder if we should leave Tresting's office for somewhere more secure.

Tresting sucked a breath through clenched teeth. "Agreed. Soon as Checker's milked all the intel he can, my vote is we walk in the front door."

"With guns," I said.

"Yeah," said Tresting. "With guns."

eleven

HAVING SEEN enough of Checker's data to give Tresting the benefit of the doubt on whether he was stark raving mad—not to mention feeling much more worried about this case and what I'd stumbled into—I elected to get a few hours' sleep while we waited on Checker's intel.

"I think I'll take a turn on your couch," I told Tresting. I wanted to be here for any updates.

"Sure thing," said the PI. "I gotta make some calls anyway."

"How were my programs?" asked Checker as I stood up, a hint of challenge in his voice. "Fun reads? I strive for elegance."

I pretended he wasn't provoking me. "Yeah, impressive. Markov chain Monte Carlo, smart way of doing it."

Both men stared. Checker's jaw had dropped open slightly. "Cas Russell, your hotness level just went up by about thirty percent," he said finally.

Score one for Cas, I thought. "I read statistics papers in my spare time. Hey, Tresting, where's your loo?"

He pointed, still speechless.

I used my moment of privacy to text Rio an abbreviated update, sending him the office park address Checker had tracked Dawna to and a quick heads-up about our plan to go in. When I came back out, Checker and Tresting were deep in quiet conversation. I wasn't sure, but I thought I heard them switch topics when I reentered the room, and I hoped they had been talking about me. It's satisfying when I make people nervous.

I stretched out on Tresting's couch, my hand under my jacket comfortably near my gun, and had a split second to register that my headache had started to come back before I was asleep.

I woke to a shouting match.

Full daylight streamed around the office's still-closed blinds. The monitors of Tresting's computer were dark; instead, he was standing behind his desk having a vociferous argument with a short, stocky woman I'd never seen before. She had a round face I might have called cherubic if her eyes hadn't been blazing with anger, and she was quite well kept, with neatly styled dark hair, impeccable makeup, and a coat I recognized as "expensive." I had a hard time guessing her age; I figured it as late-forties-but-looks-younger.

I sat up and rolled my neck, embarrassed I hadn't woken when she'd come in—usually I'm a light sleeper. But then, usually I haven't gone two days without rest.

"I pay you to keep me updated!" the woman was shouting.

"That's what I'm doing now, Doc," Tresting answered, obviously trying to keep his cool.

"You *found her* and then you lost her! You knew where she was and instead you go chasing off after—"

"That's not what—" Tresting tried to cut in.

"She killed my husband!" she cried.

Oh. Leena Kingsley. "I thought you were supposed to be a diplomat," I said without thinking.

Kingsley spun to glare at me with the full weight of her attention, and I'll be damned if I didn't lurch back a few inches from the fury radiating off her. I remembered belatedly that she'd seen her whole Foreign Service career come tumbling down in flames. Oops.

Kingsley rounded back on Tresting. "And as for bringing in someone else—"

"She's another professional who had information—"

Nice of him to put that spin on it.

"California law expressly prohibits a private investigator from sharing any information related to a case without prior consent of the client!" Kingsley snapped.

"California law also prohibits PIs from trespassing on private property, or drawing firearms on unarmed citizens, or pretending to be anything other than a PI to get information," Tresting said, crossing his arms. "I don't believe you've expressed any displeasure with me before."

I hadn't known those laws. Arthur Tresting was one naughty PI.

"They killed Reg," Kingsley spat, her voice trembling with fury. "Try to remember that. It may not be *personal* for you, but finding out what happened is the single most important thing in the world to me. Have you ever loved anyone, Mr. Tresting? If so, try to put yourself in my shoes."

She spun on her heel and stalked out of the office. Tresting slumped into his chair, his head sagging.

I thought Kingsley was being a bit hard on the poor man. It was obvious to me he'd been driving himself into the ground investigating this. "Good thing you didn't tell her you spilled about her case while we were pointing guns at each other," I said.

"Shouldn't have at all, really," he admitted. "Everything's gone upside down and backwards. The doc, too. First time I met her, she was the soul of diplomacy, thought I'd never see anything disturb that poise. And now she's . . ."

"Unhinged?"

"It's been a trying case," he said.

"She's very . . . dedicated," I offered.

"You're not seeing a tenth of it. You know, we both started getting death threats, anonymous, after this whole thing started—not sure if I should be insulted no one's tried to follow through, by the by—and she always laughed. Said if someone killed her, they might start taking her husband's death seriously."

"Really?"

"Yeah. Some guy even threatened her son once. She got him a bodyguard and didn't look back."

"Wow."

"Yeah." Tresting leaned back in his chair and closed his eyes. "She's a trip. Can't even say she's the craziest client I ever had, either, though this is by far the craziest case. Glamorous life of a private eye, huh?"

"Speaking of, what *does* a PI license let you do?" I asked, curious.

"Huh? Well . . . loiter."

"That's it?"

"Pretty much."

I felt a strong urge to snicker.

"Though sometimes people see the license and think they have to answer questions," Tresting amended. "Authority figure and all that."

"That's why I have a fake one," I said.

"I didn't hear that."

I went to use the washroom, and took the time to splash water on my face and rinse out my mouth. When I returned, Tresting's monitors were back on and he was talking to Checker. "Good timing, Russell," he said.

"I think I've narrowed down your search," Checker told me. "It fronts as a travel agency, which makes a good cover for tons of international calls. But the security on their intranets is ridiculously intense. It's—"

"Did you crack it?" I interrupted.

He twitched. "I will. A little more time—"

"We know it's the right office, though?"

"Statistically, the suspicious activity—"

"Yes," said Tresting, over Checker's annoyed squawk at being interrupted again. "That's his way of saying yes."

"Then let's go."

"I feel appreciated," grumped Checker.

"Thank you," I said to him with sweet sarcasm, and turned back to Tresting. "Now let's go."

Checker gave us a hearty middle finger and cut the connection.

"He'll be standing by for when we get in," Tresting assured me. "In case we can get him remote access. Shall we?"

"Can you get him to cut the security cameras for us first?" I wasn't likely to forget how easily Checker had been able to find Dawna and me on the Santa Monica footage.

"Asked already. For some reason the building security system is down today. Been down for the last few hours."

I studied his grim face. "You think they have something going down?"

"Only one way to find out. Mind giving me my gun back?"

Tresting drove; I sat in the passenger seat and tried to keep from fidgeting. I'd never gone into a place with someone else. It felt odd, itchy, like a variable I had no control over. I tamped down both that and my headache, which had reappeared with a dull throb as we drove—this wasn't the time to be distracted. Fortunately, I'd had enough practice with hangovers to ignore headaches pretty easily.

Once we hit the right block, Tresting parked his badass truck on the street in favor of not being locked in a nine-dollar-per-hour garage, and we walked in the front door of the office building. An attendant in the lobby nodded at us with a mild frown—probably because we both looked like we either belonged to the same fight club or made a habit of walking into doors together—but Tresting nodded back in a friendly sort of way and went up to the directory as if he belonged there, and the attendant went back to his crossword.

We took the elevator up to the third floor, neither of us speaking, and found our way down a carpeted hallway of anonymous doors to suite 3B. I raised my eyebrows at Tresting and put a hand under my coat. We split to either side of the door and he reached out to open it.

The door handle refused to yield under his fingers. Locked.

We looked at each other. Clearly the travel agency wasn't an active front, if potential clients couldn't walk in. Tresting gestured for me to stay on my side of the doorway and raised a fist to knock loudly. "Building maintenance," he called.

Nothing.

He tried again. Still nothing. I didn't hear even a rustle of movement from inside.

I mimed kicking in the door. I'm excellent at kicking in doors. Tresting, however, held up a hand to stop me and pulled out a set of lockpicks. His way was less conspicuous, I'd give him that.

I stayed ready in case the occupants of the office could hear us and were quietly preparing. Tresting picked the lock with astonishing speed, almost as if he were inserting a key instead of some squiggly pieces of metal, and raised his eyes to nod at me. I nodded back, and he twisted the handle and pushed the door open.

My gun leapt into my hand, but I had nothing to aim it at. We stared numbly.

Someone who looked like she'd played the role of receptionist was sprawled just inside the door, her throat slit so deeply she was almost decapitated. Blood saturated the carpet in a massive, soggy pool around her.

Tresting had his weapon out, too, and we stepped into the room, covering every angle and carefully avoiding the soaked carpeting. Tresting elbowed the door shut behind him, and we crept into the office suite.

My stomach folded in on itself as we passed down the row of desks. A young, sandy-haired man at a computer had been disemboweled. The women in the next two cubicles looked like they'd tried to run. One had fallen on her front, but her head was twisted all the way around so her sightless eyes stared up at the ceiling in frozen horror.

We turned the corner and found the conference room. The blood had turned it into a grotesque modern art painting.

The men and women seated around the conference table had been older, well-dressed corporate types. All except one were tied to their chairs, cloth gags choking their corpses, the lone exception a middle-aged man with a .22-inch-diameter hole in his forehead. He'd had a better fate than the rest. The mathematics arranged itself in brilliant arcing lines of red, the spatter patterns showing me exactly how they had all suffered.

I'm not squeamish, but I closed my eyes briefly.

"Here," said Tresting's voice, and he handed me a pair of latex gloves he pulled from a pocket. He'd found some plastic bags in a bin somewhere, too; he shook bits of shredded paper off them and put them over his boots, handing two more to me. "Forensics are good. Rather not go down for this."

I tucked the plastic mechanically into the tops of my boots, and we cautiously approached the scene. I tried to deduce something useful from the carnage, but my mind drew a blank; I could see only parabolas of blood fountaining to end in gruesome trigonometry, infinite repetition from too many points of convergence—angles of impact, speed of slashes, over and over and over again. . . .

I could see everything. It meant nothing.

Tresting hooked a Bluetooth over his ear. It wasn't hard to figure out whom he was calling. He succinctly described the scene and started carefully pulling wallets from those around the conference table, reading off their IDs.

I forced myself to detach, to observe, running my eyes over the unhappy victims and trying like hell to ignore the mathematical replay, but nothing could make this scene better. I saw limbs bent in unholy directions, shallow cuts carving lurid designs in skin . . . one woman had been partially flayed. The stench in the heavy air clogged my nostrils, gagging me.

The brute horror here wouldn't tell me anything useful. I escaped back into the outer offices, doing my best to avoid looking at the bodies, and attacked the cubicles, dragging open desk drawers and filing cabinets.

I needn't have bothered. Cabinet after cabinet revealed rows of hanging file folders, telling me some paper trail had been here, but every one of them swung empty—even the paper tabs labeling the folders had been pulled. The desk drawers mocked me with more of the same. I tried the computers next—when the first one refused to start, I crawled around to the back to find the hard drive missing, the connectors still dangling. I took the time to check around the back of every computer in the place, but they were all gutted. The private offices showed much the same story except sans corpses; apparently everyone important had been in the conference room.

Bits of paper from a shredder littered the floor here and there as I moved through the suite. I eventually found the shredder in question, an industrial-strength behemoth, but the bin beneath it had been cleared out. I figured out why when I found the office kitchen.

A large metal filing cabinet had been turned on its side against the doorway, with plastic garbage bags duct-taped across it to create a seal, and the impromptu levee held back a pulpy white goop that drowned the entire kitchenette to the level of my waist. The caustic odor of chemicals assaulted my senses, and I coughed and hugged one arm across my nose, blinking watering eyes. Though the tap was no longer running, rags in the sink drain showed how the place had been so easily flooded, and then some sort of mad chemical mixture had been thrown in along with . . . shredded paper.

Someone had wanted to be very, very, *very* sure no one reconstituted the data from this office. Hell, it wasn't like most people could piece back together shredded documents in the first place; certainly no one could do it easily—except me, that is, but it seemed both egotistical and too coincidental to assume this destruction was for my benefit. Why would anyone go to so much extra trouble?

"Hey, Russell," Tresting called.

I carefully avoided the corpses in the outer office and wound my way back to the torture chamber of a conference room. Tresting stood at the far end, examining an empty chair. "Look at this," he said, and I stepped around to oblige him. Sprays of blood crossed the edges of the chair in multiple places, but the seat and back were clean.

"Someone was sitting here," I said.

"Haven't seen Dawna Polk anywhere. Could be her?"

I narrowed my eyes at the chair seat, trying to remember the measurements of Dawna's hips. I hadn't been paying too much attention, but I estimated, measuring in my memory. "No. This is too wide. I'm guessing a man. Or a large woman." I squinted at the blood spatter surrounding the empty chair, the numbers spiraling to find their sources in midair, a person-shaped outline of shimmering red. "Whoever it was got tortured, too."

"How can you tell?"

"The spray," I answered, not wanting to go into it.

"Think our perps turned kidnappers," said Tresting. "They wanted information—forced the vics to talk, most likely while their coworkers got tortured or killed." He reached over to the nearest woman and lifted the side of the cloth gag with a gloved finger. "Take a look."

He was right. Blood stained the skin underneath the cloth, and nowhere near any of her own wounds. The smearing made it harder to judge, but from the angle I guessed it had come from the man across from her.

Maybe this investigative stuff was worth something after all.

I told Tresting what I'd found in the rest of the office suite. "Unless they have data on an outside server somewhere, it's cleaned out."

"Think we better head out, then," he said grimly. "We can keep an eye on the police investigation."

"When do you think they'll find it?"

"Right after we leave, when I call in a tip."

I rolled my eyes.

"Can it, Russell," Tresting growled. "This is too big."

He had a point. Of course, considering what we knew of Pithica, this was probably too big for the cops, too.

twelve

WE DROVE in silence almost all the way back. When Tresting found a space on the street a few blocks away from his office, he yanked the truck over into it, shifting gears so hard my teeth rattled. As he turned off the engine I reached for the door handle, but Tresting's voice stopped me.

"Russell."

"Yeah?"

He made no move to get out. "Been thinking. This wasn't Pithica. Not their style. And they wouldn't do this to their own."

"New player, then?" I thought of Anton's garage, of the men in dark suits at Courtney's place. I saw the massacre in the office building again, my mind skittering away from the details. Maybe this mess had reached the point where I should throw in with Tresting for real, share everything. I opened my mouth.

Tresting slammed the heels of his hands against the steering wheel. "*Dammit*, Russell!"

I bit back on my other intel. "What?"

The look he shot me was positively poisonous, for no reason I could fathom.

"*What?*" I repeated.

"You told him, didn't you."

"Told what to whom?" Where did Tresting get off thinking he had a say in my business? It wasn't as if I had a whole lot of friends to blab information to anyway; the only person I'd been in touch with at all was—oh. *Oh.* "Wait—you think Rio did this?"

He gave me a long, level stare, his jaw clenched, his eyes mirroring the pain and anger of the victims in the office building.

I swallowed. Had it been Rio? *And so what if it was?* Stumbling upon that kind of . . . work . . . I would be lying if I claimed it had been pleasant, but it wasn't news to me what Rio was capable of. I was well aware of his methods. *And if anyone deserves them, it's Pithica. Isn't it?*

Tresting was still staring at me as if I'd betrayed him. I tried to ignore the squirming sensation in my stomach that felt remarkably like guilt.

Of course I had to tell Rio we were going in, I insisted to myself. *He was tracking Dawna; if we ran into each other working at cross-purposes . . . that's how people get killed!* I started to bridle under Tresting's judgment. He did not have the high ground here, I told myself. He didn't. "I told you," I said. "You work with me, you work with the people I trust. I don't know if Rio had something to do with this, but—"

"Get out."

"We can still work toge—"

"Get out of my truck."

I did. Tresting got down from the other side and slammed his door with much more force than necessary.

I decided to try for professional. "I'll call him," I volunteered. "If he did go in, I'll see if he got any information out of the office. I'll let you know."

The tension in Tresting's posture cracked, and he whipped his arm around, bringing a fist down on the hood of his truck so hard he dented it. "How can you stand there and say—after what we saw—" He shook his head over and over, as if warding off the devil. "No. No. Don't call me, Russell. Just don't. We'll solve this without you or not at all." He cleared his throat. "It's not worth it."

Something stung inside my chest, a sharp and unfamiliar pain.

It wasn't only Rio he thought a monster. "I understand," I said. My lips felt strangely stiff. "I won't bother you again."

Tresting's condemnation washed over me as he turned away, disgust and contempt and horror simmering in his wake. He strode off.

The stinging feeling got worse. I took a deep breath and told myself it didn't matter.

I waited for Tresting to disappear down the street and then followed in the direction of his office, looking for the sports car I had driven here the night before, but someone had jacked it. Not surprising, considering it was way too nice a car for the area and I had already done half the job for any aspiring car thief, but still, talk about an annoying end to a rotten morning. I briefly and pettily considered taking Tresting's truck, but that was beneath even me.

A group of teenagers was using the street I had originally parked on for skateboarding practice. I sighed and started back along the sidewalk, looking for a nice witness-free place to steal a ride home.

A shot rang out, followed closely by several more.

My mind triangulated in less than half a second. Tresting's office.

I flew back the way I had come. The gunfire beat out an irregular tattoo—one fully automatic weapon, and three, no, four semiautomatics or revolvers. People on the street cried out to each other and rushed to get indoors, grabbing out mobile phones—the cops would be on their way, then, but I added response times and travel times in my head—too long, too slow.

My boots pounded the cement in time with the staccato gunfire as I dashed around the corner to Tresting's alleyway, my brain bursting into echoes and trajectories and telling me exactly where the shooters were: one, two, three, four, five. Two gunmen against the near wall of the upstairs office, three more ranged out toward the other side of the room. One could be Tresting, but with the blinds still closed I had no way of figuring out which. I had to get inside.

Second-floor office. Cinder-block walls, locked and reinforced door, barred window. With a little time and the right leverage I could blast through any of the three, but which was fastest? Which?

The window, it had to be the window. Estimates of bolt depth and wall strength ricocheted through my head. Tear the bars off. Crash through. *Yes.*

Instead of racing for the outside stairway up to the door, I veered for the opposite side of the alleyway and turned my mad bound into a leap, catching the bottom rung of the fire escape there with one reaching hand. The iron bit into my palm as my body weight jerked against it, and then I was swarming up the metal.

I drew my SIG as I flew across the first landing and tore up the next flight of stairs. Across the alleyway, Tresting's window was inset in the wall past where his stairway ended at his office door, a sheer two-story drop below it. As I blew past the same height, I fired at the window without slowing.

Bang-bang-bang-bang.

I hit the next landing up, vaulted over the rail, and jumped.

My leap took me high in an arc above the grimy pavement twenty feet below, a long moment of weightlessness before my shoulder slammed into the concrete wall above Tresting's window. Time seemed to slow. In hundredths of a second I was going to fall; my margin for error was almost nonexistent. I looked down at the two-story drop below me, equations unspooling in my head, the acceleration of gravity tumbling through every incarnation of every possible assignment of variables, and I flattened my arm against the cinder blocks, forcing friction to delay me the slightest touch. Vector diagrams of normal force and gravitational pull and kinetic friction roared through my senses. Just before gravity won and sucked me into a two-story plunge to the alleyway below, I dropped the SIG.

It outstripped me by the smallest fraction of a second, and as it fell between the bars and the top lip of the wall above the window, I shot out my left foot and came down on it with my entire body weight. The frame of the handgun slammed against the bars on one side and the top lip of the window on the other with all the force a simple machine could harness, and became my very own makeshift crowbar.

When I'd fired from across the alleyway, I'd been aiming at the four bolts fixing the bars to the wall. A handgun round wasn't strong enough to break them, but it made a heck of a drill. With the drilled bolts and the massive leverage, the bars scraped in their sockets and then shrieked out of the wall.

I had no time to gather myself. My left foot leveraging against the falling bars was the only thing keeping me from tumbling twenty feet and splatting on the pavement. I kicked away from them and smashed my upper body into the naked window.

No chance I'd keep from getting cut; I needed all the math I had to generate enough force to break the glass from this direction. I crashed into the room shoulders first, the blinds coming down with me in a shower of broken shards. As I fell, I windmilled my legs to catch the shooter who'd been standing closest to the window—she wasn't Tresting; I scissored my legs with a snap and took her out before I hit the floor.

I had no weapon anymore, but I scooped up a piece of broken windowpane in each hand, spinning as I came up. *Not Arthur*—the glass left my hand, *not Arthur* again and the other piece of windowpane found its mark, the boy dropping his gun and clutching at his throat as he fell. I glimpsed Tresting across the room taking cover behind his gun safe and whirled to face the last hostile, who screamed inarticulately as he brought his Glock around. I dove and rolled over the desk, grabbing at one of the tall, treelike houseplants as I did—my roll translated into centripetal acceleration as I spun the plant with me and let fly like it was a slingshot. Heavy clay pot hit face before he had time to get a shot off. Heavy clay pot won.

I let my body complete its roll over the desk and landed on my feet. "Tresting?"

He emerged shakily from behind the safe and stared at me with wide, unblinking eyes, his Beretta twitching in his hand.

"You all right?" I asked.

He kept staring.

"Are. You. Hit?" I enunciated. Was this what they called shock? I wouldn't have thought Tresting would go in for shock, being an ex-cop and all.

"That window's two stories up," he said.

"That's right," I agreed. "I guess that's why they call you a private eye. Now, seriously, are you okay?"

He touched his right bicep; blood glistened on his fingertips. "Graze. Lucky, I guess." His eyes flickered over the scene. Four bodies. Broken glass and dirt everywhere. "It had *bars* on it," he whispered.

"Yup." I'm not going to lie: I like impressing people. Especially people who've just walked away from me in the street and told me they never want to speak to me again.

thirteen

"YOU'RE BLEEDING," Tresting managed, once he had found his voice again.

"So I am," I said. I have a hyperawareness of my own body; all the math in the world won't help me if I can't match calculation with reality. I can make estimates about other people's anatomies, but mine I know every detail of at any time, and I knew I'd sustained five shallow cuts on my face, neck, and hands, and that none of them were worth worrying about. "So are you," I added.

Tresting half shrugged and kept his left hand pressed against the graze as he crunched across the glass-strewn floor to crouch by the nearest of the corpses. He reached out to place his fingers against the boy's wrist.

"They're dead," I informed him. I wasn't entirely happy about that. I was only now registering just how young they were—four teenagers, a girl and three boys, probably around fifteen or sixteen. Kids.

I hate it when bad things happen to kids. Especially when I'm the bad thing.

I also noticed something else. "They're all Asian." It seemed strange. "Did you rob a Chinese restaurant or something?"

"They're Korean," corrected Tresting. I made a face; I couldn't tell the difference. "And gang members." He pointed to a blood-smeared tattoo on the hand of the boy next to him as he stood.

I almost said, *So?* but something pinged in my memory about Koreans and African Americans and race riots. I made a mental note to ask the internet at some point. "Oh," I said instead.

Tresting moved over to the window. I didn't miss how he glanced out through the shattered panes and then at me, disbelief still sketching his features. I felt rather smug.

He crouched down again to touch the girl's wrist, checking for a pulse I knew wouldn't be there. I looked away.

The sounds of the street filtered up through the broken window, traffic noise and horns and people going about their days. A light breeze accompanied them, stirring the air in the office and making the cuts on my face start to sting.

"Thanks," said Tresting suddenly.

The word parsed oddly, as if I were listening to a foreign-language speaker say something and knew it wasn't coming out the way he intended. "Sure," I said.

Tresting stood back up and regarded me with a slight frown, as if I were a puzzle with a new twist. "They would've killed me," he said. "This neighborhood, cops would've been too slow."

"Yeah," I agreed.

"I don't . . . Thanks," he said again.

I looked around the ruined office. Depression had neatly replaced the smugness. "They're kids," I whispered. Maybe I was the monster he thought I was after all. "They're *kids*."

"I know," he said heavily, and it sounded like he did.

I took a deep breath. "What now?"

He hesitated. "I don't know. Something's different. First time Pithica's targeted me."

"You think this was Pithica?"

"Korean gang members trying to hit a black PI in a bad neighborhood," Tresting recited. "Cops would write it off as a hate crime."

"So? Maybe it was."

"You saw the data, Russell. Hell, you've been attacked."

I waited, but he didn't say anything else, as if daring me to figure it out. I thought about the cases from Kingsley's journal. A few of the strange deaths had involved gang violence, sure—drive-by shootings, or people caught in the crossfire in places gangs shouldn't have been active. But Checker had connected a lot of other deaths in the file to Pithica that had nothing to do with gangs—suicides, freak accidents, muggings gone wrong—

My thoughts ground to a halt. "They don't want it investigated."

Tresting pointed a finger at me, as if to say, *Bingo*.

"They're killing people in ways the police can write off easily," I realized. "Close the case."

"Senseless tragedies," he agreed. "Don't know how Polk got Kingsley to write that note, but if it wasn't for Leena—" He broke off. "Shit. Leena."

He strode back to his gun safe, spun the combination to open it, and started reloading his Beretta. "You armed?"

"I will be in a minute." I picked my way through the debris and slipped weapons out of the lifeless fingers of Tresting's teenage attackers. The girl by the window had been toting a TEC-9 illegally converted to full auto; the others had two Glocks and a cheap and ugly Smith & Wesson semiautomatic. Jesus, it was irritating enough they had to be so young; couldn't they at least carry nice hardware?

Tresting had his phone to his ear as he reloaded; he left a terse message for Dr. Kingsley to take her son, get somewhere anonymous, and call him back. He hung up and holstered the Beretta, then reached back into his safe to hoist out a shotgun that I didn't need my math ability to tell was far too short to be legal. He wrapped it in a spare shirt like a bundle of curtain rods and completely ignored me when I raised my eyebrows at him.

"Your prints and DNA are here," he said instead. "That going to be a problem?"

"They'd need something to compare 'em to," I answered. "How about you?"

"I'll wake up in an alleyway later and claim amnesia."

"You don't want to stay like a good citizen and help with the investigation?"

"Not when the doc might be in danger." He relocked his safe and grabbed a duffel behind his desk to stow the wrapped shotgun in. It still stuck out slightly, hopefully not too obviously.

Sirens sounded in the distance.

"Better dash," said Tresting.

"For an ex-cop, you're very cavalier about the law, aren't you," I commented, heading for the door.

Something dark shadowed his face. "Law's never done me much good."

We crept down the outside stairway in a hurry; I scooped up my battered SIG from the ground and we made it to Tresting's truck at a fast walk. The engine came to life with a reluctant shudder; Tresting swung out into traffic and immediately pulled over to make way for five police cars, their sirens wailing and lights flashing. I watched them pass us, trying to keep a poker face. Tresting pulled back into traffic and then reached across to his glove compartment to grab a burner cell still in its plastic packaging. He tossed it in my lap.

"Call in an anonymous tip on the doc. I'll give you her address."

Which would ensure we'd run into the cops when we arrived. "Really?"

"Forty minutes in traffic. Call."

I cast around for something sharp to use on the vacuum-packed plastic—the math said I wasn't getting in otherwise—and found a ballpoint pen on the floor of the truck to pry it open with. "You call, then."

"I'm driving. Isn't safe."

"*Really?*"

"For the—we can't afford to get pulled over! Just make the damned call. And put your seat belt on."

"*Now* you want to be law-abiding?" I muttered, but I did as he asked, punching the buttons a little harder than necessary. I relayed the address Tresting gave me to the dispatcher and hung up when she tried to ask my name.

"Does her son still have that bodyguard?" I asked Tresting.

"Far as I know. And he'll be at school right now. Good. Don't think they'd risk something at a school."

"We still don't know who 'they' are," I pointed out. "Or what they're after."

"There's an agenda," Tresting said, his jaw clenched. "Don't know what, but they've got one for sure, and we're monkeying it up, lucky us." He gave me a brief, almost calculating glance. "You especially, I think."

"What are you talking about? I just stumbled in on this, thank you very much. You're the one who's been working it for months."

"Yeah, but I think they were happy to see me chasing my own tail. Entertainment, probably, for all the headway we were making. You show up, and . . ." He slammed down a little too hard on the brake as we approached a red light, and the stupid seat belt tried to garrote me. "I tracked Polk for months, and they don't care about saving her hide from anyone till you hook up with her. Then they're after you posthaste, she disappears, and a day later I got a target painted on me too? Don't believe in coincidences."

He was right. Dammit. After all, I hadn't exactly randomly chanced upon this mess. Rio's words came back to me: *What interests me more is who made such a concerted effort to draw you into this. . . .*

"Got anything you want to share?" said Tresting. His tone wasn't hostile, but it wasn't neutral, either.

"Hey, I've been playing catch-up from the beginning," I said. "You still know way more about this shit show than I do."

"Well, you know something. Maybe you don't realize. Or maybe they want something from you."

"I'm not special," I objected.

It was a stupid thing to say. Tresting wasn't an unobservant man, and my little display while rescuing him hadn't been what one might call "discreet." He didn't answer right away, shifting gears with feeling and jamming down the accelerator to cut rudely onto the freeway. Then he said what I'd been dreading.

"At my office. Not that I'm not appreciative, but how the hell . . . ?"

I sighed. My usual response, that I'm really good at math, wasn't going to suffice in blowing off a guy like Tresting. He seemed the type to worry at something until he got every last kernel of fact about it.

"I jumped," I said, deliberately obtuse.

"Two stories."

"No, stupid. From the fire escape."

He digested that. "And pried off the bars."

"With my SIG. It's a good crowbar. Metal frame, you know." I was proud of myself for not making a dig about cheap polymer piece-of-crap Glocks. I'm the soul of tact.

Tresting looked like he was searching for another question to ask. "Damn. If I hadn't been there myself . . ."

"I train a lot," I lied.

"In being Spider-Man?"

"Among other things." At least he hadn't actually seen me leapfrog the alley. I was a lot faster than most people imagined.

"Damn," Tresting said again. Then he hazarded, "Military?"

I blinked. "What?"

"Your background. Ex-military?"

"I seem *military* to you?"

"Oh-kay, so not ex-mil." There was a pregnant pause.

"School of hard knocks," I supplied, trying for clever.

"Hey, that was my alma mater, too," said Tresting. "But apparently you graduated summa cum laude or something."

"Gesundheit," I said. "Hey, stop PI-ing me or next time I won't come save your sorry ass."

I didn't expect that to stop him, but for some reason it did, and he dropped into a thoughtful silence.

Relieved, I took the opportunity to shoot Rio a cryptic text to see if he had any new updates. The bloody corpses played through my vision again, the stench in the air heavy and metallic and cloying. Those people were dead anyway; was I hypocritical if I hoped it hadn't been Rio?

Then who else?

I thought of Anton. I'd assumed Pithica had been the one to come after him, but the explosive fire didn't fit with their usual MO. A stunt like that wouldn't fly under the radar; it would demand investigation. Same with the massacre at the office suite, I supposed.

Rio wouldn't have gone after Anton, however. I felt sure of that. He wasn't bothered by collateral damage to innocent people, but he would never make a concerted hit against a decent man and his twelve-year-old daughter. It was impossible. He himself might be capable of such an act, but his God wasn't.

Who was?

One fact was inescapable. No matter who had come after Anton, the office workers, me, Tresting, or Courtney Polk, Tresting was right: none of it had happened before I had gotten involved. Correlation didn't imply causality—but it was also possible I was the kiss of death. *You know something,* Tresting had said. *Or maybe they want something from you.* I thought back through my retrieval clients, but I'd been doing this only a few years, and I couldn't think of any past cases that had been strange or unusual enough to have a connection to Pithica. Certainly I didn't think I knew anything worth killing for.

And the only thing special about *me* was my math ability. Which was cool, sure, and occasionally made me into some sort of flying squirrel on crack, but in the grand scheme of things, even I wasn't conceited enough to think I was worth as much trouble as some people were putting in to stop us.

Things weren't adding up. And for someone with an overpowered math brain, things not adding up meant a serious problem.

fourteen

WE ARRIVED at Leena Kingsley's house fifty-two minutes after we'd left Tresting's office. The drive had been mostly silent. Tresting was lost in his own thoughts, and I figured our détente was so touchy and fragile that going into a possibly hostile situation wasn't the time to mess with it.

Tresting cruised by the first time without slowing. A cop car sat on the street outside, but only one, and its lights weren't flashing. The small house was still—no sign that anything was amiss, and no neighbors gawking. It didn't look like there had been a shoot-out here.

Of course, that didn't mean anything. This was a nice residential neighborhood, with well-groomed yards and picket fences and rose-bushes, and Pithica liked subtle.

Tresting circled the block and then pulled over a few houses prior to Dr. Kingsley's. He reached into the duffel he'd brought the shot-gun in, pulled out a scope, and held it up to one eye. "Can't see much," he said after a moment. "But there's movement. Think she and the cops are talking."

"Do you think they'd come after her with police there?"

"Seems stupid."

"We wait, then?"

"Think so."

We sat in the truck, tense and silent.

About twenty minutes later the door opened, and two uniformed LAPD officers came out onto the porch. Leena Kingsley saw them out, speaking politely. They gave her a last nod and good-bye and headed back to their patrol car. But instead of staying on the street and watching the house as I'd expected, the black-and-white pulled away from the curb.

"They're leaving?" I cried. "I called in a death threat!"

Tresting shrugged. "Police are busy."

As the patrol car cruised past us, without meaning to I twitched my face away from their line of sight.

"Stop flinching," said Tresting. "That's a good way to get noticed."

"I wasn't *flinching*," I protested.

Tresting shook his head in disgust. I opened my mouth, feeling absurdly defensive, but he was already getting out of the truck. I told myself I could clean his clock in a fight any day, and in fact already had, and checked on the weapons tucked into my belt under my coat before following him out onto the sidewalk.

We'd taken only a few steps when a man in a suit stepped out of a black sedan and started briskly up Kingsley's walkway. We both stopped for a split second and then simultaneously began walking faster.

"Door-to-door salesman?" I muttered.

"Don't think it's a coincidence he waited till the cops left," Tresting muttered back.

The suit reached the porch and pressed the doorbell. As Dr. Kingsley pulled the door open, he reached into his suit jacket, and I already had a gun out and aimed before we saw he was only flashing a badge and ID at her. Leena Kingsley spotted us over his shoulder at the same time.

"What's going on?" she asked, her eyes going back and forth between Tresting's face and my gun.

The suit turned, a lanky white guy with a scraggly beard, and saw the barrel of my newly acquired Smith & Wesson in his face. He stumbled back a step, immediately raising his hands in the air. "Miss, please put down the weapon."

I'd thought he was familiar when he first turned, but now I definitely recognized him: Mr. Nasally Voiced, one of the fine examples of humanity who'd been sacking Courtney's place. *Oh, hell.*

Tresting grabbed the leather badge holder out of the guy's hand and scrutinized it. "FBI?"

The man nodded. "Agent Finch. Now, please put down the weapon."

FBI? That didn't track at all, not with what I'd seen him doing earlier. "No," I said. "Let's go inside."

Tresting either agreed with me or wanted to present a united front. He gestured Finch ahead of him, and Leena Kingsley apprehensively stepped back to let us in.

I glanced back at the street as I went inside, but nobody was stirring. With luck, our little cowboy stunt had gone unnoticed. I kicked the door shut behind us; Tresting was already closing the blinds in the living room.

"Sit down," I ordered our new friend.

He did so, sinking onto an upholstered chair, arms still raised. "What do you want?" he asked calmly.

"To know who the hell you are, first of all," I said. I could feel Tresting's eyes on me, questioning. "Ten to one the badge is a fake," I told him. "Now, who are you?"

"I'm SSA Gabriel Finch," the man repeated. "I'm here to speak with Dr. Kingsley—"

"Check him," I directed Tresting.

He came forward and patted down the man quickly and efficiently, finding a mobile phone in his pocket and a Glock in a shoulder holster. Glocks. Why did everyone like Glocks?

"Please," Leena Kingsley broke in, "what's going on?"

Tresting stepped over to her. "I was targeted," he said in a low aside. "Worried about you and Ned now. He at school still?"

"Ye-yes." Kingsley inched closer to Tresting, her posture tense as she regarded my tableau with Finch. "You think he isn't who he says?"

"Possible," said Tresting neutrally, looking at me.

"I assure you, I am with the Federal Bureau of Investigation," Finch repeated, much more tranquil than I wanted him to be. "Now if you'll put down the weapon, I'm sure we can sort this out."

"Courtney Polk," I cut in. "Skinny kid, frizzy hair. What do you know about her?"

"Nothing," said Finch, with a poker face I would have killed for.

I smiled slowly. "Oh, see? You just lied to me. That's a bad idea."

"I'm not lying," said Finch guilelessly. "I have no idea what you're talking about."

"Miss Polk killed this woman's husband," Tresting said, tilting his head at Leena. "You got any information at all about her, this is not the time to withhold it."

"That's true," I said. "You don't have to worry about me making holes in you; Dr. Kingsley'll put your head through a wall."

"I, uh . . ." said Kingsley miserably, and trailed off.

That pinged me as all wrong, considering the firebrand she had been that morning. Out of the corner of my eye, I could see Tresting staring at her in confusion. Oddly, so was Finch, with the first sign of apprehension he had shown the whole time.

"Please finish, Dr. Kingsley," said the would-be FBI agent, his nasally voice suddenly sounding strained.

Her face tensed as if she didn't like being in the spotlight. "I was going to call you," she said to Tresting.

He reached out and touched her elbow, steadying her. "About what?"

She started twisting her wedding ring back and forth on her finger. "I . . . I want to call off the investigation."

What the . . . ? Dr. Kingsley wouldn't have given up this investigation voluntarily—

"What's going on?" asked Tresting gently.

"Nothing," said Kingsley, shaking him off. "It's just—I've done so much thinking today. I can't do this anymore." She drew herself up and turned back to Finch and me. "Whoever you're with, Agent Finch, if this is about Reginald, it's done. I'm taking my son and moving back to Washington."

Agent Finch went white as a sheet.

"Somebody better start explaining fast," I declared into the silence. When nobody spoke, I waved my gun a little. "Hey. Kingsley. This morning you bit our heads off about this being the most important thing in the world to you. What gives?"

"It was—it is—it still is," she faltered. "But I think that needs to change. I need . . . for my son's sake. For my sake. I can't keep doing this to us." She took a deep breath. "This has gone on long enough. We need to rebuild our lives, to move on. I have to try."

I didn't buy that for a hot second.

"Dr. Kingsley," said Finch, very tensely, "may I ask if you've had any visitors today?"

Her brow furrowed. "Um . . . two police officers; they said they'd had another threat. I've had a lot of threats since this started," she explained to nobody. "It's one of the reasons . . ."

Tresting crossed his arms. "Doc, the first time you got a death threat you called and asked me what kind of shotgun to buy, and then told me to bug your phone and said you hoped they'd keep calling so they'd give something away."

"You see? This is why I have to stop this," she pleaded. "It's madness. It's been like an addiction. I can't—"

"Please," interrupted Finch. "Did you have any other visitors today?"

"Well, you, I suppose." She looked at Tresting as if asking for help, but his eyes were pinched, and he said nothing. She waved her hands weakly. "That's it. No one else."

"Dr. Kingsley," said Finch, "this is very important. Can you recount your entire day for me?"

Getting no help from Tresting, Kingsley looked at me. I gave her a slight shrug. It was unnerving that Finch seemed to have taken over completely while still being at gunpoint, but I very much wanted to see where this was going. "My whole day?" she finally repeated.

"You saw these characters this morning, yes?" said Finch, nodding at Tresting and me. "You can start after that."

She glanced around at the rest of us again, as if wondering when the world had gone mad. "Well, I came home, and then I suppose I took a nap. Then someone was knocking—those police officers—and I spoke to them for a while, and then just as they left, you arrived."

"Thought you said you did a lot of thinking on all this today," said Tresting.

Her expression twitched, confusion rumpling her features. "Yes. No. That is, yes, but not—it's been between everything else."

"Do you remember lying down to take your nap?" asked Finch.

"Well, yes," said Kingsley. "I suppose I do . . . ?"

She blinked and looked away from us, her words trailing into silence.

"You keep using the word 'suppose,'" said Finch after a beat. "Are you not certain, Dr. Kingsley?"

A red flush began creeping up her neck. "I don't have to answer these questions."

"Please, Doc," said Tresting. "Bear with us. Something hinky—"

She straightened her spine, recovering some of her prior imperious fire. "I told you I'm done. I'm sorry, Mr. Tresting, but this mad crusade is over. Leave my house, please. All of you."

I didn't know about Tresting, but I wasn't leaving until I had some answers. And I thought I knew who could give them to me.

I stepped closer to Finch, tilting my Smith & Wesson so the front sight lined up with his forehead, right between the eyes. "You know what's happening here, don't you."

Finch took a breath. "Please take that weapon out of my face."

I hesitated, then lowered the gun. It wasn't like I needed it anyway. "Now, what the hell is going on?"

He wet his lips. "Someone got to Dr. Kingsley. That's all I'm at liberty to say."

Hell if I was going to let him stop at that. "Someone *who?*"

"Pithica," said Tresting.

fifteen

My hand tightened on the grip of the Smith & Wesson—I itched to have a target again, but who was my enemy? Or what? "I say again," I addressed the room at large. "What the *hell* is going on?"

"I interviewed Senator Hammond's assistant," said Tresting. "From Kingsley's, Reginald Kingsley's, notes. Same thing, almost word for word. Assistant remembered the senator saying he 'supposed' he had a lie-down. Except then he about-faced on a nuclear arms treaty."

"So someone from Pithica is telling her to say this," I said.

Tresting was watching Dr. Kingsley very closely. "Or something."

Kingsley drew away from him. "What are you implying?"

Tresting didn't answer. "What do you say, Agent Finch?"

"Unfortunately, this is need-to-know," said Finch. "What connection do the two of you have to Dr. Kingsley?"

"Unfortunately, that's need-to-know," I parroted back at him, and raised my gun again. "You know something about Polk, and about Pithica, don't you? You're going to tell us."

"This has gone far enough," said Kingsley. Her voice was firm again, with the strong charisma of authority, and it was hard to believe she didn't mean it. "Leave, all of you, or I'm calling the police."

Tresting reached out and grasped her shoulders. "Please, Doc. Talk to me. What happened today that made you change your mind?"

She twisted back from him, fury clouding her features. "Let go of me! This is my decision. Mine, not yours, and not anybody else's! How dare you imply someone talked me into it?"

"'Cause nothing else makes sense!" cried Tresting. "Doc, you've been in my office almost every day for the past six months bullying me about this case! You moved across the country; you got Ned a body-guard, for God's sake—and now you say you're giving up?"

"That's exactly why I have to! This—this *obsession*, it's destroyed my life. I have to let go of it!"

"But we have a lead now," I argued, gesturing at Finch. "This guy knows something. I saw him at Courtney Polk's house. Don't you want to know—"

"No!"

The absolute denial rang through the room, unqualified and final. Something echoed in my memory.

Kingsley took a breath, resettling her composure. "I'm done. Please, just leave."

"Holy shit," I said.

"What is it?" asked Tresting.

I ignored him and turned to Finch. "Okay, how's this? If you don't tell us what's going on, I will bring you somewhere and tie you up and call someone who can make your worst nightmares come true." I met his eyes squarely, never mind that something inside me was start-ing to feel creeped out and terrified, and my headache had returned with a pounding thunder. "And then I think you'll spill everything."

"Wait," said Tresting, his voice quick and panicked. "Don't—"

The man really had to do something about his fixation with Rio. "Stop getting your knickers in a twist; I don't mean him." I was about to step off a cliff, and the vertigo was dizzying. This was little more than a shot in the dark, but I was right. I knew I was right. "I have a phone number," I said to Finch, "for Dawna Polk."

Finch blanched.

I'd thought he had gone white before, but now all the blood drained from his face as if sucked away, leaving him gray as a corpse behind his scraggly beard. It threw me off-balance; I tried to cover with more bravado. "I'll do it," I pressed. "I'll leave you somewhere, and I'll call her."

"You don't want to do that," Finch croaked. "You don't know what you're dealing with."

"Oh, really? Why don't you tell me then, Mr. SSA Finch?"

Sweat had broken out all across his face, exacerbating the grayness. He rolled his gaze desperately toward Tresting, but the PI's expression was unreadable. "I . . . I can get you a meeting with my supervisor," he offered finally. "Please."

I began to be more than a little unnerved by his reaction. The man was folding like a wet piece of cardboard. Who the hell was Dawna Polk? Christ, my head hurt. "Fine," I said. "Let's go."

"You'll come with us," added Tresting. "We'll set up a meet in a neutral place."

"Yes, all right, okay." Finch sounded so desperate that I wouldn't have been surprised if he'd started offering up friends and family as human sacrifices to us. "We can do that."

The doorbell rang.

We all jumped.

Tresting went to the window and peeked around the closed blinds. He swore softly. "Cops."

I looked at Leena. "Can you go out and tell them nothing's wrong?"

Tresting shook his head. "Too many. Shit. They already think something's going down here. Someone must've seen us pull a weapon."

Finch raised a hand weakly. "I can take care of them."

I snorted. "I wouldn't trust you to give me a Band-Aid for a paper cut."

He let out a strangled laugh that had no humor in it. "Believe me when I say that I'm currently viewing you as a child playing with a nuclear missile. This is above my pay grade, and I don't care who's holding the gun, but I'm not letting you out of my sight if I can help it. Even to be arrested." He held out a hand to Tresting. "My badge, please?"

"What are you going to do?" I demanded.

"You are free to listen in," he said, picking up a receipt that was lying with a pile of mail on the coffee table and scribbling "STING OPERATION IN PROGRESS" on the back of it. He folded it into his badge holder and stood up, some of his previous equanimity returning. "Now, I suggest you all stay out of sight." Without waiting for our response, he moved toward the door.

It looked like I was either going to let him try this, or things were going to get violent. Normally I'm in favor of violence as an easy answer, but with cops involved—fuck.

I kept my gun out and ready, but stepped back.

The living room was separated from the house's foyer by a wide, open doorway. I tucked myself into the corner just on the other side of the archway from the door, where I'd be able to hear every word. Tresting herded Leena to the opposite side of the living room, where they'd also be out of line of sight from the porch.

I heard Finch unlock the door and swing it open. "Is something wrong?" His nasally voice had the tone of a concerned homeowner.

The cop on the doorstep hesitated way too long. I imagined him taking in Finch's badge and the scribbled-on receipt and trying to figure out what to say. "Uh, we had a report of a disturbance," we finally heard. "Do you live here, sir?"

"Yes, I do. Uh, my wife was screaming at me a little while ago for breaking some plates; maybe the neighbors heard it."

"Very well, sir," said the officer. "Sorry to have disturbed you."

"No problem, Officer." I could hear people moving around outside. "You all have a good day, now," called Finch, and shut the door.

He hurried back into the living room. "We're in trouble," he said. "Someone give me my mobile back, now."

Tresting squinted at him, but did as he asked.

Finch hit a few numbers. "Indigo," he said into the phone. "Verification needed, Los Angeles Police Department. Eight five oh three two bravo." He paused, then added, "And Saturn. Used Redowa as a threat. They want to meet."

I snapped my fingers in his face. "Cut out the code words, super-spy. What's going on?"

He whirled on me furiously. "Look, missy, they've got SWAT out there. They're not going away just because I waved a badge at them. And meanwhile you and your friend are a couple of children playing at something you know nothing about, and you're going to get a lot of people killed unless *I* clean up your mess here, so now would be a good time to *shut up*." He turned back to his phone. "Yes, sir. . . . Yes. No objection. I'll let them know. . . . Thank you, sir."

He hung up the phone and I punched him.

"What the *hell*!" cried Finch. His nose was fountaining blood. It was getting all over his suit.

"That's for calling me 'missy,'" I said. "Now, clearly you have some super string-pulling powers, so I'm not actually that worried about those police anymore. Like you said, that's your mess now, with my thanks. What I *am* worried about is you thinking this is your game to run. It's not. So I'll thank you to talk to me like the heavily armed person I am."

Finch glared at me, trying to stanch his bleeding nose.

Tresting touched my arm. "This gets us nowhere," he murmured.

"Maybe," I said. "But it felt really good."

Tresting shook his head at me slightly, warning me back, and I felt a flare of resentment. He had no call to tell me how I ought to conduct myself. This wasn't *his* game to run, either.

"Everybody calm down," Tresting said to the room. "One crisis at a time. Let's find out what's going on." He pulled out his phone and hit a button; as soon as someone picked up, he said, "We're at Kingsley's place. Everything's under control, but I'd like some intel." There was a slight pause, and then the person on the other end swore copiously and creatively, loudly enough for all of us to hear over the speaker. Tresting winced and held the phone away from his ear a little. "I said everything's under control," he tried to insist over Checker's tirade. He looked at the rest of us. "Be right back."

He headed through the foyer and into Leena's kitchen, trying to get a word in edgewise. He didn't close the door, however, instead leaning against the counter, still in sight of the living room. I wondered if he was keeping an eye on me to make sure I didn't punch anyone else.

The rest of us stood uncomfortably. I tried not to think about Dawna Polk and what she might have done to Leena Kingsley.

What she might have done to me.

Fuck. My head pounded like someone had driven an ice pick through the back of it.

Finch was still bleeding on Kingsley's carpeting. "Can I get him a towel?" she asked hesitantly.

"No," I said.

Dr. Kingsley went over to the window and peeked around the blinds. "It looks like the police are leaving."

I studied her. She was walking and talking and functioning like a normal human being. But then, I had been, too. "Are you going to call them back after we leave?" I asked.

She shook her head, not meeting my eyes. "Just don't bother me again. I want to be done with this."

Pithica never wants an investigation, I remembered.

Leena Kingsley couldn't be threatened into submission. Killing her to keep her quiet might have made people look more closely at her husband's death. So someone had done something else to silence her. Something that had made it seem like she'd changed her mind on her own.

Something that Dawna Polk had also done to me in the coffee shop, when she'd asked me where I would be.

Drugs? Hypnosis? Was I still under her influence? I had a feeling Finch knew, and he was going to tell me or I would beat it out of him.

The fact that Pithica had acted now scared the shit out of me. Kingsley had been on this crusade for months, and today they had suddenly decided to kill the PI she'd hired and convince her to give it all up? Sure, maybe Tresting's investigation had started to close in on something important, but Tresting was right: this was all happening right after they had hooked up with me. Dawna had targeted me to go in after Courtney and had targeted me on the road to Camarito, and I was a fool if I didn't assume she was targeting me now. I just didn't know why.

Tresting came back into the room, hanging up his mobile and tossing a roll of paper towels at Finch, who caught it clumsily and started mopping up his face.

"What's up?" I asked.

"Trouble." Tresting hesitated and glanced at Finch before continuing, but probably decided that this guy had enough connections to find out everything on his own anyway. "Turns out the neighbors didn't see our hostage dance. The cops who were here earlier got back to the station and saw composites of two people suspected in a brutal multiple homicide at an office building. Happened they recalled noticing two suspicious characters who looked mighty similar to the sketches in a truck outside an address they just reported to. Told you not to flinch," he added to me.

"Wait, so this is *my* fault, Mr. Let's Report Everything to the Proper Authorities?"

He shot me an expression of thinly veiled disgust. "Good news is they haven't ID'd us, just got composites from the lobby guy at the building." He turned to Leena. "Doc . . ."

"I told your new friend already, I won't tell anyone anything." She sounded exhausted. "Just make this go away, please."

He hesitated, then nodded. I supposed there wasn't much else he could do but trust her. "Guess we better get while the getting's good," he said to Finch and me. "They going to find out you're not a real FBI agent and come back?"

It was Tresting's turn to get a baleful glare.

"I'll take that as a 'maybe,'" the PI said, unperturbed. He reached out and touched Leena on the shoulder. "Doc. If you need anything, anything at all, or if anything starts to seem . . . I don't know, strange, or something frightens you—you call me, okay?"

She appeared to pull herself together slightly. "I . . . thank you. For sticking with me as long as you did. Maybe you can relax now, too."

Fat chance of that, I thought. Tresting was never going to give up this case, whether he had an active client or not. He looked like he wanted to say something else to Leena Kingsley, but finally he just nodded at her once before moving away. He checked out the window to make sure the coast was clear and then pulled open the front door.

"Okay, folks, let's walk all normal-like," he murmured as we followed him out. Considering that we'd now *all* been punched in the face recently, we would have been a sight to see, but any gawking neighbors had gone back inside already. Tresting led the way, and I lagged behind, watching Finch for any sudden moves. He was busy shoving a clump of paper towels against his nose, however, and didn't seem inclined to try anything.

"We'll take my truck," said Tresting.

"It's two-hour parking," Finch protested in a muffled voice. "Let me—"

"Oh, Lordy, a parking ticket. Won't kill you," said Tresting, officially making him my new favorite person. "Now get in."

We crammed Finch and his blood-covered suit in between us. "Understand something," I said to him as Tresting shoved the truck into gear. "You are to keep your hands in sight at all times. I am faster than you, I am stronger than you, and the hand you see under my coat is on a gun that is pointed at you. If you try anything—"

"Yeah, yeah, I get the message," he groused.

"Good. As long as we're all on the same page."

sixteen

As WE drove, Tresting directed Finch to dial his superiors on the burner phone and put them on speaker. "I'll do the talking," the PI instructed, in a tone that brooked no argument.

The voice that emanated from the mobile was a calm, charismatic basso, and I recognized it immediately as Finch's boss from the sack of Courtney's place. "May I ask with whom I am speaking?" the voice inquired.

"No, you may not," said Tresting, and he went on to give detailed directions to a picnic area in Griffith Park.

"It may take me some time to get there," the man warned.

"Shame," said Tresting, "seeing as we'll only wait half an hour. See you soon." He nodded at me, and I reached over and hit the button to end the call. We were turning onto the streets adjacent to the park by then, and Tresting pulled off and swung into a parking area. "Let's walk from here."

He led the way up a winding road into the park. Cheerful hikers and joggers passed us frequently, half of them with energetic dogs and most of them in the dreadfully fashionable athletic gear that seemed to be the uniform of choice for active Southern Californians. Our current state got a few double takes, particularly Finch's obvious nosebleed, but like true Angelenos, they all decided to mind their own business.

We reached a large picnic area with red stone tables, sparsely populated with only the odd family fighting over snacks and sandwiches. Tresting led the way to a table some distance away from anyone else and gestured for us to sit. Finch sat on the bench; I perched on the table to face the opposite way as Tresting and look out over their heads to scan the wooded area behind the picnic area, my hand under my jacket. The ice pick in my head hadn't gone away, but I forcefully ignored it.

About twenty minutes after we arrived, Finch cleared his throat. "There he is."

I tried to keep my gaze as wide as possible while I turned to catch the guy in my peripheral vision. I wouldn't have recognized him right away from my glimpse at Polk's house—he had dressed casually in jeans and a sweatshirt this time, and didn't seem at all out of place in the park. Combined with his appearance as a fiftyish clean-cut white guy, in good shape but not attractive enough to turn anyone's head, he was in all ways most emphatically someone who would go entirely unnoticed.

He kept his hands out of his pockets and slightly away from his body as he approached. Smart man. Tresting stood up as he reached the table.

"Mr. Tresting," the man said in greeting.

I glanced sharply at Tresting, but he was already nodding to concede the name. "Thought you wouldn't have trouble with that."

"Your identity was easy enough to deduce. Your associate, however . . ." He extended a hand to me. "May I ask whom I have the pleasure of addressing?"

I snorted. "You can ask. And who are you?"

"Call me Steve."

At least he was obvious about it being an alias. I jerked my head toward Tresting. "So, Steve. Now that you know who he is, are you going to make trouble for Arthur here?"

"Well, I suppose that depends."

"On what?"

"On whether the two of you are determined to make trouble for me." He sat, laying his hands against the top of the picnic table deliberately—and overdramatically, in my opinion. "Let me be frank. I could not care less about any police trouble in which you two have ensnared yourselves. It would frankly be a waste of my time to become bogged down with aiding local law enforcement in their Gordian investigative practices; that is quite beneath my interest. I do, however, very much care about any involvement you may have with the organization known as Pithica."

"Why?" said Tresting.

"Before I can answer that question, I must know how deeply you are involved with their agents."

Tresting narrowed his eyes. "All right," he said after a moment's hesitation. "I got a niggly feeling you're going to know all of this within the hour anyway, so I might as well tell you. I got hired by Dr. Leena Kingsley to look into her husband's death. Fell down the rabbit hole, and here I am."

Steve turned to me. "And you?"

"I'm helping him," I said.

"I'm afraid that's not good enough."

"She's the one who said she would call Dawna Polk," said Finch; through his bloody nose her name sounded more like "Dodda Po." "She used her to threaten me, boss. She *knows*."

Knows what?

"I did glean something of the sort from your message," Steve said to Finch. He turned to fix his attention on me in a way that made me want to turn and run. After shooting him first. "So. Either you are one of Pithica's agents, or you truly have no idea what you are dealing with."

I felt Tresting's eyes shift to me. "I'm not working for Pithica," I said, more for Tresting's benefit than for our agency friends. "As a matter of fact, they tried to kill me."

"Yet you somehow not only know the woman calling herself

Dawna Polk, but know that she is dangerous—a combination of knowledge that makes you very, very . . . special."

"Why?"

The man calling himself Steve hesitated very deliberately. I was starting to think that he practiced being deliberate in front of a mirror. "Because people who speak with Dawna Polk see only what she wishes them to."

"Yeah, well, clearly I'm not the only one who figured it out. You and your little band seem to know exactly what her deal is."

"Because I have not spoken to her."

The light breeze in the park suddenly felt very cold.

"Neither has Mr. Finch," Steve continued. "Neither, I pray to God, has anyone else who works with us, because if they have, we are already lost."

"You don't trust your own people?" I asked, my mouth dry.

"It is not a matter of trust," he said. "Dawna Polk is . . . for lack of a better word, she is what one might call a telepath."

There was a moment of silence. Then I snorted out a laugh. "You're putting me on."

"I assure you I am not."

"That's ridiculous. Telepathy doesn't exist," I informed him.

"Please explain," said Tresting.

Steve opened his mouth, and the pounding in my head resurged—this time along with a visceral, shriveling dread. More than anything else in the world, I wanted him *not* to explain. I wanted to mock him and call him an idiot, because what he was saying didn't make sense; it couldn't make sense—my body tensed. I had to keep myself from launching over the table and knocking him flat before he could speak, or, failing that, putting my hands over my ears and humming very loudly, because *I didn't want to know*—

"Some people are born into this world with certain talents," said Steve, his baritone as calm and deliberate as ever. "People who are . . . one might call them emotional geniuses. Charismatic brilliance on the furthest edge of the bell curve. Under normal circumstances, some of them become the most successful of businessmen. Others are con artists. Others movie stars or cult leaders or the greatest politicians of their time. Believe me when I say that only a handful of people in a generation have this capacity on the level of which I am speaking."

No. I wasn't going to take this seriously. I didn't care how emotionally adept someone was; she was still human. To assign her supernatural mental powers was an impossible fancy—

"Enter the wonders of technology," Steve continued. "Someone, somewhere, found a way of refining this ability and sharpening it. We don't know how. Before, a person like Dawna Polk might have had the potential to lead nations and inspire millions. Instead, she has been altered. Enhanced. She can observe the slightest movement of your face, take in the smallest quickening of your breath, phrase a question in exactly the right way, and whether she reads it from the twitch of your eyebrow or you voluntarily tell her yourself, she will know exactly what you are thinking. More than that, whatever ideas she plants in your brain, you will walk confidently into the world determined that they are your own. She is, for all intents and purposes, a telepath, capable of taking any information you know and molding you to her will in whatever ways she desires, and as far as we know, her abilities are absolute and have no defense."

Absurd, I told myself, trying to ignore the cold trickle of sweat on the back of my neck. This was absurd. I took in a breath to deny his story categorically, to announce my complete disbelief in anything so fantastic—but then something in the back of my brain clicked, so suddenly it jarred me, and the world shifted. . . .

I had no idea what I knew or why, but some spark deep in my memory, perhaps in the subconscious web of interrelated knowledge we call instinct, had connected and fit together and God help me but I believed him. More than believed him: I knew with freezing certainty that he was right.

Dawna Polk was a fucking psychic.

Fuck.

"That is Pithica," our narrator concluded. "They employ other agents as well, of course, who have been so indoctrinated by those with these mental powers that they are the most fanatical of followers, but people like Dawna Polk are at the heart of what they do. Our organization opposes them. I tell you this because you need some basic understanding of our dilemma here."

"What dilemma?" said Tresting.

Steve spread his fingers, pressing against the stone tabletop. "The only reason we are able to exist is that Pithica does not know that we do. They *cannot* know. We have only managed as much as we have against them by taking swift and thorough measures against anyone who might reveal us to them."

Oh, *shit*. I straightened where I sat, every nerve ending firing to alert status.

"You, either as targets of Pithica or as people who have . . . interacted . . . with them"—Steve's mouth twisted on that word— "are an obvious liability to us, now that you know of our existence."

His calm tone hadn't changed. In fact, he spoke like someone who did not care one whit that we had chosen this meeting and this location, someone who didn't even care if we walked away from the park today, because no matter where we went, dispensing with the danger we posed would be as trivial as flicking an annoying fly from his arm.

My hand tightened on my weapon beneath my coat, and Tresting shifted beside me, rebalancing himself on the grass. If it came to a fight here and now, I would win, but killing Steve would mean nothing. Who else from their organization was here? How far could they reach?

"However," Steve continued, turning to focus on me alone, "it is also of utmost interest to us how you managed to walk away from Dawna Polk with the knowledge that she was something other than what she presented. That is . . . astounding, in a word. Almost unbelievable. It would be a great asset to our task if we could discover how you were capable of such a thing." He leaned forward on his elbows, pressing his fingers together and addressing me over them. "If you will agree to cooperate with us fully, in all ways, we will help you, along with Mr. Tresting and anyone else who has been involved in this with you, to disappear and start a new life elsewhere."

"Strong-arming our intel, then? No quid pro quo?" I spoke more lightly than I felt. "What if we don't want to enter your demented witness protection program?"

"Please believe me when I say that if either of you sees Dawna Polk again, you *will* give us away to her. Knowing that, what would you have us do?" He spread his hands, as if to say, *Sorry, but there you go.* "The offer to help you disappear is an exceedingly generous one. You will have to be removed entirely from civilization, and be overseen by some of our own people on a constant basis to ensure you will never attempt to contact Pithica on some embedded suggestion from them. It will be an unspeakable consumption of our resources, and is not generally an opportunity we extend. I strongly suggest you take it."

"You usually just kill people, huh," said Tresting. He sounded off-hand about it, but the words crackled at the edges, and I was getting to know him well enough to hear the outrage under his casual tone.

"We do not take it lightly. Ever." Steve's face tightened, his jaw bunching. "We exist in subterfuge and obscurity. We only act when our hand is forced."

"Real gentlemen," said Tresting.

Steve folded his hands on the table. "You will tell us what you know about Pithica, and you will disappear," he informed us, his calm, charismatic tone as ominous as a death knell. "Whether you do either of those things voluntarily or not is your decision, but they both *will* happen, one way or the other."

"Wow," I said. "You and Pithica deserve each other." I hadn't moved yet, but the adrenaline was slamming into my brain, shutting away the revelations about Dawna Polk to deal with later and focusing on how to escape our current situation alive. The smartest thing to do might've been to accept their offer and play along, discover what we could, and then escape from the imprisonment they were calling protection. But I was a terrible liar—and besides, I didn't feel good about our chances once we entered their custody.

The next obvious solution was to take out both men and run. But the minute I did, we'd have to dodge this organization's crosshairs for the rest of our lives. Could we take Finch and his boss hostage instead, use them to negotiate for getting ourselves off the target list? Unfortunately, I had the distinct feeling their employers had a broad definition of "acceptable losses," even when it came to their own.

My jaw clenched, and the metal of the Smith & Wesson dug into my palm. There had to be a better option.

Tresting had his head cocked to the side, still seemingly casual. "I'm thinking you're an international group," he said to Steve. "Banding together to protect the global power dynamic from Pithica's influence, or something. Off the grid, not even answerable to the people who set you on this crusade of yours. Am I right?"

"I'm afraid I can't tell you any more about us," said Steve, still far too calm, "regardless of whether you take our offer. The less you know, the less you would be able to give away. Now, I must have an answer."

"Well, you see, that's a problem," said Tresting, and I felt a surge of goodwill toward him. Did he have a plan? Maybe this working together thing wouldn't turn out to be so bad after all.

The man called Steve sighed. "Please don't make this difficult, Mr. Tresting. Not to be callous, but it's not even your decision."

"Oh, I have a problem, too," I said immediately. "Right here. Problem. You look up 'problem' in the dictionary, you'll find a picture of me putting a gun to your head, which is what I'm considering doing in about three seconds."

"Did I not make myself clear? If you don't—"

"Oh, you were perfectly clear," said Tresting. "Perfectly. Only, see, this here's the problem. Just a little one, but—I got a guy on the out-side, who knows everything we know, including about running into Mr. Finch here. If he doesn't hear from us, bam, it all goes public. Everything, including you gents."

Steve twitched. "You're bluffing."

"Willing to take that chance?" said Tresting.

"If you begin throwing Dawna Polk's name and face around openly, we will be the least of your problems." The ominous edge in Steve's voice had turned darker, more deadly. "Besides, Mr. Finch has been with you since you discovered our involvement. You never had the opportunity—"

"He did make a phone call, boss," interrupted Finch with a wince. "And she ID'd me from Courtney Polk's house. It's possible they made us there."

His boss gave Finch a look that promised repercussions would come later and took a deep, steadying breath before moderating his tone. "I told you our offer extends to the people with whom you've been working. Believe me, whoever this is, we can find him, too, and he can disappear along with you both—in whichever manner you choose."

I ignored the very real fear settling in the bottom of my stomach, and decided to follow my other gut feeling, which was telling me to get out of here now. "Points for creepy," I told the guy whose name wasn't Steve, pleased with how unconcerned I managed to sound. "We'll think about helping you, but it's sure as hell not going to be on those terms. We have your phone number already—don't call us; we'll call you."

"You're making a mistake."

"If I had a nickel for every time someone told me that," I mused. "Bye now."

I glanced at Arthur, but for once we seemed to be in complete agreement. I hopped off the picnic table and we backed slowly away. Finch and his boss watched us go, not moving from the table. Their tranquility was unnerving. It meant they didn't have to be worried.

We headed onto the winding road. I saw a thick, knobbly stick by the side of the pavement and picked it up, twirling it experimentally. I looked back. Perfect. The picnic area was almost out of sight. Nobody on the path here would find someone tossing a branch that odd, and nobody back there would connect me with it. I twirled it one more time to build up the exact right centripetal acceleration and let it fly. Way back in the picnic area, barely visible now, the butt end of the branch smacked into Finch's temple and bounced off at just the right angle to whack his boss across the ear. They both collapsed.

"Might buy us some time," I said to Arthur, who was starting to get the freaked-out *my window had bars on it* look on his face again.

His eyes went down to my chest, and widened. "Or not."

I looked down to see the bright pinpoint of a red laser sight dancing there.

Oh, hell.

seventeen

"PLEASE COME with us," said a nondescript woman, appearing with an equally nondescript man right next to us.

"Laser sights? *Really?*" I said to her in disgust. "What is this, a cheesy action movie?"

She smiled slightly. "They are more for you than for our people. An incentive to accompany us, if you will. I'm sure it has been explained that we prefer not to kill you."

"It's just so hard to take you seriously now," I said. I felt the breeze on my cheek and calculated wind speed, trajectories springing up in my head. Assuming the snipers were dialed in correctly . . . I casually rocked my weight back. The bright red light was several seconds in correcting.

"Thought we went over this with your boss," said Tresting. "We're not coming, and if you try to force us, things will go bad for you people. Seemed like he got it."

"He gave us no signal to let you go."

Tresting glared at me.

"Oops," I said. "My bad."

"We would prefer it if you came with us. However, I have been authorized as to alternatives," the woman informed us.

"I have an alternative," I said. "Tell your snipers to back off, and they get to live."

Tresting and I each got an additional laser dot joining the first. Two for each of us. Goody.

"I recommend you come with me," said the woman. She didn't have any visible weapon, but her casual clothes might have been concealing one, and the same was true of her partner. Both of them stood with their weight square and their hands free. They were ready for a fight.

Of course, so was I.

The last few hours had been nothing but subterfuge and conspiracies and deep secrets and threats in the dark. The fact that I finally had an enemy pointing a gun at me again was *glorious*.

This was an enemy I could fight.

I took one last glance at the four dancing laser dots. To the close observer they stretched into slightly elongated ellipses, and the angle automatically backtracked for me, extending upward infallibly, four lines of sight to our four snipers. Excellent. I hoped one of the clowns in front of us had a high frame rate camera, because otherwise they were going to miss a spectacular feat.

"Well, I warned you," I said. I slipped back a step and whipped both hands across my body and under my coat, drew before anyone could react, and fired two shots with each hand.

The red dots disappeared from our chests.

One of the passing hikers screamed.

Pandemonium erupted. The woman and her partner tried to grab us and to reach for their own weapons, but they never had a chance. Tresting gave the woman a vicious uppercut that dropped her like a sack of potatoes, and I brought my right-hand gun back down to the man and fired, but the gun didn't go off, so I kicked him in the face instead. I gave Tresting a shout and a shove with my shoulder and we started racing down the lane. Pedestrians screamed behind us— someone yelling for help, someone else yelling for the police.

I shouted for Tresting to follow and skidded into the woods, realigning what I remembered of our arrival in my mind and pelting down through dry leaves in a shortcut to a parking area we'd passed. At least, I hoped we were aiming at the parking area—my memory wasn't perfect, but I could estimate, and I drew lines and angles through the woods and *yes, there!* I stumbled out among the cars, shoving my guns back underneath my jacket, and dashed to a van with nicely tinted windows. I jacked it so fast that by the time Tresting scrambled up next to me the passenger door was already open with the engine thrumming to life. I pulled out onto the street toward the park's exit before he had even gotten his door shut and tried my best to drive sedately despite my pulse hammering away at 163 beats per minute (well, 163.4, but I was the only one counting).

For the second time that day, we pulled over to let police cars scream past on their way into the park. I didn't start to breathe normally until we were back in traffic on Los Feliz and headed toward the freeway.

Night was falling, and I flicked on the van's headlights as we merged onto the 5. Beside me, Tresting made a quick call to leave a message for Leena Kingsley—he told her he didn't think she was in danger, but the stakes were going up and maybe she should get gone just in case—and tapped out a couple of text messages before taking the batteries out of both his smartphone and the burner phone we had used to call Finch's boss. Smart man. My phone was already in pieces in my pocket, even though only Tresting, Checker, and Rio had the number. Less trackable was always better.

"Did you really tell Checker about Finch?" I asked.

"Asked him to check on the name for me; that's all."

I laughed. "Good show back there, then."

"I'll make sure he's up to speed. Good insurance policy, sounds like, and Checker's thorough. Won't be easy for them to get around him." He paused, and his voice became weighted. "Course, I don't have the full story."

I felt a little bad about that. "I took Courtney back to her place to pick up some cash," I explained. "A bunch of men in suits were there searching for something. Two of them were Finch and our friend Steve."

"They find what they were looking for?"

"I don't think so. But it's how I knew he wasn't a Fed—none of it exactly struck me as FBI procedure. Plus, one of the guys was British, and Finch had some other accent, too. He only started to sound American when we saw him at Kingsley's."

"Yeah, I got that he wasn't American," said Tresting. "Kept using the word 'mobile' for his cell phone. Knew you were on the money with him from that."

I frowned. "Is that strange? I say 'mobile' sometimes."

"I noticed that," said Tresting. He didn't elaborate, however, instead switching topics entirely. "And Dawna Polk?"

Cards on the table, I supposed. Dawna Polk . . . even the thought of her name was enough to make my throat close bitterly, and for my stupid headache to begin throbbing again. I swallowed. "She mojo'd me the last time we talked. I told her exactly where I was headed next and didn't even notice."

"But you sussed it out later."

"Yeah. It took a lot. Rio knew me well enough to see it and prod until I connected that something was wrong." I hesitated, then added, "She did a number. She had me utterly convinced she was harmless."

"You didn't mention this before."

"Well, yeah; it was embarrassing. I thought she had drugged me. I didn't start to put it together any more than that until we were talking to Kingsley."

"But you did put it together. Seems our new friends think that's a touch improbable."

I frowned, watching the road. "If what they say is true, I don't know why I was able to. Or how. All I know is that resisting her seems to come with a nice side effect of chronic headaches." I paused. "And that I definitely wouldn't want to talk to her again."

Tresting sat back and digested that. I felt like brooding myself. This whole thing was far beyond anything I usually dealt with. We had another global organization after us now—another one with tremendous resources and no compunction against violence. Not to mention the whole "Dawna Polk, Functioning Psychic" thing. . . .

The twilight had nearly turned to full dark while we inched forward in traffic before Tresting spoke again. "Where you headed?"

"I keep a few places around the city in case I need to get off the grid, but I figured we'd drive around and swap cars a few times first," I answered. Go Cas, ever prepared.

"Russell," said Tresting, "I don't think I can work with you."

Dammit. Not this again. Maybe I could make him understand. "Look, I know you don't like Rio—"

"No." He rubbed his forehead with one hand, like someone with a migraine coming on. "Well, yeah, that's an issue. But it's not him, Russell. It's you."

Something constricted inside me. "What does that mean?"

He took a deep breath. "Life is cheap to you."

I started to get angry. "Those snipers had rifles pointed at us. It was self-defense."

"Yeah, and why was that? Your little trick with the hunk of wood? Violence isn't always the best choice, you know. If you didn't—"

"We don't know he was going to tell them to let us go," I countered, bristling. "Maybe he was going to give the order to shoot on sight instead. Did you ever think of that?"

"Maybe," said Tresting, "and maybe we could've gotten out of there without anyone hurt at all if we'd just walked away. Without anyone else dying. And without another dozen eyewitnesses fingering us for a crime."

"You don't know that," I argued. "Any of it could have gone either way. And I did just save both our lives—*again*—so a little gratitude might be in order!"

"Gratitude?" He shifted in his seat to face me. "You caused the whole damn situation in the first place! And shooting off a bunch of rounds in a crowded park—what if you'd hit an innocent?"

"I knew I wouldn't," I tried to defend myself. "I'm really good at what I do—"

"Which is what?" challenged Tresting. "Killing people? Threatening people with guns? Punching them when they insult you? That what you're so good at?"

I fumed in silence for a minute, revving the engine hard and then slamming on the brakes every time traffic moved a few inches.

"You got some good in you," Tresting said quietly. "You do. But you also scare the shit out of me."

Usually I enjoy scaring people, but for some reason, hearing Tresting say that gave me a crumpled feeling inside. I didn't like it.

"And you're a smart kid, shit, maybe brilliant, but for some reason your first solution is always to pull the trigger," Tresting continued after a moment. "And I can't work with that. I can't."

"I don't go around killing innocent people," I said stiffly.

"That guy just now, in the park," said Tresting. "You went to shoot him."

"Piece-of-crap gun misfired," I said. "Look, he was trying to grab us or kill us, one of the two—"

"Yeah, and that's another good reason to avoid that sort of fubared situation in the first place: what if you got a jam in the middle of capping those snipers? Or if there was more than four? But that's not even my point. First you tried to shoot him, and then . . . I don't know where you learned to fight, but you kicked him so hard . . ." He swallowed. "Shit. I was almost sick on the street right there."

I thought back. I'd been in the throes of adrenaline at the time, but now I could remember the feeling of his face collapsing against my boot—I cut off that line of thought. "He was a threat," I insisted stubbornly.

"And now he's dead, isn't he," said Tresting. I didn't answer. "What about our buddy Finch and his boss? They dead too?"

"No," I said. "It would've been too hard to get the leverage from that distance."

"Listen to yourself," Tresting said, his voice cracking.

They're enemies, I told myself. *Taking out an enemy is not wrong.*

"How about me, back in that motel bathroom?" Tresting said. "Just couldn't get the leverage then either?"

I didn't answer.

"Too small a space, I guess," he filled in for me after a moment. "Lucky me."

"You were threatening me with a gun," I pointed out angrily.

"The rate you do that yourself, it should count as a hobby."

I accelerated and slammed on the brakes a couple more times.

"Drop me in East LA somewhere," said Tresting.

"Pithica's after you," I reminded him, trying to keep my tone neutral. "And the police. And now these guys—without me around and whatever they want from me, they'll just kill you."

"I'll be fine."

Right.

I pulled off the freeway and found the seediest-looking neighborhood I could to park the van in. We both got out, Tresting giving his door handle and seat belt a quick wipe-down with a napkin as he did so.

"I guess this is good-bye, then," I said.

We stood awkwardly.

Then Tresting spoke, with an obvious effort. "Thanks again for saving my life, back at my office."

I shrugged a little too harshly. "We're even."

"Russell."

"Yeah?"

"Think about what I said, okay? You're a good kid. You don't have to be like this."

"I like how I am just fine," I said.

"Take care of yourself."

I shrugged again.

He turned and walked away, leaving me on a graffitied street corner that smelled vaguely of human urine. My adrenaline had faded into listless fatigue.

Well, I supposed it was time to steal another car and head to one of my bolt-holes. Cas Russell, ever prepared.

I sighed.

Why did people have to be so complicated? I thought of Dawna Polk's superpowered human relations ability, and a spark of jealousy twinged. Dawna Polk would have known how to say exactly the right thing so that Arthur *understood* her. He'd have been eating out of her hand.

I, on the other hand . . . well, I could have killed him in less than half a second, but that didn't help at all. In fact, a niggling voice in the back of my head reminded me that such an attitude was what he was taking issue with in the first place.

Why am I even upset? I wondered. I was used to being on my own. I'd never concerned myself with what anyone else thought of me before. Why now?

Fuck, I thought, I'd started to care. Somewhere in this whole mess, I'd started to care about Arthur—whether he lived or died, what he thought—Jesus, I was even feeling *friendly* toward him.

Well, there was an easy solution to that, clear and simple: stop caring.

And I'd better make a mental note never to make such a stupid mistake again.

eighteen

I DECIDED to walk for a little while to clear my head; the night air felt good—and, I'm not going to lie, I sort of hoped someone would try to mug me, but nobody did. Eventually I ended up near a metro station, and on a whim I elected to travel legally for once. I tended to forget LA had a metro system.

I took the line up to Union Station, where I stopped at a tourist stand to buy a large and obnoxious "I ♥ LA" T-shirt, a baseball cap, sunglasses, and a tote bag, and then found a toilet to change in. The sunglasses covered half my face, including most of the bruising that made me look like I had raccoon eyes, and with the baseball cap and loud T-shirt and sans tall black guy next to me, I was sure I wouldn't catch anyone's eye as matching certain witness reports. The T-shirt was thin, so I rolled up most of my hardware in my jacket and stuck it in the tote bag, leaving only one of the Glocks tucked in my belt underneath my clothes.

I rode the subway for a while after that, zigzagging the city and letting my mind go blank. I didn't want to think about Arthur, or Leena Kingsley, or Dawna Polk and what she might be capable of doing. I didn't have much I could do about any of it anyway.

Courtney Polk was probably dead. Maybe I should drop the case and disappear into the woodwork—I didn't precisely live on the grid anyway; I could get a new set of IDs and head off to a new city, and just let Pithica or anybody else try to track me down. I could leave Steve and his people chasing Dawna Polk, and the police chasing their tails, and Arthur and Checker doing whatever the hell they wanted, and Pithica could keep playing its merry game—I didn't really care. And screw Courtney. Dawna had hired me to rescue her under false pretenses anyway and hadn't even paid me.

The thought of abandoning Courtney gave me a squirmier feeling than anything else. I'd never broken a contract before. My priorities probably proved Tresting's point about me being a bad person.

I tried not to think about that either, or what Tresting had said to me. *Your first solution is always to pull the trigger. . . .* That wasn't a bad thing, I insisted to myself. It meant I survived, and would keep surviving. I needed to keep reminding myself of that, because Arthur's words kept echoing in my head, tedious and ugly and irritating. *Life is cheap to you. . . .*

I rested my head against the dark train window, exhausted. My trail was clear as far as I could tell; some sleep might finally be in order. Maybe everything would look better in the morning. *Fat chance of that.* More likely everything would be far more apocalyptic in the morning when I wasn't strung out on fatigue. Too drained to bother stealing another car and driving a long distance, I switched trains to head back toward Chinatown—I had a little hole of an apartment paid up a few blocks outside of it. I fell into a doze on the way there and almost missed the stop.

It was the middle of the night when I finally reached my bolt-hole, and I was almost afraid I wouldn't remember where it was. But no, I found the ugly, run-down building and the outside door that led into the room I kept there. I studied the address and concentrated; I had an algorithm for where I hid keys that used the house number and the letter count of the street as inputs. I measured with my eyes and leveraged up the appropriate brick—ah, there it was.

I barely got inside the room before I collapsed on the thin mattress in one corner and fell asleep. At least I didn't dream.

I woke up in the middle of the next morning. The room was still dim; heavy curtains hung over the one small window that was too grimy to see through anyway, but I could hear traffic out on the street and someone yelling in Chinese, and my watch told me it was after ten. Fuck. I'd slept for a long time.

I sat on the thin mattress and ate some cold breakfast out of a can while I tried to think. I had a lot of people after me right now. Fortunately, none of them knew who I was, and I was as prepared as a paranoid crazy person could be for needing to stay out of sight, hence places like this that I kept paid up and stocked with food and basic medical supplies. I had a box of other necessities here, too, hidden in a nook carved out of the drywall: a bundle of cash and another firearm at the very least. My bolt-holes varied with what supplies I'd stashed in them, but they all had the basics.

So potentially I could do what I'd thought about last night and disappear. The easiest way out would be to lie low here indefinitely, then stuff a bunch of cash in my pockets and get the hell out of LA. Switching my base of operations to another big city would make no difference at all to me. I had no reason on earth not to get out, and every reason to run as far as possible from a place where a lot of people seemed to want either to kill me or to scramble my brains into an omelet.

Like Dawna Polk.

I shivered and wrapped the bed's thin blanket around myself, pulling it tight. The chronic headache had resurged as a dull throb. Dawna Polk—a woman who could look at you and read anything she liked from you, no limits, easy as you please. A woman who could pluck out your deepest secrets. A woman who could compel you to do anything. Believe anything.

I remembered how I'd felt after I'd spoken with her, when I was defending her to Rio to the point of irrationality. I had felt perfectly normal. Every thought, every reaction, had seemed to follow logically from the last. As far as my brain had been concerned, *Rio* had been the person acting strange. It had taken Rio's pushing, and consequently me doing something wholly and appallingly out of character, for me to realize something was wrong—and if "Steve" was to be believed, even that wouldn't have snapped most people out of it.

Of course, the most obvious question was also the most terrifying one: aside from getting me to tell her my immediate plans and making sure I didn't look too closely at her, had Dawna Polk *suggested* anything else to me?

How could I know any of my decisions since talking to her were my own? How could I even be sure I hadn't been contacting her and then purposely forgetting about it? Leena Kingsley was proof that Dawna was capable of obliterating or changing any memory I thought I had. All of reality was suspect. I couldn't be sure of anything.

The feeling was paralyzing.

I tried to think back through everything that had happened so far. It all sounded like me, and no odd blank spots struck me, but if I was compromised already, then that meant nothing.

I had a desperate urge to talk to someone who knew what I was supposed to sound like, to check myself and figure out which way in hell was up. I needed to talk to Rio anyway, I thought; we needed to touch base and compare notes, and with Tresting turning his back on me, I needed every lead I could get—and Rio might have new information.

Of course, he'd also been tracking Dawna Polk. If he'd talked to her, too . . .

I suddenly felt strangled, like I was having trouble getting air. If Dawna Polk had sought to meddle with Rio's faith in God—if she had shaken his moral compass even in the slightest—

Fuck.

"Get a grip, Cas," I said out loud.

I couldn't sit here wallowing in indecision. That itself might be what she wanted. I still had to make choices, and hope like hell they were mine to make.

Do the math, I told myself. *How many variables? How many possible paths? She can't have microscopic control; it's not practical.* The thought let me breathe a little easier. Dawna Polk might have some foothold in my head, but there was no way she could have predicted every event that would happen to me and implanted her preferred reaction to it. At least, I hoped not. *And are you really so egotistical that you think you merit her full-time puppet mastery?*

It depended on what she wanted with me, I supposed, which brought me back to wondering why she had even called me in the first place. It was clear Pithica already had the resources to pull Courtney out of the cartel's clutches if they had chosen to. So why me?

I mulled it over for a while, but I had no idea. The only possibility I could think of was what Steve had said—that I had shown some sort of unusual resilience to Dawna's techniques. Maybe Pithica had known that somehow and wanted to test me on it. Was this all an elaborate game to see whether I was capable of shaking off their influence? Or—Steve had said Pithica had some normal human agents; could everything have been a strange way of recruiting me? Maybe each interaction was supposed to build up some web of faith in Dawna and Pithica until I was their thoroughly domesticated de-livery girl.

I shivered again.

But that didn't make sense either. If that were the case, Dawna Polk was failing miserably at her indoctrination effort. Pithica had done nothing but try to kill or brainwash both me and the people I'd been working with since I'd rescued Courtney; I feared and dis-trusted them now more than ever, particularly Dawna. It would be nice to assume they were making mistakes, but that seemed like wishful thinking. No, I was missing something.

Dammit. I wasn't sure how to begin to unsnarl this whole mess— like I'd told Tresting, I wasn't an investigator. I didn't usually need to figure anything out beyond how to get through a locked door.

I definitely needed to get in touch with Rio. And sooner rather than later.

I left most of my small arsenal under the mattress, disdaining the shoddy guns for the Ruger I had stashed in the wall, and set out to find an electronics store.

It was coming on noon when I finally got back to my bolt-hole with a couple of new prepaid phones. I stuck one in my wall stash as a backup and dialed from memory on the other. Rio picked up on the first ring.

"It's Cas," I said.

"Cas," said Rio, and I could have sworn he sounded relieved. Odd. "I've been trying to reach you."

"I burned my phone," I said. "What's up?"

"Have you seen a paper this morning?"

"A newspaper?"

"*Yes*, Cas, a newspaper."

"No need to get sarcastic," I said. "I'm part of the internet generation. No, I haven't. Why?"

"You're in it."

That brought me up short. "What?"

"Or rather, a bruised, if accurate, composite of you."

"I didn't do it," I said, feeling sick.

He paused a moment too long. "I know."

"What's that supposed to mean?" I demanded.

"Beg pardon?"

"That tone," I said. "You hesitated. What's going on?"

"Nothing. It also says you're a person of interest in a shooting in Griffith Park."

"Oh, that one I did do. Do they have any leads?"

"Not that they mentioned. Cas, you have to keep a lower profile."

I felt unfairly put-upon. "I didn't ask for this!" I reminded him. "Someone dragged me in, remember? And now people keep trying to kill me! The police are only after me because I tried to kill them back!"

Silence over the line. Then Rio said, "Cas, what's wrong?"

"What, other than *people trying to kill me*?" Fear shot through me as I remembered one of the reasons I'd wanted to call Rio in the first place. "Wait, am I acting strange? Do I seem off to you?"

"You are very defensive."

"Unusually defensive?" I pressed.

"Cas, what's going on?"

"It's about Dawna Polk. We found out why she made me act . . .

when she talked to me; she can . . ." I didn't want to say it. Saying it would make it real. "We met a group working against Pithica. Rio, they say she's a real-life telepath. They say she can make you believe anything." My words sounded crazy to my own ears. "You probably think I'm insane. *I* think I'm insane."

"No," said Rio. The word was slow and deliberate. "I believe you."

I digested that. "You knew," I said finally.

"Yes."

"When I started acting funny the other night—you already knew what she was."

"I suspected."

"You *knew* and you didn't tell me?"

"Cas, I have been trying, to the best of my ability, to keep you out of this."

"Why?"

"These people are not to be trifled with."

"I'm very good at trifling," I said.

"I'm serious."

"So am I."

"Cas, believe me when I say that you are not prepared to deal with them."

First Arthur, now Rio. Did everyone think I was a child? "I've already beaten them," I reminded him. "Several times."

"You have not been their focus. And you have been lucky." He took a quiet breath. "Please, Cas. Stay out of this."

I felt myself frowning. Rio had never made a request like that of me before. "You're the one who told me to go consult with Tresting," I pointed out.

"To be perfectly honest, I had no idea he would prove so competent."

"So you tried to send me on a wild goose chase."

"Yes."

"Why?"

"I told you, Cas. Pithica is far too dangerous. You now know part of the reason why."

"So it's true, about Dawna." I swallowed against a dry throat. "She can do that—she *did* do that, to me."

"Yes."

"How much can she do?"

"She could make you believe black is white. She could make a mother kill her child and enjoy it."

The words parsed in my head, but they didn't make sense. *"How?"* I breathed.

"She plays on emotions. Expertly. Small influences, but her targets eventually feel and believe whatever she wishes them to."

"Small influences that can drive people to *murder*?"

"For an act that defies her target's psychology in the extreme, it is true that it would take her time, not a single conversation. Months, perhaps, depending on the person she targets."

"But you're saying even a strong enough person can't—"

"Strength does not enter into it," he corrected. "It is—I suppose you would say psychology. What you would call a weaker mind might prevail for longer, simply because it may be more comfortable with the mental contradictions her influence would produce. Or it might fold immediately. Each psychology is unique, and each will itself respond differently according to what she attempts."

"And there's no way to fight it?" I pleaded.

"None that I am aware of."

I pulled the blanket from the bed up around myself again, wrapping it close. I still felt cold. "How can I know if I've been affected?"

"It is nearly impossible to tell, because you will rationalize whatever she has made you believe. You are concerned?"

"Of course I am."

"Walk me through the course of events since I saw you last. It is not foolproof, but I shall tell you if I observe inconsistency."

And it would be good for him to have my intel in any case. I took a deep breath and started with Courtney Polk going missing, then described my night with Tresting, finding the office workers, Leena's abrupt change, and the meeting with Finch and Steve. Rio listened quietly. I shared everything, up to and including my final conversation with Tresting.

"I think that's why I'm feeling so defensive," I finished unhappily. "Unless Dawna Polk *has* been messing me up again. But he was so— he was so patronizing." And since he had implied I was not only a thoughtless kid, but one who went around killing people . . . "Rio, am I—do you think I'm green? Do I act like it?"

He seemed to think for a moment. "In some circumstances. You can be impulsive."

I wanted to curl up in a corner and disappear from the world. So much for being good at what I did.

"You are young, you realize," Rio continued. "I am given to understand that impetuosity is to be forgiven in youth."

"I'm not that young!" I protested. "Stop making excuses for me. Tresting's right. Part of my job—I hurt people. I can't mess up and then call it a learning experience!"

"You are, perhaps, asking the wrong person about that," Rio said. "I myself have learned many things by killing the wrong people."

I picked at the hem of the blanket. As much as I trusted Rio, I didn't want to be him. Didn't want people like Arthur Tresting to think of me that way. Didn't want to live with being that type of person. "Rio . . . did you do the office building?"

He barely hesitated. "Yes."

"Off the text I sent you?"

"Yes."

I swallowed.

"Cas, if it helps, they were not the wrong people."

I thought about how young the receptionist had been. Whatever mistakes she had made, her youth had not excused her from Rio wreaking God's vengeance.

"Cas?" he said.

"Did you learn anything?" I asked quietly.

"Yes. Many things."

"You aren't going to tell me what they are, are you."

"I would hardly have gone to such lengths to keep them from you only to divulge them later," he answered.

I thought of the shredded and pulped papers. "Right."

"What you shared with me today is valuable also," said Rio. "I shall put it to good use. And although I cannot say for sure, I do not believe Dawna Polk has influenced you further."

"Oh . . . good. Thanks."

"Of course."

"Are you trying to take down Pithica?" I asked.

"Yes."

"And you want me to stay out of it."

"Yes. Will you?"

I closed my eyes. I had no leads. Tresting wasn't talking to me. Courtney was gone. Rio wouldn't help me. I had no allies, and nothing to follow up on.

"All right," I said.

Rio's tone when he answered sounded awfully like relief, even though I knew that wasn't possible. "Thank you, Cas. God bless you."

nineteen

I HUNG up the phone with Rio and found myself with nothing to do. Giving up on investigating Pithica meant I had zero obligations. I still felt bad about dumping Courtney's case, but between Dawna masquerading as her sister and Tresting's evidence that she had killed Reginald Kingsley, it seemed clear she was as hopelessly snarled up in Pithica and its machinations as it was possible to be. Which meant I didn't feel *too* bad.

So I'd go with the obvious decision. I would lie low here for a week or two until the bruises and cuts on my face healed, which would help change my appearance from the composite, and then skip town. I wondered where I'd go; no city seemed more appealing than any other. Chicago? New York? Detroit? Maybe I should leave the country. Mexico was only a short hop away.

I lay back on the mattress and stared at the ceiling, and the bigger problem hit me.

I was off the job.

I wasn't working anymore. And I don't do well when I'm not working.

The numbers simmered around me. I tried to avoid acknowledging them, instead staring into space and yearning for some alcohol. How had I not thought it necessary to stock some hard liquor in my bolt-holes? Or even something stronger? The prospect of being stuck here for days with no liquid medication, with only myself against my brain . . .

I gave myself a mental slap. *Idiot. You can last for a few days. It's only a few days!*

The quiet room seemed to mock me.

If I stayed here a week . . . one week was seven days—168 hours—10,080 minutes—604,800 seconds—

I became hyperaware of every breath, each one counting out another one of those seconds before everything would collapse, before I would fall—no, not counting another second, counting another 2.78 seconds. 2.569 seconds. 2.33402. 2.1077001. 1.890288224518154 . . .

I clenched tingling hands into fists and tried to slow my breathing, to curb the rising tide of panicky dread. Technically I was still on *a* job, I told myself: hide and then escape the city. Focus on that.

For a few moments, I hoped I might fool myself.

I tried to unfocus my gaze, to concentrate on nothing, but my eyes locked on a crack in the ceiling plaster where something had banged against the dingy paint job. Numbers started to crawl out and through the spiderweb of cracks, a teeming, boiling mass—forces, angles, the entropy time-lapsing into the future and the past . . . the mathematical outlines of the impact and fracture and deterioration refined themselves further and further, the corrective terms layering themselves over each other until the units were so small they had no physical meaning, and they filled my brain, overflowing it—

I squeezed my eyes shut and flopped over onto one side.

An instant of blessed darkness.

A car horn sounded outside. The decibel level spiked in my head, the oscilloscope graph expanding and buzzing through my thoughts. My heartbeat thudded through me, each beat approximating periodicity—the waves broke apart, crashing and layering against each other, each amplitude spiking separately and adding another term to the Fourier series, sines and cosines repeating themselves and correcting in minute iterations. My skin stretched too tight, hypersensitive, every neuron registering forces and pressures, gravity and atmosphere crushing me between them, acting on my clothes against me and through the mattress below me, where Hooke's law pushed back with a hundred tiny springs—

I jumped up and moved restlessly around the room. Every step was a thousand different mathematical interactions. I tried to channel it, wear it out: I ran up walls, flipped over, then vaulted into a one-handed handstand on the worn carpet. The forces balanced themselves immediately and automatically, the vectors splaying out in all directions like countless invisible guy lines. I started moving, kicking my legs back and forth as fast as I could, spinning on the spot, switching from one hand to the other, leaning myself away from my center of mass as far as the physics would allow, the calculations a swirling maelstrom around me.

Two hours later (2 hours, 17 minutes, 46.87539260982311157 seconds . . .), I was at the counter of the nearest grocery store buying as many bottles as they had of the highest-proof alcohol I could find.

"Having a party?" said the long-haired, pimply kid at the register. I thrust cash at him desperately. He counted with agonizing slowness. I was having trouble focusing on him; the image of his lanky frame slid back and forth between wavelengths of visible light and an infinitely complicated imbroglio of movement and forces, a stick figure of vectors.

"Keep the change," I got out. He shouted after me, something about needing an ID, but I was already toppling out of the store and into the parking lot. I'd swallowed half the first bottle, the alcoholic burn lighting my esophagus on fire, before I became aware of the busy crowds surrounding me and the afternoon sun stabbing me in the eyes. My breath heaved in and out, but the alcohol was doing its work to take the edge off, its depressive effects calming the numbers until they were their usual manageable background hum.

"Excuse me, miss? You can't do that here." A security guard in a reflective orange vest was approaching me, an older white man with a bristly haircut, his gut pushing over his belt.

I took a deep breath. "I'm good . . ." I tried to brush him off. "I'm good."

"Miss, I'm going to have to ask you to leave the premises," he said, his superior tone already grating on my nerves. "Did you drive here?"

"No. I walked. I'm good." And Tresting thought my first response was always to punch people. *See? I can behave.* "I'm good. I'm leaving."

Another security guard strode quickly out of the store, a tall woman built like a brick. "Ma'am, the cashier says you didn't show an ID for the alcohol." She registered the half-empty bottle in my hand. "Ma'am, you can't drink that here."

"Yes, I've *heard*," I said grumpily. "I already told him, I'm leaving."

"Ma'am, could we see an ID, please?"

I put down the bottles and felt around in my pockets, in my pants and then in my jacket. And felt around again.

Shit.

I always carry a few fake IDs; I never know when I might need one. But along with my Colt, the Colombians had taken everything in my pockets when they'd captured me three days ago, and replacing my ID had completely slipped my mind. My scrambling fingers found that over the past few days I had accumulated a knife, several spare magazines, some loose ammunition, a couple of grenades from the other night, and a bunch of cash, but no IDs.

"I, uh, I forgot it," I said. "Look, I'll leave the booze, it's fine." I'd self-medicated enough already to stabilize my world for the moment. I could go back and check the Chinatown apartment to see if I had an ID in my stash in the drywall; I probably did. I raised my hands in a gesture of surrender and took a few steps back.

The two security guards looked at my half-drunk bottle on the ground. Then they looked at me.

"I swear I'm over twenty-one," I said reasonably. "I'll just go, okay?"

"Ma'am, please stay there," said the female security guard. She pulled out a walkie and started speaking into it.

Okay, this wasn't great. If the police showed up, I would have a lot of problems, starting with the illegal Ruger tucked in the back of my belt and the grenades in my pockets and ending with being accused of mass murder once someone noticed I matched their suspect. Of course, these morons wouldn't be able to stop me from leaving; they weren't even armed. But I wasn't exactly succeeding at keeping a low profile. I sighed and started glancing around for the best avenue out.

Someone screamed.

I turned to see a dark-skinned, curly-haired woman with her hands over her mouth. "You caught her!" she shrieked at the security guards. "The psycho from the paper! You caught her!"

A lot of people were suddenly staring at us. The security guards looked thrown, as if this were more than they'd bargained for when they'd had the gumption to detain me for suspected underage drinking.

"Everybody stay calm," declared the female guard.

"Oh my God," breathed her colleague, the blood draining from his face as he took in my features. "She *does* look like it."

"Look like who?" the female guard demanded tensely.

"The—the woman who killed all those people—"

The two guards began backing away from me, clearly deeming that their rent-a-cop duties weren't worth risking their lives against a homicidal maniac. The woman had her walkie at her mouth again and was speaking very fast. It might have been a coincidence, but I heard sirens start up from not too far away.

A fair crowd of not-very-bright onlookers now surrounded me at a healthy radius. Some people pulled frantically at their children and hurried away; others stared blatantly. I saw at least two people surreptitiously pull out mobile phones.

This situation was not going to get any better. Time to get out of here.

I glanced around. The crowd—how had it grown so fast?—meant making a dash through the parking lot would be tricky. But my back was to the building, and that was child's play. I spun and leapt. A display of potted plants rose against the wall right behind me; I ran up the shelves like they were stairs and launched myself toward the roof, clearing the eaves in a dive and rolling back to my feet on the flat rooftop. Shouts erupted behind me as I ran. Too easy!

I launched myself off the back of the supermarket's roof without slowing and landed in another roll in the alley behind it, where I sprang up into a fast jog. *Where to now?* That was a good question; the composite was clearly good enough for random people off the street to recognize me, whether or not they had any hard evidence from the office building—

Evidence. Oh no.

I'd left a half-drunk bottle of alcohol at the grocery store. One that had my fingerprints and DNA all over it.

Idiot!

They'd be able to put me in the system. I'd get linked with the deaths of the Korean kids at Tresting's office and who knew how many other places where I'd left some remnant of forensic evidence without knowing it.

Calm down. Will it really mean anything? They'd still have to find you.

But I'd be in the system, my prints and DNA matching a face.

How much would it matter? My information was probably in the system somewhere anyway, I reasoned, if from nothing else than the incident at Arthur's office. Would it make such a difference that it would no longer be quite so anonymous? That it would now match my mug shot, that it might get linked to Rio's massacre of the office workers?

I had to go back, I decided. Just in case. After all, who knew what the consequences would be? I might regret it forever if I didn't, and it would be simple enough to go back, grab the bottles, and dash away again.

I wheeled around to dart back down the alley the way I had come. A quick sprint brought me back toward the rear wall of the supermarket—

I stared in shock. The place was already swarming with cops. Since when did LA response times get so good?

Lights flashed around the corner, and I slipped in between two dumpsters as three police cars screeched into the alley behind me, unexpectedly cutting off my escape route along the ground. *Shit.* Why did things have to get complicated?

And then a low thrum started just on the edge of my hearing and began building, vibrating through the air louder and louder and louder.

A helicopter.

Seriously?

Okay, this might be . . . bad.

I might be in some real trouble here.

twenty

My BRAIN zigzagged through my options. Unlike most of the people I ended up on the wrong side of, law enforcement never seemed quite like fair game as targets. Well, unless they were dicks, but these people were just doing their jobs. *See, Tresting? I don't always go around killing people.* And I had grenades, too! Set a few of those off and I'd have more than enough chaos to escape in.

It was tempting, now that I'd thought of it.

Okay, so plan B was blasting and shooting my way out of here. I needed a plan A.

The uniforms were multiplying like the supermarket was a kicked anthill. I didn't just need a plan A, I needed a plan A *fast*.

A trickle of nervousness bled through me. This could be bad. Most violent situations I ended up in did not happen on busy downtown streets with lots of innocent bystanders, and as for police, I'd never done more than kick the odd uniform in the head while making an escape. The idea of a large number of law enforcement casualties made me . . . uncomfortable. Not to mention that it was the worst way ever to keep my head down; if I blew up this many cops, they'd probably have Homeland Security out here after me.

My mobile buzzed in my pocket.

Only one person had this number right now. It had to be Rio. "Not the best time; I'll call you back," I answered in a whisper.

There was a pause. Then a voice on the other end said, "It's Checker."

"Wha—this is a new phone!" I hissed. "How—?"

"Oh, I'm all-powerful," he said. "Hey, so I—"

I didn't have time for this right now. I hung up on him.

The phone buzzed immediately with a text message: NEED UR HELP

What he needed was to learn to spell correctly. I moved my thumb to turn the damn phone off entirely.

PLS VRY IMPORTANT

I sighed. Checker was the most annoying person I'd ever met. Evading arrest. Will call back later, I texted, and pocketed my phone again, turning my attention back to the problem at hand.

Grabbing the evidence I'd left would probably be too complicated now. Dammit. I could have gotten away clean if I'd just kept walking, and now that I was boxed in, even escape was looking difficult. My hiding place felt more transparent by the moment, and I couldn't think of any way out that wouldn't lead to some version of a shootout. Which I would win . . . but at what cost?

Taking to a roof meant exposure to the helicopter—helicopters now; a second had joined the first—and trying to cut down the alley would make me the target of the three bajillion and counting cops on the ground. *Seriously, you guys went to this much trouble just for me?* I wondered if I should be flattered or frustrated that someone finally wasn't underestimating me.

My phone buzzed, distracting me again. Swearing colorful curses at certain computer hackers in my head, I pulled it out to turn it off.

U NEED HELP?

I stared at the words. It felt like the setup to a really bad joke, one in which the next text would read, HA HA, JUST KIDDING, UR SO STUPID. The little computerized letters burned into my eyes.

Cas! Stop it! No time! I chided myself.

But was he serious? Why would a guy I'd had barely any interaction with want to help me?

Maybe it wasn't so unrealistic. After all, he seemed to need me for something. He could be trying to offer a quid pro quo, an "I'll help you, and then you're going to be obligated to help me." Or he might assume he was charging me for it and that we would settle up after. Either of those explanations aligned much more reasonably with my expectations of human nature . . . but in a way it didn't matter, because what could he possibly do to help me?

Unless . . .

Maybe he could forge something—some order, some directive, that would clear the police out of the area without anyone getting hurt. It was worth a try. I stabbed my phone with my thumb to dial.

Checker picked up on the first ring. "Turn yourself in," he said immediately.

The world trembled. There, there was the punch line. First Tresting, now Checker. *"What?"* I breathed.

"Turn yourself in. It's the easiest way. I'll have you out as soon as I can push some paper."

It took me a moment to catch on, and when I did, the jerk back from the self-pity and resentment I'd been starting to build up almost gave me whiplash, leaving me confused and embarrassed and angry about having felt anything so maudlin as emotions at all. Not to mention that Checker's plan just *sucked*.

"That's your solution?" Even though it was still hushed, my voice was more furious than I meant it to be. "Turn myself in and wait for you to fake a release order? No!"

"You're not in the system anywhere yet, right? Then I'm telling you, I've got this! Just don't say anything to anyone while they're questioning you. Not a word, okay?"

"I am not getting myself arrested!"

"I promise you, I will get you un-arrested! Now go!"

"And let the authorities get a record of me?"

"I'll un-record you," he insisted.

"Not a chance!"

"For the love of God, you are unbelievable!" he exclaimed. "Do you have any idea what kind of a situation you're in? I'm tracking it in real time here, and I didn't know LA *had* that many police resources. Either Tokyo called about an enormous lizard, or they think you're a domestic terrorist who—"

"Can't you make them go away?" I demanded.

"Sure, I'll wave my magic wand and, oh, wait, no, we don't live in a mystical fairyland. But fortunately for your pwned self, we do live in a mystical bureaucracy land, and I'm telling you, go surrender. I swear to you, I have it covered."

"Thanks, but no thanks," I said. "I'll find another way."

"Another *way*? SWAT's moving in! I already faked a 911 call from a few blocks away saying someone had seen you and they had enough people on the ground to cover it; some poor Pakistani girl got tackled by mistake and I would not have wanted to be her. You are in deep trouble! Are you *seeing*—"

"I'm right in the middle of it, thanks," I snapped in a whisper. "Look, can't you just issue some fake orders or something? All I need is a distraction."

"'Can't I just'—no, I can't 'just'! Not on this scale! Not fast enough!"

"Getting arrested is not an option," I hissed. "End of discussion. If you don't have anything else for me—"

"You'll what? Teleport?"

I was glad I could count on myself, at least. "I can shoot my way out if I have to."

"*Shoot* your way—? What the—I don't even know why I'm helping you," he groused.

"Then don't," I bit off, and hung up, turning off my phone for good measure. Calling him had been a bad idea after all. If shooting my way out was plan B, getting myself arrested was at least plan Double-Y-and-a-Half.

But he said he could get you back out, said a small voice in my head. And even if he couldn't get me cut loose quietly, I'd be able to break myself out in short order anyway . . . and leave the police with an even more complete record of me, I thought. Getting arrested was a *bad plan*.

Not to mention that it would mean depending on a guy I barely knew to pull through for me in a complicated gambit. I'd never trusted anyone aside from Rio to have my back, and I wasn't about to change that habit now. No, I was much better off relying on myself, even if it meant violence. Grenades it was.

Your first solution is always to pull the trigger, said Arthur's voice in my head, sadly.

"Shut up," I whispered. I started measuring avenues of escape and blast radii with my eyes.

Life is cheap to you.

Shut the hell up!

I had a hand on one of the grenades in my pocket, the weight of the Ruger firm and solid against my back. I couldn't depend on anyone else, I reminded myself. Myself, my skills, my gun—those I could rely on. Those were all I had.

Except in this case someone had offered me another way out. An insane, uncomfortable way that I really hated, but a way out.

One that didn't involve hurting anyone.

You're a good kid. You don't have to be like this.

"Shit," I said aloud softly, and even to myself I sounded pitiful.

I peeled off my jacket and wrapped the grenades, gun, and spare magazines in it. Then I squeezed back along the cinder-block wall behind my hiding place among the dumpsters and inched out until I could roll under a nearby parked car and wedge the whole package into the exhaust system. I measured tensions and pressures with my eyes: it wouldn't be falling out unless someone started taking apart the undercarriage. I took note of the plate so I could track down the car and get my toys back after this was over.

I squirmed back to the dumpsters, turned, and snuck along the wall toward the rear of the supermarket, putting some distance between myself and where my hardware was hidden. I was unarmed now, and it was not a good feeling.

Fuck. I can't believe I'm doing this.

I crouched for a whole minute at the end of the wall, still off the beaten path of all the police officers, one more parked car between me and them. I tried to will myself out, but it was like stepping off a cliff. Harder, because I could probably do the math fast enough to survive stepping off a cliff. *I can't do this,* I thought.

If Checker doesn't come through for you, you can always get yourself out, another voice in my head reminded me. *This isn't all that big of a deal. You won't be in a much worse position than you are here.*

Not a big deal? I'd be getting arrested*!*

I'd be putting myself in someone else's power. In the authorities' power. Voluntarily. They would be able to take whatever they wanted from me. It was lunacy.

Maybe, if you do this, he and Arthur will work with you again.

I wasn't sure where that thought had come from, but I suddenly knew how much I wanted it—because they were still working the Pithica case. I'd told Rio I'd drop it, but in that instant I knew I couldn't: I had unfinished business with Dawna Polk, and Courtney might still be out there, and Pithica . . . Pithica had a lot to answer for, and I was staying on the case until they did.

The resolution made me certain.

"Christ, this better be worth it," I muttered, and stood up, my hands in the air. "Hey, you, officer people! Uh, don't shoot; I'm unarmed!"

Boots stampeded on the pavement all around me, and I heard one or two pump actions chamber off to my left. Within seconds, I was surrounded by a ring of blue uniforms in bulletproof vests, a wall of police bristling with semiautomatics, mostly Berettas and Glocks.

I sighed and raised my hands higher. I really hate Glocks.

twenty-one

I WAS reminded just how much this was a *bad plan* when I had to let a couple of overzealous, hulking male officers tighten cuffs against my wrists and manhandle me into a police car. Forcing myself into helplessness made me feel exposed, as if acting vulnerable somehow made it so. I suppressed the urge to kick their ribs in, and dearly wished they knew how much self-control it required.

I mollified myself by calculating escape routes. Particularly ones involving permanent injury to certain meathead cops.

They drove me to a police station in a caravan of cop cars and jostled me inside. Someone patted me down—again—and they took my fingerprints and mug shots. I kept involuntarily flinching away from it all, from these people who thought they lorded power over me, these people who were prodding and recording and keeping a piece of me here forever.

Checker better do as he promised.

The booking officer kept trying to get my name and information, but I ignored her. Finally they brought me into a small, stark interrogation room, handcuffed me to the table, and left me alone, though I was sure someone was keeping an eye on me from behind the long one-way mirror.

"Hey," I called after a few minutes of waiting. "I have to go to the bathroom."

There was no response for about ten minutes, and then two female officers came into the room—one short and black and one tall and Hispanic, with identical tough-as-nails expressions—and took me without speaking. I didn't really have to go, but I'd need to get rid of the alcohol I'd chugged eventually, and I wanted to get a better lay of the land anyway in case I did need to break myself out. Yeah, I could do it, I concluded. Harder without grenades, but I never claimed I wasn't up for a challenge.

I wondered how long I should wait before taking the situation into my own hands. Checker had already taken too long for my taste. I contemplated asking for my phone call so I could harass him.

After I waited in boredom in the interrogation room for a while longer, they brought me out into a lineup, where I stood in a row with a bunch of other short, dark women and stepped forward and back when ordered to. Then they brought me back to interrogation and I waited some more. Really, it was a ridiculous amount of waiting—I would have been tempted to make a joke about my tax dollars, if I paid taxes. The quip made me think of Anton, a sharp burst of painful memory. One more score to settle.

I sat back in the hard metal chair and tried to relax. Well, at least I was back on the job, not stuck in my flat in Chinatown with nothing to occupy me. Ironically, waiting in handcuffs for the best chance at escape from police custody was a far better headspace for me than being at loose ends: this was the type of situation my mind could handle, even after I'd metabolized all the alcohol that had started the whole fiasco. Better this than being alone with my brain.

Yeah, I had a problem.

Finally, the door opened, and a dark and statuesque detective entered the room. "I'm Detective Gutierrez," she said, and sat down across from me to open a folder in front of her. "You're in quite a lot of trouble. If I can, I'd like to help you out."

I wondered if her implied offer meant they hadn't found any hard forensic evidence. Maybe their plan was to push for a confession and deal because they weren't sure they had a case—at least, not one a good lawyer couldn't tear apart by pointing out how all short, brown women would look alike to most people. Or maybe they thought Arthur was the better catch. In the theme of racial profiling, he did have the scary black man image going for him as the chief perpetrator.

Or maybe she wasn't making any offer at all, but merely employing a tactic to coerce me to talk.

"We have an eyewitness who saw you at 19262 Wilshire Boulevard yesterday morning," Detective Gutierrez continued. "What were you doing there?"

I stayed silent, letting my mind drift, toying with whether I would give Checker a few more hours or arbitrarily decide his deadline had been ten minutes ago.

Gutierrez kept asking questions for quite a while, the same ones over and over and over again. I tuned her out. She got in my face a bit for a change of pace, then stood up and left the room. They let me sit for almost an hour before she returned, this time with a partner, a younger male detective who kept condescending to me and then tried to play good cop while Gutierrez got aggressive, but I was about as responsive as a rock. I thought about asking for a lawyer, but figured if I did that they'd chuck me in a prison cell until one got here, and the interrogation room was probably marginally more comfortable— and easier to escape from, if Checker didn't come through. Besides, I didn't mind being talked at.

I hadn't been keeping track of time too closely, but it had to have been getting on in the evening when a knock came at the door. Gutierrez stood, gazing at me stonily before stepping outside. Her partner leaned back in his chair and smirked at me, as if that would bother me or something.

After a minute, Detective Gutierrez came back in with some papers, a sour pinch to her mouth. "You're free to go," she said.

The decree was so sudden and so without fanfare that my brain took several seconds to catch up.

The other detective jerked out of his superior slouch, equally shocked. "What?"

"It isn't her." Gutierrez snapped the folder in her hands shut. "Miss, one of the officers outside will process you out. We apologize for the inconvenience."

Dazed, I wondered if this was what being around civilized people was usually like: that they would give up their power over someone just because the evidence said so. Gutierrez uncuffed me, and I sort of nodded at them as I beelined for the door.

"What do you mean, it isn't her?" I heard the male detective demand of his partner as I stepped out. "We can't just let her—"

"Must've been a false ID. They got a match on this girl and verified her whereabouts all day yesterday. Nowhere near the crime scenes."

"Then why didn't she say anything?"

"Apparently she's not quite all there. Brother takes care of her," Gutierrez said.

"We can still hold her for—"

"No. Look who her family is."

After that I didn't hear anything else.

Bloody hell. It was this easy?

They had me sign some paperwork, which I did with a shapeless scribble, playing into whatever slightly mentally challenged character Checker had created for me and allowing me not to have to know what name I was supposed to have.

"Do you need us to call someone for you, Ms. Holloway?" one of the officers asked.

"No, I'm good," I said, feeling this was exceedingly anticlimactic.

"Okay. You be safe, now," he told me, and I stuffed my cell phone and cash back into my pockets and headed out of the police station a free citizen.

I forced myself not to run, walking away from the station at a moderate pace instead and figuring I should put some distance between myself and a building full of officers before stealing a vehicle. Night had fallen, and it was late enough that the usual bumper-to-bumper traffic had died down, the cars whizzing by in blazes of red taillights. An almost-full moon hung above the busy city, gazing down like an enormous white eye.

My phone buzzed as I hit the sidewalk.

U OUT?

I punched the "send" button to dial back.

"Oh, I'm good, aren't I? Tell me I'm good," crowed Checker in my ear.

"Sort of slow," I said, affecting nonchalance.

"Slow? *Slow?* Do you have any idea how much paperwork I had to forge here? This was *record breaking.* I never do 'slow' unless there's cuddling afterwards."

"Are you my brother?" I asked.

"Dear Lord, I hope not, considering what a turn-on your knowledge of statistics is. But I might've pretended to be. We have very important parents, by the way. Everything go smooth?"

"So smooth. Infinite differentiability, in fact," I assured him, maybe just to be a little funny.

He cackled. "I knew I liked you."

I cleared my throat. "What about—they took my fingerprints and everything. . . ."

"Disappearing as we speak."

Was that even possible? "Wow. Uh, thanks," I said. Checker, I decided, was a good person to know.

"Sure thing. You made it easy; having nothing in the system meant I had a window to work with. So, how does it feel to be a free woman?"

I took a deep breath, intending to say something about an arrest in the civilized world being kind of a letdown, but the truth was, it felt good not to be trapped in the station anymore. And Checker had made it so I didn't have to hurt anyone this time around. The copy of Tresting who had taken up residence in my head was starting to keep track.

"How much do I owe you?" I asked, to cover the fact that I was having feelings.

"Oh, on the house," he said. "I owed you one for saving Arthur anyway, and besides—"

"We were even already."

"Maybe *he* was, but I'm kind of grateful you kept him kicking, too, so, no charge."

"Oh." I mulled over whether I was okay with that. I don't like owing people any favors.

"Just don't tell Arthur. He, uh, doesn't like it when I do things like this."

The mention of Tresting's self-righteousness soured me. My conscience deciding to take on his persona was frustrating enough; I didn't need the real-life version harping at me any more than he already had. "I don't get it," I complained. "I've seen him break more laws than I can count, and he gets all hung up on the littlest stuff."

"Hey, he's good people," Checker said sharply.

"Inconsistent people," I muttered.

"Cas Russell, you may impress me with your knowledge of Bayesian probability, but don't insult Arthur to me, okay? Just don't."

Apparently I'd hit a nerve. Oh, brother. "Uh, okay." When he didn't say anything, I probed, "You still there?"

"Yeah." I couldn't read his tone.

Best get back to business. "Didn't you need my help with something?" I'd help him with his favor as payment, I thought. Then we'd be even.

He sighed. "Arthur isn't going to like that I'm asking you this, either."

"Asking me what?"

"He needs backup."

Oh, good. Backup I could handle. "Sure," I said. "On what?" If Checker was inviting me back onto the Pithica case, that wasn't even a favor—I would jump at the chance. Even if it meant working with Tresting again.

Checker hesitated, then said in a rush, "Polk's tracker came back on."

"It did? Where is she?"

"The signal's here in Los Angeles."

"Why would she have flown back h . . ." I trailed off. "You think they figured out we had a GPS on her. You think they found the tracker."

"It doesn't make any sense otherwise. Why would it go off-line and then pop back up again? Here?"

"But that doesn't make sense either! If they make it that obvious it's a setup, why would they think we would be stupid enough to—"

Checker made a strangled sort of noise.

I groaned. "Tresting's going in, isn't he."

"That would be a yes."

"He thinks they're waiting for him, and he's going in anyway."

"Hence the needing backup."

"Okay. When and where?"

There was a short beat of silence, as if Checker had expected a different response, but he recovered quickly. "I'm texting you the details now, including the location and the tracker frequency. Satellite imagery was no help, unfortunately; it only shows some buildings in the middle of the desert. As for when . . . he's going in tonight."

I looked up at the stars. "Uh, it's night already."

"Yeah."

"So, I'm in kind of a hurry here, huh."

"He left a few hours ago," said Checker. "I tried to stop him."

His words had become heavy with worry. It made me feel strangely isolated—no one gave a damn if I decided to make a suicide run. I wouldn't even be missed; I'd disappear into the fabric of the Los Angeles underground as if I'd never existed.

"I'd better get going, then," I said, starting to walk faster. "Anything else I should know? Is anyone else with him?"

"I swear, I tried to get him to call in help. He got all idiotic nobility complex on me about not wanting to involve anyone else."

That might have been why Tresting hadn't phoned his other contacts, but I was pretty sure he'd had a different reason for not calling me. It made me perversely eager to save his bacon again. I wanted to rub it in his face. "Gotcha. Anything else?"

"Is it true?" Checker asked. "What Dawna Polk can do?"

I swallowed. "Yeah. I'm pretty sure it is."

He didn't say anything for a moment.

"Are you still there?" I asked.

"Yeah."

"Hey, listen," I said, trying not to let his concern for Arthur irritate me. "Stop worrying about it. I'm on my way."

"Thank you. Really—thank you. I owe you big-time. Anything you need, really, just say the word."

Well, that might be a useful favor to call in someday. But first I'd have to make it through the night. After walking into a Pithica trap. Goddamn Tresting.

"And watch yourself, okay?" Checker added.

I blinked. I hadn't expected him to be concerned for me, too. I doubted he would miss me if something happened, but still, it was . . . nice of him.

"Oh, don't be stupid," I said, a little too brusquely. "I'll be fine."

twenty-two

I HAD to move fast.

The location Checker had sent was out past Edwards Air Force Base, way out in the desert north of Mojave. Not much out there, I thought—nothing but rocks and dunes and endless sky. Good place for an ambush.

The car with my Ruger and grenades under it had probably been driven off by now. I'd grab Checker's help to track it down later, if I lived that long. I was still near enough to the Chinatown apartment to swing by; all I had left there were the crap guns from the day before and a knife, but that was better than nothing. I armed myself in less than five minutes, grabbed a few protein bars and a light jacket from the meager tangle of clothes I had there, and headed northeast in a stolen sports car.

I called Rio from the road and hit a voice-mail box. I gave him all the details, then hesitated, wondering if I should apologize for breaking my word to stay off the case. After all, I had told him I would keep my head down right before doing a spectacular job of exactly the opposite.

"I've got to go in," I finally said to the recording. "I, uh—I hope that doesn't interfere with any of your plans or anything." I didn't have a choice, though. Stupid Arthur Tresting had forced all our hands.

I went well above the speed limit the whole way, but it was still almost three hours before the GPS in the sports car told me I was nearing the coordinates Checker had sent. The location was off any roads, but I circled around and barely made out the outlines of an unmarked half-paved track leading into the desert. I paused the car, switching off the headlights and letting my eyes adjust to the dimness.

Cell service had dropped out miles before. I was alone out here, driving into what was almost certainly an ambush. Shit. I might pack a whole lot more punch than Pithica was expecting, but if they sprang a trap before I saw it, I'd be just as dead as someone who didn't know any math.

As long as I had an instant to react, however, I'd have the edge. And Tresting didn't have a chance without me, I reminded myself. I took a deep breath, every sense alert, and nosed the car forward down the makeshift road.

The GPS said I was still a few miles away. The car crunched over the rocky ground, the empty night rolling by quietly to either side. Before long a handful of buildings rose ahead, a ghost town looming out of the desert: a couple of boarded-up businesses, a graffitied gas station, a string of warehouses that had probably encouraged the town to grow here in the first place. Darkness cloaked all the buildings, and they sat heavy with the stillness of the long since abandoned.

I let the sports car roll to a stop and watched from a distance. Nothing moved. The moon lent its gray light to the emptiness, but only showed each hulking, shadowed building as darker and more vacant than the next. I sat for a moment, measuring out likely places for danger to come from, extrapolating probable threats. Snipers? Possible, though they didn't have many vantage points here; the lines of sight danced through my senses and crossed at poor angles. Mines in the road, as the motorcycle gang had tried? A bomb that would obliterate the entire town, one already set to detonate, one I would never even see before it went off?

That was all more dramatic than Pithica's preferred MO, though. Maybe they wouldn't care how they took me out; after all, I lived off the grid anyway, and no one would miss me. But wouldn't they want a better explanation for Arthur's demise? How much would they care about disguising it?

I wasn't keen to find out. My current objective was to find Tresting and leave. We could return with a much better plan than sneaking in haphazardly and separately in the dark.

I goosed the sports car forward, the tires crunching on gravelly asphalt. As I came to the outskirts of the town, a familiar shape rose out of the darkness and distinguished itself: Tresting's truck.

I stopped the car and slid out, drawing the Smith & Wesson. I reached out with my other hand to press against Tresting's hood. The engine was cold. He'd been here for a while already.

A slight scuff in the dirt. I spun and dove to the side in a crouch, bringing up the Smith—

I recognized the silhouette and let my finger up off the trigger. "Tresting. Shit."

He lowered his weapon at the same time I did. "Russell? What are you doing here?"

"Backing you up." I straightened, staying wary. "Checker called me in."

He sucked in a breath. "Course he did."

"What's the situation?" I asked, keeping my eyes on the darkened buildings.

He turned back toward the town. "Not rightly sure. Nothing here."

My spine prickled. "What do you mean, nothing?"

"Been through the place three times," Tresting said. "Was real leery of surprises the first time through, but . . . nothing."

That didn't make any sense. "What about the tracker?"

"Haven't found it yet. Looks to be in the second warehouse there"—he nodded toward the hulking buildings—"but the signal's not precise enough for me to pinpoint. Searched the place top to bottom, and can't find anything."

"Show me," I said.

I let Tresting take point, trailing him to the warehouse. I kept my gun drawn, my senses wired, but the street stayed empty.

Tresting led the way inside, prying up a metal roll-up door with a loud screech of steel. I glanced around sharply, but our surroundings didn't give a twitch in response.

I ducked into the warehouse, my eyes straining against the leaden darkness inside. A few grimy skylights let in scant moonlight, but didn't provide any more contrast than outlines of gray on gray. Someone had tried to refurbish the inside of the warehouse, badly, and had never finished—flimsy walls attempted to partition the vast floor space and formed a maze of unceilinged half rooms, as if a giant had approximated an office cubicle jungle with cheap Sheetrock.

"Could be anywhere," said Tresting softly, his voice echoing. "Might be hopeless."

"I think we can narrow it down," I said. I'd taken great care to pay attention to the coordinates Checker had given me, and to what the GPS had read when I stopped the car. I did a quick extrapolation in my head given the precision of the tracker—it had to be the northeast corner. "This way," I murmured, heading in that direction.

Tresting seemed as nervous as I was, even after having searched the whole place already. This time he hung back while I led, watching our six in a semicircle as I found a way through the wide aisles between the drywall.

"It has to be somewhere past here," I said, and then realized I didn't hear Tresting's footsteps behind me anymore.

I slipped to the side and whipped around, gun barrel first.

Tresting had disappeared. Instead, a slender silhouette was stepping out of one of the unfinished rooms and raising delicate hands in the air.

Everything went cold. Even in the darkness I recognized Dawna Polk.

"Hello, Ms. Russell," she said. "My people have Mr. Tresting. Please put down your weapon, or unfortunately he will be the one to suffer for it."

He said he searched the building. He said he searched the building! Where had they been hiding? And *why*?

"You have questions," acknowledged Dawna. "The reason we did not show ourselves before now was that we were waiting for you."

How could they possibly know I would show up?

"We made some educated guesses about human nature," she answered with a small smile. "We're quite good at that."

But what did they want with me in the first place? And why not just kill us?

"I shall explain everything in good time," said Dawna. "But you are quite correct; we do wish you to accompany us whole and unharmed for the moment. Your new friend Mr. Tresting is more expendable, so please, put your weapons on the floor."

Jesus Christ. She was reading my mind.

And to make everything orders of magnitude worse, they'd grabbed Arthur so quickly and quietly I hadn't heard a whisper of it. Some serious muscle must be lurking in the shadows—I'd fought alongside Tresting; he was no slouch.

And now Pithica had him.

A flicker of doubt throbbed through my brain, a question that needed answering, an assumption to dispute. But I didn't have time to concentrate on it. Dawna Polk had given me a command.

I lowered the Smith & Wesson slowly and placed it on the cement floor, keeping my hands away from my body as I stood back up and struggling not to think.

"Really, Ms. Russell?" said Dawna, a hint of humor in her voice.

"It was worth a try," I said aloud. I reached around to untuck the Glock and the TEC-9 from my belt and leave them on the ground, too.

"Everything," said Dawna. "It's almost as if you doubt me."

I slid the knife out of my boot and left it with the firearms.

Dawna lowered her hands. "That's better," she declared, and I felt a sharp pang of frustration. Rio had warned me, but something in me had hoped his stark description an exaggeration. Mind reading had seemed too absurd, too unbelievable. But here was Dawna Polk, able to see exactly what I was thinking as if she'd cracked open my skull, to look at me and *know*—

"Yes, I do," Dawna said briskly. "Now, we do know you can be . . . an effective person, even unarmed. Please believe Mr. Tresting will continue to be a hostage to your good behavior." She raised her voice slightly. "Take her, please."

More shadows glided out of the surrounding rooms, black-clad bodies punctuated with the distinctive hard angles of the well armed. If I had been here alone, I might have looked for a way out, even with Dawna reading me—might have tried to get away even if the mathematical expectation read death. But if I made a move . . . *goddamn Arthur*. I shut my mind away from calculating escape routes and let gloved hands pull my wrists behind me; the plastic bite of a zip tie cut into my skin.

This was why I should never care about another person's welfare, I thought.

"Oh, Ms. Russell. Caring about others is what makes life worth living," Dawna chastised me.

I squinted at her. I might not be psychic, but I couldn't hear any irony in her words. She seemed to believe that.

"I do," she said. "Now, I apologize for the less than ideal treatment you are about to receive. But you and I have a lot we must talk about."

She nodded to her people, and I felt a gentle shove of a strong hand on my shoulder. I took the cue and walked out among the press of heavily armed bodies, out into the night and into the back of a white van that had materialized from nowhere.

As the van rumbled to life and rolled away from the ghost town, I tried not to think about what Dawna had said. She wanted to talk to me.

She wanted to *talk* to me.

My chest felt tight, and I couldn't get enough air.

Dawna Polk wanted to talk to me.

Raw terror began crackling around the edges of my thoughts.

Calm down, I ordered myself. *Think. Strategize.* Dawna wasn't here now, only her faceless black-clad people who surrounded me silently, armed with M4s in their hands and sidearms on their thighs, and their well-armed discipline was trivial. Eight people became nothing when I had mathematics on my side. But the sure knowledge that Tresting was in a similar windowless van surrounded by equally armed guerrillas stayed me; Dawna had told me she would kill him if I didn't cooperate, and I believed her.

I needed a way out for both of us.

But if I couldn't find one, how long would it take Dawna to turn me inside out, to destroy everything I was and replace it with whatever personality she chose? How long before she scraped my brain free of any errant opinion, made me a parrot for Pithica's goals? If her earlier influence was any indication, I wouldn't even notice it happening. I would become a puppet who blithely continued to think herself a real human being.

Panic rose, flooding my brain with static, crowding out any attempts to plan. A new and unfamiliar emotion dragged at me—*helplessness*.

I had never been helpless. I'd never faced any threat I hadn't been confident of overcoming eventually, not with my abilities—

My abilities. Did Dawna know what I could do? If she didn't, if I managed to hide it, I might have just the edge Arthur and I needed to escape. Did I have the slightest chance of it? Had I already given myself away?

Dawna could read any thought off my face; I had no hope of masking any information she might seek from me. But she wasn't seeing every last bit of knowledge in my brain, was she? Surely that would be impossible. If she knew every last fact in everyone's head at every moment, the deluge of information would overload her. Might I potentially be able to shield something from her, something like my math prowess, if I simply didn't think about it?

Yes, because it always works to try not to think about something!

I squashed back the panic and racked my brain for ideas. If Dawna asked whether I was a superpowered math genius who could make like a one-woman army, a twitch of my eye would tell her yes, but unless she already suspected as much, she would have no reason to ask, would she? The question would be so far outside her fundamental assumptions; it would never occur to her unless I gave myself away. I couldn't turn off seeing the numbers, but if I refrained from calculation as much as I could, would it be possible? Mathematical connections made themselves apparent to me all the time. Letting that sense lie latent would be as insurmountable as turning off my hearing—or, more accurately, trying to ignore everything I heard. Could I damp it down enough to hide it?

Wait. What if I did the opposite? Dawna likely didn't know a great deal of mathematics; she wouldn't be able to tell the extent of my abilities unless I connected them to reality. If I focused inward instead—well, *not* thinking of something might be almost impossible, but *thinking* of something was a much easier strategy, and focusing on innocuous trivialities might crowd out every thought I didn't want to have. Messy computation would provide the perfect static, which meant I didn't have to bind back my mathematical capability—I would instead hide it in plain sight.

Not to mention that if I provided enough white noise in my brain, I might not only have a chance at camouflaging my math skills, but potentially keep other stray thoughts from surfacing as well. If Dawna asked what I was trying to hide, the answer would truthfully be *As much as I possibly can.*

She might see through the guise right away, of course. But at least now I had something to try.

Over an hour later, when the van pulled to a stop after rolling downward for several long minutes into what felt like an underground parking structure, I'd filled my brain with unending computations of the nontrivial zeros of the Riemann zeta function. If that ceased to occupy my full concentration, I threw in constructing a succinct circuit and calculated a Hamiltonian path in it at the same time, and also tried to keep up a run factoring a string of two- and three-hundred-digit numbers, one after the other. It was math—but it was normal, uninteresting math, heavy computations I hoped would weary Dawna with their tedium the moment she saw them, dry manipulations of numbers that would frustrate her as an obvious strategy to hide something else.

Most people's eyes glazed over the instant equations came on the scene. I hoped Dawna Polk would be no different.

twenty-three

I KEPT up the computational white noise as the paramilitary troops
brought me out of the van, refusing to look at the mathematics for
escape routes even for interest's sake and pointing all my concentration inward. Forcing myself to ignore the math drenching my surroundings strained my brain, but even though Dawna herself might
not be in evidence yet, I was sure security cameras were recording my
every microexpression. If my ploy had even a chance of working,
I didn't want to let up the effort for an instant.

The guards marched me down several flights of stairs and through
a series of bare cement hallways to a door with the weight and thick-
ness of a bank vault's, which they manhandled open to reveal a cellblock with a row of empty jail cells. Concrete cinder blocks formed
the back wall, but iron bars partitioned the cells from each other and
from freedom, leaving no privacy for the prisoners. My captors
ushered me into a cell near the middle of the row and surprised me
by cutting the zip ties around my wrists before sliding the bars closed
and locking me in. Then they left—not far, I felt sure—save one guard
who stayed at attention at the end of the cellblock.

I peeked mathematically and quickly discarded every option for
escape; even I'm at a disadvantage when I start out locked in a cell

with no assets. I sat against the concrete wall and went back to my Riemann zeta calculations, chugging out another few decimal places for the imaginary part of the latest *s* I was contemplating.

The door at the end of the cellblock opened, and my heavily armed friends reentered, this time with Tresting between them. More bruises purpled his face than before, and a trickle of blood marked a split lip. The bruising struck me as odd somehow, but instead of trying to calculate why, I buried myself in a Hamiltonian path analysis.

I scrambled to my feet.

"Hey, you all right?" Tresting called.

"Yeah," I said, keeping my mind whirring on my succinct circuit and another Riemann zeta root in the background. "You?"

"Yeah."

He left off speaking for a minute as the guards hustled him to the cell next to mine; they cut his hands free as they had done for me and locked him in impersonally. Once they had left again, Tresting turned toward me, rubbing his wrists. "I'm sorry," he said, all weighty and heavy and undoubtedly sincere. "So sorry. My fault, all of it."

"Not really," I answered. I honestly didn't blame him; I had known full well what I gambled when I went in after him. "They must've hidden somehow till I got there. She obviously had this planned."

"Not what I meant," he said. "Knew it was a setup. I shouldn't've . . . just got desperate. Didn't want to lose the lead, you know?"

"I know," I said. "It's okay."

"No. I heard what she said. They set the trap for you, but on your lonesome, you might not've been dumb enough to fall in. Was me who got us caught."

"She played us all," I said. "Human nature, she said, right? She can predict when we'll be stupid."

"Maybe."

"It was my fault I was there just as much as yours," I said. "I came uninvited in the first place, remember?"

He exhaled sharply and unhappily. "Any idea why they want you?"

It was a good question. Two nights ago they'd tried to kill me with no questions asked, and now they had set a trap for me? The only good guess my earlier brooding had come up with was that this all had to do with my minimal ability to break away from Dawna's brainwashing after the fact. Of course, considering how easily she had gotten to me during our meeting at the coffee shop, and how profoundly the effect had lasted before Rio's insistent intervention, I didn't have much hope of the supposed resistance helping me out now.

"I guess I'll find out," I said.

"Yeah." Arthur was looking at his hands, still reflexively rubbing them against each other. "You know, you could've run, when they threatened me."

"No, I couldn't have."

He glanced at me and then nodded, as if he understood what I meant.

Absurdly, I felt as if I had passed some sort of test. "Besides, you would have done the same for me," I pointed out, embarrassed.

"Yeah, but I got a reputation for self-sacrificing idiocy to uphold."

"Well. We all have our flaws."

He huffed out a breath that sounded almost like a laugh, and any tension that had remained after the last time we saw each other slipped away. Arthur went to sit down on the floor, leaning back against the wall, and I joined him on the other side of the barred partition dividing our cells while I factored another hundred or so integers. Most of them were easy, but I'd just hit a frustrating one that might be a semiprime.

"What do you think's going to happen here?" asked Arthur after a while.

"I think Dawna Polk is going to come talk to us," I said. "And then we're going to do whatever she wants."

"You got a plan?"

The Euclidean algorithm flickered through each subsequent remainder, subtracting and dividing and subtracting. "Resist as much as I can, I guess." Of course, Dawna could make me think I was resisting when I was doing exactly what she wanted me to do. We would both be her babbling lapdogs eventually.

What had Rio said? That the conversion would take time, if her goal went fundamentally against her victim's personality? Months, even, for a result opposite to the person's psychology?

What was my psychology? Axiomatic, probably, but I'd already witnessed her ability to rewrite those axioms to let me rationalize anything. I had no defense against her. Neither of us did.

"Never been one to consider suicide an appropriate solution," said Tresting beside me, "but in this case . . ."

I snapped my head around to look at him. Killing myself hadn't even occurred to me. "Well, I guess that's one way to avoid her influence," I managed.

"Avoid it, and make sure she could never make me do anything to my—to anyone I cared about. Or anyone else."

If his main concern was being used as a tool to hurt others, then he was definitely the better person. "I . . . if you want to do that, I can make it quick," I offered, the words dry in my mouth.

"Thank you," he said quietly. "I'll let you know."

We lapsed into silence. Eventually I curled up on the cement floor and tried for some sleep. One of the guards brought us food and water every few hours, and Arthur was graceful about turning away when I needed to use the steel toilet affixed to the wall. The wait was humane, if tedious.

I noticed my chronic headaches had gone away. Instead of being a relief, their sudden lack only spurred my anxiety. The headaches had come on whenever I resisted Dawna's influence—what did it mean that I didn't feel them anymore?

Fuck. I buried myself in more mathematics. It was all I could do.

Busy with my constant stream of monotonous mental arithmetic, I didn't bother to keep track of the time, but at least a full day had passed before the door at the end of the cellblock opened again to reveal a familiar frizzy-haired and freckle-faced figure.

"Hi," said Courtney Polk, coming down the cellblock to face us.

Arthur and I stepped forward in our cells. "Hi," I said warily.

The staggering number of question marks surrounding Courtney surged to the front of my brain. Was she in league with Pithica and

Dawna? If so, how much through her own free will, and how much through Dawna's psychic brainwashing? Had she really killed Reginald Kingsley, and if she'd done it under Dawna's influence, how much could she be held accountable?

Who was she? Was she still my client? And if so, what on earth could I do for her?

"I'm sorry you have to go through all this," said Courtney, waving a hand at the cells. "It's for your own good and all, but I'm still sorry."

"What do you mean, it's for our own good?" I said cautiously.

"Well, my sister. She's helping you." The corner of her mouth quirked up in a friendly smile.

Arthur and I glanced at each other.

"Helping us how?" I said.

"Become better." She spoke like it was the most obvious thing in the world.

"That what she did for you, sweetheart?" asked Arthur.

Courtney's smile blossomed. "It's what she does, my sister. She's amazing. The most amazing person in the world. I was so lost before she helped me."

This conversation was surreal. "She's not really your sister, you know," I blurted.

Courtney didn't seem bothered. "She is in every way that matters."

"I didn't see her helping when the cartel snatched you," I said.

"Of course she did. Didn't she hire you?"

I boggled. Well, I supposed that was one way of looking at things—if Dawna weren't a *freaking psychic*.

"She couldn't get me out of there herself, but afterward she came to get me as soon as she could," Courtney explained.

I found my voice. "Let me drop a little knowledge on you," I said. "Your sister can do pretty much anything she wants. She could have walked into that compound and walked you right out of the cartel's custody if she'd wanted to, but for some reason, she didn't. I'm sorry, but all you are is a pawn in some huge game she's playing." I took a deep breath. "Look, I said I'd help you. I'm still willing to."

"That's nice of you," said Courtney delicately, in the same

transparently fake way I might have if a high school student had offered to tutor me in arithmetic. "Really, I appreciate it. But Dawna's fixing everything, just like always. No faraway island. No running away. And my life's going to have meaning. Real meaning."

"Doing what?" I said.

"Helping her." The smile was back, her eyes sparkling.

Arthur cleared his throat. "Sweetheart, what does your sister want to do?"

"What else? Change the world."

I bit back an incredulous exclamation about vacuous truths. "Change the world *how*?" I pressed instead.

"Make it better. What else!" Courtney almost laughed at my slow-wittedness. "So many horrible things happen in the world. Like the drug cartels. But not just them. People doing awful, cruel things to each other, people starving, and war, and Dawna and everyone else are working to put a stop to all that. They're doing so much good. And I'm going to help them, and I hope you will, too."

"Wait. Let me get this straight." My thoughts whirled. "Dawna's goal is to *make the world a better place*?"

Courtney blinked at me. "What else would it be?"

I had been thinking along the lines of being an evil mastermind and making everyone her slave. Although perhaps such a dystopia was the same thing in her mind, if she forced all her slaves to play nicely together and made sure they all had enough food . . . after all, I thought ironically, wouldn't that make for a mighty peaceful world?

Some detached part of my brain wondered what Courtney had been like before she met Dawna Polk. Whether she had been anything like this Courtney, or whether that original girl was gone now, forever. "If you're all wanting to be such good people," I probed, "then why are Arthur and I locked up here? Shouldn't you let us go?"

Courtney bit her lip. "I—I like you. I do. And you tried to help me out a lot, in your own way. But people like you . . . you shouldn't be on the streets." She regarded me sadly. "You hurt people. I've seen it. And you've killed people, and you steal for people, and—we're trying to change the world for the better, put away the people causing all the chaos, and right now, you're one of them." She scrunched up her face uncomfortably, then added to Arthur, "And I don't know you, sorry, but I'm sure Dawna has a good reason for having you here, too. She always does."

"But you said you hoped we'd work with you—you all," I protested, knowing I'd lost the argument before I even began.

"Yes, we do, after you turn away from all of that. Dawna will help you." She was smiling again. It was eerie.

"What if I already have?" I tried in some desperation. "Turned away from the dark side, and all that? You've explained it, uh, really well, and I, I want to change and come and join you. I've seen the light, I swear. Will you let us out?"

The words sounded so cringingly insincere to my own ears that I wasn't surprised when Courtney laughed gently. Apparently being brainwashed didn't make her stupid. "When it's for real, when you really do want to join us, I know we'd love to have you. *I'd* love to have you. And Dawna, she's so forgiving, and—well, she's really the best sister ever." Her smile had gone all glowing and hopeful. "I think she's going to come and talk to you pretty soon. She'll be able to help you. You'll see. I'll come visit you after?"

"Sure," I managed. I wanted to rage at her, to lose my temper, but all I could muster up was pity. Pity for Courtney, and fear for myself.

Courtney's face lit up even more. "Great! I'll see you then, 'kay? It was nice to meet you," she added to Arthur, despite never having introduced herself, and then she turned and tripped off down the cellblock.

"In a way, she's right," said Arthur as the door clanged shut behind her. "People like you and me. In a perfect society, we wouldn't exist."

I wasn't in the mood for philosophizing. "When we live in a perfect society, you let me know."

He leaned his back against the bars across from me. "Well, sometimes I'm not sure I even make it a better one. Lord knows I try, but . . . well. I do lots of things I'm not proud of these days. Suspect I won't weigh out so well on the scales of judgment my own self. Maybe she's got a point."

I turned on him incredulously. "Do you really think what Dawna does is—"

"Not saying it's justified," he interrupted, still in a contemplative tone. "But if she really is trying to improve things—I dunno, she could have worse targets than you and me."

"What about Courtney?" I said tartly. "What about Dr. Kingsley? And Reginald Kingsley? And all those people in his file? And who gave Dawna Polk the right to choose in the first place, anyhow?"

"Calm down. I'm not saying I agree with all the methods here. But a greater good thing that got out of hand . . . well, makes some sense, yeah? And if we are talking greater good, I'm not sure you and me would be on the side of the righteous, is all."

I didn't know what shook me more—that Arthur seemed to be able to see the side of the woman who currently had him locked up pending brainwashing, or that he was including himself on the same ethical level as me. After he had come down on me for my relative immorality the other day, hearing him so insecure about his own inconsistencies of principle was vaguely shocking.

Maybe that's why I said what I said next. Maybe it was the impending certainty of my mind getting twisted into pretzels that made frank soul baring suddenly more appealing. Or maybe I figured it didn't matter what I said to Arthur anyway, as his mind was about to get twisted into pretzels, too.

"Whatever your scales of judgment are, you'll weigh on them a sight better than I will," I admitted, my voice cracking a little. "You at least try. I . . . I survive." I swallowed. "I've been thinking about it, and you were right, before. I don't think a whole lot about the people I hurt, and killing someone who's threatening me—it's always been the smart thing to do. You pointed it out yourself—I would have killed you too, back at the motel." I felt as if I were making a deathbed confession. Perhaps I was. "I don't think I'm a very good person," I added softly.

"You're wrong about one thing," Arthur remonstrated gently. "You didn't kill me."

"Only because you're right—I didn't have the leverage."

"No. Talking about after. You knocked me out, and then you left me alive."

"You weren't a threat anymore."

"Yes, I was," he corrected. "And you knew I could be."

I frowned. He was right. Mathematical expectation had been that I was in the clear, but he had started out by pointing a gun at me, and the probability he would have been able to come after me again had definitely been nonzero. In point of fact, he *had* come after me again. Why had I left him alive?

"I thought you were a cop at the time," I remembered. "Murdering law enforcement—too many complications."

"And that's why you didn't do it?"

"Well, no." The idea of dispatching him once the immediate threat was over hadn't even crossed my mind, which seemed oddly illogical of me, looking back. "I guess the smart thing would've been to consider it."

He chuckled. "You on some crusade to make me think poorly of you?"

"Fine," I conceded peevishly. "So I don't kill gratuitously. That's a high recommendation. I'm sure it's the standout essay God gets on 'why I should get into heaven.'"

"Don't sell yourself short, Russell. World's a big place, and you got a lot of people beat just with that."

"What happened to telling me I'm too violent and immoral?"

"Well, you are. But maybe so am I. We're neither of us angels, I guess. And I don't know; I think there's hope for you. Maybe for me, too."

"That's comforting," I said. "What's your point, then? That we're not the good guys, but Pithica should still let us go because we're not the worst of the bad guys either and there might even be some hope of redemption?"

He smiled at my phrasing. "Just ruminating here, honest. Maybe we're all shades of gray—you, me, Dawna Polk trying for her greater good. . . ."

I thought of what Dawna Polk had done to me, to Leena Kingsley, to so many other people—and what else she would do to Arthur and me very soon now.

"No, I'm pretty sure we kill Dawna as soon as we can," I said, "and redemption be damned."

Arthur chuckled again. He probably didn't realize I was serious.

twenty-four

When Dawna finally came, she came for me.

Two of her black-clad troops arrived in the cellblock and courteously requested I accompany them. I glanced at Arthur; his expression was heavy with worry.

I took the barest of moments to glance out from behind my shield of tedious arithmetic to evaluate the weighty, locked door at the end of the cellblock and wonder if I could jump the guards (probably) and get Arthur and myself out and through the door in one piece before an army of troops arrived (unlikely). As much as I preferred to go down fighting, committing suicide via an almost zero-probability escape attempt appealed to me about as much as bashing my brains out in the cell did. Waiting for a more opportune time was the obvious answer . . . though it might be hubris to think I could survive even one interview with Dawna and stay an intact person.

I stepped up the arithmetical white noise in my brain, filling every neuron with a mess of calculation, so much I had trouble juggling it all.

The troopers took me down several cinder-block corridors and through a few more heavy metal doors, and then up a lengthy ride in an elevator that opened into a well-furnished hallway of what appeared to be a luxury estate. We stepped out. The carpet was so thick under my boots that it not only muffled all sound of our passage but had its own spring, and the paramilitary troops looked strangely out of place against the spotless decor and tastefully framed paintings.

They led me down several plush corridors before finally ushering me through a shining set of carved double doors and into a library, where one gestured for me to sit at a long table. Rows of stacks spread out to either side, every shelf filled with hardcovers in pristine condition.

"Please wait here," said one of the troopers, a woman with a stark military haircut. "In the meantime, we have been instructed to remind you, with apologies, that your friend's continued well-being is contingent upon your choices."

"Yeah, I get it," I said. I wondered how far Dawna thought she could push me using that leverage. Hell, she probably already knew exactly how far. I peeked at the math around me again—the probabilities bounced into a much more favorable array, tantalizing me with escape, but I still believed that Dawna's threat was good and that they would hurt Arthur very badly if I tried. I wasn't ready to risk that.

I sat in the comfortable, well-upholstered chair and waited, counting the time, overflowing my brain with pointless mathematical grunge work. My chaperones retreated to the door but stayed in the room, presumably prepared to shoot me or tell on me if I tried anything.

The small part of my mind that wasn't cycling through repetitive NP-hard and EXPTIME algorithms wandered. Why the heck did Pithica have a library here? What was this building to them? As in the hallways, the decor here struck me as luxurious but impersonal; maybe the room was only for show—though why anyone would need a library for show, I had no idea.

"It's not a pretense," said an articulate female voice. I jumped, reflexively stepping up my arithmetic mental scramble. Dawna had entered the room, the thick carpeting muffling her elegant stilettos. She stood with her hands clasped behind her back in a light approximation of parade rest, wearing a crisp business skirt and blouse. Her gracefulness made me feel positively trollish as a human being. "I have a library here because I enjoy books," she continued with a small smile. "I have a particular proclivity for first editions."

"Ironic," I said, my voice coming out a little croaky. "I think Courtney Polk's at least on her third."

Dawna turned and nodded to her guards; they about-faced and left the room, closing the doors softly behind them. She stepped over and sat down across from me, folding her hands in front of her on the table. "Courtney . . ." She pressed her lips together. "When I found Courtney, she was . . . broken. Beyond depressed. Drugs, pills, no job, and no skills to acquire one."

"So you got her a spot as a drug mule," I said, chugging through another Riemann zeta root as I spoke. "Great upgrade."

She smiled slightly. "The cartels put up a good front, but on the whole we've defanged them. In almost all ways, they work to serve our ends now, not theirs. In working for them, Ms. Polk was truly working for us."

"Wait, you took over the *drug cartels*?"

"Yes," said Dawna. "Eventually we'll phase them out entirely, of course, but for now they provide us with the means, in many ways, of accomplishing our objectives. Their resources, the networks they have in place already—they have been very valuable to us."

"Your objectives," I repeated. "Which are?"

She raised her eyebrows. "World peace. Didn't Courtney speak to you?"

"Yeah," I said slowly. "She did mention that."

"Well?" She opened her hands, inviting. "What do you think?"

I factored another integer. What did I think? I thought this wasn't at all how I had expected this interview to go. I had been anticipating—

"'Brainwash' is such an ugly word, Ms. Russell. Come, you're an intelligent person. Why would I waste effort forcing you into something you will so easily see the logic of yourself? All I want is to explain what we do here. Once you understand, I believe you'll want to join us voluntarily."

"You locked us up," I pointed out.

"See it from my perspective," she said reasonably. "You and Mr. Tresting have been operating on the assumption that we're some sort of monstrous conspiracy, when nothing could be further from the truth. I admit you even started causing some trouble for us. I wanted the chance to explain to you what we're truly about."

"And if I don't agree to drink the Kool-Aid, then are you going to let us go?"

"Well, it hardly makes sense to do that if you're going to work against us, does it? Not when our efforts are bettering so many, many lives." She spoke simply, articulately, earnestly. "Ms. Russell, we lift countless people out of poverty and starvation every day. We're bringing down violent crime globally, effecting drastic change in cities that have never known any other reality. We've headed off nuclear crises and tamed dangerous insurgent groups into nothing, made brutal warlords impotent or helped raise up revolutions against them. Millions of people suffer less every day because of what we do—real, tangible people who can work and love and live their lives now—because of us."

I shook my head, trying to dispel her magic, to wrap myself in my internal mathematics and use it to ward off her spell. "You kill people," I reminded her doggedly. "Arthur and his tech guy tied a long list of murders to you. And you *do* brainwash people; I saw what you did to Leena Kingsley, and I'm pretty sure you brainwashed Courtney into killing Kingsley's husband and making it look like a suicide. Oh, and you've tried to kill Arthur and me both. Not the best way to convince me you're all sunshine and rainbows."

Dawna inclined her head. "I won't deny any of that. But I urge you—Ms. Russell, I believe you're intelligent enough to perceive the larger picture. What we do—we use surgical strikes. Precision. One life, compared to the thousands more whom that one execution will save. Or a single government official changing his mind on an issue he doesn't even fully understand, and thus averting tensions that would build to a world war within a year. We find the butterfly that would cause the hurricane, and clip its wings to save millions—can you truly tell me this is wrong?"

"And what gives you the right to decide who lives and who dies?" I challenged her.

"We all have that right, Ms. Russell," she said sadly. "Every one of us. We are only unequal in the power we wield. Pithica has great power, as do I. I and others like me—we divine connections few can, and we have the strength to alter them. If I chose inaction, I would be choosing death for all those people I would otherwise save. Any decision I make condemns some and not others." She leaned forward. "I can see what a rational person you are, Ms. Russell. You must see the logic here, that if I did not step forward, I would be making a choice in favor of all the suffering I could prevent, as surely as if I had caused it myself. So I would instead ask, what would give me the right to refuse that responsibility, when I can help so many?"

"No," I said weakly. My head was spinning. Her philosophy seemed so *logical*, so mathematically correct, but it had to be inconsistent somewhere. It had to be. "No. That can't justify what you do."

She nodded as if she had expected that response. Hell, she probably had. "In that case, I would like to pose a question to you. If you regard aggression as so unjustified for any greater good—forgive me if I beg you to consider an inconsistency." She waited a beat that was almost apologetic before plunging on. "You call us evil, yet you seem to accept the same behavior quite readily in your friend."

I almost laughed. "What are you talking about?" Half of Arthur's problem was that he wasn't willing to be violent *enough*, even in self-defense.

"I was not referring to Mr. Tresting," Dawna corrected gently.

A sudden sick feeling condensed in my stomach, and for the briefest moment my grasp on my internal mathematics wavered. "He's not my friend," I said, ignoring the something in me that didn't like to say it out loud.

"Perhaps not," said Dawna. "But you are his."

The sick feeling intensified. I said nothing.

Dawna seemed to be waiting for something, gazing at me with her eyes slightly narrowed—I ensured my brain was still as occupied as possible with its mundane algorithmic litany, wondering what she sought, what she *saw*—but after a moment of silence she broke the tension and leaned back in her chair. "Ms. Russell, I would like it if you would trust me. I know it does not come easily to you, but perhaps I can help. I beg you, ask me anything. I swear I shall answer you honestly."

I found my voice. "Like it would mean anything, that you promised not to lie."

"True, you have no way of being sure of my word. However," she added, with the slightest hint at a conspiratorial smile, "at least you will know what answer I choose to give you."

Jesus Christ. I stared at her, my mouth dropping open slightly. She knew me better than I knew myself. As much as I was opposed to going along with her on anything, I was constitutionally incapable of not taking her up on such an offer. More information was always more information, no matter how little I trusted the source—after all, I would at least be able to file away the particular answers she chose to give me as the answers Dawna Polk would choose to give me. And that could tell me something, right?

Ridiculous. Was I honestly thinking about trying to match wits with someone who was literally psychic?

And yet, she was offering to tell me anything I wanted, and that meant I had to ask. I had to know.

Oh, hell.

"Fine," I said, redoubling my brain's furious churning through its mental mathematics as I tried to dispel the sinking certainty that I was about to play right into Dawna's hands. I fancied I could feel the ground giving way beneath my feet, but I couldn't stop myself. "To start off with, your high-and-mighty motives are all well and good, but I want to know what kind of game you've been running on me in particular. And why. You say that trying to kill me or locking me up is all for the greater good because I'd make trouble, but you're the one who dragged me into all this in the first place, remember? If you own the cartels, why let someone you've brainwashed into being your pawn get captured by them? And why fake a contact from Rio to hire me to get her back out? It doesn't make any sense."

"Ah. Yes, that needs some explanation. It was not a case of allowing Ms. Polk to be captured so much as it was engineering it."

What? She had set it up?

"Yes. Courtney Polk—bless her, we already had her working for the cartels, and she was perfect for this role. You see, we needed someone who might conveniently be taken captive. And who might conveniently be worthy of rescuing."

Be worthy of . . .

The pieces were starting to come together, even with half my thoughts busy at pointless arithmetic. "It was a test." As I said it, I was sure. "Courtney didn't know it, but she and the cartel, they were all your people all along. You were testing me."

Dawna hesitated, almost as if embarrassed. "No. We, ah, we weren't testing you."

And suddenly I understood. "You were testing Rio."

She inclined her head slightly.

They hadn't cared about me at all; I was only another pawn. Somehow, the game had always been about Rio. "You wanted to see if Rio would rescue her," I said slowly, feeling my way through. "You already knew he was working a cover. And when he didn't . . ."

"You are unusual, Ms. Russell," said Dawna. "You may not be aware of quite how much. The relationship you have with Mr. Sonrio is— well, in point of fact, you are the only person we have found who *has* a relationship with him. When I sent you in after Ms. Polk, we wanted to see how far he would go. For you."

The puzzle was taking shape, fitting together as neatly as the Hamiltonian circuits I had going in the back of my head. "You told the cartel I was coming. You made sure I got caught. I thought it was too convenient."

She smiled at me. "Truth be told, you were far more skilled than we had anticipated. That was when we first started to discuss recruiting you, as well."

"Instead of just having extremely well-armed bikers kill me off afterwards?" I asked pleasantly.

Her color heightened a touch. "I must apologize for that. We mistimed that attack. It was meant to be another gauge of Mr. Sonrio's response to imperiling you."

Right. Though presumably they hadn't much cared if I bit it, either—especially not after I had name-dropped Pithica to Dawna in the coffee shop. "So, all of this. Calling me in the first place. You were—what, studying Rio?"

"Yes."

"And what did you learn?" I asked.

"He surprised us. He let you go."

I raised my eyebrows. "I had to knock him out with a chair." We looked at each other for a second. Dammit. "Fine. If Rio hadn't wanted me to escape, I probably wouldn't have. Okay, then why Rio? Why are you so interested in him?"

She scrutinized me for a hairbreadth before answering. "We need someone like him."

"Seems like you've got your own private army already," I observed.

"Ms. Russell," said Dawna delicately, "I am not sure you are fully aware of Mr. Sonrio's skills. His ability to be effective—it borders on the unrealistic. He has destroyed entire governments. Leveled armies. Found and obliterated terrorist cells the intelligence agencies of several continents were chasing their tails trying to pursue. He has altered the course of nations. A lone man." Her voice was calm, factual, and very serious.

Huh. So that was what Rio did in his spare time. I'd had no idea he was that impressive. I'm not going to lie: I was jealous.

I forced myself to chew over the math of a path problem, and didn't answer.

"He has, on occasion," Dawna continued, "turned his considerable skill set against organizations similar to Pithica. They did not fare well against him." The corners of her mouth turned upward in a shadow of a wry smile. "You can see why we do not want to be his latest target."

"I think the ship's already sailed on that one," I said.

"We are still hoping to change his mind."

Change his mind. Fuck. If Dawna could say one thing with confidence, it was that she could change anyone's mind.

Except—

Wait a minute. If they'd pierced Rio's cover back with the cartel, and had known where he was, then why wasn't he Pithica's obliging tool already? He hadn't known who Dawna was until she'd put the whammy on me; he wouldn't have recognized her as a threat. She could have walked in and done her ESP thing on him without arousing the least suspicion. Unless—I felt my eyes widen.

Dawna smiled at me. "Your deduction is correct. My insights—those that help us relate so well to people—they fail us here. Mr. Sonrio is, as I am sure you know, a special case."

Holy crap. They couldn't control Rio. They couldn't control Rio! *Note to self: To avoid being vulnerable to telepathy, become a psychopath. No, bad plan, Cas.*

"Hence all the experimentation," I breathed. "You were trying to see how he'd react."

"Precisely," said Dawna. "Science would tell us what our intuitions could not."

I cleared my throat, almost afraid to ask. "So, what did science tell you?"

"Our research could fill three textbooks," she said, still smiling. "But I shall give you the short version. Our insights—we see people's emotions. What they feel, what they desire; we see it and empathize with it. Mr. Sonrio's psychology was simply foreign to us before, but we believe we now have a better understanding of him. He is not driven by emotion in the same way as others, but he does have . . . needs."

No. No, no, no, no, no. *Rio's immune. You just said Rio's immune!*

"Ms. Russell, please; you insist on such a dramatic view of us! I assure you, all we wish to do is talk to Mr. Sonrio, as I am talking to you now. Discuss our views with him. His goals are so similar to our own; I think once he sees our point of view, he will agree to a mutually beneficial working relationship."

If they got Rio . . . even discounting the insane accomplishments Dawna claimed he had to his name, I knew what Rio could do, what he was capable of that most people weren't, and it didn't have to do with his skills.

If Pithica got to Rio, I wasn't sure anyone would be able to stop them.

"Ms. Russell," said Dawna, that earnest passion back in her voice, "I know you haven't yet been wholly convinced of our motives here. But don't you think it could only be a good thing for Mr. Sonrio to have another check on his . . . inclinations? You know him—you know we would help him be a better man. As his friend, you must want that."

Like all of Dawna Polk's arguments, it seemed so *reasonable*, such a perfect compromise. But for some reason—perhaps because I'd known and trusted Rio for so long, and it was *Rio* I trusted, not a Pithica-aligned Rio—I couldn't find myself agreeing. I wasn't even sure why.

"You have a very special relationship with him," Dawna observed.

Yes, well, I trusted Rio, which meant I could rely on him, and for his part, he wasn't actively annoyed by me. It was a nice symbiosis. Generous of her to call it a relationship.

For the second time in our chat, Dawna seemed to be waiting for something, but I had no idea what.

I brushed aside my momentary puzzlement and reordered my thoughts on the number field sieve I had going in the background— and the next question I wanted to ask Dawna. "Okay. So you were trying to run psych experiments on Rio and I got caught in the middle. Fine. What about the other group working against you—the international one? What's their game? And what were they looking for at Courtney's house?"

"At Courtney's house? Oh." She thought for a moment. "I do not know for certain what they sought, but at a guess it was a keepsake I gave her. It was something of little importance, but I will admit I led Courtney herself to believe it needed protecting."

"Why?"

"I wanted her to trust me. There are many ways of earning such trust, and granting it yourself is one of them."

Then whatever they'd tossed the cottage for, it was meaningless. A stupid trinket Dawna had given to Courtney to make her feel trusted. "What about Anton Lechowicz? Was Pithica involved in his death?"

"Not to my knowledge. I'm afraid I don't know that name."

"And Reginald Kingsley? Everything in his file?"

Dawna shifted suddenly. "Excuse me." She pulled out a sleek cell phone and examined it briefly. "I apologize, Ms. Russell. I have an urgent matter I must address. Perhaps we can continue this interview later?"

I had so much else I wanted to ask . . . so much more I needed to know . . .

"And I promise I shall give you the chance, the next time we talk," Dawna said with a regretful smile. "Ms. Russell, I have to say, it truly has been enjoyable having this dialogue. It is so rare that I can discuss our goals in so frank a manner with another open-minded person. I hope you'll at least think on what I've said here."

"Oh, I'm sure I'll think about it," I answered. "But don't get your hopes up." The retort felt good. As annoyingly logical as her arguments had been, I had survived our talk and was still instinctively blowing her off. That had to be a good sign, right? And I still had my layer of obfuscating mental arithmetic going, too. Maybe my slight resistance to her was helping.

"You really do have quite a false impression about what we do," Dawna told me with patient exasperation as she stood up. "I assure you, my insights into human nature do not work quite the way you seem to think they do. We just finished a very civil conversation, don't you agree? And you feel no different than you did before."

It was true. I felt a small spike of self-doubt.

"Please question your assumptions about us, Ms. Russell. I don't know where you got such ideas, but we are not the monsters you think we are. We'll speak again shortly."

And with that, Dawna Polk smiled at me and left the library.

twenty-five

"WHAT DID she do?" asked Arthur in a low voice after the guards had—politely, as always—ensconced me back in my cell next to him.

"I'm not sure." I frowned. "She . . . talked to me. And I guess I talked back. We had a conversation." A few hours ago the idea had been terrifying, but it didn't seem so bad anymore. After all, nothing had really happened, had it? I couldn't figure it out.

"What about?" Arthur asked.

"You know, Pithica's out to save the world, all the crap Courtney told us already." I didn't mention Rio. No need to get Arthur on his high horse again.

Arthur leaned back against the wall, staring at the ceiling. "Think it could be true?"

I felt the same spike of niggling self-doubt as during my conversation with Dawna, along with anger at Arthur for reinforcing it. "I don't know," I snapped.

We lapsed into silence. The guards brought food and water. The light didn't change, but I tried to sleep.

The sound of the metal door at the end of the cellblock woke me from a not-quite-doze against the wall. I registered a couple of soft thumps and the clack of rifles against the floor—I jerked awake, scrambling to my feet.

Rio stood in front of my cell like a larger-than-life dream, two black-clad guards sprawled behind him, unconscious or dead. Instead of his tan duster, he wore black fatigues matching the uniform of Dawna's troops, complete with the same assault rifle and sidearm. He pulled a small explosive charge from a pocket of the vest, packed it into the lock on my cell, and took a step back; the lock blew with a pop and a clack of metal, and Rio gave me a friendly jerk of his head as if to say, *Come on already.*

"Him, too," I said as I pushed the cell door back, nodding at Arthur.

Rio glanced at Arthur, then back at me. "He could be theirs by now."

"She never talked to him," I said quickly. "Only—only me. Rio, he's coming with us."

If he had hesitated, I would have started breaking Arthur out myself, but one thing I loved about Rio was that he never wasted time arguing or wavering. Less than five seconds later, Arthur was out as well, and we hurried after Rio down the cellblock. I paused briefly as we stepped over the fallen guards to relieve one of his M4 and sidearm; Arthur did the same with the other body. They were dead, I noticed. Definitely dead.

Rearmed, we followed Rio into the corridor at a quick trot. "Security system?" I asked.

"Compromised," he said. "We should be clear until after we're out."

"Subtle of you," I observed, a little surprised—"subtle" didn't usually describe him.

"This was a trap, Cas," Rio explained without turning back to me. "The Lord's wrath has patience."

Oh, hell. *How could I have been so stupid?*

Dawna had already told me this was all about Rio. Interring us here had nothing to do with me or Arthur or recruiting us to

Pithica—we were only bait to catch their bigger fish. Which meant, fuck, Rio had played right into their hands by coming after me . . .

. . . which, apparently, he knew, and he had figured out a way to get in and out without them realizing the time had come to spring the ambush. I imagined the hammer of Rio's vengeance would fall on this place once we were well away.

Rio unlocked the door to a dim stairway and gestured us down ahead of him, farther into the subbasement. "You have a way out?" asked Arthur nervously. Rio didn't deign to answer him.

We descended two more levels and were heading down another featureless corridor when Rio raised a fist to stop us. "They know I'm here." He had pulled a small device about the size of a cell phone out of a pocket and was examining it. "They have pinpointed us. Three groups closing in." He looked at me. "Are you up for this?"

I hefted the M4, puzzled he had to ask. "Of course."

"Stay here. You'll get in our way," Rio instructed Arthur, tossing me a pouch of grenades.

Arthur tried to sputter something in response, but Rio and I were already charging.

It wasn't even a contest.

There is something beautiful about the high-speed math of a gunfight. I've heard other people opine that gunfights are confusing and disorienting, but to me, they always happen with perfect clarity: every bullet impact leads back to its source, every barrel sweeping through with its own exact trajectory. A firearm can shoot in only one possible direction at a time, after all. I could always see exactly where they aimed, as if the predicted flights of the rounds were visible laser beams, and I could always move fast enough to step easily out of the way.

The M4 pulsed in one hand, Rio's grenades becoming fragmenting islands of destruction as thrown from the other. I fired as I ran, every muscle in my body coordinating in a precision dash to send my projected path leaping between the ever-changing, ever-crossing lines of danger. One shot, one kill.

I had thirty rounds in the M4. I didn't need them all.

Less than a minute later we were striding through the carnage on our way toward another stairwell; I slung the bag with the remaining grenades over my shoulder and redrew my sidearm from where I'd stashed it in my belt, reaching down as we hurried through to snag some spare magazines for the M4 off the bodies.

Arthur picked his way through after us, looking vaguely sick. He stumbled to a halt. "Hey," he called in a hoarse voice. "Hey. We need to stop."

I turned back. "Tresting, what the hell—"

His words came out strangled. "She's going to obliterate the whole building."

I looked at him blankly. Looked, and noticed he had a cellular phone in his hand.

A phone. When had Arthur gotten a phone? I hadn't seen him pull one from any of the guards. . . .

He held it out to Rio. "She wants to talk to you."

Rio's face was unreadable. "Ah," he said. "I see."

"I'm sorry," Arthur whispered to me. The hand holding the phone was shaking. "So sorry."

Horror shorted out my brain. "No," I said. *"No."*

"Cas—" tried Rio.

"You've been working for them this whole time?" I cried.

"No—it's not like that—"

"You betrayed us!" My M4 swung to point at Arthur. "You—!"

Rio placed a cautious hand on my weapon, shifting it off-line. "Cas, it isn't his fault. Dawna Polk did talk to you, didn't she," he said to Arthur.

"I'm sorry," he said again, wretchedly. "I'm sorry, Russell."

I had to restrain myself from hitting him.

"Give me the phone," said Rio. He hit a button and held the phone out in front of us, raising his voice slightly. "Go ahead."

I recognized Dawna Polk's mellifluous voice on the speaker immediately. "I must say I'm impressed."

Rio was silent.

"You evaded extensive security measures. We only knew you were here thanks to our friendship with Mr. Tresting."

I wanted to scream.

"I hope you know that is a vast compliment, Mr. Sonrio. We were extremely prepared for your visit, and you still slipped in undetected. Mr. Tresting's involvement was a contingency we never thought we would have to use. May I ask how you infiltrated us so effectively?"

"I'm certain you shall figure it out eventually," said Rio evenly.

"As it seems you are also more effective than even we expected at evading capture by our people—"

I snorted.

"—we have been forced into our endgame rather abruptly."

"Annihilation of your own base," confirmed Rio. "Quite cold of you, Miss Saio."

There was a short silence on the other end. "I'm sure you understand," Dawna said after a beat. "You have been causing us a great deal of trouble. We would strongly prefer to talk you out of it, but failing that, we must cut our losses. I would regret the collateral damage, but it would be a fair trade for putting an end to the difficulties you insist on giving us."

"You flatter me," said Rio.

"Modesty does not become you, Mr. Sonrio," she responded, a hint of a smile in her voice.

"Let Cas go." I looked up at him in surprise. So did Arthur. Rio's expression was as blank and flat as ever. "Let Cas go, and I shall enter your custody willingly."

"I apologize if you were under the impression that this was a negotiation," answered Dawna. "Please disarm yourselves and exit the building. All three of you. If not . . . well. I admit I do not know the technical details, but my advisers assure me nothing will survive the blast, not in a wide radius. I recommend you don't take too long to decide." She hung up.

"She could be bluffing," I suggested weakly, not believing it myself.

"She could be," said Rio, "but I would not doubt Pithica has the resources for such a move, however extreme. I suggest we operate under the assumption that she can and will carry out her threat."

"What now, then?"

"She has outmaneuvered us. I believe we do as she asks."

"You can't turn yourself over to her!" I cried.

"Cas," he said, putting a hand on my shoulder. "Trust in God's plan."

Nausea rolled through me. If God had planned this, He shouldn't have been put in charge of anything, ever.

·.·˙·.·˙·.·˙

THEY SEPARATED Rio from us almost immediately and stuck Arthur and me together in one cell this time, back on our old cellblock. I refused to look at him.

"I'm sorry, Russell," Arthur tried again pleadingly once the guards had left us. One of them had taken up a post at the door, as before. The dead bodies were gone.

"The hell you are," I bit out. I had been the one to insist he come with us. Rio and I might have made our escape if he hadn't inter-fered. *Or maybe Dawna just would have brought the building down on top of us.* I pushed that thought away. "What did she offer you? Did she promise you money? A place in her new world order?"

He choked. "It's not like that. She just—she *explained*. They needed you, but they promised not to hurt you, I swear."

"What are you talking about?"

"I don't know if Pithica's right, or if it—I don't know any more than you do," he said, anguished. "Could be they're not right or wrong. But some things aren't gray in this world, Russell—some things aren't gray."

He wasn't making sense. "Yeah, she brainwashed you," I said sar-castically. "Seeing it now." It didn't make me any less angry.

"No, I'm telling you," Tresting implored me. "That's not what—"

"When did she even talk to you?" I snapped.

He looked even more stricken.

The question had been offhand, irritated, but then realization hit me like a pile driver.

They needed you, but they promised not to hurt you, I swear. And: *Nothing here. Searched the place top to bottom.* How did an extremely observant private investigator miss Dawna's paramilitary army?

"Son of a bitch," I whispered. Dawna had gotten to Tresting back in the town. Of course she had. Obvious, so obvious, and yet I hadn't even considered the possibility, because Dawna had made sure I wouldn't.

She'd made Tresting lead us both into her hands in the first place. She'd found the buttons to push in his psyche within hours by playing on . . . what? *Some things aren't gray in this world, Russell—some things aren't gray.*

"You son of a bitch," I growled. "You were trying to help her get Rio."

"Russell," he begged, "I had to help—the man is—"

I did hit him then, so hard his head whipped around and his body smashed against the bars on the far side of the cell. Then I turned and gripped the iron bars in front of me as hard as I could so I wouldn't turn back and kill him.

He might not have been able to prevent Dawna from getting into his head, but he'd made it easy as hell for her. All because he wanted Rio dead just that damn badly.

They left us in the cell for days. I couldn't help wondering what Dawna still wanted with us—hadn't we only been her bait to entrap Rio? Maybe she'd kill us when she got around to it, or maybe she did want to recruit us for real, but was prioritizing her bigger catch.

I thought a lot about what she'd said about Pithica working for the greater good. I still didn't know what to believe, but it didn't much matter to me right now. She had Rio, and that decided me; I'd be damned if I would let my doubts about whether Pithica was all right as an organization keep me from backing him up and getting us out of here.

Unfortunately, every idea I thought of to break out came up short computationally. With the guard at the end of the cellblock, anything I tried would have to be fast enough to avoid being shot, and in order to neutralize the guard first I'd need something both of sufficient mass and small enough to throw. Every option I thought of I had already considered, calculated, and discarded during our first round in here. Too bad I hadn't known about Arthur's secret mobile phone before, I thought sarcastically. A phone would have made a perfect projectile.

Whatever. Eventually there would come some change, some break. Dawna would bring me to talk to her again, or one of the guards would have a bout of laziness, or something else would happen, and when the window of opportunity hit, I would be ready.

Three days after Rio's abortive rescue attempt, Dawna Polk came to see us. She stood in front of our cell and spoke to me as courteously as she always did. I'd slammed my walls of mathematical white noise back up, although at this point I wasn't sure they were doing any good; she never seemed bothered.

This time was no exception. Her mind appeared to be concentrated wholly on whatever she was here about; she barely made eye contact. "Ms. Russell," she said, very formally and with no hint of irony, "I want to apologize for what is about to happen here."

"What's that supposed to mean?" I asked. "Are you finally going to kill us?"

"I'm not a sadist," said Dawna quietly, avoiding the question. "I want you to know I sincerely regret doing this to you."

Arthur edged forward. I ignored him; we hadn't exchanged three words in as many days. "What's going on?" he asked. He had taken hold of the bars and gripped them like he planned to dent them. "You promised not to hurt her. You promised."

Huh. Brainwashed-Arthur's primary motive might be getting Rio offed, but he was still concerned about my welfare, such as it was. Who knew.

Dawna nodded to the PI. "I did say that. I'm afraid it cannot be helped. My apologies to you, as well."

"You can't—you swore to me—" Tresting's eyes darted around like a cornered animal's. "Take me instead," he offered suddenly. I blinked at him in shock. I hadn't realized he was *that* concerned. Or was this his "all life is valuable" shtick? Whatever the reason, Tresting was hyperventilating, tension cording his body. "Whatever you're planning, whatever you need someone for, take me instead," he implored Dawna. "I did this, my doing, I—leave her out of it. Please."

"Unfortunately, that is not possible." She turned back to me. "You, Ms. Russell, are the anomaly, so it is you we must use for our test. I do apologize, once again."

The anomaly. She was talking about Rio—and my relationship with him was her anomaly. "You think you have him," I whispered, suddenly cold. "You think you found a way."

She inclined her head. "For which I must thank you. His belief in God was the key to our understanding. No one else might have known such a thing about him."

"I never mentioned that," I croaked.

She smiled pityingly. "Oh, Ms. Russell, you know who I am. You didn't need to." Of course. "Mr. Sonrio has indeed agreed to work for us," she continued. "I did expect it would come to that, considering the vast overlap in our mutual goals, but it was you who put us on the right track, so again, thank you, Ms. Russell. I believe we shall be able to satisfy his . . . needs, and the good he will do with us will save so many lives."

Tresting made a strangled sound. "Wait. You wanted him to *work for you?*"

I wanted to laugh in his face, even though I had never felt less amused. "What, she didn't tell you? She doesn't want to keep Rio from going around killing people, she wants to harness him for herself. Why did you think they wanted him alive?"

"I thought—" His face froze in horror. Oh, the irony. He'd been expecting Dawna to stop Rio, not recruit him. Well, wasn't this funny, in a way that made me want to scream.

Dawna ignored him. "I hope you will be comforted, in the end," she continued to me, "to think of the good your friend will be doing with us, and the part you have played in it. But I hope you understand— we do have to be sure."

"You mean you still can't read him," I translated. "You're trying to make sure you control him, but you can't read him. And I'm the only person he's had a predictable response to."

"'Control' is such an ugly word," said Dawna. "Instead let us say, we must be certain he is truly on our side. I *am* sorry."

"And if he isn't on your side?" I challenged her.

"Oh, I doubt that will be the case, Ms. Russell. But if he is not, then . . . well. In that case it would be time to cut our losses. So if it helps, you can also be comforted by your friend being spared by your sacrifice."

"You twisted woman!" Tresting cried, finding his voice. "*Twisted*—I can't—I believed you!"

Dawna smiled at him. "Rest assured, Mr. Tresting, if I have time or inclination, I am sure I can bring you around to our point of view again quite easily. We are doing what's best, after all."

"I will never trust another word you say," declared Tresting hotly.

A thread of frustration entered Dawna's voice. "Oh, of course you will. For goodness' sake, you would come back to us in a heartbeat as soon as I—" She stopped and put a hand to her temple. "I am so sorry, Mr. Tresting. It's been a trying few days. I assure you, this must be done, but we can discuss it afterwards. Would you prefer to be in another room?"

"No," growled Arthur.

"As you wish," said Dawna. She nodded to both of us, her composure back in place. "I shall return shortly."

Arthur rounded on me. "Oh, God," he cried frenziedly. "Oh, God. What's she gonna do?"

I had thought it obvious. "She's going to have Rio kill me."

Arthur froze.

"Well, there might be some torture first or something, but only if Dawna has the stomach to ask for it."

He threw up.

twenty-six

"THIS IS my fault," Arthur kept mumbling, doubled over and retching. "I—she convinced me, oh, Lord—I *listened*—why did I listen? Oh, God, I trusted her—"

"At least we know that once our lovely Dawna Polk seduces someone, she can shove him back the other way if she wants to," I said. "Congratulations, it looks like you've been unbrainwashed. Though if you ever sell out Rio again, I will fucking kill you."

His expression was stricken. I wasn't even sure he heard me.

I sighed. "Besides, shouldn't I be the one who gets to freak out here? All you're doing is having a guilt complex meltdown. I think the impending death thing trumps that."

"How can you be—you're cracking jokes?" He sounded broken.

"What would you like me to do?" I asked. "Panic?"

To be honest, I wasn't sure why I wasn't panicking. If Dawna had gotten to Rio, well, then he would kill me. But as soon as I had realized the implication of her words, it was as if she'd explained she wanted to set pi equal to three on pain of death and expected me to take it seriously.

I trusted Rio. I trusted him completely. So Dawna telling me he would kill me was like insisting in perfect seriousness that black was white, or one equaled two, or the theorems in Euclidean geometry didn't follow from the axioms. And given her skills, she could probably get me to believe any one of those before she would ever convince me Rio would kill me. The idea didn't compute. And as if the very thought had caused an unending error message in my brain, I didn't feel any reaction to it at all.

The door at the end of the cellblock opened again, and Dawna reentered, this time with Rio behind her. He still wore the same black fatigues and had his hands cuffed in front of him, but he walked normally and to my relief appeared uninjured. Behind them crowded in six of Dawna's troops, all with their weapons trained on Rio. Dawna wasn't taking chances: if Rio refused to kill me, she had already said she would finally write him off, and I fully believed she would have her troops drop him with neither delay nor remorse.

Arthur sidestepped in front of me.

What the hell? "What are you doing?" I demanded.

"I gave us up to her," he said, his face a rictus of desperate guilt. "I did. I thought—doesn't matter. Russell, this is my doing, and they aren't killing you without doing me first."

I rolled my eyes and swung an arm into his solar plexus.

He literally flew off his feet and collapsed against the barred partition on the other side of the cell, wheezing mightily but nicely out of my way. "Being stupidly heroic is just going to get you killed," I told him, and then proceeded to ignore him. I needed to concentrate.

We had arrived at a moment in flux, a moment for my window of escape to open and for me to smash our way out of here. The variables were fluctuating, and Rio had arrived to back me up. I would find a way out, and I would find it now.

The six troops stayed alert and trained on Rio, and Dawna was watching him closely too, not looking toward Arthur or me. Rio wasn't quicker than a bullet, not with six M4s already aimed at him, but if he had a sufficient distraction . . .

"Hello, Cas," he said.

"Hi, Rio," I answered. Muzzle velocity, the troopers' reaction times . . . all too fast, still too fast. Dammit.

"Cas, you know what I have to do, don't you?"

Rio could take six men, but not if he started out handcuffed and in all their sights. And trapped on the other side of the bars, no matter how we played it I would need a few seconds' delta before I would be able to escape and help him. If he attacked Dawna or her troops, we would all die. I looked, and did the math, and looked again, but no matter how I jigsawed every equation, I found no window, no opening.

Impossible. How had this happened? I always had options. Always. I did every equation again, reset my reference frames, and did them once more. Nothing. We had no way forward except one.

Rio had to shoot me.

Fuck.

"Cas?" said Rio.

"Yes," I said. The word came out choked. "I know."

"It would be my preference not to harm you," Rio said quietly.

"It's okay," I whispered. I kept searching desperately, but the values surrounding us were steadying, reaching a new equilibrium in which everything came up checkmate. Mathematically, we had no other choice.

Oh, Jesus, I wished we did.

Dawna pulled out a revolver and handed it to Rio—.38 Special, it looked like. Rio took it between cuffed hands and opened the cylinder. "One round," he observed.

Dawna said nothing. We all knew he would not need more.

He snapped the cylinder closed again, drew the hammer back, and lifted the gun. Even cuffed, his hands folded sure and firm around the grip, and the barrel stayed rock steady as it leveled its deadly blackness with my heart. My eyes tracked it, measured, the numbers snapping into place.

I didn't have time to prepare myself. I took a deep breath, looked into the tiny yawning bore of the gun, shifted minutely, and met Rio's eyes. He gave me a slight nod, a barely visible movement of his head.

And fired.

The explosion of the gunshot was deafening, louder than any gunshot I'd ever heard. Everything seesawed, vibrating and melting. I was staring at the ceiling. I was on the floor. How had I gotten on the floor?

Someone was shouting, and a dark, frantic face swam above me. And then something welled up inside me, a burning swell, taking all other sensation with it—*pain*—

"I am pledged to your cause," said Rio's voice, remote and irrelevant. Someone answered him, but I couldn't hear what she said, and it didn't seem important.

The pain surged, unimaginable, overwhelming—it rose up and enveloped me, smothering; I drowned in its red clouds until it was all I could see, all I could feel—

A hand slapped at my face. I barely felt it. The air wobbled, waving in long, slow frequencies that collided and blurred. Someone was hitting me. I tried to tell him to stop, but my mouth didn't work.

"Russell, come on, girl! Stay with me!"

Not going anywhere. The thought amused me for some reason, but things weren't working well enough for me to laugh.

Somewhere, either close by or far away, or possibly both, I heard movement. A voice gave directions, and people started breaking up, moving around. Dawna dismissing her troops, a final thread of lucidity in me knew. The shadows moved and mutated as they shifted away.

And then everything exploded in a cacophony of noise.

It was thunderous, terrible, threatening to pull me under. Gunfire shattered the air, each blast erupting through my whole head, and too much light, and people shouting and screaming and crashing and breaking, and a woman's scream, and my head felt like it burst apart and the world fractured and spun, tearing me apart with inertial force. . . .

The ground fell away. Someone was lifting me. I tried to fight back, but I couldn't, and then the pain blazed up and shattered me again, redoubling, whiting out everything else.

I wasn't aware of much more after that; I blinked in and out of consciousness. I caught vague sensations of being carried, of rapid movement, of jerking to a stop and several voices shouting. Every new slice of awareness layered on another spasm of agony, until my thoughts stuttered incoherently like a badly tuned radio, the screeching overwhelming any other sound until I wanted only to turn it off—

The floor vibrated now. The air, too—so loud it shook me apart, and I wondered if this was what death felt like until the word "helicopter" floated through the strands of pain. Then time skipped again and the vibration of a different vehicle rumbled through me, a car, and two men were arguing, shouting: *You shot her!* and *She aimed for me* and *I don't expect you to understand.* And part of my brain heard Rio's voice and thought, *Good, he got it!* even though if he hadn't, I wouldn't have been alive to think those words.

The next time I wavered to semiconsciousness I was lying still, on something soft, and I could tell I was very, very drugged. I struggled for a moment against the layers of mental wool before giving up; the warmth of unconsciousness hovered right below me, beckoning me back.

Arthur's face swam into view. I had just enough awareness to think, *Huh, weird,* before the world melted away again.

twenty-seven

MY SENSES stayed foggy for a long time. I kept seeing Arthur's face during my intermittent spurts of consciousness, which my brain still thought was strange, but eventually it adapted. Rio was around, too. I became vaguely aware of Arthur making a fuss about letting Rio near me, which didn't make any sense. Rio and I went way back. Arthur must not know that.

He also must have forgotten how Rio had saved all of our lives. And had kept his hand steady, which had saved me. If he weren't such a good shot, shooting exactly where I aimed . . . the thought struck me as funny. I started to giggle, but it hurt too much.

Odd that Arthur would forget all that; he'd been there.

Occasionally I registered the presence of a third person, a middle-aged black woman who must have been a doctor. I tried to push her away the first time I figured out she was there, but I didn't think the signals even made it out of my brain.

Time seemed slippery, too much of an effort to hold on to. Half the time I thought I was awake but then realized reality wasn't Hausdorff, and what kind of topology was I in anyway if Twinkies were allowed? And the totient function was a rainbow, a beautiful rainbow and the greatest mathematical discovery of all time, but if you put a Möbius strip in the fourth dimension could a rabbit still hop down the side?

I became more lucid slowly; maybe they were weaning me off the drugs, but I stopped thinking I was the next Erdős every time penguins waddled through my dreams on a four-colored map. I slept or floated, the world still foggy but solid now, which was a vast improvement over it being wibbly.

The disorientation cleared enough once for me to see Rio's face as he changed my dressing. His movements were swift and certain, and his lips moved in the whispered litany of a prayer.

"Rio," I slurred. "You're a good friend."

"I'm not your friend, Cas," he said quietly. "You know that. Don't ever think otherwise."

I did know. Friends cared about you. But friends also knew you well enough to communicate without words, and did things like save your life and then stay by your side and take care of you while you were injured. Did it matter that Rio didn't care about me, as long as he acted like he did, and always would? Did it matter that he did it for other reasons, for his own grand religious reasons, instead of because he felt any sort of affection for me?

Plenty of people were generous and kind and giving only because they thought it was the way of God. They were still good people. What was friendship, after all?

I slipped back to sleep.

The first time I woke enough to have a real conversation, Arthur was back. "Hi," I rasped.

He was instantly attentive. "Hey, Russell. How are you feeling?"

"Fuzzy," I answered. "Where's Rio?"

His lip twitched. "Out."

"You still don't like Rio?" I frowned at him, trying to string the right words together. "He saved all our lives. He saved *me*. Again."

"He shot you!" burst out Arthur.

"Because I told him to." How could he not get it? "I knew I could line up a nonlethal shot."

"A nonlethal—! Russell, do you have any idea how gunshots

work?" He took a deep breath and visibly calmed himself. "That was absolutely, positively a lethal shot. Any gunshot can be lethal. You get hit in the leg, it can kill you." His voice cracked. "Russell, he shot you in the chest and you almost died, and if the bullet hadn't bounced and missed your heart—"

"I *made* it bounce," I told him thickly. "It bounced 'cause I told it to."

Arthur looked like he wanted to cry.

I ended up drifting off again at that point, but the next time I opened my eyes, feeling a good deal more alert, Arthur was still beside me, almost as if he hadn't moved. It was kind of creepy. "How are you feeling?" he asked immediately. "Up to eating something?"

"Don't you have a job?" I said.

"Pithica was the only case I was working on."

I couldn't help thinking it strange that he kept hanging around. The last I remembered, we'd been at each other's throats and he'd been swinging between trying to get Rio sold into slavery and having a massive guilt breakdown over getting me killed. "You don't have to be here," I told him. "You can go if you want."

"I'm not going to leave you alone with a . . . with someone who shot you," he said darkly.

I started to sigh, but it hurt too much. They'd taken more of the drugs away, I realized. "We've been over this," I said. "It was the plan."

"Getting yourself shot is not a plan."

"It allowed Rio to get us out of there," I argued. "Any other option would have gotten one of us killed."

"This one almost did get you killed!"

"But it didn't." He was making me tired, and my whole body ached. "You said something about food," I reminded him, even though I wasn't hungry.

Arthur hurried off to make me some soup, and I fell back to sleep.

When I finally woke again I was starving, but Arthur wasn't in his usual spot next to me. I could hear his voice, though; I looked over to see him on the other side of the room, leaving a quiet but intense voice mail for someone.

I pushed myself up a few inches and looked around. I was in a spacious studio apartment, and not one I recognized; it must have been Arthur's or Rio's. An IV stand stood beside my bed, with a long clear tube that wound around until it ended in a catheter taped into the back of my hand. On the way it passed over a crumpled pillow and blanket on the floor—someone had been sleeping close enough to keep an eye on me. Probably Arthur. Jesus.

The man in question hung up the phone and saw I was awake. "Hey. You're looking better."

"I'm feeling better," I said. "What's been happening? I take it we got away clean?"

"Your, uh, your *buddy* got us out—he took out the troops and took Dawna Polk hostage. Turns out she's so valuable we managed to swing trading up to get out. I got the impression only a handful of 'em can do the mental jazz; they didn't want to lose her."

"I suppose she's one of Pithica's higher-ups, then, huh."

"Yeah," he said, sounding unsure and unhappy.

"So you let her go?"

"Your friend was the one calling the shots, but not much choice on that one."

"He's not my friend," I said automatically.

Arthur made a face. "What, then? He owes you money? You owe him money? I can't figure it out!"

"Then ask when you can tell me why it's any of your business." There wasn't a chance in hell I would tell him how Rio and I had met. That wasn't his to know.

The apartment door opened at that moment and Rio himself came in. He was back in his customary tan duster, and water slicked the mantle in dark patches. Apparently it was raining outside—I couldn't hear it. It made me wonder how long I'd been out; the rainy season in Los Angeles doesn't usually start until December or January, though sometimes it was months earlier.

"Hello, Cas," Rio greeted me when he saw I was sitting up. "How do you feel?"

"Like I've been shot," I answered.

He nodded. "Understandable, given the circumstances."

Arthur threw up his hands in what I could only have described as flailing.

"But I'm getting better," I told Rio, ignoring Arthur. I felt more energetic, and I was awake, which was a change, and the numbers surrounding me weren't quite as sluggish as they had been, and I knew the answer to how fast I was metabolizing the drugs, so things were looking up.

"Thanks be to God," said Rio. He came over and checked the IV bags hanging above my head.

I thought the thanks were due to Rio, myself—oh, all right, Arthur too—but I was sensitive enough to Rio's beliefs that I didn't say it out loud. Instead I said, "I heard you made a daring rescue." Arthur mumbled something about getting me food and retreated to the kitchen area at the far side of the room.

"It was not hard once you provided the opportunity," answered Rio.

"Dawna Polk's that important, huh?"

"The people with her skills are the core of Pithica. They are rare and precious to the organization. It is their greatest resource weakness."

I mulled over that tidbit of information. In hindsight, this meant I might not have needed Rio's help at all. I could have taken Dawna hostage in her library without blinking. Heck, I could have taken her hostage back at the town where they had first captured us. Why hadn't I at least tried? All I could remember thinking was that they had Arthur and therefore I had no other options. . . .

"I could have gotten us out," I blurted.

"No," said Rio.

"I could have. I had plenty of opportunities around Dawna—"

"Do not fault yourself, Cas. She can make herself safe from anybody."

Oh. Right. I never would have considered attacking Dawna as an option because she had made sure I didn't think of it. I wondered if I'd had other escape options, too. It was hard to think back; I'd been so certain at the time.

Rio pulled up the chair that Arthur usually occupied. "You said before that she talked to you. Will you tell me what about?"

Well. At least she hadn't mind-zapped me during that part. I kind of wished she had—it would make my doubts easier to swallow. "She talked about Pithica," I admitted softly. "How it's all because they want to make people's lives better. How they want to make the world all peaceful and wonderful for everyone."

"Did you believe her?"

I picked at the blanket across my knees. "I'm not sure."

"I see," he said.

"She didn't brainwash me," I insisted. "It wasn't like that. I remember everything. She just . . . she had a lot of really logical arguments."

"Cas," said Rio, "she had logical arguments for you because you respond to logical arguments."

I was confused. "What other type would someone respond to?"

"It's clear you don't often converse with other people," said Rio with a hint of irony.

"Oh, and you do?"

"Touché," he said. "Cas, she used the method of argument that would most appeal to you. With another she might have used emotional appeal, or irrelevant facts, or fallacies of any stripe."

He was missing the point. "It doesn't matter what she would use on anyone else," I said. "She *had* logical arguments. The logic in them doesn't go away just because she wouldn't have mentioned it to someone-not-me."

"She had what *seemed like* logical arguments," Rio corrected. "People can pretend to logic to perpetrate almost any reality."

"Except when you dig deep enough, that kind of 'logic' always has deductive flaws," I contested hotly. "This was different. I think I would know."

"Are you so sure?" asked Rio.

"Of course I'm sure! I'm perfectly capable of differentiating—"

I stopped. Rio was smiling.

"What are you laughing at?" I asked crossly.

"We can keep going until you call me names again," he said.

My brain screeched to a halt. I had been getting steamed up at him again, and for no reason except—"Oh," I mumbled. "Sorry." I buried my face in one hand. The familiar—and suddenly welcome—thudding of a headache started up in the back of my skull. "She did get to me, didn't she."

"Only in the incipient stages. If you keep out of their way from now on, it will be of no consequence. If they cannot find you, they cannot do anything. Will you stay off the case this time?"

But she had logical arguments. She had logical arguments! Was there a flaw? Could I find it?

Rio, though not psychic, seemed to know what I was thinking. "Cas. It is much more difficult to apply logic to morality than you sometimes believe it to be."

"That's stupid," I muttered, but without any vitriol, and without any real belief behind the words. "You should be able to axiomatize everything. How else can you know right from wrong?"

Rio was smiling again. "If you're asking me personally, you know how. *Sumasampalataya ako sa iyong tsarera.*"

"What does that mean?" He didn't answer me, but I knew already. "God's not my thing," I said.

"It doesn't matter," he countered. "Whether you believe or not, it remains that there are no mortal answers to these questions, and any claimant thereof must therefore lie." He sounded so calm. So sure.

I'd never talked philosophy with Rio before. I had always assumed his blind faith meant he hadn't given it much thought and he would parrot Bible verses as his version of argument . . . but apparently I was wrong.

The pending migraine notwithstanding, I started feeling better about my tangled feelings regarding Pithica as an organization. I was less sure than ever of the right answer, but if Rio was correct and a right answer might not even exist, then I didn't have to plunge wholesale after where Dawna's logic led. At least not right away.

"Thanks," I mumbled. I realized something. "You think Pithica's pretty bad, don't you?"

"Yes."

"Why?"

"Cas, the Lord could force us all to peace and righteousness if He wished to. Our world would have no war, no pain. Instead, He gave us free will."

Huh. That wasn't a bad way of looking at it. "But you could argue that Dawna's using her free will," I pointed out. "Even if it's to take away other people's."

"And like all those who use their freedom to harm others, she sins in doing so."

"Oh." I mulled that over. Because Rio was the only religious person I knew, I tended to forget that mass murder wasn't supposed to be in the playbook. Except . . . Dawna was doing the exact same thing Rio did: hurting people to make the world a better place. "But what about what you do? I thought—your God . . ."

"Cas, I am a condemned man in the eyes of the Lord," he said. "I have sinned far too gravely."

Shock rippled through me. Rio believed in God and also believed that he was going to go straight to hell? "But you . . ." Words failed me.

"Do not think me such a tragic figure, Cas. I am too weak to my baser desires. The least I can do is use them to do God's work."

I was stunned. Not that I believed in heaven or hell myself, but the fact that Rio did and still thought no matter how faithful he was, the former was closed to him—I couldn't imagine living that way.

Rio had given me a lot to think about. It was so strange—Dawna had seemed so *right,* her logic absolutely inescapable. Rio had only brought up more questions, and not even entirely consistent ones, and if possible everything was less clear than it had been and I was developing a killer headache to boot, but at least I knew the muddy snarl was my own thoughts on the matter.

"Did our friend Miss Polk discuss anything else with you?" Rio asked.

"Not really. Mostly she just offered to answer my questions."

Rio looked far more serious about that than I would have expected. "I see," he said again.

And the realization blazed through me, viscerally painful, my recovering wound hot with agony and every nerve ending on fire. By asking her questions . . . by asking her questions, *I had been willingly telling Dawna everything she wanted to know.* I had asked about what I had thought was important, and in asking about it, I had thought about it, and in thinking about it . . . Jesus Christ, if she had let me keep going, I would have asked her about *everything,* given away the smallest detail of everything I knew, as far back as I could remember.

But she hadn't been interested in any of that. She had stopped our session even though I was still ready to spill a lot more than I already had. Thinking back, I realized with horror that she had taken the time to converse with me on only one topic: Rio. She had turned the conversation toward him at the very beginning, and then taken all the information I had.

"Oh, God," I said. "I—I'm so sorry. Rio, she only wanted to talk about you—" Dawna was a bloody *psychic;* I had given away every last morsel I knew about Rio in that conversation; I was sure of it. Tresting's treachery was nothing compared to what I had done. "I told her . . . I told her—" I was so *stupid.* The only person in the world I could trust, and I had spilled my guts about him at the first opportunity.

"Cas, calm yourself," said Rio. "I expected that. I do not think you could have given away anything of harm to me. Take me back through what you spoke of, as nearly as you can remember."

"It doesn't matter," I said desperately. Why couldn't he hate me? "She's a mind reader! She got everything!"

Rio raised his eyebrows. "She had me her prisoner and could not use anything you gave her to any effect. What does that tell you?"

It didn't matter whether she had hurt him with it; I had still betrayed him. I turned away.

Rio sighed, the barest susurration of breath. "I promise you it is of no consequence to me. Melodrama does not suit you, Cas."

Melodrama? I had just proved myself completely untrustworthy, and he was calling it *melodrama*?

"In fact, considering why I am insusceptible to her influence, had you been able to resist her, you would now have a far more significant worry."

I still felt wretched, but that almost got a laugh out of me.

"Now, humor me, Cas. Take me through your discussion with her. I don't believe there is any cause for concern."

twenty-eight

Now that I was awake, the hours passed slowly. I discovered I detested convalescing. It was extremely boring. The one saving grace was that I was still technically on a job, at least enough to satisfy my messed-up brain. Despite my discussion with Rio about what had gone down with Dawna, I still hadn't talked to him or Arthur about what our next step would be regarding Pithica.

Of course, Rio still wanted me off the case. Ordinarily someone else's objections wouldn't have stopped me, but I had a sneaking thread of suspicion that he was right, that dealing with Pithica truly was out of my league. I'd never felt that way before, and I didn't like it.

Presumably, Rio was still going after Dawna himself, but he wasn't telling us about it. Arthur, meanwhile, was mired in some sort of guilty cognitive dissonance between what Dawna had convinced him of at first and what she had inherently convinced him of later by trying to have me killed in front of him, and seemed perfectly content to hover over me as I recovered. He spent a lot of time on his phone, too, though I never heard him reach anyone.

As for me, I decided to defer my decision on what to do about Pithica. If I could fool my brain for a while longer into thinking I was still working, that was fine by me. I still couldn't figure out if I wanted to charge after Dawna Polk with everything I had or run as far away as possible and hope she never found me. Not to mention that some part of me still thought her logic might be right and Pithica might be a pinnacle of moral rectitude and I should do everything I could to help them. It was confusing. And I got a headache whenever I tried to think about it seriously.

Rio had given me a secure laptop to use, and I spent the hours reading up on the latest papers in recursion theory to give me something to focus on. It was marginally interesting.

On the fourth day after I'd woken up and been able to keep track of time effectively again, I remembered my email and went to sign in. I didn't use email much. The only person I talked to about anything other than business was Rio, and he was strictly a phone person. The only thing I used email for was to get messages about potential jobs, though most of the people who knew to contact me did it via a permanent voice-mail box. Likewise, I used email more as a message drop than for anything else.

I did have three overtures for possible work, all old clients or people who had been referred by old clients, which was how most people found me. Two looked dead boring, the other only vaguely intriguing, but at least they would keep me busy if I ducked off Pithica. Provided I stayed in LA, I thought—I might have to go back to considering a disappearing act if I decided to run. My autoresponder had already taken care of the "on a case, will reply shortly" messages and none of the circumstances sounded urgent, but I took the time to dash off replies anyway, telling them that I was currently busy with a job but that I was potentially interested and would be in touch.

That left one message, from an address I didn't recognize. I clicked on it, frowning a little. It was encrypted. I passed my public key around to anyone who wanted it, but I didn't know many people who would have sought it out, let alone used it. I decrypted the text—and my whole body went cold, like a ghost had reached out and touched my soul.

The message was from Anton.

All I could do was stare at it. The seconds ticked by, and I still stared. First of all, Anton never sent email. Despite being a professional information broker and probably owning more computers than I had guns, he had been something of a Luddite when it came to living in the modern world. He hadn't even had a mobile phone. I always picked up a folder full of printouts from him in person, and though I had always assumed part of that had to do with much of his information coming from places that weren't accessible via clickable URLs, I also figured Anton simply liked dealing with the world through landlines and hard copies.

Second of all, he was dead.

That part was still true. I looked at the time stamp and thought back, then shivered—he'd sent this less than three minutes before the first explosion had gone off.

I finally took a deep breath and read the words. The email was only one line long:

penny's real excited. wants me to send you this right quick. her find.
—anton
p.s. "p" = "pithica" we think

One file was attached. I opened it. I felt like my fingers should be shaking, but they were perfectly steady.

The file was text only, and looked like a response to someone:

```
To: 29814243
Re: Missing flash drive
    >>his wife, he must have had an unbreakable hid-
ing place. Lost cause at this point?
    All sources verify P. has not found it. If they are
still searching, so are we.
    H. suggests it may have been removed from the scene
but not handed over. Unlikely, but the zombies they
use, it's possible. Pursue that line. Let's hope it
was a blind spot.
```

The beginnings of adrenaline had started tingling through me. I read the message again. The mention of a wife . . . could that mean . . . ?

"Arthur," I called. He was next to me in a flash; I tried not to roll my eyes. "Arthur, was anything missing from Kingsley's crime scene?"

"Yeah. He had a USB drive he always wore around his neck, but they never found it. Was one of the things that made the whole thing weird—the doc said he never took it off."

The email was definitely talking about Kingsley, then, and he'd had a flash drive with . . . something . . . on it, and Pithica had been going crazy trying to find it. And apparently so had someone else, whoever had written this message. . . .

My thoughts constricted in horror. As far as we knew, the only other group working against Pithica was Steve's. And he had as good as told us that they would obliterate anyone who found out about them in order to protect themselves from Pithica.

Oh, God. Anton.

Penny.

"I found the drive, you know," said Arthur morosely. "Too bad it was useless."

It took my brain several seconds to catch up with his words, and then I cried, "You *what?*"

"Found it. In Polk's house, once I tracked down she was the killer. Was only a few weeks ago."

"What was on it?"

"Couldn't tell; it was all coded up. But it's useless."

"How do you know that if it's encrypted?"

His face was all moon-eyed hopelessness. "Asked Dawna Polk about it. She said it was nothing."

Holy crap. "Arthur, where is the drive now?"

"Checker's got it. I'm going to get it back from him and toss it, though."

"Arthur! Arthur, no, that's—that's not you talking; that's—Forget it. Have you talked to Checker about this yet?"

He sighed. "I can't reach him."

I was suddenly having trouble breathing. "You can't reach him?"

"No. It's strange, you know? He usually answers. I can't reach . . . I can't reach anybody."

Oh, crap. Oh, fuck. How had I not thought of this before? Shit, *I* had mentioned Checker in my generous tell-all to Dawna, and I had only just met him. Arthur worked with him all the time.

"Arthur," I said carefully, "don't freak out, but did Dawna ask you about Checker?" Would it matter? Could she have seen everything anyway, whether or not she had asked?

"No," Arthur answered. "Well, not until after I mentioned him. She was real interested. He's a heck of a guy, you know?"

"Oh, no." I pushed back the blankets and scrambled up. "Oh, God."

"Russell, stop! What are you doing? You can't get up!"

"The hell I can't." I tore the medical tape off the back of my hand and slid out the IV, ignoring the dark blood that welled up. It would clot. "We have to find him. Now."

Arthur shook his head. "You're not allowed to find Checker. It's part of his security whatsis, you know—clients don't get to know where the Hole is."

"Arthur, this is very important." I grabbed him by the shoulders. "Where Checker lives—he calls it the Hole?" I took a deep breath. "Do you know where it is? I'm not asking you to tell me, but do. You. Know?"

He looked like he was thinking it over. It was wildly disconcerting, like watching a five-year-old child in a grown man's body. "Of course I do. But I'm not telling you, so don't ask."

I physically shook him. "Arthur! We have to find him, now! *You* know, so Dawna knows, and Pithica's coming after him!" We might be too late already.

Arthur shook his head again, adamantly. "She wouldn't hurt him. She was just interested."

"No! She would definitely hurt him! She lied to you, remember? About Rio? About not hurting me?"

His face clouded. "Yeah."

"And it made you doubt her motives, right? Remember?"

"Yeah . . ."

Thank goodness Dawna hadn't had another crack at him after undoing her own work. He would have been a Pithica-loving robot. "Arthur, listen to me. You don't have to believe me, okay? But you do have to go see Checker, now. In person."

He frowned down at me. "You feeling better enough for me to leave for a while?"

Oh, Jesus, did I ever. "Yes! I promise! Now go, right now!"

He shrugged me off. "Don't know what you're so hyper about, but okay. I am kind of worried I can't reach him." He grabbed his coat off a chair. "And I can get that flash drive back off him, too."

Oh, brother. Was I this bad under Dawna's influence? How on earth did I fix this? Rio always seemed to be able to talk me out of it, but Steve had implied I was highly unusual that way, and I still didn't know why. I shuddered to think what Arthur would have been like if Dawna hadn't had me shot.

"You lie back down," Arthur admonished, pointing at me as he headed toward the door.

"Cross my heart," I called after him.

The door closed. I found my jacket and gingerly zipped it; if it was still raining out I probably didn't want to get the bandages wet. My boots were by the door.

It was indeed still raining, the continuous, drenching downpour that was the hallmark of Southern California's wet season. The flat we'd been in turned out to be back in the congestion of Los Angeles proper, and Arthur, honest guy that he was, got on a bus. Since I stole a car, it was mind-numbingly easy to follow him, even through miles and miles of red lights and stop-and-go traffic.

After three line transfers and over two hours, Arthur disembarked from the latest bus line near Panorama City and started walking. I ditched the car and followed, hunching against the rain and turning up the collar of my jacket to block the deluge. Arthur was one of those people who was always glancing around and checking his surroundings—it probably came with the whole being-a-PI thing—and his observational skills would have caught most tails, but I'm very good at following people.

I trailed him onto a residential street, where he turned into the driveway of an unremarkable one-story house with a ramp installed over the porch steps. Arthur bypassed the house entirely and circled around to a side entrance of the garage.

As he reached it, he stumbled to a stop and staggered as if he'd been knifed.

My brain short-circuited. I dashed forward, next to him in an instant. "What is it?"

He blinked at me through the rain. "Russell! What in the hell— you shouldn't—how did you—" His voice kept cracking, as if he weren't sure how to form words anymore.

I turned to the garage. The doorjamb next to the lock was splintered, and the door stood open a few inches, letting the wind and rain pour into the dark emptiness inside.

twenty-nine

ARTHUR DIDN'T seem to be able to move. I reached out and nudged the door all the way open, stepping into the dimness. My boots squelched on soaked carpeting.

The inside of the garage was finished, and was the room I had seen during our video connection with Checker. A counter around the perimeter of the small space served as one long computer desk, and brackets rode up the walls, supporting more monitors and tower frames. Checker had probably half again as many computers as Anton crammed into about a quarter of the space, but whereas Anton's machines had been a sprawling mess of half-open cases and loose circuit boards, Checker's cluster was much more fastidiously organized.

At least, it had been.

Someone had torn the place apart. Computers had been rent open willy-nilly, every hard drive in the place yanked, and I saw a number of loose adapters in empty spaces where laptops had probably sat. All the monitors were dark, and one LCD was smashed, the cracks spider-webbing outward from where something very hard had struck it. Something like a crowbar or a tire iron.

I swallowed.

Near the back, soot blackened the desktop in several places, and metal frames twisted where they had been on the periphery of small explosions. I bent to look more closely in the dim light. A dark brown smear and smudged handprint told their own story.

Arthur edged into the room behind me. "Oh, Lord," he whispered. "Oh my God . . ."

"Let's check the house," I said.

The back door of the house was still locked, so I kicked it open, ignoring the twinge from my chest wound. Someone had beaten us here as well: multiple black bootprints tracked through every room, and drawers were upended and furniture overturned in a search that had as little regard for Checker's living space as Steve's men had shown for Courtney's.

Steve's men. This could have been them again. Or Pithica. Or both.

"Did I do this?" mumbled Arthur. "Did I?"

"I don't know," I said.

Orphaned adapters and Ethernet connectors told us Checker had kept no shortage of computers in the house, either, but everything from laptops and tablets to ebook readers had been swept up and taken. I wandered into the living room. A flat-screen TV dangled crookedly on the wall where it had been knocked askew, and a snowdrift of papers from an emptied file cabinet made half a mummy of a guitar on a stand. It looked like Checker had had a pleasant place, before he'd been abducted.

"Russell," Arthur called.

I found him in the washroom, frowning at the sink. "What is it?" I asked.

"Toothbrush," he said. "Toothbrush and toothpaste are missing."

"So?"

"Seem weird to you? Kidnappers or killers, and they take him a toothbrush?"

I mulled it over. It did seem weird.

"My God," said Arthur suddenly. He pushed back out of the washroom, dashed to the front door, and flung it open to dive out onto the porch, his head swiveling from side to side as if he were trying to see in all directions at once.

I followed him out. "What is it?"

"Blue Nissan. You see a blue Nissan anywhere?"

I got what he meant immediately. This was Los Angeles; of course Checker owned a car—but the driveway was vacant, and the garage had been converted into his hacker cave. So where was it?

I peered through the sheeting rain into the street. Parking wasn't bad in this neighborhood, and cars were sparse. I didn't see a blue Nissan.

"He got away," I breathed. Maybe.

Arthur pounded a rain-slicked fist against one of the porch's pillars. Then he sank onto the porch swing and rested his head in his hands.

I had a thought. "Hey. Where have you been leaving him your messages?"

"Got a few numbers for him," Arthur mumbled. "Tried 'em all."

"Whatever you think is the most foolproof one, dial it now."

I sat down next to him as he pulled out his cell; he wiped a wet hand on the porch swing's cushion to dial with marginally drier fingers before handing the phone to me. Over the drumming of the rain I heard a recorded stock voice of a British woman tell me the party I was trying to reach was not available and to leave a message after the tone. Said tone chimed.

"It's Cas Russell," I said. "I'm, uh . . . I'm here with Arthur, and we're kind of hoping you aren't dead." I swallowed and thought again of Anton. "We both got whammied by Dawna Polk, but I'm pretty much back to normal. At least according to someone I trust. Arthur's still a basket case, but I think he's getting better."

Arthur reached out and tried to grab the phone away from me, but I leapt up off the swing and danced backward. "Call us back, okay? And whatever you do, don't give Arthur back the flash drive. Dawna convinced him it's meaningless, but I'm pretty sure it's important."

I hung up.

"He hasn't called me back." Arthur sounded sore. "What makes you think he's going to call you back?"

"Let's wait and see," I said. "Should we go back to the flat? It's drier."

He stood. "Can I have my phone back now?"

"No."

"Why not?"

"Because if Checker calls back, I don't want you to answer."

Arthur hunched into himself. "Really think he's okay?"

I looked out at the rain. I hoped we were right, but realistically? "I don't know," I said. My chest was aching badly now. "Let's go back, yeah? I've got a car."

"And where did this car come from?"

"I bought it."

"Liar."

He allowed us to drive back anyway.

Only a few roads out from Checker's place I took a right turn and said, "Don't look now, but we're being followed."

Arthur flicked his eyes to the side mirror. "I don't see anything," he said after a few more streets of watching the tragic comedy that is LA drivers trying to navigate through pounding rain. "How can you tell?"

"Game theory," I said. "The white sedan isn't driving selfishly."

"They staked out Checker's place," Arthur guessed. "'Case we came back."

"It's okay," I assured him. "They're not after us; they want us to lead them back to Rio. I can lose them." I juked the steering wheel to the side and slammed on the gas, shooting through the next intersection just as the light changed. Arthur yelled. In the rearview mirror, an SUV crashed spectacularly into the passenger side of the white sedan, and brakes screeched as three other cars skidded on the wet streets, spinning to a stop and completely blocking the intersection behind us.

"What the hell!" cried Arthur.

"We'd better switch cars," I said.

"You could've gotten us killed!"

"Please. That was child's play."

"You might've gotten other people killed!"

"At those velocities it would have been their fault for buying death traps." It was true, though I hadn't thought it through in so many words beforehand. I decided against telling Arthur that. "We should probably relocate our hideout to somewhere outside LA."

Arthur covered his eyes with one hand. I almost felt sorry for him.

By the time we arrived back at the apartment, I could tell my body temperature was edging up into a fever. We squelched inside, and I went to dig out some dry bandages. Arthur, no matter how irritated he might be with my methods, started mother hen–ing me again and pulling out another bag of IV antibiotics.

When the phone in my pocket rang loudly, however, the clean bandages hit the floor as I scrabbled at my jacket. Arthur was squeezing the IV bag in his hand so tightly it looked like it might burst. I finally got the phone out, almost dropping it in my haste to hit the button before it went to voice mail. "Hello?"

"Cas Russell? Is that you?"

"Yeah, Checker, it's me." I was grinning myself silly at Arthur. "Good to hear your voice."

He was slow in answering. "You said Dawna Polk got to you. Both of you."

"Yeah. It turned out that going into a known ambush was a *spectacularly bad idea*," I said pointedly in Arthur's direction.

"Don't take this the wrong way, but . . . how do I know you guys are still you?"

That was a very good question. I sat down on the bed and thought about it. "Huh. Yeah, I guess I wouldn't trust me right now either."

He made a sound like a hopeless laugh. "That makes me feel better about you than what Arthur's been saying. His messages don't sound like him at all; I've been going out of my mind. Is he okay? You guys got out, right?"

"Yeah, we escaped, and then Arthur betrayed us, and then I got shot, and then we escaped for real." I had to jump up and duck away from Arthur, who was trying to grab the phone again. "Dawna had me shot in front of Arthur, though, so she kind of messed up her own mojo there. He's in a state."

Checker was sputtering. "You got *shot*? Are you okay?"

"Yeah, fine. Arthur's been smothering me. I think he feels guilty. 'Cause it was, you know, his fault." I peeked at Arthur. He looked ready to murder me. "He still seems under the influence a bit," I told Checker. "But he's lucid enough that he hasn't been calling Dawna to come get us, so I think he'll probably be all right." I had already figured that the only reason Rio had let Arthur stay was that he'd needed the extra hand in helping me back from the brink of death— as a general rule, Rio didn't like working with other people if he didn't have to—but it occurred to me that he probably would have kicked him to the curb anyway if he'd judged Arthur was still enough of Dawna's tool to be a danger. It made me feel better about Arthur's chances.

"Oh," said Checker in a small voice. "Okay."

I winced at his tone. I wasn't the only one Arthur had betrayed, and Checker had known him a hell of a lot longer. "He really couldn't help it, you know," I said, adding in a spurt of honesty, "Uh, neither of us could. I would have given you away too, if I'd known how." I thought of Rio and was flooded with shame again. "Don't blame him."

"Oh, I know *that*," Checker brushed me off. "You guys were going after a mind reader, duh, of course I got somewhere safe. It's Arthur I'm worried about; what did she—"

"Hang on, you weren't even there anymore when they broke in? But—we saw blood, and it looked like there had been a struggle—"

"Yeah, uh, sorry if I scared you guys. I figured with multiple groups in play, whoever came by first would think the other one had beaten 'em and then go after them instead of me. I think it worked, too; I proxied into my home security, and by the way, these people are truly evil, the way they'll tear apart a perfectly nice computer that never did anything rude to them—"

"Wait, you staged your own kidnapping? That was all you?"

"Well, the Hole was my work, mostly, though when whoever-it-was came they scavenged everything that was left. My poor network! I'm going to have to rebuild it from scratch. And I have no idea why they felt the need to break into my house. Talk about unnecessary."

"They were probably looking for the flash drive," I said. "Everyone knows you have it now."

"Yeah, what's the deal with that? Arthur, he—he left me like seven messages about it—"

"He did, did he?" I looked up from the phone conversation to glare at Arthur. "Tresting, really? No wonder he didn't call you back."

"What?" demanded Arthur, all innocence.

"She really did a bad job on you if you're coming off that programmed." I talked back into the phone, explaining to Checker. "Dawna tried to convince him it was meaningless, but I got a source says Pithica's still trying to recover it. I think it might be important. Did you crack it?"

"Yeah, a few days ago; it's mostly numbers. What do you mean, she programmed Arthur? How bad is he? Is he going to be okay?"

"He's, uh . . . well, I'm not an expert or anything." I tried to figure out how to answer. "I think she only influenced him with regards to this case. He seems as annoying as usual otherwise. I think maybe just don't trust anything he says about Pithica, and if she doesn't get a chance at him again . . ."

"You really think he'll be all right?" His voice sounded tinny over the line. "He'll be—back to himself?"

"I'm guessing there's a good chance." It wasn't a comforting answer, but what else could I say? For all I knew, Dawna had twisted up Tresting's mind permanently. "Go back to the drive. You said it's numbers?"

He cleared his throat. "Yeah. Lists of numbers—gigabytes' worth. I haven't been able to find a pattern yet."

Numbers. "I'm good at numbers," I said. "Email it to me."

There was a pause. "Done."

"Wait, how do you know my email address?"

A hint of his former humor returned. "I'm all-powerful, Cas Russell. Didn't I tell you?"

I rolled my eyes. "Yeah, you mentioned it once or twice."

"I'm like Oracle, Mr. Universe, and Elaine Roberts all rolled into one. Nothing can hide from me! Oh, uh, speaking of, I think I found Dawna Polk."

"Wait, *what*?" I turned away from Arthur and lowered my voice. "What do you mean, you found her?"

"Sorry, 'found her' as in 'figured out who she is,' not physically located her. Arthur left a name in one of his messages—Saio, he said. I did a search. Well, a lot of searching—"

"Checker. Spit it out."

"It was decades ago. A Daniela Saio. Her parents were famous fortune-telling psychics—"

I snorted.

"I'm on your side on that, but here's the interesting part," said Checker. "When she was ten or so, Daniela got more famous than her parents. Psychic extraordinaire. The toast of Europe. She was brilliant at it."

"Brilliant at making people believe her rigmarole," I said.

"I told you, I'm *with* you, but you're not seeing this. She was doing that when she was *ten*."

The air in the room suddenly felt heavy. "And after that?"

"That's the weird thing. She just dropped off the face of the earth."

"And then what?"

"And then nothing, that's what I'm telling you. For years. I found two other recent aliases for her in other countries, both as airtight as the Polk one, and who knows how many others might be out there, but in between—"

"What happened to 'nothing can hide'?"

He hissed in frustration. "I'm still working on it."

"So wherever she went in between, that's where she . . . what, got trained up? Injected with psychic superpowers?"

"I don't know," said Checker. "But wherever she went when she was ten, I'd bet an original mint-condition Yak Face action figure it had something to do with Pithica."

I digested that. "You think Pithica took her."

"Find genius kids and recruit 'em young," he said. "It's one theory. The skills she had already, well, anyone who could get her on their side—and then considering they were able to give her this crazy boost in psychology? Someone was thinking ahead."

A strange ringing was buzzing in my ears. "She was just a kid."

"Huh?"

"They took her when she was just a kid."

"So?"

I closed my eyes, took a breath. "I don't like it when bad things happen to kids."

"Right, well, I'll keep looking. Maybe I can find something that will help us fight the adult version."

"Yeah," I said. "Okay. And I'll check out those numbers. See what I can make of them."

"Sure," he said. He sounded subdued. "Hey, tell Arthur . . . tell Arthur I'm worried about him. And tell him he shouldn't worry because I took care of the other thing." He hung up abruptly. I was left staring at the phone, emotions roiling.

"He didn't want to talk to me, huh," said Arthur. His hands were shoved in his pockets, his expression miserable.

"Don't take it personally," I said.

"Hard not to."

"Yeah." I didn't know what to say to that. "He said to tell you he's worried about you. And, uh, he also said to tell you not to worry because he took care of 'the other thing.' What other thing?"

His whole body relaxed, tension easing out of every line. "Nothing. Doesn't have to do with this case."

His tone screamed it was something private. Since I was nosy, I didn't respect that. "I thought you didn't have any other cases right now."

"It's personal, Russell."

"Fine." I'd bug Checker to tell me later, if I remembered. I cast about for a change of subject. "Let's check out these lists of numbers, yeah?"

"They won't mean anyth—" Arthur tried to insist, but I interrupted him with a glare.

"Go—go dry off," I instructed tiredly. "I'm going to waste my time looking at a completely meaningless file. Okay?" He looked as though he wanted to argue, but he complied.

I pulled over the laptop and opened it. Sure enough, a new email showed bold at the top of my in-box, encrypted with my public key. I sighed. It wasn't like my public key was secret, but the fact that Checker had had it on hand was just annoying.

I uncompressed the file, and the computer locked up for a full sixteen seconds while it opened. The thing was long. *Very* long. And as Checker had said, it consisted mostly of contextless numbers, some of them arranged into tables, others spinning out into protracted lists. I scrolled through pages, and pages, and pages.

I let my eyes unfocus. Let my brain relax. The numbers slid over each other, rearranging, realigning. Some joined into armies, others popped up and shouted, drawing attention to themselves. Patterns crossed and recrossed. Numbers. Numbers. *Numbers . . .*

"Cas."

I looked up. Rio stood over me, his hand on my shoulder. Arthur, clean and dry, was watching me with some concern. I realized that I was still quite wet and very cold, and that my whole body ached and wanted to start shivering. But it didn't matter.

"Cas," said Rio, "keeping the bandaging clean and dry is medically important."

"Yeah," I said. "Rio, I know how to take down Pithica."

"How?" asked Rio.

My lips twisted into a feral smile. "By using math. We're going to destroy them *economically*."

thirty

"WAIT," SAID Arthur. "Say that again?"

"The numbers Kingsley had," I said. "They're far from meaningless. The patterns in them—they're Pithica's finances. All the accounting, money laundering—"

"Dawna told me they didn't mean anyth—" Arthur tried to insist.

"How complete is this information?" said Rio.

"Staggeringly complete." I looked back at the file, at the small rows of type, pages and pages and pages and *pages*—I swallowed. "Rio, their operation is so much bigger than I ever—I had no idea."

He didn't comment. I had a distinct feeling he *had* known.

"And economics, it drives everything." The idea was still forming, but the solidity of the math filled me with confidence. These numbers coiled with power, ripe for exploitation. Not to mention that the ice pick was beginning to thump away at the back of my skull again, and the headache only made me more certain. "The sheer amount of resources Pithica needs—if we can cut off their revenue stream . . . assuming we can get accurate information," I added loudly, since it looked like Arthur was going to protest the veracity of the flash drive's contents again, "we could cut them off at the knees."

"Yeah, but can't they just ask for more money? Anyone would give it to 'em," Arthur pointed out. "They could ask Bill Gates—"

"Pithica operates in the shadows," said Rio. "That must be the reason they have constructed such an elaborate diversification of resources in the first place."

"Yes, but it's more than that," I argued. "The amounts here—their yearly income is equivalent to the GDP of a small country."

Arthur made a face. "How could they hide all that?"

"That's why their resource structure is so complicated," I said. "The money laundering, and layering, and—the number of accountants they must have had over the years to build all this, it's staggering. It's like looking at the code to an operating system." Rio and Arthur both looked blank. I wished I were talking to Checker instead. "Complicated," I clarified. "It's very complicated. And whoever put all this together in one document was . . . well, a colossal idiot, but on the other hand, I don't think Reginald Kingsley realized what he had his hands on. I bet he only knew it was something crazy and important. And it's probably what got him killed. If he hadn't found the drive, Pithica wouldn't even have looked at him—their activities are too massive. They don't sweat the small stuff; they're too big to care about most of us." I nodded at Rio. "You should feel complimented, I guess."

"But they went after Leena," said Arthur. "And they did go after you, and me—"

"Only after we were on to Dawna," I reminded him. "And she only approached me because of my connection to Rio. Arthur, you and I are ants compared to this." The scale of it gave me a dizzying vertigo, like looking up at a massive skyscraper. "But we're in luck, in a way. Pithica is so massive and sprawling, and I think that's why they've made mistakes. First, they botched Kingsley's murder—Courtney must've been convenient because she was already brainwashed and in the area, but she lost track of the drive, or didn't hand it over, or something. They should have sent someone competent, or, hell, Dawna should have gone herself, even if Kingsley seemed like a minor player. Maybe they didn't know what was on the drive till later."

"If Dawna was the one, his suicide note might've sounded like him in the first place," said Arthur.

"Hell, it would have been real," I agreed. "Courtney probably—I don't know, threatened his wife or kid or something if he didn't write it. Forced him somehow. But Kingsley managed to tip his wife off, and she hired you, and I doubt that was even on their radar, no offense, but then you met me—"

"And you knew about Dawna," finished Arthur. "Which, actually something important."

"But I wouldn't have suspected her at all if it weren't for you," I said to Rio. "And I think that's the second mistake they've made— Dawna going after Rio full tilt, herself, because she put an enormous amount of time and resources into it, and she made a bloody mess of it. Not only did she not take out Rio as a threat, but we got out with way more information about her and Pithica than anyone's ever had on them."

"And you think you can use this information," said Rio.

"It's numbers," I said, waving a hand. "I absolutely think I can. With a little help." I picked up Arthur's phone.

Checker answered on the third ring. "Cas?" he said. The pause before he spoke was long enough for me to tell he really didn't want to talk to Arthur yet.

"Yeah," I said. "I figured out the numbers. It's Pithica's financial empire."

He let out a low whistle. "You're kidding."

Finally someone who understood what this meant. "Nope."

"I feel like a dead man walking just knowing that. Uh, irony not intended."

"Irony?"

"I can't walk." Oh, right. I'd forgotten he used a wheelchair.

Frighteningly, he did have a point. Once Pithica found out what we'd discovered, we would rocket straight to the top of the hit list. "Well, we just have to use it before they get to us," I said.

"How? Steal all their money?"

"They'd just come after us and steal it back," I pointed out. And

I was pretty sure they'd win. It wasn't a good feeling, knowing someone else could beat me.

"What's the plan, then?"

"Wait a sec, I'm putting you on speaker." I hit a button and put the phone on the table so I could talk to Rio and Arthur and him all at once. "The advantage on our side is that they're drawing from thousands and thousands of accounts," I said, feeling my way through the logic as I spoke. "So if we cut them off everywhere at once, they won't be able to recover fast. They'd have to rebuild their whole infrastructure."

"Double-edged," said Rio. "Such diversification also means we cannot take out their resources simultaneously. Too many targets."

"I don't know. I think we can," I said.

"How? Bring the Feds in?" Arthur rubbed a palm against his chin as if he couldn't believe he was entertaining the possibility the flash drive might contain viable information. "Could work. Feds are slick at taking down money-laundering operations. You give 'em the evidence, they could bring them down."

"No, that has the same problem as stealing the money ourselves—single fail point," I said.

"Pithica eats criminal investigations for breakfast," agreed Checker from the phone. "They could divert one without taking a breath. We saw that in Kingsley's notes."

"It's down to us," I said.

"I was afraid you were going to say that," said Checker.

"Chin up," I told him. "We're very smart."

"Well, yes, but—"

"Here's what I'm thinking instead," I plowed on. "With this many revenue sources, they can't have brainwashed so many people. They must be . . . siphoning, or running front businesses, or fake charities, or whatever else huge criminal organizations do." I raised my eyebrows at Rio. "Right?"

"A reasonable hypothesis."

"So, here's a thought. What if we can alert everyone they're stealing from that the money isn't going where they think it is? Then *they* slam the lids on the revenue streams. And we can potentially send a hundred thousand security alerts at once with the click of a button. What do you think? Is it doable?"

Checker took a moment to answer. Arthur was frowning and still rubbing his temple; I couldn't read Rio any more than usual, but I got the impression he was thinking very intently. Their opinions didn't matter, however—for sheer plausibility, I needed a computer expert's assessment.

"Potentially," Checker said at last. "Pulling it off isn't as easy as you make it sound, especially if all the different fronts funnel money to them in different ways. But maybe we can build algorithms to sort those into rough categories of attack—"

"The sample space isn't large on a computational level," I reminded him.

"True. We won't need to worry much about efficiency or scalability. Quick and dirty will do the job; the question is whether we have enough commonality here to make 'quick and dirty' work."

"We do," I said. I had an intuitive grasp of the math already; it was laying itself out in patterns in my brain like beautifully crafted knitwork. "I can tell we do. If you can write the code, I can do the math."

"Well—we can try it. But no promises."

His reply might not be the resounding enthusiasm I'd hoped for, but at least he'd said yes. "You'll see. We can do this."

Checker cleared his throat. "Cas, pick the phone back up, please."

I avoided catching Arthur's eye as I did so. I levered myself up off the bed, making a face as my wet clothes pulled against my skin and my chest wound twinged, and walked between Arthur and Rio to head over by the windows. "You've just got me now," I said into the phone.

He came straight to the point. "I can't trust you. Or Arthur."

I didn't blame him. "So we do this remotely," I said. "So what?"

He made a hissing sound. "It'll go a lot faster if we're in the same room." He was right. I wasn't sure what he wanted me to say, though—I couldn't give him any guarantees, as much as I would have liked to. "And, uh, one other problem. I think I'm going to need more processor power than I took with me, and I don't have enough cash left—I can't make a withdrawal while Pithica's trying to track me down, and—"

"I got it," I said. "Give me a shopping list. And let this be a lesson for your survival kit."

"Yeah," he said fervently. "I'm not nearly as prepared for the zombie apocalypse as I should be. Although zombies would probably mean chaos and looting and massive inflation, so cash wouldn't necessarily—"

"Hey. Shopping list."

"Right. I'm emailing it to you. Uh, thanks. I'll get you back, assuming we survive all this."

"Consider it payment for springing me from prison," I said.

"That was nothing. I had back doors built into those systems already. Just, you know, in case. Don't tell Arthur," he added as an afterthought.

"I already said I wouldn't." He might not be prepared for rebuilding computer clusters on the run, but Checker had some levels of paranoia I heartily approved of. I wondered what his history was. "So, what's the verdict? You want me to dead drop the equipment?"

"Oh, I'm sending you after way too much for that," he said. "We might as well do this in person. This is where I take the leap, I guess." His voice had gone high and uncertain. "How can you be sure you're . . . cured?"

I looked around the edges of the closed blinds. The traffic of Los Angeles buzzed by on the streets below, the cars splashing miserably through rain sheeting down from a soggy sky. My head still hurt, so I liked to think I was resisting *something*, but that was very far from a sure thing. "I'm not," I admitted.

I heard Checker take a few shallow breaths. Then he said, "I can't help wondering. How do we know this isn't part of some elaborate Xanatos Gambit?"

I left off staring at the traffic. "Some elaborate what?"

"Some sort of complicated scheme. I mean, how do we know this isn't all exactly what she wants us to do?"

It was an extremely legitimate question. "I don't know."

The conversation stalled into awkward silence. I had a pretty good idea what Checker might be thinking: Dawna hadn't found him yet. He could continue to run, and run as fast and far as he could, instead of hooking back up with us and facing the real possibility of becoming another one of Pithica's pawns.

"If it helps," I said, "it *feels* like I'm fighting her. Plus, Rio really does seem to be immune, and he thinks I'm okay." Checker still didn't say anything. "Hello?"

"Who?" The word was slow and suspicious.

My chest started to cramp in a way that had nothing to do with the healing wound or the wet bandages, and my headache suddenly felt twice as bad. I leaned against the wall next to the window. "Arthur neglected to mention I work with Rio, didn't he."

"*That* Rio?"

"I assume so."

He made a choking sound. "Some of the things Arthur said make a lot more sense now. I'm going to kill him."

"I take it you've heard of Rio, too, then."

"Heard of—!" He cut himself off. I could practically hear him mentally rearranging his impression of me in light of the whole works-with-a-mass-murdering-sadist connection. I closed my eyes, heartily tired of this. "That name," whispered Checker. "Some of the less-than-reputable people I've known, before I met Arthur—he terrifies *them*, beyond reason. It's like he's the boogeyman. People invoke his name like he's a demon or something. Cas Russell, I like you so far, but . . ."

"I trust him," I said, for what felt like the thousandth time.

"To do *what*?"

That was a good question. What did trust mean, exactly? "To have my back," I said.

"I have to think about this."

"He got Arthur and me out of there."

"He did?"

"Yes. I told you, I trust him." I tried for impatient, but the words just came out drained.

"He's after Pithica?"

"Yes."

"I have to think about this," said Checker again. "I'll—I'll call you back."

He hung up the phone and I leaned my head against the wall. The pounding of the rain reverberated through it, a steady thrum. A moment ago I'd been so hopeful, so sure we had a chance that we could do this. But for the first time I could remember, I needed help to make it happen, and nobody wanted to jump with me. Why did everything involving people have to be so difficult?

Rio came over. "Other plans notwithstanding, we should change location," he said. "Tresting told me you were made."

"I lost them," I said.

"Regardless, now that you are well enough to travel, you should leave Los Angeles. Other plans can wait. Pithica will be able to track you here eventually."

I'd been thinking the same thing back when we'd lost our tail after Checker's place, but now my feelings had snapped into orneriness. "Here's a thought," I said. "Let them. We'll set a trap of our own, figure out a way to fight back."

"Cas," said Rio.

Arthur joined him. "Leaving LA is not a bad plan, Russell. This is too big. Even if the info you think you found is legit—"

I growled at him.

Arthur held up his hands placatingly. "Might be a better idea for us to run anyway. From what you say, if we aren't causing a fuss, maybe they let us be."

Rio turned away from him slightly. "Your assistance during this has been appreciated; however, you will not be going with her. You are still compromised."

"Says the man who shot her!"

"You are free to go your own way," said Rio.

"I can? Why, thank you *so* much for the permission!"

"Cas," said Rio, "we must move you to a more secure location immediately. Preferably outside the country."

"No," I said.

"Cas—"

"Yeah, you just go and tell everyone what to do—" put in Arthur.

"Cas, I cannot impress upon you the danger of—"

"I'm not trusting you to keep her safe!"

"Hey!" The shout sent spikes of pain shooting through my still-damaged lungs, but I didn't care. This was like trying to corral wet, angry cats. Rio thought Arthur useless, Arthur thought Rio an abomination, Checker didn't trust anyone anymore, and Rio didn't trust anyone ever, apparently me included. For crying out loud, *I* was the only one who wanted to be a team player, which was so laughable it pissed me right the hell off. Not to mention the ridiculous, chauvinistic chivalry that apparently came mandatory with a Y chromosome—I was capable of wiping the floor with both Rio and Arthur at once, and they thought they had a right to dictate what I should do? No wonder I preferred to work alone.

"I'm done with this," I snapped, and hit the button on the phone to redial Checker, putting him on speaker again. "Okay, you three, listen up," I said the moment he picked up. "Pithica's come after all of us. They've tried to kill us, they've tried to brainwash us, and they've messed up our world in ways we probably know nothing about. Two of you have been chasing them for months; Rio, you've been going after them forever. I tell you I think we can finally make a difference and bring them down and you choose to give up *now*?"

"I would like to discuss your discovery," said Rio, "but first we must assure you are safely—"

"What? Out of the way? That's not your decision to make!" This was only the second time in memory I'd lost my temper toward Rio, and the first time had been caused by Dawna's influence. "I get that you're trying to look out for me or some other ridiculous notion, but that's not your call. I'm angry—I'm *furious*—and guess what? I'm going to fight back. If the three of you aren't in, then, God help me, I will figure out a way to go after them myself, and I will fucking win. And you"—I gesticulated at them wildly—"can go and do whatever you want with your meaningless little lives, run if you want to,

I don't care, but I am thoroughly sick of trying to work together on this. So if you aren't in, I'm done. I hope you all have nice lives."

The rain pounded against the walls, almost drowning out the city noise outside. No one spoke.

"Was that supposed to be a motivational speech?" said Checker finally from the phone.

"No," I said, quite cross.

"Good, because I don't feel motivated. I vote against you for team morale officer."

Arthur's lip twitched. "That mean we're a team?"

"Well, I've got a self-destructive streak a parsec wide that needs feeding," said Checker. "And war, strange bedfellows . . . uh, something. I suppose I'm in; I mean, was I ever going to say no to this? But, Arthur?"

"Yeah?" said Arthur.

"I still don't think you should know where we do this thing. At the risk of setting Cas off again—it's just good sense."

Arthur hunched his shoulders slightly. "That's okay."

"Rio?" I said.

Rio spread his hands. "If you are determined on this course of action, I will assist you." I couldn't read his expression. "However, I must still insist we at least leave the city."

"As long as it won't delay us too much," I conceded.

"Leaving the country would still be the best—"

"And would take time," I argued. "Unless you think flying commercial on a fake passport is secure enough. . . . No, I didn't think so either. Look, every day we wait on this is another day they can use to rework their financial structure."

"Is there nothing I can say to dissuade you?" said Rio.

"Nope," I answered. "You can tell me if it sounds like I'm playing into her hands, or walking into a trap, or doing something that might be Dawna Polk's lovely programming, but you're not keeping me out of this. Okay?"

"Of course I shall alert you if you appear compromised."

"And you trust him to—" started Arthur.

"Rio," I said, "do I sound like myself, or do I sound like I'm just doing what Dawna wants?"

"You sound distinctly uninfluenced," said Rio dryly. "Regrettably."

"I can hit the road within an hour," said Checker.

"Okay. We'll get the equipment in the meantime," I said. "I'll text you where to meet us."

"Just make sure it's not a walk-up," said Checker. "See you soon."

"Talk later," offered Arthur.

There was a brief pause and then a click as Checker hung up.

I bared my teeth at Arthur and Rio in something that might have been a smile. "Okay. Who feels like electronics shopping?"

thirty-one

Rio, with a disapproving turn to his mouth that said he thought a hundred and twenty miles was not nearly far enough to run, volunteered a safe house out near Twentynine Palms. He gave me the address after Arthur was safely out of the apartment. "Take the path from the road to the back door," he told me. "Do not go in the front."

"Or what?" I asked curiously.

"I have some minimal security measures in place."

"Goody," I said. "Just make sure you don't forget to tell me about any of them."

Arthur had taken off first, following my hastily scrawled directions to retrieve copious amounts of cash from various places in Los Angeles to buy computer equipment with.

"Wait, you remember where you keep your stashes with *equations*?" he'd demanded incredulously when I started giving him directions.

"It's easier than memorizing them," I tried to explain, but he just shook his head at me and departed with the list. The plan was for Rio to meet him and then drive all the equipment out, stopping to collect Checker at a rendezvous point some distance away from the safe house. Rio didn't trust anyone who wasn't him or me not to pick up a tail.

Rather than risk accidentally activating a LoJack signal, I retrieved an old clunker from a storage space that I had acquired quasi-legitimately some years ago—along with a few weapons for the trunk—and fought creeping LA traffic to the 405, where I jerked northward through the rain. I figured I'd hit the 14 and cut across, taking a roundabout route via Victorville. If I got made on the first leg, the assumption would be that I was heading toward Vegas, or maybe Mojave. I kept one eye on my mirrors the whole way, but I got out of the city clean, and eventually I left the crush of LA behind to mark mile after mile through the desert.

I reached Yucca Valley and slewed east, following Rio's directions and heading off the highway. I'd left the rain behind with the city, and the wind swirled fogs of dust across the asphalt, the tiny grains of sand pattering against my windshield and obscuring the half-hearted attempts at civilization out this way. I thought it too generous to call them towns.

I finally crawled up a steep, winding dirt track to the address Rio had given me, wheels crunching and thumping over rocks not nearly small enough to be considered gravel. The little car strained up the slope, the tires skidding on the scree, until I reached a small clapboard house clamped to the top of the crumbling plateau, its high ground commanding a view of the desert nothingness for miles.

Twilight was falling over the landscape heavy and purple as I got out of the car, and the rock formations and knobby Joshua trees cast long, stretching shadows across the emptiness of the desert. The last rays of the sun warmed my skin, but the air was already turning cold and biting in the shadows. After retrieving some guns and a stack of legal pads from my trunk, I heeded Rio and went in the back door.

The place was small but well stocked. Crates of MREs, foil packages labeled as emergency rations, and sealed bags of drinking water dominated most of the storage space and were stacked against the walls of the rooms, with a respectable number of gasoline cans keeping them company. I frowned briefly at one whole kitchen cabinet filled with hard liquor—as far as I knew, Rio didn't drink. Temperance was one of the Christian values, after all. Maybe alcohol had some survivalist purpose I didn't know about.

I also found a heavy metal door that was very solidly locked. I figured Rio stored the armaments back there. Or it was a small bunker. Or both.

I flicked on the lights to banish the shadows collecting in the corners and leaned my weapons up against a nearby wall fully loaded—a girl has to feel safe, after all. Then I picked up the first legal pad and pulled out a ballpoint pen. My chest ached, my head ached, and the long drive had drained me, but none of that mattered.

I started writing.

My longhand scribbles expanded over page after page. As I finished each one I tore it off and spread them out in order over every available surface. By the wee hours of the morning, the floor was carpeted in scrawled-on yellow paper, the walls had sheets Scotch-taped up to form an overlapping wallpaper, and the cardboard backs from five dead legal pads lay discarded in a corner while I scribbled on a sixth.

When I heard tires on the dirt road, I dropped my pen, slung a rifle over my back, and picked up the pump-action Mossberg beside it. I was pretty sure it was only Rio and Checker, but better to be safe. I slipped out the back door into the pitch darkness of the desert night, the sky crusted in stars above me.

Headlights cut through the blackness at the top of the drive. It was indeed Rio, helming a large white van with Checker in the front seat. After acknowledging my shadow with a nod—Rio was nothing if not aware of his surroundings—he got out and stepped over to flick an outside switch and bring several floodlights to life, blanching the scene in white light. I lowered the shotgun and stepped out from the wall of the house as Rio went around to the back of the van to start unloading boxes.

Checker slid his chair out from behind the seat, set it up with practiced ease, and swung himself down into it. He wheeled over to meet me, making a face at the gravelly drive and throwing nervous glances over his shoulder. "That was the longest car ride of my life," he muttered when he got close enough.

I raised my eyebrows, and he flinched at the reminder he was talking to someone in Rio's corner. I sighed. "I told you, I trust him."

"Cas Russell, not that I'm scorning your recommendation or anything, but you'll forgive me if I think you're *frakking insane*," he hissed.

"You probably shouldn't antagonize me, then," I said very mildly.

He blinked twice, opened his mouth, and then closed it again.

"Jesus Christ, I'm only kidding." I wasn't sure I liked how genuinely nervous he'd looked at the idea I might hurt him. "Look, why don't you come inside. I'll catch you up on what I've got."

I'd been writing out the math on paper specifically so I could walk him through it. He swung back to the van to grab a laptop before we headed into the house, and in minutes his fingers were tap-dancing across the keyboard while I talked.

I kept talking while I helped Rio unpack the computer equipment, and Checker either got over his freak-out about Rio or was capable of ignoring everything else when it came to computers—I suspected the latter—because he proved more than equal to multitasking, bossing us around with the authority of someone who knew exactly how he wanted his personal computer cluster to take shape and taking time out from his coding to flash around the cramped rooms and set up the network cables the right way around or slot in the correct hard drives when he deemed we were being too slow or too dull to get it right on his time schedule. He'd brought a huge stack of solid-state drives originally pulled from the Hole, along with at least seven laptops—seven I counted, anyway—and in short order, the monitors spread across the table and counters sprang to life to show Checker's customized operating system.

By the time the sun began baking the little house the next day, Pithica's revenue sources were unfolding for us layer after layer, banks and locations and names blossoming fast and furious in a text file thanks to my algorithms and Checker's coding. The skinny hacker also had a frankly surprising level of financial knowledge, which accelerated the process considerably. I could hardly believe how quickly we were aggregating the information.

Of course, nothing was as easy as all that. Rio, who had been moving around the place doing who knew what—probably setting up a Barrett on the roof or something—came back in while we were in the middle of a raging argument.

"I'm telling you, I know how this works! The notification needs to come from the banks, and we're talking at least fifteen different government agencies in a dozen different countries! I don't even know half the strings we'd need to pull—"

"So, why can't you hack them all and find out?"

Checker literally threw up his hands. "I'm not a slot machine! Do you have any idea how secure these systems are? And how much cross-checking happens? I can't hack human brains!"

"What's going on?" asked Rio. He reached into one of the stacked crates and tossed a ration bar at me as he spoke.

Right. Food. I tended to forget about that. I tore it open.

"Hey! Not near my machines!" squawked Checker.

I obligingly backed up a few paces. "Checker's pussying out," I answered Rio.

"Pussying ou—! First of all, gendered slur, *not* cool, Cas Russell, and second of all, you're asking for something patently impossible. Look, tracking's one thing, but to differentiate ourselves from a thousand different phishing scams you'd need—"

"Explain," said Rio, leaning up against the doorway and crossing his arms.

Checker swallowed and then answered while shying away from eye contact, concentrating on his monitors instead of on Rio. "Cas's idea here has two parts to it. Tracking the accounts is turning out to be . . . well, not easy, but doable. Cas's math on that is pretty spectacular, and the uniqueness of format in the account information, even though we only have numbers and amounts, is—"

Rio cleared his throat and Checker stopped like an animal in headlights, mouth working. The room wasn't large enough and was too full of equipment for him to shrink away from Rio effectively, but he certainly looked like he wanted to try.

I took pity on him. "We'll be able to get a pretty complete account list," I explained. "It's a staggering amount of data—we're tracking the money through layers and layers of banks and front businesses—but by the end of today, we'll have a huge list of the exact paths of all Pithica's revenue streams. We're talking thousands of sources here."

"But?" said Rio.

I huffed out a frustrated breath. "My thought had been to send massive tip-offs," I said. "Warn people they're being stolen from, or that their money isn't going where they think it is, the idea being that Pithica can't have more than a couple key people converted to the cause. And we can actually do that, but Checker pointed out—"

"We won't be taken seriously," finished Checker. "It's not a matter of running a scam on a single bank and convincing it we're sending legit warnings. Our account list—their network comes from all over the world."

"And the revenue sources are diverse," I said. "All different banks, all different businesses and organizations. We could send a mass communication, but it would be dismissed in less than zero time. It probably wouldn't even get past most people's spam filters."

"We lack legitimacy," said Checker. "What about this? What if I sent some sort of Trojan that . . . I dunno, does something to all of these accounts, so when they're checked on people see something happening—"

"But if you're right, nobody will check, even if we tell them to. Not for a while, anyway, and not all at once. We need everyone to jump in fright and move their money simultaneously—if the transition's slow enough, Pithica will be able to deal with it, get out in front of it—"

Checker's frustrated words overlapped with mine. "It's *verifying* the message, not delivering it. Without some virtual psychic paper that grants us authority—"

"Wait," I said.

"What is it?"

I could feel a smile starting. "We happen to know a shadowy mul-tinational organization who can pull every string in the book."

"Wha—bad idea!" Checker cried.

"Do you have a better one? We don't have time to sit on this. Pithica knows we're out here, they know we have this information—it's only a matter of time before they either track us down or change their revenue structure enough to make it not matter."

"Those guys already said they'd kill you!" Checker sputtered.

"Then they can't do much worse, can they," I said.

Checker pressed a hand against his forehead in apparent pain. "Why do I have the feeling you're going to get your own way on this? No matter how much I object to it?"

"Because I am." I turned to Rio. "Have a spare cell I can burn?"

He stepped past me into the narrow kitchen, opened a drawer to reveal a jumble of disposable cell phones still in their packaging, and pulled one out.

"Come on! You can't possibly think this is a good idea!" Checker called from over by his computers.

Rio ignored him. "You think this is a viable plan?" he asked, hand-ing me the phone.

"It's what we've got," I said.

"These are dangerous people."

"And since when do you care about that?"

He raised his eyebrows. "I attach somewhat greater value to your well-being than to my own."

Right. He attached more value to pretty much anyone else's well-being than he did to his own. We were all works of God, I thought. I wondered if he viewed us the way a security guard with no appre-ciation for art might view the paintings in a museum he'd been charged with safeguarding—bits of paper and wood and canvas mushed to-gether with some oily and plasticky stuff that someone else told him were worth protecting at any cost.

"Are you going to try to stop me, then?"

"No. You are quite capable of looking after yourself."

I blinked. He did still trust my skills, then—at least against any-one who wasn't Pithica. The sense of disgruntlement I hadn't even realized I'd been feeling against Rio faded somewhat.

"At least wait until we've finished our end of it," begged Checker. "Come on, this isn't the movies; we can't just hit 'send all.' Who knows what other difficulties we might run into."

"You're right," I said. I went over to Checker and tossed the phone back to Rio. "I should stay here and work. You mind taking a ride and making the call?"

Checker groaned.

"What do I ask for?" said Rio.

"A man called Steve," I answered. "Tell him what we're doing."

"We'll need high-level, verified alerts sent out to a variety of government organizations, both here and overseas," said Checker, giving up. "Here in the U.S. it'll be the Secret Service—I can put together a list, but with the whole shadowy multinational organization thing they have going, they might know better than we would. Some support on spoofing our messages to the banks to be authentic would be helpful, too."

"They'll want us to turn over the information," I warned Rio, remembering how thoroughly Steve's group had dismantled both Courtney's and Checker's houses. I thought of Anton and Penny, and wondered how many people would die if we handed over the data. "Whatever you do, don't agree."

"Do not worry," said Rio. "I am not accustomed to allowing any-one to make requirements of me."

That made me quirk a smile. I wouldn't have wanted to be on the other end of his phone call. "Checker, do you have a secure email address we can give them to coordinate through? Something they wouldn't be able to trace?"

He grumbled something unintelligible about signing our own death warrants, but wrote one down. I added Steve's number from memory and handed Rio the paper; he folded it carefully and tucked it in an inside pocket.

"I shall return in a few hours. Cas, if necessary, I have some armaments on the roof."

"Good," I said, and turned back to Checker, whose face was a funny shade of white. "Okay, let's finish this."

Five hours later, Rio hadn't gotten back yet, and Checker and I were almost done with our notification algorithm.

And we were in terrible trouble.

thirty-two

CHECKER HAD unearthed the alcohol in Rio's kitchen. He'd deemed it necessary, after what we had found.

"What happened to your no food or drink rule?" I asked. Not that I could blame him.

"Tequila doesn't count," he said, taking another swig. "It's *tequila*."

To be fair, the alcohol didn't seem to impair his computer skills at all; his fingers hadn't slowed on the keyboard. "You almost have my alcohol tolerance," I said.

"Well, then you should be drinking, too! I need company in my paroxysm of misery here."

"I don't drink on the job," I said. "I drink more than enough between jobs."

"Between jobs, you say?" He took another swig. "You're on, Cas Russell."

"On for what?"

"You and me. Drinking contest. Once all this is over. I bet I kick your ass."

I highly doubted that, but this wasn't the time for a pissing contest. I snapped my fingers at him. "Hey. Focus, or I'll cut you off."

"I'm focused!" he protested, and to be fair, even my math ability could detect only the barest elision in the words. "I can't do this without drinking. Too depressing."

I couldn't argue with him there.

Three hours ago we had realized—well, Checker had realized, with his uncanny savvy about finances and money-laundering operations—that the sources of Pithica's enterprises weren't merely faceless organizations. To be sure, some were innocuous front businesses, or odd governmental funds, or false charities. But others . . .

Once we figured out where some of the money was coming from, we started looking more closely. And then more closely. It turned out the lion's share of Pithica's revenue came from . . . well. From places that would have been on Rio's target list.

I stared at the monitor, feeling nauseated. "Dawna said Pithica basically owned the drug cartels," I murmured. "She wasn't lying."

"Yeah, well, did she mention the human trafficking? Arms dealing? Owning corrupt *governments*? Holy shit." Checker's fingers drummed against the keys, and a few lines of scripting spat out on the screen. He was running his predictive programs again, the same algorithms he'd used on Kingsley's data to hunt down Pithica in the first place. The same ones we'd been running now for hours, hoping for different results, ever since Checker had become suspicious of what we were looking at. "This is not good, Cas Russell. This is . . . it's not good."

Pithica's economic model was ingenious. They wanted to make the world a better place, and they were. They hadn't chosen to steal from just anybody; their benign-looking accounting was siphoning from and slowly strangling off some of the most extensive crime syndicates in the world. *The cartels put up a good front,* Dawna had said, *but on the whole we've defanged them. . . . Eventually we'll phase them out entirely, of course, but for now they provide us with means, in many ways, of accomplishing our objectives—*

No matter how we ran the mathematical models, if we let Pithica's victims keep their own money, then they got to use it. And the violence, the human slavery, the human *suffering* . . . it was going to spike off the charts afterward.

If we knocked down Pithica this way, we were going to take a whole hell of a lot of innocent people with them.

"They really are doing good," said Checker. "They weren't just saying that. Who knows how much else they've been doing? They're probably using all this money to help people even more."

I swallowed.

"I'm not arguing that they aren't Evil with a capital E," said Checker. "But—I guess—are they? Yeah, they manipulate people, and not setting aside that they almost killed you and Arthur, but . . . it's not like they're going around starting wars. More like preventing them."

"Preventing them by twisting people's minds around," I said.

"Yeah," said Checker. "But . . . maybe it's like what Professor X does, you know? I bet in their eyes they're the heroes."

"What about what they do to children? The children they take?"

"You mean like Daniela Saio? What about them? We don't even know—"

"She was ten," I said. "We know enough."

"Yeah, and what did they do to her? Gave her telepathic superpowers? Dude, I'd go in for that in a heartbeat."

I barely restrained myself from clocking him. "Take that back."

"Whoa!" He twitched away from me. "Hey, sorry. Uh, that really upsets you, huh."

"They're kids," I said. "They're just kids."

"I thought those kids were our bad guys."

"Maybe now," I said. "But they didn't have to be."

Checker was quiet for a moment, looking at his computer screens without seeming to see them. "You know, kids get hurt by the drug trade, too. I'm just saying. And human trafficking, a lot of it's children. Slavery. Child prostitution. Child porn. It's—it's not good." He scrubbed a hand over his face. "It's a zero sum game. We take out one monster, the other rises up."

"It's not zero sum," I corrected. "If that were true, taking out the drug cartels would increase Pithica's power, not the other way around."

"Stop being accurate when I'm trying to be dramatic," Checker groused.

"Well, I'm just saying. If we could find a way to take out all the corruption in the world simultaneously, Pithica would get drained of its resources, not win, which means there *is* a game theoretic payoff where both monsters die—"

"Oh, great," he shot back. "You come up with a way to uproot and eradicate all the crime syndicates and fix all social justice problems everywhere at the same time, you let me know. I'm not sure, but I think there might be a Nobel Peace Prize in it for you, if you need the incentive."

I let my head drop into my hands. "So we take down Pithica, and people everywhere suffer. Or we let things stand the way they are." I felt sick. And I hadn't even been drinking.

"I've never met Dawna and her mind mojo, and I'm still doubting doing this," mumbled Checker, toying with the label on the tequila bottle.

"Ends justify the means, then?"

"What? Hey, whoa, trick question!"

"No," I said. "It's not."

Checker frowned, considering. "You're right," he said finally. "You think you should always say 'no' to that, don't you? The saying? You say no, the ends don't justify the means. Except—when you're actually faced with the choice—"

"We say they have no right," I said softly. "Except maybe they do. The math . . ." Dawna's words came back to me, about the balance of more innocent lives saved at the expense of so few. The numbers agreed with Pithica, no question. The math was on their side.

But what if I was having that thought only because of Dawna's influence?

But what if I wanted to take her down only because I wanted to be positive she *hadn't* influenced me, so I was overcompensating—at the expense of innocent people?

But what if she wanted me to think that?

My head pounded.

"I'm not going to have a clear conscience no matter which way we choose," said Checker. He took off his glasses and leaned back, rubbing his eyes. "What about you? Still think we should go ahead with this?"

I thought about what Rio had said. About free will, and humanity's freedom to sin, and how nobody should take that away. Rio's chosen path was clear: he was going after Pithica, and shit, if other villains rose up in their wake, he'd go after them, too.

Pithica might save people. They might be saving the world. But what they were doing was still wrong.

"Let me ask you something," I said. "Would you like to meet Dawna?"

Checker jerked reflexively.

"Yeah," I said. "I agree."

He looked away.

"It doesn't matter what the results are." I was certain. I told myself I was certain. "They run the world the way they see fit, and twist around people's minds to do it, and assassinate anyone who might get in the way. We have to stop them."

"I just wish . . ." Checker murmured. "Darwin help me, I wish this were somebody else's decision."

"Well," I said, "if it helps, remember that you and Arthur first started this because you were trying to find the people who'd murdered an innocent man."

Checker picked up his bottle and contemplated it for a moment, then swirled the dregs and raised it toward me. "To Reginald Kingsley, then." He sounded like a man at his own execution. "We're going to destroy the world for you."

"And save it," I said. Save it for those who would ravage it. Checker was right. It was not a decision I wanted to be making.

I remembered what Dawna had said about the burden of making the choice, once one had the power—the decision of which lives to save, of which gray morality was better. We faced that choice now, too. And we would have to live with the results.

A tone sounded from the nearest computer. Checker moved over to it. "It's the email account we gave to He Who Calls Himself Steve," he told me. "Looks like your boy came through. With . . . holy shit, this is a lot of detail." I stood up to look over his shoulder; he was scrolling through pages and pages of instructions, details on every kind of notification and authentication to send to each type of bank, government agency, monetary fund, or business. "They gave us exactly what we need—all we have to do is incorporate it. We'll be ready to deploy within a few hours."

And we'd hit a button, and everything would be out of our hands.

A crunch on the gravel outside signified Rio's return; I went out to meet him fully armed, but he was alone and unperturbed. Evening was falling again, streaking the clouds red and pink across the broad Morongo Basin sky.

"Steve came through," I informed him. "We just got the email. He give you any trouble?"

He looked at me.

"Nice one," I said.

"Well. It seems I am capable of inspiring some fear."

Either Rio had somehow managed to develop a sense of humor or he was making the understatement of the year.

"How does your work here progress?" Rio asked, following me back inside.

Most of the time he'd been gone had been spent rehashing our moral quandary—in comparison, the programming had been easy. "It's done. Pretty much. We just have to set up and format the messages according to what we got from Steve and Company a minute ago. A few hours, tops. Have they deployed alerts to all the right agencies yet?"

"He said it would be done within two hours of our conversation, which time is now past. Your notifications will be taken seriously."

"Hey, Checker," I called as we came in. "We're good to go. Steve's sent out all the alerts. As soon as we're ready, we can—"

The lights went out. Simultaneously, all of Checker's monitors died, their glow an afterimage in the dimness, and the all-pervading hum of the electronics cut off, leaving us in sudden silence.

Checker yelled something inarticulate and possessive. He started flailing around in the grayness, trying to get his laptops restarted. Rio disappeared from my side as if he had been teleported.

I raced back outside, my foot hitting a windowsill to gain the roof in one bound. Rio was already crouched on the shingles beside a collection of armaments, peering through a scope to scan the valley.

"We're not alone," he said.

At first I thought he meant they had found us—I scanned the landscape, the empty desert snapping into a sharp relief of mathematical interactions—before I realized Rio wasn't reacting as if to an offensive. "What do you mean?"

He lowered the scope and handed it to me, pointing toward the south. "Pithica didn't locate us. This attack is widespread."

It took me a minute, but I found the gas station and small cluster of buildings just visible in the direction Rio had indicated, tiny even through the scope. People were standing around outside, milling in a way that was not quite normal, some talking, some gesticulating broadly at one another. The twilight was deep enough that some lights should have been on, but everything was dark.

"What the hell?" I said. "A power outage?"

Rio pulled the burner cell out of his pocket, reinserted the battery, and hit the power button. Nothing.

"No," he said. "Not a power outage."

"Then what?"

He squinted toward the horizon. "EMP. Pithica was warned by the alerts going out. It's protecting itself."

Rio swung down off the roof; I followed closely behind him as we burst back into the house. "Explain, Rio!" I demanded. "How the hell did they—"

"Guys, everything's fried!" came Checker's panicked voice. "They must have hit us with an EMP; it's the only thing that could've—"

"That's what Rio said!" I interrupted. "Somebody start explaining *now*!"

"EMP," said Checker. "Electromagnetic pulse, it'll fry any electronics in the radius—"

"I know that," I cut in. "I'm not an idiot. Skip to the 'how' part."

"High-altitude nuclear detonation is probably the easiest way," said Checker.

I felt dazed. "Easiest?"

"Clearly you're not up on your right-wing nutjob blogs," said Checker. "One high-altitude nuke could take out all the electronics in the United States. The good news is, no loss to human life, except of course for all of the countless people who are depending on medical electronics to keep them kicking—"

"Cars," I said. "What about cars?"

"I don't—I don't know. Most cars are computerized these days— older ones might have a better chance? I don't know—"

"We need to get out of the radius," I said. "Checker, you've been backing up in the cloud, right? If we can get to a place that's not fried, will the network be—"

"Distributed computing, it should be fine, well, depending on how much they took out—what if they *have* taken out the whole country?" Checker's voice had gone very high.

"Would they?" I wondered. "They're all about helping people. And last they knew we were still in LA. Plus, if they got provoked into this by what Steve's group did and tracked it back to them—"

A squealing noise cut me off. Rio had been digging around inside a metal box, and came up with a working radio. Apparently a true survivalist kept emergency electronics inside a Faraday cage.

Panicked voices overlapped each other on the airwaves. Rio finally found a frequency on which a crisp-voiced woman informed us that whatever "event" had happened . . .

It is unverified whether this is an attack or the result of a natural phenomenon. . . . The president is asking people to help each other out in this time of crisis and to avoid panic. . . . We now have reports FEMA and the National Guard are being deployed to affected areas. . . ."

. . . was at least localized to Southern California and parts of Arizona, Nevada, and Mexico.

"This is not their endgame," said Rio.

"You're right." Shit. I saw it too. "This is a stalling tactic. They're giving themselves enough time to hunt us down and stop us."

"They will have some plan of escalation," said Rio. "They are very efficient when they pool their resources."

"So what do we do?" asked Checker.

"*We* don't do anything," I said. "You get out of here. I'm going back to LA."

"Cas," said Rio.

"We have to bait them," I insisted. "They have to believe they've got our scent until we can get the notifications out. That's all that matters right now."

"Abort," said Rio.

"No." I turned on him, talking very fast. "What's going to happen if we do? If we run? What will their next step be? Bombing the LA metropolitan area into the ground and hoping they'll kill us somewhere in there? As long as we're a threat, they won't stop coming after us. Which means we've got only two options—either we come to them and save them the trouble, or we make good on our threat, or we do both before they mow down anyone else in their way."

I paused, out of breath.

"Do you have a plan?" said Rio, his baritone quiet in the shadowy darkness.

One was forming in my head even as we spoke. It was dangerous. Scratch that, it was insane. And it very well might not work. But I already knew I was going to go for it anyway.

"Yes. As a matter of fact, I do. And I think—I think we've got a chance to take down Dawna Polk at the same time." I took a deep breath. "But you're not going to like it."

I told them.

They didn't like it.

thirty-three

My plan depended on us being able to find a working car. If we couldn't do that, we were stuck.

Fortunately, both the van and my clunky sedan turned over on the first try. They were both old cars, so maybe they didn't have enough electronics to matter. I decided I didn't care why they still worked, only that they did.

Rio and Checker loaded into the van. "Get him out safe," I said to Rio, leaning on the open passenger window. He nodded. "How long do you think you'll need?" I asked Checker.

He was gripping his arms across his chest very tightly. "I don't know. Traffic might be backed up getting out, but once I can get my hands on a working laptop—two hours. I can finish in two."

"I can give you that," I said. "Good luck. It's all down to you now."

He shivered. "Cas."

"Yeah?"

He couldn't seem to form words.

"Spit it out," I said. "We've got to get going."

"Tell me you think you can make it," he said in a low voice, not looking at me. "Tell me you and Arthur aren't going to die for this."

That was what was bothering him? Oh. "I'm really good at staying not-dead," I tried to assure him. "It's a special talent of mine."

"Seriously," said Checker. "Please."

Maybe he was right to be concerned. After all, I reflected, I was going after an organization that had just taken down an entire metropolitan area to get to me, and I was going to put myself willingly in their crosshairs. Along with a good friend of Checker's. When I looked at it that way, my plan felt a trifle more daunting.

"Hey," I said awkwardly. I wasn't good at being comforting. "I'm really good at what I do. Ask Rio."

"He doesn't like your plan, either."

"Very true," put in Rio.

I didn't know what to say. I wasn't used to having people worried about my welfare. "Okay, you're on," I said.

Checker finally looked up at me, forehead wrinkling in confusion. "On for what?"

"That drinking contest. Once this is over. You don't know what you've gotten yourself into, I promise you."

That got a smile out of him. "Promise me you'll watch Arthur's back?"

"I promise. Now get going." I thumped the hood of the van and headed back over to my clunker as Rio made a precarious three-point turn at the top of the drive and then eased down the slope.

I put my car in gear and crawled down the gravel after them. The indicator lights flickered at me nonsensically, winking on and off. I tried smacking the dashboard, but it didn't help. Well, I'd be fine as long as the engine stayed working—I had enough gasoline in the back to get me to LA five times over.

As I drew closer to the city, however, the freeway became increasingly clogged until traffic stalled to a standstill. Full dark had fallen, and not everyone's headlights were working, leaving the lanes a weird play of shadows and vehicle silhouettes. I waited in the car for ten minutes, engine idling, the lines of cars not moving an inch, and then I got out and went to the trunk, where I pulled out a few weapons to sling over my shoulder. The driver in the minivan next to me stared in frozen horror, her face a pale circle in her window, before ducking down over her daughter in the front seat, who kept trying to fight back up so she could see what was making her mother so afraid. I ignored them.

I threaded the strap from a bag of ammo through a couple of gas cans and slung that on my back as well, and checked on the two hand-guns in the back of my belt. Then I hopped up on the roof of my car and looked out over the parking lot of vehicles. Within minutes I heard a faint rumble and saw the headlamp of a motorcycle threading through the stopped traffic on the other side of the median, headed out of LA. I ran, leaping from car to car, ignoring the squeals and screams of the drivers beneath me as my boots dented their roofs, and hit the pavement just in time for the biker to slam on his brakes. Or rather, her brakes. She squealed to a stop on the fringes of another car's headlights to reveal a woman in full gear that was head-to-toe pink, on a pink bike, with a helmet that was black with pink flames.

I swung the Mossberg on my shoulder around and pointed it right at her.

"I need your bike!" I shouted over the roar of the motorcycle's engine.

She hit the cutoff and raised her gloved hands. I gestured with the shotgun; she kicked frantically at the stand to put it down and dis-mounted to stumble to the side against a Jeep.

I yanked her pink-trimmed saddlebags off the back and threw them at her; she didn't bring her hands down quite fast enough to catch them. I swung onto the bike, restarted it, and cut between two tractor-trailers to turn the bike and start back toward LA, going the wrong way on the stopped freeway. I didn't bother stealing her helmet; the police had more important things to worry about right now.

In the side mirror, I could see the pink biker staring after me, a gawky, bright statue in the Jeep's headlights, exhaust fumes fogging her image.

I faced a long haul back to the Westside. The 10 was stopped all the way in, and when I headed down the shoulder of an on-ramp, I hit gridlocked streets of half-deserted vehicles. With no helmet on,

I could hear shouts and crashes over the motorcycle's engine, and sirens sounded from at least three directions. Los Angeles was not famous for the cooperation of its residents in times of trouble. The looting had already started.

The city was black. It was eerie: all the streetlights loomed dead and silent, every building a blank, dark silhouette in the night. Many of the gridlocked cars had been deserted, and the residents who had taken to the streets had become the monsters who came out at such times. One hoodlum ran down the pavement shouting, smashing a crowbar through car windows. He ran straight at my bike, swinging as I barreled between the stopped vehicles, hollering a wordless ber-serker cry. I took my left hand off the clutch, rolled the throttle all the way open with my right, drew one of the handguns, and shot him in the head. He crumpled in the tight space between the cars, and I swerved around his falling body, the math giving me just enough room.

I was two streets away from the apartment I'd been holed up in with Arthur. The final block was bathed in the pulsing red of police lights, their deadly brightness reflecting off pavement still wet from the recent rain. I could see officers with nightsticks out, shouting and trying to corral belligerent rioters. None of them paid the least bit of attention to me. I pulled the bike over, raced up the stairs to the flat, and burst through the door to find it dark and empty. Arthur wasn't there.

He wouldn't have gone back to his home or office, not with all the people after us right now, and with no working cell phone, I had no way of contacting him. But despite my lack of observational prowess when it came to the human condition, in the short time I'd known Arthur I had figured out a few things about him. And I had a sneak-ing suspicion that in a time of crisis he'd try to find somewhere to be of help.

After that, it didn't take long to find him. I just went to the nearest ER.

The place was chaos. The whole ER was a mess of screaming, jostling, crying people who had swarmed the hospital entirely until they swelled out onto the sidewalk in a pawing, pleading mass. The hospital was as dark as everywhere else—apparently their generators had been fried—but people had dug up working flashlights and some battery-operated lanterns, and I saw some of the nurses battling the commotion with glowsticks around their necks.

Tresting's composite might still be on police "most wanted" boards, but that didn't seem to matter to him. He had thrown himself into the crisis with authority, and was currently rescuing the ER staff from drowning by being a booming voice of order—keeping people neatly triaged, calming screaming voices, and soothing hysterical parents. The staff was going to hate me for pulling him out.

I pushed through the mob of bleeding and coughing people. "Tresting!"

He turned, and his eyes went wide. "Russell! Get those out of here!"

I had forgotten I still had several large firearms slung on my back. I glanced to either side to find a circle of space had formed around me, people shrinking back and staring. The dancing flashlight beams threw the pushing crowd into a seething knot of flesh and shadows, its humanity hidden in the darkness. I grabbed Arthur's arm and hauled. "Come on, then."

Fortunately, Los Angeles had other things on its mind than a private citizen who wasn't currently using the firearms she was carrying, and nobody tried to stop us from heading anonymously back out into the night.

"Russell, what the hell is going on?" demanded Tresting as I hurried him along the sidewalk. "Didn't work, did it? That thing you were trying to swing with the damn flash drive?"

"We started," I said. "Long story short, Pithica caught wind of it and decided the quick way to stop us was to knock out every computer in LA."

"They did this . . . ?" Arthur's mouth dropped open. He shook himself. "Thought you left LA. Didn't think I'd see you back here."

"Well, we didn't want you to know—Pithica brainwashing and all that—but LA's a big enough city to disappear into."

He nodded, not questioning it. "Checker okay?"

"Rio's looking after him."

Tresting's expression soured.

"Hey, he's safer than anyone I know that way," I said severely. "Look, I've got to finish getting our program out. I need your help."

"Thought I was a liability," he said.

"Desperate times, desperate measures. I need backup."

It was fortunate he didn't know me better. He didn't question that either. Instead he just took a breath and nodded, back in crisis mode. "Where to?"

"Los Angeles Air Force Base," I said, leading him around the corner at a quick trot. "They're the people most likely to still have a working computer. Hop on." We had reached the pink bike.

Arthur looked from me to the bike. "Your color."

"We have working transportation; don't knock it." I unslung the Mossberg and handed it to him along with a pistol. "Warn me before letting loose with the shotgun."

"Will do," he said, accepting the weapons and climbing up behind me on the bike.

"And hang on," I instructed. "I'm planning to take the corners a little tight."

We weren't far from LAX and the air force base. At least not the way I rode. As soon as the green airport signage began popping up and wallpapering the streets, I pulled over to ditch the bike.

"What's the plan?" asked Arthur, shaking his legs out. He didn't otherwise comment on my driving.

"Break in," I said. "Find working equipment. Finish the job. Elegant in its simplicity, isn't it?"

"What about all this?" Arthur swept a hand toward the darkened, violent streets. "Can we fix it? Restore the power?"

"Power's not the problem," I said. "It's an EMP. They fried every circuit board from here to Phoenix. Anything run by a chip will have to be replaced before it'll work again, even after the power comes back online."

He seemed to get it. "That's why the cell phones are out, too."

"Yeah. I'm guessing landlines might still work as long as they weren't fancy cordless phones with a power connection—well, assuming something somewhere along the way in the telephone network hasn't started being run by a computer. And shortwave radio would still work." That was the sum total of Checker's and my combined knowledge and guesses about postapocalyptic emergency communication. I hoped the base would have one or the other. And I hoped Arthur was listening to me.

"I can't believe Dawna—" His mouth twisted, and he ran a hand over his face.

It was exactly the opening I needed. "Well, she'll have more than enough to occupy her soon. Rio managed to poison her, you know. Back when we were all captured. A bad poison. Time release, but she'll be starting to feel the effects right around now and be dead within a few days. Christ, what a relief." I bit my lip. I was talking too much, but then, I'm a very bad liar.

Arthur didn't seem to notice. He went still. *"What?"*

"Yeah. There's an antidote, but once she starts showing symptoms, it'll be too late. Come on, let's head." I kept him in the corner of my eye, wondering if he would turn the shotgun on me, demand the antidote to take back to Dawna. But he didn't seem to be that far gone.

Hopefully he'd be just far gone enough to warn her.

thirty-four

WE LEFT the motorcycle in a park a few blocks out and I led the way at a jog, hoping I remembered the layout of streets correctly in this part of Los Angeles. I didn't have the city memorized, but I'd had enough close escapes that I had made a point of swallowing large portions of the road map, especially the areas near the airports.

Of course, the moment we skidded around the corner onto El Segundo, we ran straight into a gang of looters shouting raucously and hurling Molotov cocktails through the windows of a large sporting goods store.

They saw us. One of them catcalled. Another drew a knife. I shot him before he finished the motion.

The shouting stopped as if the looters' voices had been snuffed out. I saw another guy start to reach into his pants and shot him, too. One of his mates started screaming profanity at me, and my handgun barked one more time—I had far more bullets than I had patience.

The looters all froze. The sporting goods store started to catch fire, the flames roaring upward and backlighting them into aggressive silhouettes.

By that time Arthur had the shotgun up on my left. "Get out of here!" he shouted.

The gang scattered.

I started to move forward, but Arthur grabbed my arm, hard. "The air force base," he said. "We're not killing anyone. Looters who try and attack us, that's one thing, but we're not killing men and women just doing their jobs."

His grip was powerful enough to leave a bruise, and his stance said he would stand his ground unless I shot him, too. Part of my brain noted this as impressive, considering that at this point, he had to know how pitifully his skills stacked up against mine—not to mention I was still holding a pistol with which I'd just shot three people, and had a G36 assault rifle slung over my shoulder.

I searched his face. He'd go down fighting for this. "Okay," I said.

His fingers tightened, the muscles around his eyes pinching. "Promise me."

"I said okay!" Behind me, flames rose in the store in a *whoosh*, punching up through the second floor, the heat scorching my exposed skin. "I promise, all right? Come on!"

He let go of me, and we dashed.

As we slipped onto the edges of the base property, I caught sight of flashlight beams dancing through one of the far buildings in a beehive of activity. That building must be the nerve center of whatever disaster response they had going, I thought—farming out personnel to help local authorities quell the rioting, coordinating logistics during the crisis. While, I hoped, maintaining some sort of emergency communication with the outside world.

We hurried into the complex. With the personnel all concentrated elsewhere, this end of the base was mostly deserted. Only one young man in fatigues tried to challenge us, running forward through the dark and shouting; I pulled my otherwise useless phone out of my pocket and threw it. He collapsed to the pavement as if his strings had been cut.

Arthur's expression tightened.

"What? He's not dead," I snapped.

We hurried toward one of the central buildings, a looming white-and-glass edifice that probably housed offices. I took a moment to get my bearings, turning toward the southeast. Yes, this was the one. Perfect.

"Let's split up," I said to Arthur. I gestured toward the far-off flashes of light and movement. "Whatever communications equipment they've got is probably that way somewhere, where all the people are. Go do your PI thing, figure out if they've got a line to the outside world and how we can get access."

He hesitated, and I literally held my breath.

"Where are you going to be?"

"I've got to jury-rig some working hardware. I'm going to look for a server room in a Faraday cage, maybe try to cobble together some unfried equipment." I was improvising the technobabble, but it sounded good. "Meet me back here on the top floor."

Before he could respond, I drove the butt of my rifle through the glass of the door next to me, the pane showering down with a crash. Arthur winced and glanced around, but no alarm sounded. As I'd suspected, security was at least partially down. "Top floor," I reminded Arthur, and ducked through the broken door.

The halls inside were dark and cavernously empty. I didn't waste any time: I broke into the first office I came to, unscrewed the back of a dead computer, and yanked out all the circuit boards. When I'd asked Checker how much Arthur knew about computers, his answer had been, "Well, he knows how to use a search engine, which is sadly more than I can say for a lot of people." I didn't know too much more than that myself when it came to hardware, but Arthur didn't know how much I didn't know.

I collected an armful of as many sufficiently electronic-looking doodads as I could and headed for the stairs. The ground floor had been deserted, but in the stairwell I ran into one surprised-looking woman in a civilian suit who would sleep off her concussion hidden in a dark bathroom stall. *See, Arthur? I'm keeping my word.*

Fortunately, the top floor was just as empty as the bottom one had been. As per Rio's instructions, I found the southeast corner, which turned out to be a conference room. It was slightly less dark than the rest of the building by virtue of the two walls' worth of windows that let in whatever moon and starlight Southern California had tonight. I dumped my armful of circuit boards and ribbon cable on the table and left to find another nearby office; within fifteen minutes, I had amassed a large pile of random electronic hardware as well as four laptops, a pair of scissors, a utility knife, a roll of duct tape, and a screwdriver. I surveyed my stash.

"Time to be a motherfucking genius," I muttered to myself, and set to work.

I wondered if Arthur would come back and find me. I wondered if the people I'd sent him for would find me first.

I wondered if he'd do what I needed him to in the first place. If he'd try. If the base personnel would take him down before he had a chance.

Enough time passed in the dim conference room that I started to wonder how much longer I should give him until I should assume my plan had failed. How much longer until I should start coming up with other options. But then I heard a quiet call from somewhere down the hall: "Russell?"

I drew my gun and didn't move, in case he wasn't alone. "In here," I called, equally softly.

A single set of footsteps approached from down the hallway, and Arthur came in, still carrying the shotgun. "They got communications," he reported. "Think I see a few ways in, but it'll be tricky. How long will you need in there?"

"Not long," I said. "Couple of minutes, at most. I'll, uh, I'll be able to let you know in a second." I put my gun down and picked up the utility knife. While Arthur had been gone, I'd had time to twist wires between a whole mess of the circuit components until they twined into an overlapping tangle, as if Checker's Hole had upchucked on the table. I'd opened the cases of two of the laptops as well, spreading their guts into the jumble. Now I picked up a bundle of wires and started stripping the ends with confidence.

"What can I do?" said Arthur.

I badly wanted to know if he'd made the call, but I couldn't ask. "Watch the door," I said instead.

He moved over and did so, Mossberg at the ready. "We going to have to move all of what you're working on over there?"

Shit. I hadn't actually thought that far ahead, given that this was a fake plan and all. "Uh, yeah," I said. "Or, no, not all of it. I've got to find the pieces here still working. Some bits are fried more than others."

"You can do that without power?"

"The laptop batteries still have juice," I said quickly.

Fortunately he seemed to accept that.

I tinkered pointlessly with the components for another twenty minutes, long enough to begin resigning myself to suspecting we'd underestimated Arthur after all. But then he straightened in the doorway.

"Russell. We got incoming."

I was by his side in less than a second, swinging my weapons to bear, a small part of my brain cataloging that Arthur hadn't fired yet and whether that might mean he had become Dawna's tool entirely—

But when I reached the doorway, I realized why a gunfight hadn't exploded. Dawna's mooks were here, but they weren't attacking.

Dark silhouettes moved in the corridor, but down by the far end, crouching in doorways and against the wall with the spiky shape of weaponry outlined in the dimness. They were holding a line well back from us, not advancing. Yet.

Arthur must have sensed me raising my weapon, because he reached out to check my arm. "Might be that's worse for us."

I hesitated. Arthur's divided loyalties notwithstanding, he did have a point. Presumably, the troops weren't attacking because they knew Dawna wanted me alive. She needed what I knew about the imaginary poison and its equally imaginary antidote, which was the same reason she wasn't blowing this building into a crater from safe up in the atmosphere. It might not be in our best interest for me to force her troops into pulling their triggers.

Especially as that might interfere with the real plan.

Still, my fingers twitched. The enemy was here. Surrounding us. Filling every escape route with their strength to give them the best possible position to spring their trap.

Their presence wasn't exactly unanticipated. Still, every instinct clamored for me to smash our way out. Press my advantage. Clear an escape route.

I forced myself to turn away from the door and edged over to the windows to survey the ground outside. I wasn't surprised by what I saw there either, though that didn't stop the G36 from leaping to my shoulder by instinct. Figures in black fatigues swarmed the pavement below, taking up positions in a bristling perimeter.

I tried to keep a mental count of where they were. They might not be trying to kill us right now, but even if this all worked the way we wanted it to, Arthur and I might end the night up against an army. I totaled up my ammo in a one-to-one correspondence with the heads outside—I'd have to get creative, but I'd give us at least sixty-forty odds, and that included getting Arthur out without too many holes in him.

I consciously kept my eyes directed at the ground, trying not to flick my gaze up to the skyscrapers looming over the next few blocks. Rio had told me not to look, but it took an effort. If the troops decided to clear those buildings as well . . .

Well, in that case we were all done for.

The movement outside slowed.

Arthur's voice came tightly from the doorway. "We got another way out?"

We weren't going anywhere, not yet. I retreated into the room, back to the computer components scattered across the table.

"I have to fix this," I said. I lowered the rifle and forced my fingers to unclench themselves from the grip. It took an effort. My brain refused to stop calculating how many tenths of a second it would take for me to be ready to fire again.

"Russell—" started Arthur.

"It's important," I said mechanically. I turned my back on him and picked up a circuit board as if it had meaning. It was a PCI card of some kind. I didn't even know what it did.

I took the utility knife and started prying tiny microchips off it. They went flying into the chaos of components with tiny *pings*.

They weren't so loud that I couldn't hear the footsteps in the hallway.

Not the soft, heavy tread of combat boots, but the click of heels. Sure and steady. Coming this way.

Past the armed perimeter, closer and closer, uncannily loud and impossibly dangerous.

Arthur was silent, and didn't fire.

I gripped the utility knife so hard my hand started shaking. I still held the PCI card in my other hand, but my brain was buzzing with something I was fairly sure was horror, and I couldn't even remember what I was pretending to be doing with it.

Why had I thought this would be a good idea?

The approaching footsteps overwhelmed the space, crowding out every other sound, every other thought.

In my peripheral vision, Arthur moved back from the doorway. A shadow fell past him, a thin blade of darkness, as a figure entered the room.

"Good evening," said Dawna Polk.

thirty-five

I KEPT my eyes on the circuit board in my hand, as Rio had told me.

"You have something I need," said Dawna, her voice silk. "I'm here to retrieve it."

Rio had also cautioned me not to speak, but she was impossible not to respond to. "I could beat your men."

Dawna laughed lightly. "They're not here for you."

Rio. The troops were here in case Rio arrived. She could beat me all by herself.

Her shadow moved as she took another few steps into the room. I felt her gaze on the back of my neck, tracing every knot of my posture, every breath of movement that revealed to her the smallest strand of thought. Piercing my skull.

Rio's voice echoed in my brain, telling me under no circumstances to let her see my face, making me promise, impressing upon me that the slim probability we had of this working existed only as long as I kept my head down. I felt myself turning and tried to stop, tried to deny her, to keep her limited to my body language—*don't look up, keep your eyes away, don't ruin everything, we're so close—!*

No words, no precautions, no plans, made any difference, not against her. I turned and met Dawna's eyes, and the moment I did, the smallest datum that she might have been lacking snapped into place.

She knew everything.

She knew that Checker was far outside the county, that he was the one scrambling to stream our code, that I had left it all in his hands.

She knew that she had never been poisoned, that Rio and I had invented the story so Arthur would feel compelled to call her and tell her where I was, because Arthur's messed-up brain was still sympathetic enough to her not to want her dead. She knew we had chosen such a story so she wouldn't bomb the building outright and kill us all once she found out our location.

She knew that I was bait, that I was here only to draw her out, that I'd been confident setting myself in the pit of the trap because I could beat or evade anyone she might send down outside of herself.

And she knew that Rio was at that moment taking aim with a high-powered rifle directly at her head.

None of it should have mattered. She shouldn't have had anywhere left to go. She was unarmed, her troops still a distance back, and even if she'd had a weapon and the skill to go with it, nothing should have made any difference against a sniper. We should have been able to beat her, once and for all, at last: Rio was one of the few human beings on the planet mentally capable of killing her, and we'd lured her into his sights.

Almost.

I didn't know precisely where Rio was, but I had glimpsed the heights of the nearby buildings, could draw the array of lines that might angle through the windows to target anyone in this room. Even with the most generous of estimates, Dawna Polk needed to take half of one step more.

And because I knew it, she knew it.

My chest felt like it folded in on itself, my vision tunneling. It had been pure folly to think I could outwit her. I'd trapped myself and Arthur and Rio, here at the end of the line.

Now Dawna would do . . . whatever she liked with us.

She smiled and took a step backward, well out of the danger zone, and flicked her eyes to Arthur—

—who spun with the speed of an action hero and aimed the shotgun exactly at my center of mass.

And I, someone who could have turned Arthur Tresting into a smear on the carpet without so much as thinking about it, who could have disarmed and incapacitated him in a fraction of normal human reaction time before he ever got the gun on me—I didn't stop him.

My breath came short in my throat, frustration blinding me. I *knew* what Dawna was doing, knew she was somehow silently and subliminally convincing me not to act, but trying to fight her was like pushing back against a phantasm. My resistance wilted away as if it had never been. I still had a rifle slung on my shoulder, a handgun shoved in my belt, but my hands stayed soft and useless at my sides.

Dawna twitched her head at Arthur and me. As if in a dream, we sidestepped closer to the windows, until the dim ambient light outlined us clearly. The troops outside had increased into a black-clad wall.

Sealing us in.

"Call him down," Dawna said.

I knew who she meant, and I couldn't disobey. I gestured at the windows, beckoning at Rio from a thousand yards away. The barrel of Arthur's shotgun stayed steady on me, a wide bore of death. His jaw was tight and sweat had begun slipping down his temples, but Arthur didn't like or trust me nearly well enough for his internal battle to mean much. He knew it, I knew it, and Dawna knew it.

I imagined the rationalizations she must be building inside his head right now, starting with the fact that I worked with Rio and escalating through every dead body I had left in our wake the past weeks. If she told him to kill me, I'd be lucky if he did me the honor of hesitating.

Rio had told me this was a bad idea. I hadn't listened.

"You thought you could trap me," Dawna said. She sounded more surprised and amused than angry. "How perfectly . . . quaint. Whatever gave you the idea you might succeed?"

I didn't want to answer, but the words came anyway, cracked and hoarse. "I had to give it a shot."

And our plan had almost worked. Almost . . .

Until we'd missed.

"I'll admit, we fell for the first part of your little ruse," Dawna said. Her voice became derisive. "Your arrogance is unbelievable. You fancy it noble to assassinate me, and thus you are willing to let so many millions of others suffer and be killed—all because *you* have the gall to judge that they should, because *we* are somehow evil for helping them."

Dawna had never before spoken to me anything less than politely. It jolted me.

"You think me incapable of your brand of anger? You have already caused me an unconscionable expenditure of time and resources. And if your programmer friend is even partially successful, you will bring about untold casualties. You condemn us for playing God, yet you decide to toy with the same forces when you have no concept of the fallout." Her words whipped at me, cold and furious. "Do you have any idea how many people all over the world would die if your little plan were to be successful?"

"At least one," I managed to riposte, but it came out strangled. No small part of me had started to wonder if she was right.

Pithica does kill innocent people, I tried to remind myself, thinking of Reginald Kingsley while I stared down the barrel of Arthur's gun. But the justifications were growing slippery, like a proof with scattered missing steps I couldn't quite drag out of memory.

Stopping them . . . is not . . . wrong . . .

I heard a noise at the door and glanced over, but it wasn't Rio, only one of Dawna's paramilitary troops. I hadn't seen her summon him.

"Track down the programmer," Dawna ordered him. "He'll have driven east from Yucca Valley. Check electronics stores along the edge of the blackout zone for break-ins; he'll need a computer. This is our top priority—put all other units on it."

The trooper nodded smartly and left again.

Shit. Checker. Even through all the sudden doubts, my stomach curdled in dread.

"Oh, dispense with the drama," Dawna said with disgust. "They're not going to kill him. Your coconspirator has some skill; he's already been deemed to be useful enough to come and work for us."

The dread froze into horror.

"I grow tired of your judgment," snapped Dawna.

"Then stop reading my thoughts."

She fell silent.

I was still doing my best not to look at her, not that it mattered anymore. Instead I strove to refocus my attention on Arthur. I'd caught a movement from him out of the corner of my eye, right while Dawna was castigating me, as if the shotgun had twitched slightly. I tried to think about that without looking directly at it, like studying a shadow instead of turning toward the sun.

Rio appeared in the room.

He materialized so suddenly and quietly that I could have sworn Dawna started slightly. He was unescorted by any of her guards, and I wondered how he had come through her perimeter—the troops down on the pavement outside had shown no movement, and I'd heard nothing from the hallway. But that meant little when it came to Rio. The men and women who'd been standing watch inside the building might easily be unconscious or dead.

Or maybe they'd run. People sometimes did, if they'd heard Rio's name before.

Dawna might have been thinking the same thing, but she recovered in less than a breath. "I'm glad to see you were wise enough to listen," she said, her voice cool again. "If you had tried to kill me, Ms. Russell would be dead."

Rio lifted one shoulder in a minuscule half shrug, as if to say, *Maybe, maybe not.* His hands were empty and held out to his sides.

"Yes, perhaps you would have been skilled enough to rescue her and still accomplish your assassination," Dawna said. "It seems I was correct in thinking you would not risk it."

"Quite a chance to take," I spoke up. I couldn't help feeling a squeezing frustration. Some part of me had still harbored a last hope that Rio might pull a rabbit out of a hat and save us all.

"Not terribly," said Dawna. She turned away from Arthur and me to address Rio. "You really are predictable in your own way. Did you honestly think this would work?"

Rio shrugged again. "It was a gamble I judged worthwhile."

"You shouldn't have told Ms. Russell your plan, then. She gave you away."

"Regrettably unavoidable," said Rio. "It was her idea."

"Then someone else should have played your bait."

She wasn't wrong about that, but there hadn't been anyone else.

"So fascinating, that you've gone to such lengths to save her and then permit her to walk directly into the lion's den once more," Dawna continued to muse. "An enigma. You'll forgive my curiosity; I see so few mysteries in people."

Rio doesn't "permit" me to do anything, I almost said aloud, but the words stayed on the edge of my tongue, because I realized—Dawna was well and truly ignoring me. She hadn't responded to my radiated anger or to my silent retort. Her attention was all on Rio.

And Arthur's gun twitched again.

I hadn't imagined it. Arthur was staring fixedly at the shotgun in his hands as he pointed it at me, all the muscles in his face vibrating with tension. A bead of sweat trickled down his neck and slid under his collar, and as Dawna continued her calm conversation with Rio, the barrel of the Mossberg began to shake with tiny tremors.

Dawna thought she'd taken care of us. She'd dismissed us as a solved problem.

Go, I urged Arthur silently, trying not to make my thoughts too loud. *Go, go—keep pushing*—the shotgun hadn't wavered enough yet, but I drew out the spread pattern of the buckshot, rebalancing my weight, standing ready. . . .

"I would love to know what you have done to her," Dawna was saying to Rio. "Inspiring such loyalty. She has no idea, and you aren't telling me. Of course, the weakness seems to go both ways."

"You brought me down here," said Rio. "What do you want?"

"You, of course," said Dawna. "I had still thought to harness your power, but unfortunately my colleagues have deemed our lack of success in that area quite indicative. The decision has been made that you are a liability with too little potential for turning to an asset."

"In simpler language, you are going to kill me," Rio said.

The floor felt like it dropped out from under me.

No. *No.*

A cascade of possibilities for violent action brute-forced their way through my consciousness with lightning speed, but Arthur's finger rested on the shotgun trigger, and any move I made—but I had to do *something*, even if I had a trivial probability of survival, I had to—had to—

"I admit I have little stomach for such acts," Dawna continued, turning to move toward Arthur and me as if she were on a leisurely stroll. "Unfortunately, Mr. Tresting is otherwise occupied at the moment, and I think convincing Ms. Russell to do the deed would take more time and energy than we have here, don't you? Though the irony would fascinate me. I suppose I could call one of my people, but—" She reached Arthur's side and drew the handgun I'd given him from his belt, checking the chamber and flicking off the safety. She might not like getting her hands dirty, but she knew her way around a pistol. "You are a very dangerous man when Ms. Russell isn't being threatened. I think it better to err on the side of completing things without further complication."

She didn't cross back to him. She was too smart to get close. Instead, she stood square and leaned her weight into the balls of her feet, her stance rolling into careful, solid isosceles triangles, and raised the gun.

Arthur's shotgun wavered to the side and dipped down.

Not far. Not far enough for it to make a difference for anybody else. Not far enough even for anyone to say he wasn't aiming at me anymore.

But just far enough for me.

I dove in, ducking to the side and snapping my elbow forward to smash into Arthur's temple. He crumpled. My hands came around the shotgun, faster than raising my own rifle—it flowed out of his dropping hands and into mine in the smallest fraction of a second. The mathematics roared through me in a torrent, every motion a thousand interacting vectors in space as the barrel snapped into alignment and I squeezed my finger against the trigger just as Dawna half spun back toward me.

The scene crystallized in my vision. Arthur, next to me, eyes rolling back in his head as he fell bonelessly toward the floor. Dawna, pistol still pointed at Rio, but shock and horror on her face as she thrust one hand back at me. Rio, who'd begun moving the instant I did, his coat flaring as he launched himself at Dawna from across the room.

"Oh my God!" Dawna shrieked. *"I know what you are!"*

Every muscle screeched to a grinding halt. My finger stopped half a millimeter from firing.

My vision doubled. Dawna's voice still echoed in my head, but she hadn't spoken, at least not out loud—no time had passed. Arthur collapsed one centimeter more, falling to meet the floor; Rio's advance flew forward in slow motion; and Dawna still hadn't finished turning to face me, but suddenly she was everywhere. Under my skin, inside my skull, clawing away at the layers of my brain. She stripped me to the atoms, tearing every last shred of my person from its moorings to be scrutinized and cataloged—she saw the parts of me I didn't know existed, read me like she had a detailed manual of my soul, tore me apart and undid me until I had no sense of self anymore.

"I see now," she whispered, and again it took no time at all. Somehow I knew what she wanted to say to me in the space of a thought. "I understand. I should have looked more closely before. If I'd had any reason to think you were . . ."

The double image of her reached out and then splintered a thousand times, and somewhere in my head, I screamed.

Dawna laughed. "You told me everything. Of course you told me everything, except what you didn't know yourself. So cunningly hidden, even from you."

"What are you talking about?" I tried to say, or at least my dream-self did, my thought-self trapped here in Dawna Polk's world.

She lifted her hands, and my neurons flowed through them like water, reflecting the delighted sparkle in her eyes. "It's brilliant work. Seamless. It had to be one of us. So much makes sense now. Your relationship with Sonrio. Why you're more resistant to me. And all your . . . unusual . . . efficiency."

She looked back at her real self, her physical self, the one whirling in shock between two armed and dangerous people, and smiled. "Unluckily for you and Sonrio, I don't need a weapon to hold you hostage, Ms. Russell. Especially now that I know exactly who you are."

She plunged one hand deep into my consciousness. Held it in her fingers. Squeezed.

"I regret this, Ms. Russell." The words echoed through pain and darkness, as every shard of awareness, every perception of reality, began to flake away. It hurt, a yawning, delocalized pain that I tasted in all my senses. "It will be somewhat brutish. Now. *Remember.*"

thirty-six

Until now, I had only had an inkling of what Dawna Polk's powers could do. Now the full weight of her focus drilled into me, crushing me to the core, plumbing my soul to its gritty dregs. Her previous work had been a scalpel, seamless and precise—now she wielded a sledgehammer.

She didn't care to manipulate anymore. Only destroy. And I didn't have the slightest chance against her—probability zero.

She had won.

I was peripherally aware that time was still frozen, that we were operating in the breath between thoughts. Physically, I couldn't even move, because I didn't have *time* to move. We played her game now.

"Let us start with an easy one," my mental image of Dawna said, and when she smiled, her teeth stretched into the fangs of a monster. "Sonrio. The degree to which you trust him defies all sense. Where did you meet him? *Remember.*"

It was like the crack of a whip. I buckled, my world spinning.

Rio refracted into ten, twenty, fifty Rios, all surrounding me. All strangely, subtly different. Different clothes. Different scars. The subtle variations in haircut and facial hair and age that came from knowing someone over a period of years.

"He . . . he saved me," I tried to say. That was the right answer. The truth. Wasn't it?

"From what?" Dawna taunted.

"From . . ."

The scene fractured like broken glass. One of the Rios appeared beside me, a hand shooting out. I tried to react but my dream-self was too slow, my body molasses.

Rio's arm flashed into me—*into* me—through me. His face blurred and stretched, becoming demonic. I grabbed at his arm, scratched at it, suffocating, but he wasn't Rio anymore.

Instead he was an older woman. Someone I both knew and didn't, with a scar through her eye, wearing a white coat and holding a syringe.

"Protectors," she said. "The halberd against any who would threaten. That's what they wanted. That's what they'll get."

She swung the syringe overhead like an executioner's sword. It cleaved into me, and my face hit red tile.

I didn't know where I was. I didn't know *who* I was. Connecting one thought to another seemed an impossible entropy, like I had tears in my brain and I was trying to hold the pieces together and call it whole.

Someone crouched beside my face. A slender, well-dressed woman, with dark European features. She reached out and brushed a sweaty lock of hair back from my eyes. When had my hair been long enough to fall in my eyes? That felt wrong.

"Oh, Ms. Russell," the woman said. "Or whatever your name is— we'll get there. This is such fun; I'm feeling almost nostalgic."

Dawna. The name drifted up like flotsam among wreckage, along with another word. *Enemy.*

She heard me and smiled. "Oh, you try so hard. To be truthful, here you might have a chance at fighting me, if you weren't already fighting yourself."

She snapped her fingers.

I was standing again. A man stood beside me. Someone I didn't know, and yet I did. He had bronze skin and dark hair he kept running his hand through, nervously. "You won't need it," he said. "You won't need it. It's just in case."

I picked up a pen. I didn't know what I was supposed to do with it.

"Write it," the man said urgently. "You have to."

I started to write. The words came out gibberish. The paper caught fire in my hands.

I yelled and flung it from me, and the walls erupted into flame. I threw myself down, choking, arms flung over my head, but my skin blistered and blackened—

Reality spun, a roulette wheel loaded like the chambers of a pistol.

"I have to hand it to you," Dawna said. She stood in a field and picked petals off a daisy. *Love me, love me not. Kill me. Kill me not.* "Your brain has the most inventive ways of trying to destroy you. It's impressive."

"What are you doing to me . . ." I croaked out. I had a fleeting awareness of reality: the room at the air force base, pointing a shotgun at Dawna, for all the good it would do me. But also trapped in this surreal field, dirt and leaves filling my mouth, the blades of grass stabbing my skin . . .

"Oh, I'm doing very little," Dawna answered. "I'm just . . . shall we say, unraveling someone else's work. Picking at threads, as it were. The rest is all you."

My own consciousness. The past and its buried memories rising up to ravage me.

But if we were in my mind . . . this might be Dawna's world, but it should be my turf. Shouldn't it?

Dawna's eyes widened just before I dragged myself up, and I briefly wondered if she could see my intentions writ large on the walls of my brain. I launched myself at her. It was a drunken stagger, and she sidestepped easily, but I didn't miss the burst of uncertainty in her eyes. In a flash I understood—her impulses bled through to me here, just as mine bled through to her—but I didn't have time to contemplate it.

Dawna straightened, going taller and taller until she was a spiked caricature, a comic book arachnid with only vaguely human features.

"You want to dance, Ms. Russell? Let's see what's behind door number three."

And she flung open a door—a wooden door that had appeared freestanding in the grass. I tried to duck away, but light blazed out, obliterating Dawna and the field and me.

I was at a desk, writing. Formulas dribbled from my pen, letters and symbols and lemmas and squared-off boxes to mark the conclusions. The next steps poured out as fast as I could move my hand.

"You have a call, V," said a girl's voice. "It's your mother." Her accent wasn't American—from somewhere in Africa, I thought.

"Not now." I was busy.

She poked her head in. A teenager, her skin a dark brown black, her hands calloused and burned with half her nails ripped off. The hands suited her; they were who she was.

"You're failing," she said.

"No, I'm not—" Panic clawed at me. The formulas crossed themselves, becoming nonsense.

"You're *dying*," the girl said mockingly, and suddenly she had become the woman in the white coat. "Acceptable losses!" she crowed, howling.

I lowered my head and tried to write faster, to solve this, to *solve it* because everything could be solved if only I—but the variables had become meaningless, squiggles contorting themselves into something vile. And then they became English words, over and over, in my own hand, repeating like a message in a horror movie—

Do not

Do not

Do not do not do not try try try do not try do not try

I wrote faster, the ink bleeding in black pools.

"It's just in case," said the anxious, dark-haired man again. "Write it. Just in case. Before I kill you."

Do not try do not try do not try to

"I made a deal with the devil," he said. "You should be grateful."

He's not the devil, I thought. His name's Rio.

Do not try to do not try to do not try to

remember

I raced through a jungle. Wet tree branches slapped at my face, water streaming in my eyes. Gunfire in the distance. "Get to the summit!" someone shouted, and a Dragunov sniper rifle was smooth and slick in my hands. I ran harder and the rifle was gone, the world flashing bright, the air searing my skin with its heat, and the sun glancing off the unforgiving glare of a desert, but the sand and dust swirled and drained until I tripped on concrete and windmilled, sprawling, waiting to hit.

The cracks of memory opened, and I fell into the abyss, one clacking over the other in the echoing distance. Burying me.

"Stop this," said a man in another time and place, where time was still passing. "Let her go."

"And allow you to kill me? I think not," answered a woman, but her voice was drawn and strained. "She's my hostage. You can move fast, but I will think faster, I promise you."

"If you continue to hold her this way much longer, it will kill you anyway," the man said. "You know it as well as I do. It is of no importance to you whether Cas lives or dies. Leave her."

"Your life," the woman ground out. "For hers. You want to end this? End it. I'll leave them. You have my word."

No . . .

Everything was a jumble, my life, my name, my memories. I beat back against the weight of half a hundred thousand days, of another existence I'd never lived and didn't want.

Do not try to remember

Something caught the edge of my consciousness. A realization I'd had a moment and an age ago. *I can. Fight back. My mind . . .*

Fight her.

Dawna's eyes caught me, and a thousand Dawnas turned on me in unison, but I smelled her fear. It seeped through my collapsing mental landscape even as a vise tightened on my awareness, any bubbles of coherency bursting and bleeding.

Remember.

I curled on a bed, every muscle knotted in agony, my throat raw from vomiting. "She won't survive," someone said.

I tore through the memory like it was wet tissue, tore through my own disintegrating mind, not caring about the destruction I left curling blackened in my wake. The smell of fear swelled, bitter, mixed with a trembling fatigue.

"Swear that you'll repair what damage you've done here, and I agree to your terms," said Rio's voice.

"As well as I'm able," answered the vise crushing my brain, echoing from everywhere, but I fastened on to the one strand of reality in it, the scent of *person* and *enemy* and *memory*.

Do not try to remember under any circumstances.

"No!" screamed Dawna, and she swung at me, her fist becoming a chain becoming a metal bat. The blow glanced off my shoulder, and I staggered. Dawna Polk's image fractured and then realigned.

"You're in my head," I panted raggedly. "You play by . . . *my* rules . . ."

And I rewrote my axioms.

Everything was slipping—who I was, where I was, why I was fighting—but I fled back to the one bit of mathematical solidity I had left. She'd drowned me in too many layers of unknowns, torn out any abstraction barriers that could keep me afloat—so I flattened us. Simplified us. Made radical, limiting assumptions. My infinite mental dimensions dwindled from n to two to one, one linear timestream of hardcoded information.

The peripheral noise receded into white space and vague outlines. Only Dawna solidified, she and I, here in the small patch of brainspace I'd reclaimed.

I'd have only a moment. I felt her grope through her fatigue and rear back to strike, to take this last shard of logical coherence from me.

I balled up every sense of self I had remaining and *negated* her.

The strike was too weak. I knew it as soon as I hit. I'd needed to annihilate her, and I hadn't. My two worlds jarred back together and I saw her stagger, but I couldn't press any advantage because I was falling, too. The shotgun clattered to the ground along with my rifle.

My skull glanced off the edge of the table on the way down, but the stars that flashed in my vision only joined the others that were already there.

I'd bought only a second. Not enough to do anything but make her angry.

A second, however, was all Rio needed.

He flew in like a hawk diving from the heavens, his duster flaring behind him and a knife appearing like an extension of his hand. He wrenched Dawna away from me and slammed her into the opposite wall, the knife to her throat.

My muscles were cement. I tried to focus my eyes, but my senses jittered and hitched. The room was too dim and then suddenly too bright, too quiet and then roaringly loud, and no, wait, what was happening?

The roar collapsed into the wave form of helicopter blades, the brightness a searchlight blanching everything into stark whiteness. I felt barely aware of it all even as it shook me apart, the room canting like it wanted to make me vomit and the numbers blurring together in a confused mass. The muffled boom of a megaphone clogged the air, someone shouting unintelligibly, and out of the corner of my eye I saw some of Dawna's troops materialize at the door as well, and I thought, *That's it, it's done, we're dead, dead, dead*. But Rio dragged Dawna back with him and the troops paused—talking only, reporting something to her with their guns on Rio, and they were angry, their news grim—

Even with the tables so rapidly turned, Dawna had been calm in her defeat, poised to flip it all back and take us down. But as soon as she heard her troops' report she struggled against Rio wildly, filled with a rage I'd never seen in her, shouting—shouting at me—her face contorted in fury—"*Millions will die because of you!* Is that what you wanted? *Is it?*"

He did it, I realized. *Checker did it.*

We'd won.

I scrambled for cognizance, trying to make the world go right again. But all I found were scabbed fragments. My consciousness froze and spiked and stiffened, the moment of respite I'd bought myself from Dawna folding in on itself.

She was no longer in my head. But that wasn't what had been killing me.

The tattered, torn-open memories yawned, tentacles groping for me, constricting my lungs until I couldn't breathe. Images flashed, scent and sound sucking me in and overlapping with reality until I lost my grip on both.

I registered a last awareness of the standoff: Rio with Dawna, her troops surrounding us, Arthur unconscious beside me, and I thought, *I have to,* and then I couldn't anymore.

Somewhere in a thousand echoes, I ran and dove and fought and laughed and killed. I smelled gunpowder and dust and breathed in seawater, leapt and bled and tore myself open on barbed knives. The wind rushed by and then tunneled into darkness, and Rio was there, always Rio, with a hundred other people I both knew and didn't, and I swore loyalty to them to my dying breath even as I crushed them.

I tried to claw back to the top of it all, but the more I groped, the more everything splintered. Burned. Dug its teeth back into me until I screamed.

"It's important," the dark-haired man said.

Do not try to remember under any circumstances.

I fell into darkness.

thirty-seven

REMEMBER . . .

Remember what? The thought slipped through my grasp, insubstantial as smoke.

Someone was talking, saying words, too many words, too many questions. *Shut them out shut them out shut them out—*

My breath wheezed in and out, my hands flexing and grasping against the floor. I clutched tighter into myself, curled up on my side.

Where am I? . . . Who am I?

Consciousness returned in slow intervals.

It was night, and the room was still. The math shimmered around me, a comforting background hum. Dawna Polk and her troops and her helicopter were all gone. Just gone.

So was Rio.

Arthur's face swam into focus above me. His expression was furrowed with concern, though his eyes still weren't quite focusing properly. Concussion. That's right.

Dawna had . . . what? My thoughts creased. Arthur had . . . and I had grabbed his shotgun and . . . and then . . .

And Rio had been here.

I tried to cast back and put it all together, but my memories of the confrontation had jumbled into confusion, strange images that slid around until they gave me motion sickness. The harder I tried to pin anything down, the more the images tumbled apart and dwindled away. Rio. And a dark-haired man—but no, he hadn't been here. Dawna had been here. And she had—done something to me—I grabbed futilely for the connections, the shreds of recollection. Vertigo shot through me as I lost my bearings—

"Russell?" Someone was talking to me. I couldn't remember who. "Russell? Hey, Russell, you all right?"

"Arthur," I mumbled, his name coming back to me again even as other thoughts slid away.

"The very same. You hurt?"

It took me a while to muddle out what he was asking. I had to concentrate. "No."

I heard him take a quiet breath, a sigh that sounded like relief. I wasn't sure if I'd told him the truth, but figuring out the right answer felt too difficult right now.

"What happened?" I said instead.

"Checker did it," answered Arthur. "Sounds like whatever you two were on about, it worked. Knocked Pithica off their game something good, from their reaction here." His voice faltered, as if he didn't know whether we'd done right or not.

I didn't know either.

"Dawna?" I said. "She . . ." We'd had a plan for her. We'd failed, hadn't we? She'd . . . "Rio!"

Sudden fright spiked through me. Where was Rio? I sat up so quickly that my brain crashed and melted inside my head, the room spasming, and I would have fallen over again if Arthur hadn't caught me. Rio had been fighting Dawna—and then—what if—

"Whoa, whoa there. I gotcha. Just breathe."

"Rio," I repeated urgently. "Where is—did they—?"

"Hey, sweetheart. Relax. It's okay. They didn't get him. He—saved us." His voice sounded strange on the last words, as if they didn't fit into his mouth correctly.

"How?"

"Made a deal," said Arthur.

"What kind of a deal?"

"Hey. Hey, relax. It's okay." Arthur was still holding my shoulders so I didn't fall over, and his grip was strong and comforting. "He offered them immunity."

"He's okay? He didn't—she wanted him to—"

"He's fine, far as I know. Went his own way, I think. Told me to get you home." Arthur sounded bemused at that last bit. "I wasn't real with it my own self, but I think he promised not to come after them again. To stop working against Pithica. Long as Dawna agreed to let us go and not come after us, either." He swallowed. "Well. I say 'us,' but you and 'anybody you're working with,' I believe were his exact words."

"I don't understand," I said. "So he—but Dawna got away?"

"Think it'd be more accurate to say *we* got away, sweetheart. He saved our lives, Russell."

"But . . ." But that wasn't what Rio *did*. He might rearrange his goals to save more innocent people, sure, but not at the expense of fighting a greater evil. He was the only person in the world with the ability to fight Pithica effectively, and even though they hadn't beaten him, he had still given them a free pass? Forever?

To save Arthur and me. No—to save me.

"You up to moving?" said Arthur. "We should probably hoof it before the authorities get here."

I closed my eyes and tried to shelve my scattered thoughts, then mustered my strength and attempted an upward direction. I didn't even make it off the ground. Arthur helped me shift so I could lean up against the wall.

"I need a minute," I said. I was breathing hard.

He settled next to me. "A minute it is. Could use one myself."

I took a better look at him. Even in the dim light, the side effects of his recent TKO were obvious. "Sorry about that."

"Well, I was threatening to kill you, so I think we're good."

Right. "So they all just . . . left?" I said. "After Rio made the . . ."

"Yeah. Your friend made her dismiss the army, and then he insisted on walking her out—said something about not giving them a chance to bomb the building. But he made her stop doing—or made her undo what she—whatever, he made her do a mojo thing on you before leaving." He cleared his throat. "You sure you're okay? What'd she hit you with?"

Remember.

"I don't know."

"Psychic attack or something?"

"Or something." Red tiles, and people in white coats. A jungle and a submarine and a Dragunov sniper rifle on a mountaintop against the setting sun, a thin black girl and an Asian boy and a windswept rooftop under a starry sky. Syringes and paper notes and people who wanted me dead.

I blinked. I couldn't recall what I had just been thinking about. Something stirred in my brain, a deep black undertow that scared me.

"Gotta tell you . . ." Arthur continued. "He let her do something else to us, before they went. Part of the deal. I was still out of it, but I think . . . I think he let her tell us not to come after her either, her or Pithica."

I vaguely remembered Dawna's face, hovering over me between the flashes of light and chaos. Her telling us never to come after Pithica again meant we never would.

"Why would he do that?" My voice cracked. "Why would he let her?"

"I don't know," said Arthur. "Like I said, I wasn't real lucid my own self. But I'm betting it's an enforced détente, of sorts. They don't come after us, we don't come after them."

"That's stupid."

"Well. I'll take it over being dead."

I supposed I would, too. But I didn't have to like it.

The world was starting to stabilize around me. I braced a hand against the wall to stagger upright. Arthur helped me. He wasn't moving altogether steadily himself, but we leaned on each other.

I breathed shallowly and concentrated on my balance, trying to remember why I felt so drained.

Dawna had done something to me. Right.

What . . . ?

The memory of her attack toppled in on itself further and further until it became a multicolored tangle, fading away and melting together as if I were recalling it from a distance of decades.

I had almost died. Why couldn't I . . . ?

Arthur tapped me on the shoulder, and I forced the thoughts away. Later. Later I could . . . something. I didn't know if I wanted to think about it.

We helped each other down the stairs and back out the broken door. My vandalism seemed an age ago. The cool night air kissed us; it anchored me, braced me in the world. The base was silent now, the activity at the far end gone. I wondered if that was Pithica's work.

"Where to?" asked Arthur.

"I've got a bolt-hole in the Valley," I said.

"The Valley," Arthur mused. "Long haul from here, shape we're in."

"I'm feeling better," I said, and I was, somewhat. I straightened a bit, let Arthur lean more of his weight on me. I thought back again to Dawna's psychic attack—or whatever it had been—but the more I tried to reach for it, the more the memories slipped. I remembered her saying a word to me . . . and then a blur . . . and we had been fighting . . .

Then Rio . . .

And I had woken up to Arthur's face.

"Sirens," said Arthur.

I wrenched myself back to the present. He was right; the high wail rose and fell in the near distance, coming closer. I did a quick Doppler calculation—less than a kilometer away.

"Might not be coming for us," Arthur said.

"Let's not find out," I answered. "Think you can cling to the back of a motorcycle?"

"I'm game to try." He leaned heavily on my shoulder, and we started a semicoordinated hobble across the pavement.

As we limped away, my brain itched, as if I were forgetting something important.

I reached, searched, trying to recall . . .

Only insubstantial shadows echoed back.

thirty-eight

It took forty-eight hours for most vital services to get restored in Southern California, and almost two weeks for Los Angeles to approach something akin to normal. Twenty-nine people died and hundreds were injured during the rioting; the number of people who died from the EMP knocking out medical devices was several times that. Whatever numbers game Pithica thought they were playing, they had a lot to do to make up for this one.

And they wouldn't be able to. At least not for a good while. We'd made sure of that.

I still wasn't sure whether we should be proud of what we'd done or not. I tried not to think about it too hard, and to remind myself every so often of what Pithica had done to people like Reginald and Leena Kingsley. And to Courtney Polk, the client I hadn't been able to rescue in the end.

I also tried to remind myself of how much I liked winning. I'm not going to lie; that helped.

We didn't manage to contact Checker for several days, since Arthur refused to let me steal a working satellite phone from the aid workers rebuilding the infrastructure. It turned out that Dawna, never having met Checker, had completely misjudged what he would do and probably never would have found him anyway. After Rio had dropped him off at his car, Checker had driven nonstop; as soon as he had hit a town where the lights were still on, he had gone, not to break into an electronics store in the middle of the night, but instead to a well-groomed residential neighborhood . . . where he had knocked on a reasonably pleasant-looking door, asked if they knew what was happening in Southern California, and told them that he needed emergency access to a computer with a network connection. Then he had offered all the cash we'd sent him off with in payment for the use of said computer. The very nice, middle-class family who lived in the house had been impressed by his earnestness (and the offer of so much money), had felt he was reasonably nonthreatening, and had invited him to set up in the living room with one of the parents' work laptops. I gathered they'd even made him pancakes and bacon for breakfast and offered to let him stay in their spare room until LA was sorted out.

Checker, not sure whether Pithica was still after him, politely declined the offer (although he did admit to accepting their college-aged daughter's number on the sly, which might have made her parents less inclined to trust him, had they known), and then sold his car to a chop shop for some quick capital and set himself up with a fake ID and some temp work in small-town Arizona while he waited for us to contact him. It turned out he was a remarkably street-savvy guy.

"What were you going to do if you never heard anything?" I asked, curious.

"Cry my eyes out that Cas Russell apparently met an ignominious and gruesome death at the hands of her *very stupid plan*," he answered.

I laughed and then told him about Rio's deal. Despite what we had done, we would be safe enough from Pithica in the future, as little sense as that all made. Checker said he'd be on a bus back to LA as soon as he could find a line that was running. "And now that it's safe for me to use a credit card again, I'm going to fill a suitcase with laptops to bring back with me."

"Leave it to you to black-market circuit boards during this time of crisis," I said.

"Cas Russell, what do you think of me? I need to repair the Hole. A suitcase full of laptops is barely a start."

I didn't mention that by meeting up with some old clients at some old haunts, I'd taken five jobs in getting people black market electronics in the past three days. Disaster was good for business.

The official explanation for the EMP hit the airwaves during the week after the event, and was some hand waving about a solar storm. I wondered what Pithica had done to pull that off. It kind of impressed me that they had done it, considering the dire straits they had to be in after what we'd pulled. But they were about helping humanity to the very end, and apparently that included cleaning up their own mess to some degree, which to them meant at least making sure nobody started bandying around the word "terrorists" or could point to a nuclear attack as an excuse to start a war with someone. The country ran fund-raisers and Red Cross drives to help the poor Angelenos struck by such a freaky natural disaster, but world politics as a whole suffered no more than it had from the last bad hurricane.

Arthur was severely concussed enough that he stayed with me for a few days in my apartment in the Valley. Since the concussion was my fault, I didn't mind waking him up in the middle of the night to ask him how many fingers and who was president. In return, he tried to nag me about taking it easy until my chest wound healed completely—something about adrenaline not being a substitute for proper convalescence—but I mostly ignored him. When he felt well enough, he took advantage of the massive chaos in the city to go in and report at a police station that he'd woken up in an alley with short-term amnesia and realized he was the victim of a crime. He filled out a police report on what had happened to his office while claiming not to remember any of it and was supported in all ways by his obvious recent head wound. The LAPD, swamped with a devastated and fracturing city, quickly filed the case away under unsolved gang-related violence.

By then a horrifically tortured man had shown up in a hospital and been identified as the sole survivor of the office massacre on Wilshire. Considering that he couldn't stop gibbering madly about an Asian devil, and that no bodies had ever been recovered from the Griffith Park shooting despite the wildly conflicting witness reports of the violence there, Arthur's and my composites got shuffled off the "most wanted" boards. I wondered if the surviving Pithica man had any inkling that he probably owed his life to Rio magnanimously getting the police off my trail.

As for Rio himself, I tracked him down a little over a week after the EMP disaster. We met in an empty subway station—the trains still weren't up and running, and the station was deserted, though someone had stopped by with copious amounts of spray paint and already graffitied over every surface. Gotta love LA.

Instead of coming down from street level, Rio walked casually into the station on the track, emerging out of the yawning darkness of the tunnel with his duster swirling around him and wearing a broad-brimmed felt hat that only enhanced the cowboy image.

Some sort of odd déjà vu echoed in my memory—Rio somewhere else, some time else, walking toward me in exactly that way—

I blinked it away.

"Are you auditioning for the Old West?" I greeted him, trying to sound normal. I hopped down off the platform to join him on the rails.

"The American frontier would suit me, I think," he said. "What did you wish to see me about?"

"The police aren't after me anymore," I said. "Thanks for not killing that guy."

He lifted one shoulder fractionally. When I didn't say anything else, he asked, "Is that all?"

"No." I'd been doing a lot of thinking since our final battle with Dawna. The memories of her attack still shifted and blurred, fuzzier with each passing day, the pieces I was able to jigsaw together making less and less sense. But the bits of it I could recall, and the deal he'd made . . . every frustrating contradiction led me not to Pithica, not to Dawna, but to Rio.

Rio was keeping something from me.

And I was going to find out what. I just didn't know how to ask him.

"Are you going to keep your deal with Dawna?" I asked finally.

"Yes," he said.

"She neutralized us, you know." Arthur and I had tested it late one night, and neither of us would be looking into Pithica ever again. We couldn't. We couldn't even try. "She told us not to come after them again, and we can't. I doubt they're even keeping an eye on me anymore. They know I'm not a threat to them." I crossed my arms, hugging my jacket to me against the underground chill. "Could you talk me out of it? Destroy their influence?" He'd done it before, after all.

"Probably," said Rio.

"Will you?"

"No."

"Why *not*?" I exploded. The possibility had been the one thing that might have made his deal make sense, if he had figured somehow that I could do more damage to Pithica in the future than he could, and therefore had a life worth trading for Dawna's—again. "Why did you make that deal, then?"

"You know why I do what I do, Cas," he said calmly. "Are we done here?"

"No. I don't care how mysterious the 'mysterious ways' are—this isn't adding up. There's something you're not telling me."

He raised his eyebrows. "I have many things I don't tell you. Would you like to know what I had for breakfast this morning?"

"Sarcasm. Nice." I swallowed. "You aren't my friend. You're telling the truth when you say that."

"I know," he said.

"So? None of this fits together. You traded my safety for Dawna's back there, and that wasn't the first time. Back when she had Arthur and me—you were trying to take down Pithica, and you had the perfect opportunity." Looking back, I wanted to scream in frustration that he hadn't taken it, even given what it would have meant. Paradoxically, I remembered how certain I had been that he wouldn't make that choice, and it made me doubt my own sanity. "You should have killed me, secured Dawna's trust, and then destroyed them from the inside out. Tell me I'm not acceptable collateral damage for that kind of coup! It would have been perfect."

I waited. He was silent.

"But you didn't," I said. "You broke us out instead." An anomaly, Dawna Polk had called me. It suddenly bothered me intensely that she seemed to understand Rio's relationship with me better than I did.

Where did you meet him? Remember.

My breath hitched. Rio narrowed his eyes, but I pressed my lips together and stared back.

Finally, he spoke. "I had other considerations. You were not aware of them."

"So make me aware of them."

"No."

"Why not?"

He was silent.

God*dammit*. Irresistible force, meet immovable object. "This goes back even further," I said. "I should have seen it right away. Back at the beginning of all this. You told me not to get involved. Why?"

"Because I didn't want you involved."

"Why not?"

Again he said nothing. The expression on his face was the definition of blandness.

"Someone who didn't know better might think you've been trying to protect me," I said. "Which I know isn't true. So I'd like some answers here. I think I have a right to know."

Amusement touched his features. "You might disagree with that."

I blinked. "What?"

"Cas," said Rio, "I'm not going to answer your questions. I advise you to stop asking them."

"Why should I? For crying out loud, I'm not asking you to tell me something that isn't my business! You know something, and it has to do with me, and I'm not going to—"

Rio tipped his hat to me and walked away, back down the darkened subway tracks. I was left ranting at the empty air.

I took a frustrated breath. "This doesn't make sense, Rio!" I shouted after him. "I don't like things that don't make sense!"

My own words echoing back at me were my only response. Rio was gone.

I sighed and climbed back up to the platform. I had one more meeting today, and I was hoping it would be far more satisfactory than this one had been.

Steve met me at an empty construction site. He looked quite a bit the worse for the wear: several days' worth of five o'clock shadow darkened his square jaw, and the purple shadows under his eyes were so deep they made his face look hollow. He had lost at least two kilos, and every twitch of his movement was that of a hunted man. A man with nothing left in the world.

I liked that look on him.

"We got your message," I said. I had told Checker I would handle it. "So much for your security, huh?"

He scrubbed both hands over his face. "They knew everything. They—when they came—"

According to his frantic email, when Pithica had knocked LA to its knees, the first thing they had done was figure out where the alerts had come from. Then they had proceeded to destroy Steve's organization with no quarter—at least, the cell here in LA. Apparently they had already been perfectly aware of every detail Steve and his colleagues had tried so desperately to keep hidden, and up until that point they just hadn't cared. Steve's group had been no more than a gnat gnawing on Pithica's big toe.

"Tell me, Steve," I said. "What bothers you more? That despite killing everyone you came in contact with, your little band of merry men was still leakier than a Swiss cheese umbrella? Or that for all your grandstanding against Pithica, you guys never achieved the annoyance level of an advertising jingle?"

"Please." His hands were working at his sides, fingers kneading against each palm. "I'm begging you. I need help."

"With what? Threatening people?"

"They killed everyone," he mumbled numbly. "Everyone who might have still been working on your plan. Gone. They were trying to stop you."

"They failed," I said. "We won."

"I can't trust anyone." He scrubbed his hands over his face again. "I was on the road when it happened, and I still—I barely got away."

I wasn't exactly going to cheer for that.

"They knew too much, too fast," he said dazedly. "I can't help but think—everything we did, I look back, and I don't know anymore. Other than what we did with you, what we were told to do—the orders we received—how can I know?"

"You think Pithica might have been giving all your orders to begin with?" I clarified, once I had sorted through his disjointedness. Well, wasn't that a delicious twist of irony.

"Or we've been playing enough into their hands for it not to matter. We were a cell system; we had some autonomy, but we . . . we clearly were not having the effect we hoped for. . . ."

"They're pretty good at the whole butterfly-and-hurricane deal, from what I understand," I said. "They probably pushed a button in Istanbul and made you hop."

"That does not make me feel better."

"It wasn't meant to."

He shoved his restless hands into his pockets. "I suppose none of it matters now. But—we did help you, didn't we? We gave you what you needed, and we suffered for it." He had the gall to straighten up then, and he looked down his nose at me. I was immediately annoyed. "Will you return the favor?"

"Whoa there," I said. "We offered you an opportunity to be a small part of the biggest advancement your stated mission has ever had. I don't owe you anything."

"Perhaps not, but—perhaps I can still be of service to you. I know a great deal of intelligence about Pithica—"

"Let me stop you right there," I interrupted. "I'm not interested." My heart hammered a little faster. The truth was, I couldn't have said yes if I'd wanted to. I took a quick breath, trying to dispel the feel of Dawna's greasy fingers on my brain. Damn Rio for not helping me.

Not that I wanted to make a deal with Steve anyway. That was too Faustian, even for me.

"Please," he begged, with all the grace of an untamed boar. "What can I offer you? I need help. I have to get away—they're coming after me—"

I highly doubted that. Pithica's move against his group had been to try to stop Checker's and my plan from completing. They had swept in and brought the hammer down where they thought it might provide a stopgap. I doubted they were losing any sleep about the collateral damage, but I would have been very surprised if they were still putting any resources into chasing after stragglers. Especially now that they had nothing left to stop. Revenge wasn't Pithica's style.

I didn't tell Steve that, though. I was enjoying the hunted animal look on him. "You only have one thing I want," I said.

"What? Anything," he promised abjectly.

"An answer." My mouth was suddenly dry, and I had to force the words out. "Anton Lechowicz. And his daughter."

He looked confused for a moment, which made a hot spurt of anger rise in my chest. He didn't deserve to forget them. But then he blinked, and looked at me, and faltered. I wondered what my face looked like. "We couldn't risk Pithica finding us," he tried to explain, the words thready.

I'd known, or suspected it strongly enough that it was the same thing, but I still felt dizzy, as if every bit of equilibrium had deserted me. "You killed two people I liked," I said. My voice sounded like it came from very far away.

"I—I'm sorry," Steve faltered. "It was one of our routine measures; we weren't trying to—and I only signed off on it; I wasn't the one who—" He stopped abruptly, confusion and guilt flaring in his eyes, as if only just hearing what he had said, that he was trying to excuse being the one who gave the order by virtue of having kept his hands clean. His mouth worked silently. Then he gathered himself, lifted his chin, and did that nose-looking-down thing he seemed so fond of.

"I am not going to apologize," he said, firming his voice. "We thought it had to be done."

"So does this," I said.

I didn't move as fast as I could have. I wanted to see his eyes widen in startled realization in the split second before he died.

The body slid to the ground with a quiet thump, and I took what felt like the first clean breath since this had all started. Pithica might not go in for revenge, but I sure as hell did.

thirty-nine

THE ODD jobs I'd been able to hustle as LA recovered dried up as we hit the second week out from the disaster—people weren't desperate enough anymore to hire me for necessities, and were still too occupied with rebuilding their lives and routines to worry about trivialities. Arthur had gone back to his own place, leaving me alone with too many thoughts—about Dawna and Pithica, about what she had been able to do to me, about Rio and whatever he hadn't told me. When I slept it was fitful and at odd hours, and the rest of the time I drank. A lot.

A week and a half after our final confrontation with Pithica, I got an email from Checker saying he'd been keeping tabs, and as far as he could tell, over seventy percent of Pithica's revenue sources had moved their money out of the organization's reach. Dawna and her people would need a long time to rebuild those resources. We had knocked them down but good.

I spent a lot of time staring out at the streets wondering when I would see crime start to spike. And then I drank some more.

I woke sober one evening, vivid dreams chasing a blurry reality, scenes so real my brain wobbled for a few seconds before settling on which world was the correct one. Nightmares had plagued me for as long as I could remember, but they had been worse these past couple of weeks.

Since Dawna.

I lay on the blankets and tried to latch on to the shreds of the dream. More and more odd, overpowering waves of déjà vu had been haunting me, particularly after I slept. Places, faces—they wavered just out of reach, the itch of forgotten memory overwhelming my brain and twisting my stomach until I tasted bile at the back of my throat. Whatever had crawled through my subconscious in my sleep last night, I had seen it before.

Or dreamed it before.

Dawna's face intruded in my mind's eye, backlit by forms and figures I didn't want to see, scenes half-forgotten, visions and memories and a world only half-real—

Pain in my knuckles slammed the images away. I'd put my fist through the drywall next to the mattress.

I wiped blood and plaster dust off the back of my hand with my shirt and dragged myself out of bed to find more alcohol. The bottles from the night before—or whenever I had last been awake—were empty, expanding in a glass forest across table and floor and attesting to my usual company.

Halberd.

I picked up a bottle with a stylized drawing of an axe on the label.

Halberd. Why had I just thought that?

The word pinged me like a fragment of another forgotten dream, a half-buried shred of awareness.

Halberd and Pithica, the memo had said, the one Anton had given me a lifetime ago. But no, something else—the word poked at me, itching, an irritating nub that wouldn't go away, echoing against the edges of my mind.

An echo in Dawna's voice? Her image swam in my memory, standing tall above me, blurred in a thousand pixelated layers. Her hands on my face, reaching into my brain—I could hear her voice, but the words overlapped in a jumbled mass.

Was I remembering something she had said while we were fighting? As she was shattering me?

Fear clenched at me. I started digging through the mess in the flat for a scrap of paper, tossing bottles and food wrappers and dirty clothes to the side while I repeated the word in my head over and over, afraid it would fade away again before I snatched the chance to write it down. I found an old envelope and a half-dried ballpoint and scribbled faster than I could form the words in my head:

HALBERD. THIS MEANS SOMETHING
IMPORTANT. FIND OUT.

The sentences floated in front of my vision: mad, mocking, absurd. They meant nothing.

Stupid. I crumpled the envelope in my hand.

Then, for some reason, I smoothed it back out and put it in a drawer. Halberd did have something to do with Pithica, after all; Anton's memo had shown that much. Foolish to think it was anything more than that, and I wouldn't be able to look into it anyway after what Dawna had done, but still . . . it had to mean something.

For some reason, I shivered.

I needed more to drink. Yes. Large amounts of alcohol sounded perfect right now. Something in me needed to get royally drunk and pass out for about three days. Good plan.

I grabbed my keys and headed for the door. I yanked it open to reveal Arthur, his hand raised to knock.

"Arthur," I said, surprised. "Hi."

"Hi, Russell," he said.

We stood awkwardly for a moment.

Arthur waved a hand apologetically. "Tried calling."

Phones. Right. I felt around in my pockets and found my latest cell phone. A blank screen stared back at me, and I vaguely remembered getting annoyed with the ringing a few days ago and turning it off. I hit the power button and saw a message proclaiming fourteen missed calls.

Oops. "Sorry," I said. "You need something?"

To my surprise, he chuckled. He had a very handsome smile. "Russell, you remind me of someone I knew once. Someone who's a damn smart cookie like you, and almost as prickly."

"Huh?"

"Might be you'll get to meet her sometime. You'd either get along like a house on fire or fight like cats. Mind if I come in for a sec?"

"Sure, whatever." I let the door swing all the way open and led the way in to flop on the saggy couch. Arthur sat down next to me. His eyes took in the forest of empty liquor bottles, but he didn't say anything, and I told myself I didn't care about his opinion anyway. "So? What's up?" I asked.

He looked like he was searching for words. "Checker's back," he said finally. "Just been to say hello."

"Oh," I said. "Good."

"You okay?" he asked. Oddly, he sounded like he cared about the answer. In fact, I was struck with the strong impression that he had come all the way here to . . . well, to check in on me. *What the hell?*

"I'm fine," I said.

"Really?" He laughed a little hoarsely. "'Cause I'm not."

Was he trying to confide in me? "I guess I'm just waiting for life to get back to normal," I said. It sort of already was, for me. Except for the dreams. But maybe those were normal, too. I was having trouble remembering.

"This case, it's the only thing I've worked on these past six months," said Arthur. "Gonna be weird, going back to doing background checks and divorce cases."

"The exciting life of a private eye?" Boy, was I glad I didn't have his job.

He snorted. "Yeah, exciting's not exactly the word for it. Usually, anyway. I work enough to take on pro bono cases for them that need it, though—those are always the better ones. Still not much excitement, but fulfilling, you know?"

I wasn't sure why he was telling me this. "Sure," I said.

"Can't get it all out of my head, though," he continued. "What she did to us. I'm not fond of being someone's puppet." The edge of steel in those words might have made even Dawna think twice, if she hadn't already beaten us.

"Yeah," I said. "Me neither."

"I can't . . ." He rubbed a hand over his jaw. "Everything I remember thinking, it made so much sense at the time. Still makes sense, if I'm honest. But there's something in me that knows chunks of it aren't me at all . . . and I'm still not rightly sure which all those chunks are; I just know they gotta be there. Think that's what scares me the most, still not knowing what was me and what was her."

"I'm pretty sure you pointing a gun at me was all Dawna," I said.

"Which time?"

We laughed a little at that, even though it wasn't funny.

"Not my usual habit, you know," Arthur said. "Greeting people barrel first. You didn't catch me in my best week."

"Well, I don't usually knock people unconscious to introduce myself, either," I said.

He affected surprise. "You don't?"

I punched him in the shoulder. Only a little harder than necessary.

"Ow!" He gave me a mock glare, rubbing his arm, and then got serious again. "Listen. Been thinking about something. Dawna—when she had us prisoner, she talked to us, both of us, for a long time."

"Yeah," I said. "Yeah, she did."

"How do we know . . . how do we know there's not any more?"

"You mean, how do we know that we don't have, what, sleeper personalities or something? That what we're thinking might not be our own thoughts anymore?"

"Something like that."

I looked down at my hands. I wasn't going to say it hadn't occurred to me. "I don't think it would be worth it to them," I said. "That level of control. She got what she wanted from us, and—well, even at the end we weren't under her total control, yeah?"

"Maybe you weren't," he said softly.

"You weren't, either," I pointed out. "You didn't give us away until we pushed you to it. And at the last minute, you took your gun off-line, when it mattered."

"Barely."

"You knew it would give me the window."

He nodded, conceding the point. "Hey, about that. What you can do. It's pretty special, huh?"

The question caught me off guard. I tried to keep my face neutral. "What do you mean, what I can do?"

He chuckled. "I got eyes, Russell."

"I'm good at math," I said. "That's all."

He squinted at me, still smiling slightly. "You gotta tell me how that works sometime."

"Sometime," I agreed vaguely.

The moment of levity faded, and Arthur looked down again. "We really can't be sure, can we?" he said after a moment. "Could be some small way. A thousand little bits she might've changed. Maybe we say she had a miss with us at the end there, but still . . . we don't know what else she might've done."

"No," I said. "I guess we don't."

"What are you going to do?"

"Well, what can we do?" I pointed out.

Arthur took a deep breath. "Keep making the best decisions we can, I guess."

And hope that nothing had wormed its way into our brains, ticking like a time bomb, waiting to make us betray ourselves. I wasn't happy about it either. But we had no way to know.

"What if we watch each other?" I said suddenly. "It's not foolproof, but it's how—well, Rio could tell, with me. We can keep in contact, warn each other if we get crazy."

He pulled a face. "Looking for excess crazy? How will I know?"

I punched him in the arm again.

"Hey!" He gave me a gentle shove in return. "Y'know, it's a good idea. Better than nothing, for sure. You got my cell number, right?"

"Yeah."

"Stay in touch, then. You know, call me, let me know you're okay. Or you can always pick up when I ring. Can't watch for excess crazy if we don't talk regular." He grinned at me, then reached over and squeezed my shoulder. "You're a good kid, Russell."

I blinked. By proposing we watch each other, I had been thinking in terms of a mutually beneficial business arrangement, but Arthur seemed to be taking it as an overture of friendship. "I . . . if you say so," I got out.

"I do." He gave my shoulder a final squeeze and then stood. "Talk soon, right?"

A sort of tight feeling was growing through my chest and throat, the same type of squeezing discomfort I got in certain death situations. Except it was kind of a good feeling, which made no sense at all. "Yeah, okay," I said.

"Give you a buzz tomorrow," said Arthur, and let himself out.

I stayed sitting on the couch, staring at the floor and feeling very strange.

I wasn't used to having friends. Friends meant obligations, and complications, and effort—

And people who check in on you, another part of my brain pointed out. *And have your back. And can watch for signs of psychic brainwashing.*

Huh.

My phone beeped.

It was a text message from Checker, newly arrived back in LA. The strange, fizzy feeling in my chest intensified.

DRINKING CONTEST 2NITE ITS ON BE @ HOLE 8PM SHARP CHECKER

And then, an instant later, a second one:

WEAR SUMTHING SLINKI

I stared at the messages. The invitation felt surreal, as if I were watching someone else's life: somebody who lived in society, some-body who did the whole "human interaction" thing, somebody who got text messages that weren't either about work or death threats.

Somebody who made friends and went out drinking with them.

Was I even capable of being someone like that?

I thought about Arthur's visit. I looked down at Checker's texts again. Maybe people weren't all bad, I thought. At least not all the time.

Maybe . . . maybe it wouldn't be such an awful thing not to drink alone tonight.

I hit "reply."

As long as my new Colt 1911 counts. See you at 8. Cas.

acknowledgments

My BRILLIANT agent, Russell Galen, is the reason you're reading this book. I owe him a hundred thousand thanks, not only for championing my novels, but for picking the perfect editor to send them to. That editor is Diana Gill, and her sharpness brought *Zero Sum Game* to a whole new level. I am so appreciative of them and my whole team at Tor—the process of bringing *Zero Sum Game* to the wider world has been the most marvelous of rides.

Before arriving at this stage, this book owes its life to the support of so many other people. First and always, so much gratitude and love to my critique partner and sister—this series owes its soul to you, and don't ever forget it. I am also incredibly indebted to the people who beta read *Zero Sum Game* for me—Maddox Hahn, Kevan O'Meara, Jesse Sutanto, and Layla Lawlor—and to those who beta read the changes to the new edition—Maddox Hahn, Rob Livermore, Elaine Aliment, Toria Rex, and Jesse Sutanto. They are the most perspicacious first readers an author could ask for, as well as being brilliant writers themselves, and I am grateful beyond words for how they've helped level up my work.

Many, many continued thanks to all the talented folks who helped make the first edition a reality, including Najla Qamber, Anna Genoese, David Wilson, and Steven Lesh. You have my gratitude forever. And a big shout-out to Sylvia Spruck Wrigley and Michael Hart for correcting parts of the manuscript according to their expertise.

Perhaps most importantly, I never realized how important community would be to my writing before I started publishing. So much love for The Menagerie, my second family, and for the incredible people who hang with me at PQ, on Codex and Absolute Write, in my Twitter circles, or in other parts of my writing and speculative fiction community. I've learned so much from all of you, and I'll keep trying to pay forward all the support I've been given.

And finally, to everyone in my life who has inspired and supported me along the way, to those who laughed at my math jokes or geeked out with me or embraced my nerddom as a feature, not a bug—thank you. This book never would have happened without you.